This Plague of Days
Season 1
The Zombie Apocalypse Serial
Robert Chazz Chute

Published by Ex Parte Press
ISBN 978-1-927607-20-6
Copyright 2013 Robert Chazz Chute
First Print Edition: June 2013
Second Print Edition: May 2014
Cover design by Kit Foster of KitFosterDesign.com
All rights reserved.
Address media and rights inquiries and reader correspondence
to: expartepress@gmail.com.
AllThatChazz.com
ThisPlagueOfDays.com

Dedicated, with my love, to She Who Must Be Obeyed, the Princess and the Prince. Only they know the sacrifices.

Special thanks to my great friend Kit Foster. He knows why.

This Plague of Days

Season 1

The Zombie Apocalypse Serial

Robert Chazz Chute

Table of Contents

Season 1, Episode 1

All words began as magic spells.

*

Things taken from us are what we treasure most.
*
You get what you deserve.

*

Journey with me down a long, twisted optic nerve,
such wondrous sights to show.
By strange harbors, roads dip and paths swerve.
We have palaces to explore, places to go,
and capricious gods to serve.
Among hanging cliffs and dangerous curves,
just when you think you're winning,
The End is The Beginning,
our humanity too precious to preserve.

~ *Notes from The Last Cafe*

Here We Sit In The Last Cafe

"Viruses are zombies," Dr. Sutr said. "They are classifiable neither as living nor dead. When given the opportunity, they reproduce using a host. Their molecules form complex structures but they need hosts to reproduce. Nucleic acids, proteins — "

The Skype connection froze for a moment before the doctor understood he was being interrupted. "—preciate your *summary*, doctor." Two men in uniform and one woman in a suit, each with their own screen, regarded him with impatience.

"The virus has grown more...opportunistic. What fooled us early on was the varied rate of infection and lethality. I suspect individual variance in liver enzymes accounts — "

The woman cleared her throat and Sutr lost his place in the notes he'd prepared for this meeting. She sighed as he fumbled with his iPad. He had too many notes and not enough time. The woman sighed and tapped a stylus on her desk. "I'm meeting with him soon, doctor. I need the bullet, please. What do I *tell* him?"

Sutr removed his glasses and closed his eyes. This was too important to stammer and stutter through. Finding the correct words had never mattered more. He took a deep breath but kept his eyes closed and pretended he was speaking intimately with his beloved Manisha. His wife's name meant "wisdom" and she shared her name with the goddess of the mind. He needed her and her namesake now. "My team and I..." He took another deep breath. "The virus has jumped."

The admiral in dress whites spoke, which automatically muted Dr. Sutr's microphone. "First it was bats, then birds, then migratory birds, then pigs and cows. What animal do we warn the WHO about now? What animal do the Chinese have to slaughter next to keep the cap on this thing? A vaccine won't help billions of Chinese peasants if they starve to death first."

"I'm very aware of the stakes, sir, but the virus has jumped to humans. I asked my contact at Google to watch the key words. The epidemiological mapping of the spread is already lighting up in Japan, Malaysia, Chechnya and I have confirmation it's in parts of the Middle East, I'm afraid."

"What's your next step, doctor?" the woman asked.

Sutr opened his eyes. "I've sent my team home. They should be with their families now. As should we all."

The man in the green uniform, a four-star general, leaned closer to his camera, filling Sutr's screen. "This is no time to give up the fight, doctor. We've got a world to save from your...what did you call it? Zombie virus?"

"Pardon me, General. It was a clumsy metaphor. My point was that viruses are dead things and I can't kill the dead. I'm afraid we lost containment. I suspect we must have lost control sometime in the last two to three weeks. Perhaps less. Maybe more. There are too many variables. This virus is a tricky one. Something...new."

The general paled. "Are you saying this disease was *engineered*?"

For the first time, Sutr showed irritation toward his inquisitors. "I don't know! I told you, there are too many variables. The loss of containment could have been sabotage or someone on my team made a mistake. Maybe they were too afraid to admit their mistake. It's possible I made a mistake and I did not recognize it as such! I've identified the virus signature, but the work will have to be taken up by someone else. In my opinion, we need a miracle. As a virologist who has worked with Ebola, my faith in miracles is absent. Nature doesn't know mercy or luck. That hope was beaten out of me in Africa."

The admiral cut in, "Look, you're already headed for the Nobel by identifying the virus. There's time before it reaches our shores.

We have to hope — " but the woman in the suit held up a hand and he fell silent.

"We do appreciate the complexity of the challenge before us, Dr. Sutr. That's why we need you. You're further along in the research than the other labs." The woman looked conciliatory now and her voice took on a new, soothing note. "We're very anxious to have you continue."

Dr. Sutr stiffened. "I've already composed and sent an email for the lab network. You'll have the entire data dump. I've made extra notes so your teams won't waste time with what hasn't worked. Dan, at CDC, and Sinjin-Smythe, at Cambridge, will coordinate my latest data to the other nodes. Good luck with it."

The woman's eyes narrowed. "You were vague about the virus gaining traction in parts of the Middle East. Have you on site confirmation, doctor?"

"Yes. I've seen the virus's work in person. Here in Dubai, in my own house. Tarun, my baby boy, died last night. My wife, Manisha, followed to see where he went early this morning."

"We're so sorry for your loss, Julian," the woman said. "Are you infected?"

"I have no doubt I will die soon."

"How long have you got, son?" the admiral said. "You've said the infection gradient and lethality is so variable…you could keep working. We could defeat this thing."

"Defeat death? I don't have that kind of time. Don't be afraid, though. I am an atheist…but…" His voice and gaze drifted away for a moment and it was clear to all assembled he spoke to himself more than his audience. "When I was a student, I found myself alone in a cadaver lab once. Seventeen bodies, each one in some state of dissection. I held a human heart there for the first time, still so muscular and strong for a dead thing. The iliotibial band is strong, too, like a fibrous, white leather strap…such awe-inspiring complexity in the human body. And so many damnable things to go wrong."

"Julian?" The woman's voice was almost a whisper, as if she were afraid to startle him from a deep sleep.

5

"Forgive me," the virologist said. "It is not the bodies that make us prisons of sadness. We will burn and bury the bodies or Nature will claim its prizes. It is those terrible reminders of what was and what could have been that will rob us of hope. That will infuse us with such fury and sadness that, for most? There is no room for anything else. Many good people will do bad and bad men will do evil. Without hope and spires, what are aspirations for? Our losses will make us wretched again. My son's unused baby booties. That is what drives me to this wretchedness."

"Doctor, you swore an oath and we, the living, still need you." The general's voice shook.

Julian Sutr's voice came firm and steady. "General, Admiral...Madam Secretary. It's entirely possible that I brought it home to them. My wife and child are dead by the virus that bears my name. I should have been an obstetrician like my mother. She brought life into the world..." A tear slipped down the doctor's cheek. He cleared his throat. "The human race has seen this before. There will be survivors. They'll have to be strong. First, they will have to weather the storm. Whoever writes this history and to whomever shall read it...tell them to let go of their expectations of how things should be. Another Dark Age is coming. If we hold on to what we've lost, we'll never be strong enough to grasp what comes next. I know I'm too weak for the trials to come."

"What is next?" the admiral asked.

The doctor gave him the amused smile of a fighter relieved to be retired from fighting. "I expect blacksmithery will be the first science to make a comeback. Perhaps in a few decades. Maybe fewer. You people ask me what you should tell him. Go to your briefing. Tell him that, in all likelihood, he is the last President of the United States."

The general and admiral startled and looked away from their screens, but the woman's eyes were steady on the doctor. "Do you have the fever yet, Julian?"

"Oh, I won't wait. I have to go looking for Manisha and Tarun." Dr. Julian Sutr picked up the Sig Sauer P220 from his desk, placed the muzzle under his chin and pulled the trigger.

Invisible, Whimsical And Losing Our Way

The moon lit the boy's face as he peered over the fence into the next yard. Jaimie Spencer watched the couple on the lawn chair. The chair's squeak had drawn him closer, curious. He wasn't allowed in the neighbor's yard, but moon shadows amid thick hedge leaves concealed him. A woman he'd never seen before sat in the older man's lap. The man, Mr. Sotherby, lay still beneath her. Jaimie could not see the man's face, but there was something grim about him, as if the couple were reluctant joggers in a cold wind. A cool hand slipped to the back of the boy's neck. Without looking, Jaimie knew it was his sister, Anna.

"Ears," she whispered, "You're being creepy again."

The woman froze and turned her head. The couple whispered to each other, too. Sotherby's voice was insistent. Hers was afraid.

Anna guided her little brother away from the hedge line. Anna did not speak again until she and Jaimie stood by their own back door. "Mr. Sotherby has brought home another one of his flight attendant friends. You shouldn't spy on them. It's wrong."

Jaimie did not look at Anna directly. He never met her eyes and he rarely spoke. Her brother cocked his head slightly to one side. That questioning gesture was a rare bit of Jaimie's body language that few outside the family could read easily. Anna told Jaimie that when he cocked his head that way, he looked like Fetcher, the cocker spaniel they'd once had. In every picture they owned of that pet, the spaniel's head was tipped slightly sideways, perplexed by the

7

camera. Jaimie thought the entire breed must cock their heads slightly sideways, hence their name. The boy loved when language was precise and logical. He was often disappointed.

"Mr. Sotherby brings home his friends. Remember Mr. Sotherby's a pilot? He gives rides to lots of people, Ears. He was just giving her a ride. That woman you saw thought she was part of a couple, but they were really just coupling."

Couple: a noun and a verb. Jaimie had read these words in his dictionary. Overlaps of meanings and terms irritated him. He wondered if his sister was trying to bother him. Anna often called him Ears when she was angry with him, though sometimes she called him that when she gave him a hug. More confusion and imprecision.

"Dad says it's a terrible thing what's happened to flight attendants," Anna said. "He says when they were called stewardesses, they were cuter. Now the older ones have a waxy look."

Jaimie wondered how the change in the name of their occupation could have changed the way they looked. He'd heard there were magic words. "Flight attendant" must have powerful, and dangerous, magical properties.

Anna pulled her little brother into the house. "Let's keep this between you and me," Anna said and then burst out in a giggle. "Mom would worry you're getting corrupted. I won't say anything and I know *you* won't."

Jaimie followed Anna up the back stairs into the kitchen. She pulled out a box of cereal and poured a bowl for herself and one for her brother. He never asked to eat but was usually cooperative if a bowl and spoon was placed in front of him.

He couldn't stop thinking about Mr. Sotherby and the woman. Jaimie liked to watch colorful patterns that flowed around people. He had seen the colors around living things all of his life. He assumed everyone saw them. The boy had seen something pass between Mr. Sotherby and the flight attendant he had never before seen. It was disturbing because it muddied their colors and made them less vibrant.

Jaimie stood at the sink and gazed out of the kitchen window as he ate. The moon hung so low and full, the tip of a distant church spire reached, its tip stretching to split Clavius, a large crater toward the base of the moon's face. The boy's mind wandered over the words *spire* and *aspire*. Surely, the terms shared the same arrogant word root. But the spire would always be bound to the Earth, many miles short of aspiration's heights. The gap between hope and doomed reality turned the boy's mind back to the naked woman in the next yard.

Small black spots had hovered between the pair like greasy flies. The black smear spoiled the usual pleasing weave of colors. There had been many of them, like a cloud of feeding insects, around the woman. They spread over Mr. Sotherby, too, reaching for him. Jaimie didn't know what the black spots were, but he sensed a yearning and purpose in their movement. They aspired to reach Mr. Sotherby and overtake him. He sensed the black cloud's aspirations would be fulfilled.

That was Jaimie Spencer's first glimpse of the Sutr virus at its deadly work. He was sixteen. He might have mentioned it to someone, but Jaimie Spencer was a selective mute. His mother didn't like that label so she called it, "How Jaimie is."

"He's a *very* selective mute," his father, Theo Spencer, said. "Jaimie has something we all lack: A super power. My son can shut up until he has something to say."

But Jaimie's ability to communicate well still waited on a distant time horizon then. Billions would have to expire — and one death would have to transpire — before Jaimie found his voice.

Toast Fortune's Smiles And Fever Dreams

The letter arrived in the late morning. Jaimie's father worked in a small library branch. Jaimie was home because the School Board and the Health Board were "in discussions" about whether children should be kept at home. Officials debated if masks should be worn while others insisted masks were too uncomfortable for children to wear all day.

Jaimie heard his parents debating, too. Jack, his mother, said she was keeping him home because she didn't want to be alone in the house. (She was "Jacqueline" to very few people, and to no one who knew her well.)

If Jaimie had chosen to speak, he would have said, "We're always alone."

Jack hugged her son and he let her because it pleased her. Jaimie knew she wanted him to speak and he occasionally pushed a word or two up past his throat, each like a stone forced through a narrow gap. Jaimie sensed his mother wanted something more from him now, but the boy couldn't guess what that might be. He ate his cereal dry from the box as she read the letter. She glanced up at him as she read, as if to make sure he was still in his seat at the kitchen table, and safe. Her hands trembled and Jaimie suspected this was a good time to say something. No words came.

Jaimie did not speak at all until he was six and then he spoke, or rather sang, words in perfect pitch. His mother credited John Lennon for her son's first miracle. After all the cajoling by many frustrated therapists and teachers, it was John Lennon who stirred Jaimie to vocalize for the first time.

"Everyone loved the Beatles," Jack said. "Somehow we never noticed that much of it is excellent children's music." The song was *Ob-La-Di, Ob-La-Da*. Jack did not hear Jaimie's first words. He sang for Anna and only his sister heard him. She whooped and leapt in the air shouting for their mother to come hear Jaimie sing those two nonsense words over and over. He never began the lyrics, as if singing the title should be enough after so long a silence.

Jack ran upstairs and slapped her daughter. "What a mean lie!" The red outline of Jack's fingers tattooed her cheek, including the thin outline of her wedding ring. She had never done such a thing until that moment.

Jaimie listened to the echo of the slap bounce off the bedroom wall. To him, the slap ended with a thin shine, the color of mustard. His mother's energies shone bright red. His sister shone yellow and crimson.

Anna screamed and whirled on Jaimie, insisting the little boy sing *Ob-La-Di* again. She was only two years older than her brother. She didn't know the surest way to shut up a selective mute is to insist he speak.

Anna was still jailed in her room, long after supper, when Jaimie sang another *Beatles* title. This time it was *Taxman*. He sang the title absentmindedly as he spun a plastic bowl on the kitchen floor, watching the after images flutter to the hollow sound as the bowl circled and shuddered to a stop.

Jack dropped and shattered a plate, wept and squeezed the six-year-old tight. That became what the rest of the family remembered, the agreed-upon and official story. However, Jaimie knew the dishes had been shattered in the sink in the late afternoon as Anna and his mother fought. Jack threw the first plate in the sink as she washed it. Anna threw the second. Jaimie listened to the screams. He caught the familiar, accusatory tone people use when they shout the same things over and over, conveying more energy than information.

Memory is a funny thing. Jaimie knew he had been in several grocery stores with his family, but they melded together as one gigantic grocery store. Such stores did not interest him. Memory shorthands the mundane. Instead, Jaimie's memory of the afternoon he first spoke was perfect. He kept the slap and held on to the shimmy of sound and light that followed. Anna held on to that slap, too, but for different reasons.

At the end of the fight, Jack wept and begged Jaimie's then eight-year-old sister for forgiveness. She bought Anna a new bicycle the next day. Jack never received her official pardon, but Jaimie's father was never told the truth of the broken plates. In their excitement in discovering Jaimie wasn't a true mute, no further questions were asked about why Anna changed so much after the boy began to occasionally speak. Theo thought it was jealousy over the shift in attention from daughter to son.

The doctors and therapists shrugged in their professional way and said the little boy must have been listening all that time he was thought to be terribly developmentally delayed.

"Mentally delayed," Anna called him.

The day of the slap, the house changed. There was more tension in the air because Jaimie's parents were always waiting for a song or at least a song title. Jaimie thought the slap made more difference to the family than his few words.

As he sat watching his mother's hands and eyes now, Jaimie felt that something was coming for them, promising to change everything again. Jaimie had heard the letter arrive in the box outside the front door. He knew there was a mail carrier, a person whose job it was to bring the mail daily, but he never saw the deliverer. His mother said the Post Office was like God in that way, unseen and capricious about delivery. She spoke about God a lot before, and during, the plague. Afterward, less so.

Bored, Jaimie left his seat and sat on the floor in a corner of the kitchen. A line of ants ferried food from a small garbage bag beside the overflowing can. The ants took the crumbs to someplace he couldn't see, though Jaimie assumed it was a place with lots of food and ant comforts and wonders. He hovered far above Antworld, outside of their awareness and time. He thought about the Post Office and what Jack said about God. He took a kernel of cereal from the box in his arms and placed the gift in the ants' path. Jaimie's mother insisted her son was made in God's divine image, so maybe, he thought, we are all gods in some small way. Or, he considered, we are God's ant farm.

Ants don't speak, either, he thought, but each nest is a city filled with mute workers and soldiers, oblivious to any handicap.

The ants reminded him of crawling in grass in autumn sunshine, back when people weren't so afraid to go outside. The radio voices called it "social distancing." Word of plague was in the air and words spread from person to person, spreading as much fear as the virus. People avoided each other, even the ones who called the worriers alarmists and conspiracy theorists.

Jaimie thought himself safe from the plague since he'd been avoiding people all of his life. The boy wondered if the worry of the spreading mind virus was the precursor to the Sutr plague, preparing everyone for the coming invasion.

That sunny day last autumn, Jaimie searched the grass, straining to pick up the cricket's chirp. Green stained his knees and the point of each cool blade prickled his bare chest, stomach and elbows as he carefully parted the green waves, focused on the small world. The boy found the cricket. He watched its beautiful yellow eyes, wondering if the insect studied him, too. If so, what did it see? Could the cricket see the full spectrum of colorful energy that wrapped his body, too?

The boy knew from watching the Nature Channel that the cricket's ears were on its two foremost legs, just below the joint. If his large ears were at his knees, the boy thought, no one would ever make fun of his ears. He could conceal them under his pant legs. There was something to envy about every small, fragile thing.

The rumble of the distant plane's engines reached him first, but Jaimie ignored the machine, his eyes focussed on the insect. Perhaps the insect watched him. Then the aircraft's quick shadow passed over him like a cool hand, a dark omen. He looked up to see the last commercial jet flights he'd ever see. They called them "air carriers". Jaimie thought those words fit well. Aircraft shrank the world enough that the Sutr virus could stretch its shroud over the Earth.

Each plane was the Sutr virus's emissary, carrying plague in its air molecules and dooming the human race to a new kind of apocalypse that would grow stronger, mutating monsters.

When Jaimie looked to the grass again, the cricket was gone, escaped to its tiny world, far from ominous shadows and safe from curious boys and reaching plagues.

Of Lost Loves And Butter Creams

A man collapsed in front of Jaimie's parents once, a long time ago. Papa Spence, Jaimie's grandfather, paid for the honeymoon. That's how they came to stand in line behind the man waiting for tickets at the Louvre.

"I had a romantic notion of Paris, as if it wasn't like anyplace else in the world. Our first day in the city, the next guy in line drops dead in front of us," Jack said. "The man was just buying his ticket, holding his hand out for change when he suddenly grabbed his left arm, and rubbed it hard, like he was trying to get something off it. After a few seconds, he fell like he'd been hit over the head with a huge mallet."

Theo searched for a pulse. Jack yelled for help. The woman behind the counter froze for a moment and watched the three tourists on the floor. She seemed to take a long time to reach out and pick up the phone by the register. Two more tourists, not a hundred feet away, came running. They were a pair of young American doctors and they took over the attempt to resuscitate the man.

"How lucky is that?" Theo said. "Two doctors, right there! As soon as they showed up, I thought things were going to work out okay. Then there was this sickening crunch! One rib broken, then two. I wasn't so sure things would work out after that."

Museum Security arrived and shooed people back, making room for the doctors to work, telling the tourists in both English and

French, "Everything is fine. Everything is fine. The problem is under control."

"I really wanted to believe that was true, but they kept saying it over and over until I didn't believe it anymore." The loud *la-la, la-la* of an ambulance drew closer, promising more help for the stricken man.

The security guards let Theo and Jack stand close, perhaps thinking they were related or thinking that the police would want to speak to them. Theo and Jack watched the unconscious man's eyes. One eye was a slit. The other pupil shot wide. It looked like an old penny.

When the paramedics arrived, the doctors stood and stepped back shaking their heads at each other. They spoke no French. One of the doctors breathed heavily, trying to catch his breath from the frantic resuscitation attempt. He turned to Theo. "His passport fell out of his pocket. I saw it. This guy's from Lichtenstein. Lichtenstein only takes about twenty minutes to cross by train...and so close to Paris, really. Everything is so close together here."

"He said it like it explained something," Theo said.

The paramedics injected their drugs and stimulants and massaged the dead man's heart. They rattled back and forth at each other and, though Jack and Theo didn't understand their words, they intuitively recognized the pattern unfolding. Life signs and orders were barked urgently at first. Then came the hard work of pushing on the man's chest. The paramedics spoke less and less as resignation set in. At last, an eloquent shrug and one of them glanced at his watch.

Jack told the story many times and she always ended it the same way. "He was on his way in. I can't get over that. Imagine dropping dead on your way *in* to the Louvre! He got up that day thinking he was finally going to see the greatest art in the history of the world."

That day in the Louvre was the first thing Jack thought of when she read the letter from Uncle Cliff. "Medical people are working hard, security people are telling everyone to stay calm and that they're in control. People are dying anyway."

Theo and Jack whispered at first, so Anna paid more attention. Jaimie paid attention, knowing parents only whispered about birthdays, Christmas presents, and death.

Everyone knew about the Sutr virus for some time, of course, but in the early days of the Sutr flu, it was not considered a serious threat. When people died in small numbers in countries far away, somehow that didn't count and went unreported. Eventually, the virus asserted itself, made itself known so it could not be ignored. Still, it was downplayed as just another flu virus. It took no more of a toll than the expected, seasonal influenza. The very young and vulnerable died. The Sutr flu killed old people crammed in nursing homes, passing the disease hand to hand.

Scary speculation in the media had lost its potency so people switched the channel, searching for news about sexy, young starlets flirting with death by meth, STDs and drunk driving. The public had heard the media cry wolf too many times to prepare for the killer wolf pack when it finally arrived.

The name Sutr was on everyone's lips by February. Scientists speculated that the plague had begun in India with cows. Riots erupted over attempts by public health officials to slaughter cows for the protection of humans. The virus might have been contained then, but when it was reported that more people had died in violent protests than from the virus, the sacred cows were allowed to live. Travel to India was restricted, but even that stopped when someone pointed out that there had been just as many deaths in the United States.

Theo said the disaster was a perfect example of the potted frog. "Put a frog in a hot pot and he'll jump out right away. Turn up the heat slowly and the frog will boil to death because, each moment, he's just a little hotter than before so he doesn't jump. He doesn't even complain. Inside, we're all frogs."

Stocks of hand sanitizer were bought up quickly and there weren't any of the little bottles to be had for any price. People washed their hands more and coughed into their sleeves as they were told by public health experts, who didn't have anything more to offer than simple hygiene.

17

Jaimie's father was unimpressed. "No one noticed Johnny Cash couldn't sing but he talked well enough that people took him for a singer. No one noticed that health experts weren't offering more than 19th century remedies."

Spokespeople for the CDC reassured the public that the dead were mostly from remote parts of the world or were already sick of something else when they died.

"Not very reassuring if you're a farmer, or a foreigner or already sick with something else," Theo said. "Sounds like, 'Everything is fine. Everything is fine. The problem is under control.'"

A curious denial stole over the coverage of the developing crisis: The news stories began to take on a sameness. People tired of the alarm bells. Some pundits turned to mocking their own reporters from cozy desk chairs in safe television studios.

"There have been too many false alarms to take the alarmists seriously," one confident commentator declared.

"Overblown," a pretty blonde woman named Megan agreed. "Many more thousands die of the regular strains of influenza every year and no one makes a big deal about that."

Jaimie watched the plague unfold. He loved television because the machine did all the talking and asked nothing of him. It was content to talk into the boy's silence. But he wondered why the TV people weren't worried about the thousands who died yearly, before the Sutr virus rose to strike down the confident and comfortable?

"Uncle Cliff wrote to warn us," his mother told the assembled family.

It was a short letter but, to Jaimie's consternation, it wasn't written in block letters. The message was dashed off with a slashing hand. Jaimie couldn't read it himself. The nuances of cursive writing were a code he could not break. Each deviation from the expected thwarted his understanding.

Cliff was Theo's identical twin brother. Though his letter was short, it sat atop a sheaf of papers that supported his claims. Jaimie could read the printed type but many of the words were unfamiliar. He went to his room and reappeared in a moment with one of his dictionaries to work through his uncle's warning.

Jaimie loved the dictionary even more than television because it is the one book that contains all others. Jaimie looked up "variant" and "adaptation" and "evolution" and "contagion".

At times, even with one finger under the questioned word and his other hand planted on the dictionary's explanation, Jaimie was lost. What exactly did Uncle Cliff mean when he said a virus could "jump"? The definition of one word led to other words. Jaimie disappeared into his dictionaries for hours, each time finding new paths to follow to new treasures he hadn't known existed.

Cliff and Theo had not gotten along in childhood and the letter seemed to acknowledge the distance between them. Uncle Cliff seemed to expect his twin to object to whatever he might say, so he sent copies of World Health Organization reports. The whispers shot back and forth between Theo and Jack for an hour as they read and reread the letter.

Jaimie caught a few of their words. His mother used the words "journey to Golgotha", which seemed to displease his father. Jaimie remembered that Golgotha, in Greek, meant *place of the skull.* Jaimie liked descriptive language.

Theo repeated the word "conflagration." Jaimie went back to his dictionary, turning pages fast to keep up.

Anna waited until the lull between dinner and dessert to steal the letter from its place by Jack's plate. When she came back to the table, Jaimie could tell she was excited: Back straight, eyes wide. "What are we going to do?"

Theo and Jack looked to each other, their faces blank.

Jack's eyes went tight, squeezing out tears.

Jaimie looked up from his dictionary and watched his father reach out and rub his mother's back in slow, warm circles. Tentatively, Jaimie reached for his mother's cheek. His hand came away wet. Thinking of amphibians on stovetops, Jaimie said one word: "Frog."

Without understanding the dark context of Jaimie's thoughts, they all laughed.

Tonight We Dream Of Claws And Teeth

Jaimie enjoyed school. He listened in class but his teachers asked little more of him than his attention. Anna said she didn't like school, but she cried when the government shuttered all the schools and decreed that everyone had to stay home.

Jack listened to the radio and shook her head when a parent called in to say that school closures interfered with his job. Daycare centers were also closed. The words "social distancing" were spoken so much that some people started saying "SD" instead.

Anna talked to a friend on the phone and complained how bored she was. Then she called another friend from school and made the same complaints. When she talked to her boyfriend Trent, she closed the door on her little brother, saying only, "Ears!"

Away from their teachers, Jaimie's classmates called him Ears, as well. Jaimie had large ears, but he thought the right one special. It pointed forward so his mother called it Jaimie's listening ear. His teachers said they wished all their students listened as well as he did. Jaimie liked that, so he didn't mind the nickname.

He didn't mind being called "retard" very much, either, because that didn't say anything about what he could do. Jaimie could listen better than anyone, and remember everything. It took Jaimie some time to realize he saw the world more deeply than everyone he knew.

When he discovered they didn't see the colors he could detect, he felt sorry for them. They spoke easily but were mostly blind. For instance, the boy saw the colors of numbers. Each flower had its own sound, gently humming to itself.

Words were Jaimie's favorite thing, though. Words had meanings everyone could understand, but Jaimie could detect the music and feel the shape of each word. As a very young child, he'd been lost in an overwhelming sea of color, taste and sensation, near to drowning. Currents and tides closed in over his head until he had to close his eyes to the beautiful onslaught. The texture of the sounds on the radio distracted him. Soft music tasted sweet. Angry voices felt jagged. Sharp words prickled his skin. Everything in the world had such dimension that Jaimie remembered everything he saw. Jaimie was the perfect witness to the end of the world.

It came to the boy that he was unique in his perceptions when he happened across *his* word in the dictionary. It had started with a random find of the word "poeticule." Wandering through the Ps, he found "perspicacity" and "perception." In the details about perception, Jaimie found a reference to "synesthesia". He followed that path to the Ss. That's where he found himself. "Synesthete."

Jaimie saw the worry lines in Jack's forehead as she listened to the radio. Her body's envelope of energy contracted and took on a washed-out yellow tone. When she turned off the radio, she unplugged it, as well. The first day the schools were closed there were only 406 cases of Sutr flu in all of Canada. There were 1,200 in the United States, only 98 in the Britain (they shut their borders early), "over 3,000" in India. (No precise numbers were provided once they got past 2,500). China stopped reporting any cases once the number rose past 4,000. Some journalists suggested that meant the true number was higher than one million in China.

Later the same week, schools everywhere shut down and it was said there wasn't a working subway train in the world. Sometimes when Jack was outside working in the garden, Theo would plug the radio back in and listen with the sound low. The voices didn't feel sharp on Jaimie's skin anymore. He felt something in the radio voices he hadn't encountered before. Fear that arrives electronically is a cool, yellow that tastes sour, like a rotten lemon.

Jaimie sometimes thought his father could see the colors because he watched the radio as he listened to it, as if he saw something more than the others. When Theo looked up, he was startled to see his son standing close. Theo unplugged the radio, yanking the plug from its socket by the wire. Theo gave a small, lopsided smile and took Jaimie's hand to pull him outside.

"You should see this," he said. "It's something I haven't seen in years."

Jack was on her knees digging in a corner of the garden. Jaimie looked around but didn't see anything different. Theo pointed up. The sky was azure, without a cloud. It was hard to imagine that anything could change under that sky or that anyone had anything to fear.

"I haven't seen this since 9/11," Theo said. "No planes, no jet exhaust. There aren't any planes up anywhere, not even the military jets or drones," he said.

"Why wouldn't they fly the drones?" Jack asked. "Robots can get viruses, I suppose, but not the Sutr virus."

Jaimie watched his father's face and recognized the indigo and violets of a new thought's inception. "They're drones. The pilots...they're um...social distancing the pilots, too."

"Or all the pilots are sick," Jack said. "It'll ease up the global warming, I guess." Jack clawed harder at the earth with her trowel.

"It's pretty early to start thinking about the garden, isn't it? There's still frost to come."

"It's something to do," Jack said. "The way things are going, we should be planting vegetables."

"No azaleas? No petunias? You love petunias."

"We'll plant what we can eat. Cliff said to get some seeds if we're going to hunker down. I got them. Cabbages are hardy, and I got lots of root vegetables. We're going to get sick of carrots, I got too many of those...but who's to say what's too much now?"

"Think we can eat it all? The kids don't even like that stuff."

Jack looked at him sharply, a rub of dirt stuck under her left eye. Jaimie hadn't seen her look at Theo that way before. "They'll eat it and like it if there's nothing else to eat. We'll be eating a lot of soup, like my parents did in the Great Depression."

"We don't know that'll be necessary yet."

"Don't we?"

"We need more data before we panic. I checked the radio. There isn't an open border anywhere now."

"Viruses don't know anything about borders. They're citizens of the world."

"The problem could be solved or contained yet."

"It could, but the people in charge don't have a great track record for solving problems. Most people are B and C students. There are a few brainiacs working with microscopes, but they're generally not the ones in charge. Think high school. The jocks ran the show. Same thing now. Get a bunch of people together to solve a problem and it's not the smartest guy who does the talking. It's the loudest."

"We're brainiacs," Theo said. "We'll be okay. We'll get through this."

Jack watched the ground and Jaimie wondered if she saw something there that he couldn't see. Did the earth harbor answers, or just the cold future?

"Last night I did a lot of googling. I already knew that every empire falls. Entropy rules," Jack said. "I'm not saying this is the end of the world but — "

"You have to be careful what you read, hon. Lots of people are screaming now."

"I'm not an alarmist," she said. "I'm saying this could be the end of the world as we know it. Things are going to change. Everything changes and I'm scared of everything changing."

"This isn't going to be that bad. People recover." Theo said. "Lots of people. Most people. We've seen this before. Spanish Flu killed 25 million, but somehow the world kept turning."

Jaimie's mother rose, bristling. The boy felt thick needles dance across his forehead and into his ears. It felt like tiny, sharp-toed ants scurrying. The light around her head went from a rich blue to a navy blue. "This isn't panic. This is what *planning* looks like. It is precisely because we don't have enough 'data' that we need to prepare for the worst and hope for the best. By the time we have enough information, it could be too late."

Theo crossed his arms and looked away. "I'm not disagreeing with you. I'm just saying we already used the vacation budget for this."

"If Cliff's wrong and it all blows away, we'll go camping this summer. It'll be good for 'em. In the meantime, I need you to help me with the yard. I'll get Anna out here, too, if I can drag her away from the phone."

He hesitated. "How much do you want to dig up?"

"A rectangle, from the swing set to the edge of what used to be my flower bed." The swing set sat in the middle of the large yard.

Theo whistled and put his hands on his hips the way he did when he was upset. "That's a lot of square footage, Jack."

"We get awfully hungry. I've got a lot of unanswered questions and your brother's got a lot of scary answers. He should know what he's talking about."

Jaimie watched his father's healthy green colors slowly turn to that now familiar sour yellow, mixed with red.

"Are you with me?" Jack asked.

"Of course," he said.

North Americans expected their doctors to have all the answers they needed when they needed them. They expected limitless supplies of all the basics and luxuries without end, too. They'd depended on technology and wealth for so long, North Americans had difficulty telling the difference between wants and needs. They had more illusions to lose, so they held on to them harder.

That afternoon, Jaimie dug in the ground for the first time. He pulled worms out of the dark, brown soil and arranged them in a line for sorting by size. He counted them and wondered what worms think about. Anna complained a lot at first and then retreated into a stony silence that felt warm and pleasant, at least to Jaimie. It was those times that he felt closest to his sister. The depth of her silence met his own, though her colors flared red around her head and in the center of her chest.

The family dug through the afternoon, overturning turf and softening the ground. Jack worked with a clawed hoe, Theo and Anna with spades and the boy with the small trowel. They broke the clumps of grass, taking turns with a new pickaxe. After half an hour, they were all shiny and wet with effort. The backyard was the family's first farm and the first time they had all worked together.

Jack's anger was a red that dulled to a blue-black bruise the harder she swung the pick. Anna stayed angry red. Theo was yellow but getting greener, like a lime.

The color around Jaimie's hands went from purple to a deep violet. Jaimie decided later that those were the hues of his purest happiness.

Tomorrow's For Promises We'll Fail To Keep

Jaimie got out of bed and listened at the crack at the bottom of the door. His parents whispered back and forth, but he could hear his sister clearly. "How bad?...How long?" More urgent whispers. Anna stomped up the stairs, passed Jaimie's bedroom and slammed her door.

When Jaimie got up early the next morning, his parents were dressed in the same clothes from the night before. Both their laptops stood open on the dining room table and Jack had a pad of paper. Jaimie couldn't read her scrawl, but Jaimie recognized the look of a list, each word or groups of words in a stack.

"I'm taking the day off work," Theo told Jaimie. "You come with me and you can push the cart and help carry things."

His mother looked to her husband, her face a question.

"He's sixteen and strong," Theo said. "We'll take the van. Give me what you've got so far and we'll go work on that. When Anna gets up, take the other car and fit what you can in it."

Jack nodded and ripped several pages off her pad. She held them out to him, but looked in his eyes and didn't let go of the pages. "Who should I call?"

"Call everyone in the family."

"Really?"

"Everyone should know. Cliff might not have been able to warn everyone. He and I have had our trouble, but he risked a lot to get the

26

word out to us about what's really going on. He'd be in big trouble sharing some of those memos, I'm sure."

"Just family? I have to call Brandy. She's my best friend."

"I count Brandy as family. Of course, tell her. It's not that we keep it a secret from anyone. It's just prioritizing who gets alerted first." He looked like he was doing a difficult calculation in his head. "We'll talk about coworkers later. I've called in sick, so we definitely can't warn any of them yet. 'k?" They kissed quickly and Theo fed Jaimie breakfast at a drive-through. The tofu sausage patty was greasy and smeared the boy's lips.

His father laughed as he wiped the boy's face with a napkin, "You're a shiny little ape."

Jaimie watched his father's aura. Theo was shiny, too. A halo of green and violet fire flared around his head as he gently wiped his son's chin.

He caught new interest in the boy's look. When he finished, Theo asked his son if he had anything to say.

The boy shook his head slightly.

"It's okay, son. When you're ready."

Most people wore surgical masks or even carpenter masks and goggles. Some had cloth tied over their faces and the people who wore eyeglasses all seemed to be steamed up so much they maneuvered through the aisles of Target in a fog. A couple people wore winter scarves tied over their faces.

Theo held Jaimie's hand. The boy stuck close to his side. No one wanted to bump into another person, but it was so busy, the crowd's press was inevitable. Theo said Jaimie "heeled like a terrier." Target was too full and only one line was open to a cashier, so they left for the mall's grocery store.

The shelves weren't as full as usual and the aisles were packed. Theo stuffed the shopping list into his shirt pocket and didn't look at it again. Instead, he grabbed a cart for Jaimie to push while he pulled another. With one hand on his son's shoulder, he guided Jaimie through the crowd and down the aisles. Instead of looking at what he was buying, Theo swept cans into the cart with one arm.

The freezers were almost empty. When Theo looked at the vegetable section he said in a low hiss, "Locusts."

All the milk — regular and powdered — was gone. Down one aisle, Theo jumped up and spotted something. He climbed the shelf to reach a big bottle of hand sanitizer covered in dust at the back, almost out of sight.

At the end of the cracker and snack aisle, a thin old woman in a black dress blocked the way. "You're taking too much," she said. Her lined face made Jaimie think of the pictures of witches he'd seen in fairy-tale books.

"Excuse me?" Theo said.

"You're taking too much," she repeated, and coughed without covering her mouth. She sweated heavily and looked flushed.

"Please," Theo said softly, but his hand clamped down harder on the boy's shoulder and Jaimie pushed the cart forward. She gave them a hard look. As they brushed past her, there was an acidic smell that came off her mottled skin. It reminded Jaimie of a dead squirrel that had been run over in front of his house last summer. The old woman glowed with fever.

The boy couldn't take his eyes off her as they pushed on. He thought of witches who kidnapped children, who pushed them into ovens and tricked them into eating poisoned apples. He watched the black dots, bigger and greasier, swallow up the woman's reds and yellows. Jaimie could barely see her face, as if the black dress was getting bigger, enveloping her in thick gauze. When she curled her thin lips back in a sneer, she revealed long, yellow teeth and bloody gums. She coughed again and Theo twisted away, turning his head, but his hand didn't leave his son's shoulder. Instead he squeezed tighter until Jaimie's shoulder hurt, urging him to walk faster.

"You're taking too much!" she yelled again.

"You don't get to say how much is too much, ma'am," Theo said. "You don't know how much I need."

Her voice followed them around the end of the aisle. "Selfish!"

Jaimie knocked a box of steel wool pads from a shelf. When the boy stooped to pick up the boxes, Theo pulled him up and urged him on.

"I see you," the old woman called. "I seen what you done!"

"Go home!" Theo yelled back. He wanted to sound commanding. Instead he felt weak, yelling at a sick, old woman. He wasn't sure she was wrong. Maybe he was taking too much.

In the next aisle, the old woman shuffled around the end, still watching. To Jaimie's eyes, she looked less like a witch and more like a seething black mass, a swarm of black insects. Jaimie recognized the word he saw as he gazed at her. It was an ominous word that had sharp edges at the ends but was soft in the middle. He had often turned to the Ws to look at the word, to feel its danger. The word was "wraith". That word tasted of bitter almonds.

Before he closed the dictionary, Jaimie looked at different words that made him feel safe and to wash away the sour almonds: "Gesture" tasted of fresh sprouts; "pastoral" tasted the way grass looks; "cheery" was a brave, golden color that tasted of orange sorbet.

They waited in line a long time. Behind Jaimie, a scared Asian woman with bright, glassy eyes held a baby in her arms. She cooed to her child in a singsong language Jaimie couldn't understand, though he understood her colors. The sugary sweetness she used with the baby covered her lemony fear.

There was only one cashier here, too. He looked like a manager. He was an older man with wispy hair that looked like it needed combing. He looked tired and harassed.

In front of Theo, a burly man in a big camouflage coat stood very straight. Many people spoke in an excited staccato, voices full of chaos, but the big man grinned through his red bushy beard as he watched the crowd. He was a blob of red and blue in a sea of yellow fear. It occurred to Jaimie that the man was enjoying himself.

The man must have felt Jaimie's stare because he looked down at the boy for a moment before giving Theo a smile. "Never think you'd ever see anything like it, eh?"

Theo shook his head. "Nope. Sure didn't."

"I did!" the man bragged. "Saw this coming a mile away."

Theo gave him an encouraging nod, glad of the distraction.

"Remember that huge power outage a few years ago? The gas pumps didn't work. I lost everything in my freezer, including twenty pounds of moose meat I'd shot the previous fall. I didn't know what to do with myself. I drive for a living. I couldn't work and I hate warm beer."

"I remember," Theo said. "Our power was out for three days and it was really hot. We slept in the basement and by the third night we were laying on top of the sheets as the heat settled on us. It felt like a wool blanket on a hot August night. We opened all the windows, but there wasn't a breath of wind."

"Yup, no air conditioning. The power was out for eight days up where I live. I had a lot of time to sit in the dark in my underwear and think. I decided I'd be ready to take care of things myself if anything happened again, hurricane, tornado, pestilence, whatever." His colors came far out from his body and Jaimie stepped back a little, feeling overwhelmed.

"You know why we gotta take care of ourselves, mister? 'Cuz nobody's coming. Like Obama said way back, we're the crazy fools we been waiting for!" His laugh shook his belly.

Theo smiled with half his mouth.

Jaimie hadn't seen his father talk with other men much at all. Theo watched the stranger, his chin close to his chest but his body faced to the side, away from the big man in camouflage.

"Things are getting kind of crazy around here. Looks like you were right to get ready. What did you do to prepare?" His father sounded casual, but his colors took on a thin feel that told Jaimie his father's interest was serious.

"Got two kinds of generators. That's where I started. It kind of grew from there. I was raised in the woods, so I already knew a bunch of what I had to know, but the deeper I got into self-sustainability...well, the deeper I went."

The line advanced a few steps. "I knew people when I was a kid who had an old house with a bomb shelter built in," Theo said. "That sounds fancy, but to lock yourself away in there would be kind of like hiding away in a small root cellar or something."

"Yeah, all that duck and cover bull — " The big man glanced at Jaimie and leaned closer to Theo, his voice low. "Survivalism gets a bad rap. The movement has been full of a lot of wackos and their macho racist bull. It was a good idea that was hijacked by a bunch of guys with a military fetish who get a little too excited about pictures in gun magazines, if you know what I mean. You listen to me on this 'cuz I've given it a lot of thought, I kid you not. They'd have been better off learning how to can their own beans and jar their own jellies instead of stocking up on more and more guns. Can't eat a machine gun and there's not much left of the bird if that's how you shoot it. The green movement has gotten more into the nature appreciation part. That's what sustainability is about. We're in for a long storm, friend. You can bet on that." The man stood straight again and looked around, as if, too late, to make sure no one had heard him.

"You really think it's going to be that bad?"

"Look around you." The stranger gestured to the crowd. "We're always nine meals away from anarchy. Grocery stores don't have more than three days of supplies on their shelves thanks to just-in-time delivery. I've been a trucker since I was twenty. I know all about just-in-time. Nobody keeps anything stored away anymore. Nobody's putting stuff away for the winter. Not like a couple generations back. People are softer now and used to so many conveniences. I don't think they'll handle it so well as our grandparents or even our parents could have."

Theo nodded, encouraging him, and the man's colors enveloped them again. The bearded man smiled broadly, glad of an audience.

Loneliness, Jaimie thought, *tastes like bland, lumpy oatmeal and makes the colors close to the heart turn to gray dust bunnies.*

"If you eat it, wear it or use it, it comes by truck and it probably comes across a border. The borders are shut down. Each nation is an island now and when the government can't help you, each man is an island. Each man is an island, at least when the chips are down and everything's gone to uh…poop." He gave Jaimie a kind glance and smiled again, revealing teeth too perfect to be real. "John Donne had it wrong, huh?"

Theo failed to conceal his surprise and the man caught his look. "Poetry isn't just for city folks, Professor. In fact, a case of beer and reading poetry in the woods go together quite nicely."

The line advanced another few feet and the man in camouflage seemed to lose his train of thought for a moment. "I didn't read much before I got into sustainability. I don't know why. I mean…I read a lot of seed catalogues and fishing magazines before. I was on a sustainability forum and somebody kept talking about Walden, you know?"

"*On Walden Pond.*"

"Yeah. You know it. Good. Go read it if you haven't, or read it again. I tell you now, Communism went under. Capitalism went under when we caught on that the brokers and bankers and the politicians were just out for themselves. Thoreau wrote the only manifesto we should pay attention to now."

Behind them, the baby began to cough. Both men hunched slightly. "Speaking of Donne…" the man said.

"Ask not for whom the bell tolls — " Theo said.

"Yeah. *Don't,*" the man replied. "Nobody likes that answer."

"I've gotta get out of this cesspool and up in isolation. My nearest neighbor up north is like five miles away."

"Where's that?" Theo asked.

"North. Just north."

They smiled at each other, but Jaimie saw some yellow creep into the big man's aura and his egg of energy took on hard edges.

The baby coughed again. Theo shifted his weight from foot to foot, anxious to leave. "You think we should wear masks?"

The man in camouflage laughed. "Looks like downtown China in here, doesn't it? Nah. Those masks don't do you any good. Viruses are small buggers and the masks these folks are wearing might make 'em feel good, but they're really only good for keeping sawdust out when you're using a circular saw."

Theo looked startled. "But they wear masks in the hospitals."

"I looked into it," the man said. "Those masks are specially fitted. They use a noxious smoke to test the seal. Even then, as soon as it gets a little wet, say from you breathing through it, it's no good anymore. I heard of some guys getting fancy gas masks and even Hazmat suits, but you can't live in them 24/7, so what's the point? The point is to rely on yourself and get through. It's not to live in a bubble."

The man looked Jaimie's father up and down, and for the first time turned his head to the side. "Can't say where I'm headed, partner. Nothing personal, but get you and your boy away from the cities. The Sutr virus is just the first wave. When the system can't clear the dead bodies anymore, the next wave is typhus or cholera or bubonic or whatever else comes with dead bodies unattended to."

Jaimie watched his father's cheeks flush. He glanced into the man's shopping cart and the man followed his gaze. The cart was full of potato chips bags and soda. "My last little luxuries," the man said. "I suppose I can shave some potatoes and fry up my own chips, but I doubt I'll be making my own soda after that runs out."

Eyeing the man's cases of soda my father said, "I hope this won't last *that* long."

The baby coughed again, and this time it wheezed a long time afterward, like it was trying to catch its breath but that race was already lost. Jaimie looked at the baby. It was a girl judging by her pink blanket. When he looked closely, he could see rivulets of black stretching out over the child's throat and chest. The baby's mother was a flare of yellow, but none of the black touched her. The mother was immune, but her immunity had not passed to her baby.

The man in camouflage finally advanced to the cashier. The man behind the counter didn't look up from the conveyor belt as he pulled the bags of chips across the scanner.

"You still taking credit cards, boss?"

"Yes, sir," said the cashier.

The man in camouflage winked at my father and smiled even bigger. "Jeez, I think I better haul ass over to the liquor store next," he said.

He waved at father and son happily as he pushed his cart toward the exit, but he was waiting outside the store as Theo and Jaimie walked to their van, pushing their carts of groceries. "Hey, friend. It was nice talking to you. I was thinking about you and your boy. I want to give you some free advice. Load up while they're still taking credit cards. Max out everything and fill up because this is the time. Don't hold back. Who knows? Our numbers might be up and nobody's coming to collect anyway. Mark my words."

"Thanks," Theo said.

"Here's an even better secret you probably didn't know. Load up even if it's not something you can use," the man said, "Load up! You see that 18-wheeler over there?" It was the only semi in the parking lot. "I was on a big delivery when I got turned back at a roadblock. Guess what that box is full of? Tampons! I've got a lifetime supply right there, all sizes. If I ever run out of anything, or if I just want some company, I've got something to trade. I'm headed north. Sometime next year things will settle down or they won't. Either way, I'm gonna come back down here and I'm gonna be the Tampon King."

"Well…good luck," Theo replied. "Thanks for the advice." He stuck out his hand to shake but the man in camouflage pulled back instead and gave a friendly wave.

"Shaking hands. You know, old son, that's a tradition that started with knights clasping sword hands to show their friendly intentions. Same with the salute, raising up the armored visor to flash a smile at a fellow knight. I think handshaking's dead, along with lots of people, don't you?"

The big man gave a cheery salute as he walked toward his truck. Jaimie had a new word for what he saw. If he had trawled through his big dictionaries in alphabetical order, he would have run across the word much sooner. The word was *aura*.

When the boy squinted, he could see two tiny black dots at the very edge of the big man's aura. They looked like black wasps, angry but waiting for their time to strike.

Jaimie thought it sad that such a big, friendly man would die along with the tradition of the handshake.

We Are All Gods In Some Small Way

Theo and Jaimie spent the rest of the morning shopping and only returned home when their van was full. Theo ran back and forth from the house, puffing. The boy had never seen him run. He emptied it as quickly as he could and then took off for supplies twice more.

At the camping store they found tents but they were for cold weather. All the summer tents were gone. The young, blonde woman behind the counter watched Theo try to decide what to buy. She finally walked up and asked what kind of camping he intended to do.

"What do you mean, *kind* of camping?" he asked.

The blonde woman did not try to conceal her heavy sigh. "Well, there's back country hiking, but you're probably thinking of campgrounds with lots of facilities. You know, like camping from your car."

"Can we make this simple? Which one should I get for four people, two adults and two kids...well, really four adults, I guess."

"That depends. Where you going and what season are you camping in?"

Jaimie watched confusion cross his father's face and his jaw hardened. He didn't know the answers to those questions, but he answered, "Summer. Maybe a long trip, like to the east coast."

The saleswoman bobbed her head. "All our summer stock is gone and the boss says there's no way to know when we'll get restocked. I can sell you a tarp. I still have some of those." My father's mouth curled and Jaimie watched thin heat come off him in a wave that

35

tasted chalky. "A tarp isn't as dry as a tent but it's something, and a tent in summer is often too hot, anyway."

"Give me a winter tent and two tarps," he said. "Anything else I need?"

When the woman rolled her eyes, he said, "Never mind, I'll browse some more and figure it out."

Theo bought a compass, a first aid kit, four cold weather sleeping bags, ponchos, several boxes of waterproof matches, a camp oven, glow sticks, a lantern, gas for the lantern and glow-in-the-dark tent pegs. Jaimie contented himself with exploring the fabric of the carpet while Theo debated about backpacks. His father picked out four huge backpacks first, thought better of it and chose two smaller packs and two big ones.

When he brought his selections to the store's front counter, the saleswoman cocked an eyebrow at him and asked if there was room for everyone to sleep in the car. "You need mats for under the sleeping bags, too. Without it, it always feels like you're sleeping on a rock or a lump no matter where you pitch the tent. The air bed is most comfortable, but you need a pump, too. There's an electric one, which I recommend."

He went back and got rolled foam sleeping mats and then handed Jaimie four plastic bags, each marked "Survival Kit." When Theo thought he was finished, the blonde woman stood with her arms crossed, considering the boy with an appraising eye. "You need this," she said as she pulled a box marked "Portable Toilet" from the wall behind the counter. Theo nodded and asked if she had any other helpful suggestions.

"Leaves of three, let it be. Never wipe your butt with poison oak. It can ruin your whole day and definitely screws up your night."

Instead of using the cash register the woman used a calculator. When she was done, she said the bill came to $3,400.

Theo hesitated, looking over his purchases. "That can't be right. I thought it was less."

"Prices went up recently," she said.

"You're gouging me? You can't do that. You have to go with the prices as marked!"

"Call it an even $2,900, then," she said.

Theo looked at Jaimie and back at the pile of camping supplies. Without a word, he handed her a credit card.

She took it without hesitating and started putting everything in bags. "Business sure is great recently. A lot of people are discovering the beauty of nature or something."

"You watch the news?" Theo said.

"Yeah, all that flu pandemic garbage will pass. We'll probably shut down for a couple weeks. I was going to spend my spring vacation backpacking in Bolivia this year but that's all screwed up. I'll head to the Rockies again this year instead. I'd rather deal with snakes than grizzlies, but whatcha gonna do?"

"Bears?" Theo said.

"The biggest."

He pointed to canisters in plastic behind the counter. "I need bear spray, too."

"Good idea. $100."

When he started to hand back his credit card she quickly added, "Cash only."

Theo dug a crisp $100 bill out of his wallet. She held it up to the light and smiled as she reached under her shirt and tucked the bill into her bra.

She helped Theo and Jaimie carry everything out to the van.

"A couple more epidemics like this and I might take a year off to backpack Australia!" she said.

Theo and Jaimie climbed back in the van and his father sat there a moment, staring at the steering wheel. Jaimie stared at it, too, but he didn't notice any change in it.

"I knew there were such things as war profiteers," Theo said. "I guess I hadn't thought all this through as things go downhill. It didn't occur to me anyone would try to profit off misery. I also never thought I'd hand over a credit card thinking there was a chance I'd never have to pay the bill. A lot of people are in denial and most everyone else seems to be in a panic. I'm lost here, J. I can't tell anyone else this, not even your mother...I really don't know what I'm doing. I've felt that way before...taking you and your sister home from the hospital after you were born. I felt this way for a long time before you got your diagnosis. But this? This feels like the first time where not knowing what I'm doing might be deadly important! This might be something I can't adapt to or fix or…I don't know…"

Jaimie buckled his seatbelt. When his father didn't turn the ignition, the boy said "Pickle!"

"Pickle" had been code in the family since Anna was a little girl. One day Jack was to drive Anna somewhere and she called out to the back seat, "Buckled?" before she started the car.

Anna misheard "buckled" and called back, "Pickle!" The mistake stuck.

Theo adjusted his mirror so he could look in Jaimie's eyes. "You have a nice voice, J. I wish you used it more."

He said that every time Jaimie spoke.

On their return, they found Anna and Jack in the kitchen surrounded by bags of groceries, mostly cans, cereal and big boxes of powdered milk. Theo let out a low whistle which Jaimie knew meant he was impressed. "You did well. I couldn't find any powdered milk."

Jack looked up from the floor where she had been sorting groceries into piles. "We got out of town and went to a bunch of smaller stores. When I looked at the grocery store and saw the parking lot, I just kept going. The panic buying hasn't set in so much out in the little towns yet, or there aren't so many people to drain the shelves. Maybe country people are just more prepared generally and have more stuff on hand."

Anna stood over her mother. "Mom says everyone else is panic buying but we're not."

Theo nodded cautiously.

"This is crazy. School's closed for quarantine and people aren't supposed to gather in large groups so the first thing we do is run out with the crowds to get a bunch of stuff?"

Jack and Theo looked at each other. "I needed you with me to help carry everything, Anna," Jack said, her defences shooting up in yellow and pink pastels.

Anna crossed her arms. "I hope you guys like powdered milk because I'm not drinking that stuff. I tried it once at summer camp and it was watery and awful."

"I hope you get to say I told you so, Anna," Jack said.

"I'm going to," she said. "I'm bringing it up at all my weddings and your funerals, too." She smiled, but Jaimie guessed she wasn't really happy.

"All your weddings?" Theo said.

"Don't be a bonehead, Dad." Anna began to march out of the kitchen but Theo caught her by the elbow. "Help your Mom put the stuff away, please. Jaimie will help me with the stuff in the van." There was a hard tone in his voice that was new.

Anna hesitated. She bent to look through the shopping bags and help her mother as if it were her idea.

At the front door, Theo paused and shouted back, "Jack? Did you find duct tape and plastic?"

"Yes!" Jaimie's mother bellowed, though I still don't know what we'll use it for!"

"Me, neither! But the governor recommended it!"

There was no more room in the kitchen cupboards. Theo told Jaimie and Anna to carry everything to the basement. A cold room with shelves for food stood near the furnace room, but Theo insisted they hide all the foodstuffs in another basement room instead. "If anyone asks," he said, "we don't have any more food than a few days' worth. If somebody looks in the logical places, we won't have much to give up. Everybody got that?"

Jaimie wouldn't understand that danger until the night the looters came and the Spencers lost everything.

Jack wanted to sort through all the supplies again and make a list on her clipboard. Instead, Theo had one more family outing planned for that day. They drove to where he worked. It was a small library branch. The libraries had closed and it was dark when they pulled into the empty parking lot.

Theo pulled keys to the big glass doors from his coat pocket and dashed ahead to enter the code so the building alarm wouldn't sound.

"There really haven't been that many people in lately, except for the computers."

The smell of stale book glue hung in the air. Theo surveyed the library. "At Hiroshima," Theo whispered to his wife, "at the moment of the blast, one of the victims was buried under a pile of books. That's how the Atomic Age began. That metaphor always stuck, you know? I wonder…if this is the beginning of the Plague Age. The experts all say we're overdue — "

"Don't," Jack said. "We'll live to find out. Somebody always survives any disaster and we're taking precautions millions won't or can't." She walked past her husband.

Only Jaimie caught his father's barely breathed words, "Everybody always thinks they're the ones who will make it."

Jaimie squeezed his father's hand. Without thinking about it, or even knowing he could do such a thing, gave Theo some of his violet energy. He'd watched his father use jumper cables to help start a neighbor's car once. The energy transfer was like that.

Theo straightened, as if sensing a mild electric current. He broke away and looked at his son, more baffled than shocked. After a moment, he set his jaw as if dismissing a useless thought and went about handing each family member a garbage bag. He gestured toward the stacks. "Anything you want. Load up. It's a free-for-all tonight. I've cracked open the vault. Go wild."

Anna and Jack headed toward fiction. Jaimie followed his father, watching as he scoured the books. He glimpsed his mother and sister through gaps in the shelves. He could tell by the way they moved that they were browsing aimlessly, letting books of interest reveal themselves.

Theo moved with purpose, searching for particular titles. The yellow that had suffused him all day (*miasma was the better word*, Jaimie thought) lifted, leaving Theo his usual vibrant blue-green.

The house seemed to belong more to his mother than his father. The public library was his father's home. Libraries were on the way out and his was a dying profession that would soon degenerate from quaint to irrelevant. However, this was where Theo knew all there was to know.

Theo found a few books on camping and a dusty book with a battered jacket on canning and making jam and jellies. A book on hiking captured his attention but he grew more frustrated the longer he looked, as if the one perfect book he needed eluded him.

Anna filled her garbage bag and she carried a few more titles stacked on one arm. She placed those on the front counter before going off to look for more. They were mostly vampire romances and celebrity biographies. Jack appeared carrying a bible in each hand. One was a King James. The other was a translation into contemporary English.

After Jaimie followed his father around the library's Outdoors section for a few minutes, Theo stopped. He looked at Jaimie curiously, and offered his hand. Jaimie grasped it and pulled him with a surprisingly strong grip toward the reference section. The boy began pulling volumes of the Oxford English Dictionary from the shelf but Theo waved him off. "That's too much, buddy," he said. "It's too heavy and takes up too much space."

Jaimie nodded and pulled out a single large dictionary, followed by a slang dictionary. He thought better of that choice and pushed it back, favoring a dictionary of Latin terms instead.

"Interesting choice," Theo said, but he did not deter his son further.

The family froze as a clatter of keys hit the front desk. "Hello?" The deep voice ricocheted off the concrete walls. "Anna? What are you doing here?"

The newcomer was Thad Krenner, Theo's boss. His British accent was thick. "Plummy" Theo called it. Mr. Krenner always wore a brown pilled sweater with a frayed collar underneath his rumpled sports jacket of the same shade as the sweater.

Jaimie never saw him without that jacket. The boy made a mental note to look up "sports jacket" in the dictionary. He couldn't think what sport Mr. Krenner played or how his tight jacket could be comfortable for playing any kind of physically demanding game. Mr. Krenner was enormous, and, though he always smiled Jaimie's way under his sharply trimmed moustache, his size and the force of his

41

booming voice frightened the boy. "Loudest librarian on the planet," Theo said.

"We're all here, Thaddeus!" Jack called.

"The Spencers are all working overtime? I'm not sure we have it in the budget to hire all of you," Krenner said.

Theo came to the front desk, a half-dozen books tucked under one arm. The family followed. Mr. Krenner looked down, eyeing Jaimie's armful of dictionaries and a picture book that showed satellite pictures of Earth. His gaze lingered longer at the garbage bag at his feet, overflowing with Anna's book choices.

"You're not preparing for a siege are you?"

"Yes," Theo said. "Yes, we are. Have you been watching the news?"

"Oh, a little bit, but there's no need to overdose on it. It seems like the media is about their business, whipping everyone up. Too much, I say."

Mr. Krenner looked to the bags of books, not looking directly at the Spencers. "You seem to be taking this stuff quite seriously, Theodore. No sense in that. This will all blow over. It's true we closed the library early today, but that wasn't my decision. The higher ups said the schools are closed so they insisted we all take some vacation time. It's unfortunate, I think. I like to take my vacations at the cottage when the leaves turn."

"I've been doing a lot of research and talking to some people who think we *should* take this seriously, Thad. We might be in isolation for a while." Theo stepped closer and put on a smile Jaimie had never seen him use at home. "You can't expect me to be locked up with the kids for more than a day or two without lots to entertain them, can you? You're an animal lover. You wouldn't do that to a dog, would you?"

Krenner laughed and Jaimie shrank behind his mother. The sound from the head librarian's throat was a clatter of various sizes of dishes. When Jaimie peered from behind Jack, he said, "That young man of yours is getting tall. He wouldn't cause you any trouble though. He's not at all a chatterbox!" and laughed again.

Theo glanced to his son and reddened. "Has everyone got what they need?" Anna and Jack shrugged and nodded.

"We'll take this out to the van. You two talk," Jack said.

Jaimie stayed with his father, slipping his hand into Theo's grip. He stared at Mr. Krenner's wide and long shoes, studying their shine.

"Theodore, really, you mustn't get yourself and your family too worked up about all this."

"We're just taking precautions."

"It's the tyranny for young people these days that they're cursed with the expectation that they'll all live forever if they can just do everything right, exercise themselves to exhaustion and eat the inedible just to squeeze a few more hours out of life. Stress gets us all in the end, and emptying out the shelves as soon as we close strikes me as something designed to cause me stress, running off with all the inventory in the night. You are not following procedures. Especially with the reference books. The dictionaries can't go home with you."

Theo squeezed his son's hand and pulled him toward the door. "You'll get over it, Thad. I hope you live long enough to get over it."

Jaimie watched the big man's certainty drain away. His aura shrank and yellows crept in at the edges, muddying his red and navy blue energies. After a pause, Mr. Krenner gave a short nod. "You think it's as bad as all that, Theodore?"

"Call me Theo. You know that's what I've always preferred yet you have always ignored my preference. It's *Theo*."

Krenner's face went pale. His eyes shifted to Jaimie and he straightened, clearing his throat, looking for words. In a cheery tone that rattled empty, he said, "We're in the lending business, after all...Theo." He stuck out his hand and Theo shook it. "I hope you'll soon find that all of this was no big deal."

"I took a risk management course during my undergrad and I've thought about this a lot. My brother's a doctor and...he told us things," Theo said. "The cost-benefit analysis makes sense. Go to your cottage, Thad. Don't wait for the leaves to turn. Go now. If I'm wrong, you can call me Theodore when you see me next and I'll smile instead of gritting my teeth."

Krenner turned away. His wave was more dismissive than friendly. Before he turned to the exit, Jaimie spotted the fleeting thin slash of black across Mr. Krenner's back. A short, sharp bark erupted from Jaimie's throat and Theo and his boss turned together to look at the boy. Their mouths dropped open, as if both stood before a grotesque fun house mirror. Krenner sought out Jaimie's eyes. The boy backed out, putting distance between himself and the man.

Jaimie was sure Mr. Krenner would not live to see the leaves change at his cottage. He might not have another day before he felt the first symptoms of the Sutr virus.

If Jaimie had taken a moment more — if he had been brave enough — he might have seen where that deadly slash of black went, and if it reached out for his father, planting its seeds for the horrific harvest to come.

As he retreated to the van, Jaimie held the Latin dictionary to his chest. The boy had opened it at random and caught one phrase which piqued his interest: *O tempora! O mores!* It meant, *these are bad times.* The dictionary entry looked like a prophecy. From the auras he had read, Jaimie was certain the world was about to get much worse.

Jaimie stepped into the car and leaned over to whisper in his sister's ear. "Spiral."

But Chaos Rules The Last Cafe

As Dr. Craig Sinjin-Smythe moved down the row of plastic cages in his Hazmat suit, his alarm grew. Six of ten of the first batch of rats were dead from the Sutr-X virus. Each white rat's cage was labeled with a code number. Sinjin-Smythe had named them all: Ernest Borgnine, Jimmy Cagney, Robert Mitchum, Burt Lancaster, Jimmy Stewart, Henry Fonda, Sophia Loren, Ella Fitzgerald, Raymond Burr and Humphrey Bogart. The rats came and went, but he named them each the same.

"Something's weird with the actors," the doctor observed. His fiancée and colleague, Ava Keres, was listening through the open mic in his helmet. He had to speak up to be heard over the fan above his head.

Dr. Keres' voice came through a little too loud. "As I've told you many times, your practice of naming them is silly, unscientific and against protocol."

"Whimsical and creative," Sinjin-Smythe replied.

"You use the same names repeatedly with all the specimens."

"Somewhat creative, then."

She sighed. "I don't deserve you."

They'd been together two years. It had been a tumultuous courtship. Ava could be imperious and lectured him on his idiosyncrasies. However, every time he had thought to break it off, she did something sweet for him.

Since he had taken her with him when he moved to the Cambridge lab, she'd grown happier and softer around the edges. Or perhaps that was the baby. She was three months along. He'd wanted her to stay home as soon as the pregnancy test stick showed two pink dots. She told him she'd consider a leave of absence at six months.

"The lab has so many precautions, the baby and I would be in just as much danger with me banging around the kitchen bored out of my skull. Besides, every day chaos is so scintillating."

Sinjin-Smythe was especially glad of those precautions as he peered into the tenth cage. "Something's wrong with Bogart. Do you have a clear picture?"

The helmet cam whirred and focused as Ava adjusted the camera's angle from the isolation lab's observation booth. "I see a rat, Craig. Tell me."

"Specimens one through six inclusively are deceased," he said.

"Expected."

"Uh-huh. Seven through ten are still alive, but Bogey isn't looking too good."

"Yes, yes."

"Sophia, Ella and Raymond are docile." He bent to peer closer. "Oh, god. The side of the cage…it's like Bogey tried to break through the cage to get at Raymond. It's smeared with saliva, feces and blood. Bogey's lying on the bottom of his cage and Raymond's cowering in a far corner."

"Anything else unusual about ten?"

Sinjin-Smythe had difficulty maneuvering in the huge isolation suit as his air hose coiled and tightened behind him. His movements were slow and deliberate, as they had to be in the High Hazard Unit, but his pulse beat in his ears as his excitement grew. "Um…his eyes are looking milky. I haven't seen that presentation bef — " The rat launched at the doctor, smacking its head against the cage door.

Sinjin-Smythe stepped back from the rodent's prison as fast as he could. Running away from the rat was irrational but involuntary. He planned to dissect Bogey's body later that day, but he wished he held the scalpel in his hand now, or a flamethrower, perhaps.

* * *

46

The hyper-encrypted, military version of Skype was a bit slow to connect. However, when his screen filled with Dr. Daniel Merritt's moon face from the CDC, Sinjin-Smythe forced his shoulders to relax. He didn't say hello. "This could be an outlier, but we might have a new variant."

Dr. Merritt was quick. As soon as Sinjin-Smythe described specimen ten's behavior, he said it sounded like rabies.

"Have any of the other nodes reported anything like that?"

Merritt shook his head. "However, there are bats with rabies in Los Angeles and reports have come in that they are becoming more aggressive of late. There have been fatalities among the homeless, but we're having a hard time determining numbers. It's a low number so..." he shrugged.

Health care and therefore epidemiological studies among the homeless were sketchy at best, especially in America. "We're working on that to get some samples and find out what's going on. Sutr's a fast jumper, so it is a concern. Perhaps when the bats take up residence in a rich, white neighborhood in the Hollywood Hills, I'll get more funding for techs on the ground."

"My rat's a fast jumper, too. I really thought it might smash right through the plastic for a moment there." Sinjin-Smythe grinned, embarrassed at his admission. "I'll have more for you after I autopsy the little bugger."

Dr. Merritt gave him a long look. "It's just the one rat, right?"

"Yes, I'm certain."

"Good." The CDC virologist shuffled some papers. "From the latest I've heard from the Middle East, one terrible strain of flu will be enough for us to deal with. The Dubai lab has gone red. Not just Julian. The whole lab's staff is dead."

"Think we can get more funding and help? Maybe pool more information with the Chinese?"

Dr. Merritt shook his head. "Nanjing went red late last night. We lost all communication with Dr. Seong's lab. Radio silence from the Chinese government. No one's sorted out what's happened yet. I assume someone on their end is working on that. Or running for their lives to hide out in a monastery in Tibet."

"And Ellen?" Sinjin-Smythe had met Dr. Ellen Harper in person at a symposium on clostridium two years previously in New York. He had fond memories of Dr. Harper introducing him to Manhattan's nightlife. If Ava hadn't swooped in on him at the same conference, it might be Ellen working with him in Cambridge instead.

"The Manitoba node remains green, but nothing new there. Go do that autopsy and get back to me with the histologicals ASAP, Craig. Tell me something new."

In the isolation unit, Dr. Ava Keres had turned off the safeties, the backups and alarms. She entered the room that held the doomed rats and hurried to the tenth cage. Bogart lay on the bottom of the cage, battered and weakened from his attacks. "I've waited years to meet you," she said, "and now you're finally here."

She slipped off her thick glove, unlocked the rat cage and thrust her bare hand at the rat. It was weak, but it snapped its jaws immediately. The infected rat's teeth sunk into the web between her thumb and forefinger. The pain was exquisite, but brief. She shook off the animal, closed the cage and retreated, holding her wounded hand tight to her belly.

Dr. Keres had signed out of the lab at the security checkpoint and was in a taxi headed for Piccadilly Circus before Sinjin-Smythe finished talking to the CDC's Sutr virus vaccine coordinator.

When Sinjin-Smythe returned to the lab, he was puzzled that his fiancée was not at her desk. Another fifteen minutes went by before he checked the ladies' washroom. She wasn't there. He tried calling, but Ava did not answer her cell.

Dr. Ava Keres had disappeared into a noonday crowd to spread the virus before he found the handwritten note on her desk:

Craig,

Words are important. Keres is not my real name, but it was chosen for me long ago. Keres is from Greek mythology. It's a female spirit of violent death: Death in battle, by accident, murder or terrible disease. Today marks the end of all your First World problems.

We are strong.
We are coming.
You deserve us.
The chaos in every day you have left will be so scintillating.
We make history and a new future.

Season 1, Episode 2

He knows where you live.

*

Everyone thinks the worst will come for someone else.

*

You fear what you don't understand.
You envy what you cannot have and do.
In each of us coils a green-eyed serpent.
If we had self-knowledge, we'd leave
each tempting apple untouched.

~ *Notes from The Last Café*

Here We Sit In The Cafe Of Despair

Dr. Craig Sinjin-Smythe stood, chewing a knuckle as he made the call. After a few rings, Dr. Dan Merritt, the Sutr Virus Task Force coordinator for the CDC, picked up his private line.

"Craig? I didn't expect you to call me back so soon. Surely you don't have the histological report already?"

"Something's wrong, Dan."

"You should be calling on the secure line, Craig. That's what it's for."

"Ava's gone."

"Ava's *dead*?"

"No. Gone. As in, out of the bloody building. Security says she left in a taxi. I can't raise her on her phone."

"What are you telling me, Craig?"

"She disabled the alarms and safeties and she left a note."

"A note? What does the note say? Fractured safety protocols and off for a nap? Tra-la-la! Back by tea time?"

"The note says...it's not good, Dan. It suggests this is a Level One."

"You know what this means. Did you go into lockdown? Are you in the isolation unit now, doctor?"

"Maybe it's not as bad as we think! The rat is still in its cage. Bogart, er...number ten is right where I left him."

"She disabled the safeties, Craig. Level One is our Defcon One. I'm sorry, but it's a breach."

"Can't we talk about this? They went to Defcon Three on 9/11. Surely…Dan…this is Ava we're talking about. Don't call it a breach!"

"Done is done, Craig. You know it's not up to me. Interpol is listening. They're undoubtedly already on their way."

There was a pause. Each man could hear the other breathing.

Finally, Merritt said, "Dr. Sinjin-Smythe. It's been an honor serving with you. I'm sorry, but you've gone from green to red."

"*Don't!* There are innocent people still in the other isolation uni—"

Behind Sinjin-Smythe, the innocuous black glass building at the edge of the Cambridge campus exploded into a bright fireball. Hell opened and thundered into the sky. The doctor fell flat and covered his head with his big leather briefcase as shattered glass and debris fell around him.

Screams from bystanders went up first. Then sirens. Before the first ambulance arrived, Sinjin-Smythe was already blocks away, removing the battery from his cell phone as he ran.

The woman in red found a comfortable seat in an empty pub just off Piccadilly Circus. Despite the warnings, plenty of people wandered about outside in the sunshine. There were no tourists — they had all rushed home before the airlines were grounded. However, Londoners came and went, tired of their government's requests that they stay indoors to avoid spreading the flu.

The woman sat, waiting. She didn't have to wait long. A man in an ill-fitting, black leather jacket sauntered in and sat beside her. He ordered a Heineken.

"Buy a lady a drink?"

The man glanced down her body. "Pardon me for saying so, but a person in your condition shouldn't be drinking, should they?"

She shrugged. "It's the best time. The baby isn't going to make it. And I just left my fiancee this morning."

"Oh, my god!" the man said. He handed her his beer. "You've had it, haven't you, love? Beastly! He couldn't handle losing the baby, is that it?"

"It's complicated."

"You're not wrong. Always is."

"Thank you for the beer. I think I'll drink this. Then I'll chew on something. Then I'll switch to Fosters. What's your name?"

"Pete. Pete Grimsby." He offered his hand and, as she extended hers, he pulled back. "Oh, that's a nasty cut, you have there." He looked at her hand and grimaced. "It's not your day at all, is it?"

"A pet bit me. It's fine. Do you have a big family, Pete?"

"Yes, I do, as a matter of fact. Since the plague, what with the economy, I lost my job. We're all packed in tight in one house. Had to get away to preserve my sanity." The man glanced at her swollen belly again and squirmed in his seat. "S'cuse me. It's bad form to be complaining to you about family right now, isn't it?"

She patted his hand. "No worries. None at all anymore."

He withdrew his hand discreetly and raised it to get the bartender's attention. "Have a cold Fosters ready for the lady, Kenny!" He cleared his throat. "Anyway, most of us lost our jobs. I got a couple of brothers — Leland and Vannever — in the police. They support the rest. If not for them, things would be dire."

"I see."

"In times like these, well…any chance you going back to your man?"

"None."

"What will you do?"

"I don't have to do anything anymore. I'll do as I please."

"What do you want to do?"

"I've been doing research for years. I'm going into education next."

"Teaching, you mean? What will you teach?"

She smiled. "I'll show you." She pointed to her throat. "Kiss me gently, here."

Pete straightened in his chair. "What?"

"You heard me."

"Darlin', you've had a tough morning. It wouldn't be very gentlemanly —"

She slapped him, hard and fast, across the face. The bartender's head came up. "Do I need to come down there and sort you two out?"

Pete was more startled than hurt. "I'm fine, but this one is crazy!"

Her arm flashed out again and grabbed the man by the hair at the back of his head. She pulled him off balance, toward her. "Kiss my throat!"

He did as he was told, she released him and he let out a laugh.

"That's good, Pete. Lovely. Thank you."

"What's your name, crazy lady?"

She looked at the floor and smiled demurely. "This morning it was Keres. But now, I think I'll call myself…Shiva."

"You do have an exotic look. It fits."

"Thank you, Pete. Let me educate you. After this, you can go tell your big family the big news." Before he could puzzle that out, she moved to embrace him. She kissed his throat, just over the jugular vein, softly. Then she wrapped her arms around him so python tight, he felt the baby kick. It kicked so hard against her belly and his, it felt like the baby must be drowning.

"Shiva, we shouldn't —" he wheezed.

"I'll just take a tiny nip," she whispered seductively. "One bite is best for now." Her teeth clamped on the meat of the muscle in his neck and she shook her head as she ripped away a chunk.

Pete Grimsby howled and pushed her back, his hands clasping the wound. His eyes went huge as he watched the blood and gore drip from the woman's chin. She smiled wider, showing red teeth.

"Careful to wash your hands, Pete. You wouldn't want that to get infected." The pistol in her hand pointed at his crotch. "Run."

The bartender was about to run, too, but she leaned over the bar and shot him in the leg, just below the knee. "Don't hobble off before you bring me another Fosters. I'm drinking for two." She wiped her chin with a napkin. "Wow! Pete was *salty*."

The bartender winced, swallowed his scream and did as he was told. She looked behind the bar. Pictures on the wall showed the bartender as a younger, thinner man in uniform. Medals hung in a box by the mirror.

"So, you were a soldier?"

"Yes. I was."

"I am," she said. "Before I let you go, I'm going to spit in a glass. You're going to fill it with water and you are going to drink it. Then run, as best you can, and tell everyone you meet about the morning you met Shiva, Destroyer of Worlds."

God Doesn't Mind Dirty Tables And Broken Chairs

The next morning Jaimie woke early to birds chirping, the blare of radio voices and his next-door neighbor singing louder than usual. Mrs. Marjorie Bendham, intent on her task, seemed to ignore the radio as she turned her flower bed with a hoe. She trilled up and down like she was trying to drown out the radio. She had been a soprano when she was young and, though she was very old now, she rarely stopped singing, even when her voice grew so weak and low, she dropped to a whisper.

She and her husband Al spent a lot of time in their backyard by the pool. Mrs. Bendham practiced scales and occasionally an aria. Jaimie did not understand Italian, but he appreciated the clear violets and blues and greens that floated out as she sang. There was something different in her voice today, a sharp yellow quaver Jaimie hadn't heard before. It seemed everyone's aura was dominated by yellow, if it wasn't already infected black. Only Anna's angry reds — "mean reds" he'd read in one of her high school books — seemed to run on the high energy of an inexhaustible fuel of emotion and gritted teeth.

Jaimie moved to the window and watched the old woman putter among her empty flower beds, disturbing gardens of dirt aimlessly. The best, clear notes sailed out as usual, but the irritating yellow vibrated and hovered, disappearing and returning around the edges of the blue sounds. Her aura was usually a muddied green and a dirty mustard yellow around her hips and knees. When she sang opera, her colors deepened to richer hues. Jaimie could feel the emotions she conveyed with her songs. Mostly, they were laments. The dictionary said a lament is for something lost, but didn't specify what. If he were a talker, Jaimie would have asked Mrs. Bendham. He wondered what she had lost.

Al Bendham was a quiet man who had worked for the government though he never said how. Jack once asked exactly what his old job had been as they chatted over the fence. He just shrugged and said, "Nothing much."

The old man was blind, which interested Jaimie since the boy saw more in the auras of others than he felt. Jaimie felt blind in his own way because the motivations of others were so often opaque to him. Despite his vast vocabulary, it seemed people had a secret language within a language. Words had too many hidden meanings and subtle implications.

For instance, at school, his teacher often lectured him about "boundaries" if he stepped too close to another student. However, boundaries were elastic things that seemed to vary by individual and circumstance. Birthday cake was good to share, but he was forbidden from eating another student's lunch. People, Jaimie decided, were disorganized and ruled by too many variables.

Since Jaimie saw more than he felt, he wondered if Mr. Bendham felt more than he could see. The neighbor spent hours listening to the radio as he vacuumed his pool. Though the radio sat on the ledge behind the screen of his kitchen window, it was turned up loud. As he vacuumed, his great head of shaggy white hair was always cocked slightly toward it. He looked like an old lion at the zoo, pacing and waiting, but with no apparent purpose beyond pacing and waiting.

Sometimes Jaimie spied on Mr. Bendham as he did Mr. Sotherby. He rarely saw Sotherby unless he spotted him mowing his lawn or playing the bouncing game with his flight attendant friends. From Jaimie's bedroom window, he watched the blind man vacuum the pool. He never seemed in a hurry and the boy found that soothing. The old man frequently cleaned the same spot in the deep end repeatedly, either not knowing when he was done or not caring.

59

The boy watched the blind man's aura. The energy was curiously disorganized at the back of his head. From a medical dictionary, the boy knew there was something faulty in the old man's occipital lobe — something that betrayed his vision. Jaimie watched and waited for him to pick his nose or dig in his ears. When he found boogers, he rolled them between his fingers and flicked them into the pool. After he dug in his ears, he smelled under his fingernails, checking for ear wax. The boy knew he was forbidden to do that, but the old man was allowed. More mysteries of human behavior. Sometimes, Jaimie wondered if he was something other than human on safari on a strange planet with customs no outsider could hope to decipher.

Mostly, Jaimie watched the old man's haphazard patterns as Al Bendham pushed the long vacuum cleaner pole around the bottom of his pool. He decided the appearance of action was more important to the blind man than actually cleaning the pool. He and Mrs. Bendham dog-paddled around in it occasionally in the evening, and sometimes their fat son (a real estate agent, Dad said) brought their little grandchildren, twin girls, over for a swim when the summer heatwaves hit.

Jaimie waited. Though the radio blared, Mr. Bendham did not appear. The boy opened his bedroom window. Cold air spilled over him. However, his mother was already in the backyard, planting seeds.

Mrs. Bendham stopped what she was doing and called over, "It's not too early for most things, but if you've got tomato plants, you should wait till the May long weekend! You'll have to wrap whatever sprouts in plastic for a while. We'll have a couple frosts yet! The weather is crazy!"

Jack stood, dusted off the knees of her pants and walked toward Mrs. Bendham, though not so far as the fence.

Mrs. Bendham smiled, her face tightening into more seams, wrinkles and lines. "You're up early, today, Jacqueline."

His mother gave a jerky nod. "Haven't slept much in two nights. You're up early, too."

"Yes. I hope my radio doesn't disturb you. Mr. Bendham doesn't feel like getting up this morning but he does love his radio.

Sometimes I get so sick of it, I turn it to classical. He objects, but he seems quite dedicated to lying down at the moment."

"He okay?"

"He'll be fine. Just a little hot. He insisted we go to the hospital last week. They couldn't find anything wrong with him, but he complains he's feeling poorly ever since."

"Oh?"

Jaimie was confused. His mother's voice sounded neutral, but her colors yellowed more. He thought if he stood beside her, he'd taste lemon juice. The boy was glad he was safe in his flannel pajamas. He instinctively drew back from the window, not so much to avoid being seen as to watch from a safer distance.

"...nothing serious," Mrs. Bendham said. "He had a checkup at the prostate clinic. Some follow-up scans and blood work. I thought we should wait, but his surgery last year scared him so he wanted to be sure everything was fine. He's the anxious type. I tell him most of what we worry about never happens. Al always says most of what we worry about eventually happens. Since the surgery, it's like he's waiting for the other shoe to drop on his head."

Jaimie knew about the surgery. Last winter he'd gone next door with his father to shovel the driveway and the Bendham's walk after a snowstorm. Theo said that in Maine, they'd use snow shovels, but heavy snowfall was rare in Kansas City, Missouri. Instead, they used garden shovels to clear the driveway and shivered in the surprising cold.

"Weather patterns are changing," Theo complained. "Even from when I was a kid I see a big change. The meteorologist's predictions can't be depended upon anymore. With climate change, the scientists say we can expect crazy storms, droughts, flooding and worse as the world heats up. I know it doesn't feel hotter today, but more heat means more evaporation which means more precipitation, so more killer storms and tornadoes. Seems like governments can't do anything besides blow things up anymore. Used to be, a debate would end. Now the arguments go on forever and the big problems never get solved."

When they were done clearing the walk, father and son stepped inside the Bendham's house to ask if the old couple needed groceries. Every lamp had a lacy bit of cloth under it. The house had a smell Jaimie associated with the dwellings of old people. Thinking of it brought back boiled cabbage doused in lavender queasiness. Perfect recall is more a curse than a gift.

Fresh from the hospital, Mr. Bendham lay on a flowery couch, a jug of green juice on a TV tray beside him. He was the most chatty Jaimie had seen him, like he was just back from an adventure and anxious to repeat it before he'd forgotten anything. Later, the boy looked up the words "retropubic prostatectomy". Then he looked it up on the Internet. The boy started eating more tomatoes after watching a YouTube video of the surgery. Something in the tomato was supposed to protect men's prostates from blowing up like a balloon and killing them. It sounded like a strange design flaw to Jaimie. The fact that a tomato could be considered a fruit by botanists and a vegetable by cooks bothered him almost as much.

"Al was in such a rush to get his checkup," Mrs. Bendham said, "but I don't know when we'll get any results. Did you hear? There are a lot of doctors and nurses who are refusing to report to work. When we were there, the hospital was packed with people, but I didn't see many white coats. There was a lot of coughing going on and the triage nurse told everyone with a fever to go home."

Jack wasn't standing close to Mrs. Bendham. It was as if they were calling back and forth across a wide stream. Still, Jaimie noticed his mother take another step back.

"A few years ago, the government tried to get the doctors and nurses to sign a pledge to go to work if there was ever a pandemic," his mother said. "As I remember, they refused. I didn't think much of it at the time."

"It's all over the radio now," Mrs. Bendham said. "Half the callers are saying they should get back where they're needed and the doctors are saying that for this to blow over, everybody should stay home. They are doctors, so I think they should go to work. Whatever risk there is, they chose it."

"Yeah, but their husbands and wives and sons and daughters didn't choose that risk."

Mrs. Bendham seemed about to speak but thought better of it.

"I should get back to the garden," Jack said.

"You've bitten off quite a bit of yard there. What are you planting, Jacqueline?"

"Oh, lots of flowers and green things," she tossed back over her shoulder. "I've decided to take this time to work on my green thumb."

That was the second lie Jaimie heard his mother speak.

At The End Of The World And Miles Away

Jaimie retreated to the books laid out on his bed. He leafed through the pages, comparing the new one from the library to the thick, old one his father bought at a yard sale. His father had reinforced the binding with gray duct tape. Until the Sutr Virus came, his life had been regimented. The doctors said he would do better in school if he knew what to expect. Now no one knew what to expect and so, very little was required of him. Jaimie disappeared into the words on the page, surrounding himself with alphabetized columns and walls. There was no boredom. Only hunger, sleep and the need to go to the bathroom could drag him from Word World.

Sometimes he looked into one word and the richness of another word waiting nearby would pull him in to taste its curves and softness — words with more than one *s* or *m* often felt like dark chocolate in his mouth.

Jaimie closed his eyes and pointed at a random page of the thickest dictionary. His finger found *cacophony*. To the Greeks, the word connoted not merely a harsh sound, but something evil. In medicine, it referred to an altered state of voice. In music, a combination of discordant sounds. School had often been a cacophony for Jaimie, but he could not detect evil. The ambient sounds in his classroom had been more like the musical definition, loud at times, but organized around lesson plans, bells and learning new things.

Next to *cacophony, cacoplastic* waited. The term referred to pathology, "susceptible to a low degree of organization." Since the Sutr Virus, the neighborhood had become quiet. It was certainly much quieter than the bedlam his classroom could descend to, but the quiet was more disturbing. He saw no one on the sidewalk in front of his house and traffic on his once busy suburban drive was rare.

The Greeks were wrong, Jaimie decided. It was the quiet that held evil. He couldn't see them, but he suspected everyone was hiding in their homes, waiting to see what came next. "It's like everyone's holding their breath," his father remarked at breakfast. Jaimie recognized the phrase as an idiom he'd heard before, but he still didn't understand it. One could only hold his breath for so long and then, if the Sutr Virus's greasy black wasps invaded your energy field, what could one do but breathe them in and feel the aura drain of light?

Jaimie dismissed the thought and delved further into the big dictionary. He got stuck on some words. Many times he could puzzle out definitions but it wasn't clear to him how they could be used in an actual sentence. He chased the trail of definitions, going from one word he didn't understand to the next, skipping around the dictionary.

After happening on several curious Latin root words in his big dictionary, he switched to his little red book: *The Guide to Latin Phrases*. Latin appealed to Jaimie because the dead language's phrases were still alive: *veritas simplex oratio est. The language of truth is simple.*

The entries were so descriptive, Latin explained things people wouldn't think about otherwise, the opposite of opaque idioms. The little red book held instructions in thinking that altered the world and gave it clarity. When he held the book, his mind stood strong, without cacophony. His Latin phrase dictionary — each phrase a concept and a poem, too — showed him how people thought, if they thought clearly.

Sine loco et anno leapt off the page at Jaimie. *Without place and date.* Since everyone went into hiding, location and time didn't matter anymore. It was one of the subtle things the plague had brought, slowing everything down, reducing each day to necessity. If death was existence without movement, living under the shadow of the plague was something like death. The disease brought the world's clock to a halt. The quiet gave people time to think. They looked up from their work and paused to consider what they were if they weren't their jobs. For many, the answer would be disturbing.

Jaimie frequently returned to the word *dirigo*. It means *I direct* or *I guide* or *I lead the way*. The book told him it was the motto of Maine, the state where his grandfather, Papa Spence, lived on a farm. The intent of the Latin word was to explain that God was in charge of everything. However, the people of Maine generally assumed their motto meant they stood in control of their destiny and "As Maine goes, so goes the nation." If time and place no longer meant anything in the face of Sutr, perhaps the people of what used to be Maine had already let go of that conceit.

No one was in charge. The world had become cacoplastic.

The siege was harder for Anna. Book glue held Jaimie together while the television tore her apart. Dr. Karen Glass and Franklin Jones died in front of her eyes.

Dr. Glass reported from India on the outbreak. She died in a huge tent — like a circus top, but filthy green — surrounded by hundreds of corpses arranged in rows of army cots. As she died on international television, the crawl along the bottom of the screen read: LIVE. She was immortalized on film with her last ratcheting breath. Anna watched it, tears rolling down her cheeks, whispering, "I watched her report...yesterday. She seemed fine just yesterday! She seemed *fine!*"

A sound technician, a pretty brown woman wearing khakis and boots, held the correspondent's limp body, crying and kissing Dr. Glass's white forehead and mouth.

"Karen! Oh, Karen!" she said, over and over.

The sound was muffled. Wind whipped at the microphone. The thick audio feed somehow made the scene more real.

"That woman must have loved her so much," Anna said. "It's suicide, kissing her bare face like that. She'll get Sutr next!"

Jack watched the screen with her daughter. "I never guessed Dr. Karen Glass was a lesbian."

"Mother!"

"What? I'm just saying I didn't know. Did you know?"

"It's not supposed to matter, Mom."

"I-I'm not saying it does matter. I just...I think that's the cameraman coughing. I wonder if her parents are watching this? It would be hell for them to get a double-barrel in the face all at once like this."

"Mom! Stop talking."

Jaimie emerged from his bedroom, lured downstairs by hunger and curiosity about what was happening. He found Anna in front of the television, a bag of cookies forgotten in her lap and a cookie in her hand, arrested in the air halfway to her mouth.

"The anchorman has it, too," Anna said.

Franklin Jones brought the crisis into focus. His death was more than a passing distraction from all the bad news about the economy. Jones had been the daytime anchor of the biggest all-news, all-the-time network on American television. When Theo and Jack wanted to know what was going on in the world, they listened to Canadian radio or the BBC, but they turned to American television channels for video.

Jones was a tall man with thick blond hair and piercing blue eyes. He had been a model in fashion magazines when he was younger. Sunlight and middle-age had cooked his skin rugged and made him look more intelligent. He no longer looked like the thin boy with a vacant stare.

Jaimie didn't pay much attention to television news programs, but Jones' accent captured him. Even through the television, his voice rolled out across the living room and the boy watched the sound waves break around him as the newsman spoke. The color was a rich blue, but the edge in his vowels made sharp white mountain peaks. Jack loved his voice, too. She said he was British via Vermont.

Jones sat behind the anchor desk eulogizing Dr. Karen Glass' sacrifice. She "served her nation and the truth," Jones said.

Jaimie looked up from his Latin phrase book. He paid closer attention to the anchor when he noticed the white peaks were gone from his voice. The edges around his tone were softer and weaker.

Jones lost his place and began the same sentence again. He stopped. "We're going to take a break now and go to commercial." He put his hand to his ear, but the camera stayed on him. He was fumbling with his earpiece when he went to the floor. Muffled voices shouted off-screen.

While the camera stayed on the newsman in the studio, an inset square at the bottom of the screen showed a confused female reporter in a bright red jacket. She stood in front of a Red Cross centre in Idaho. The color of her jacket matched the Red Cross symbol on the building behind her perfectly. Jaimie wondered if she meant to do that.

The woman held a microphone under her chin and repeated, "Frank? Frank? Frank?"

Jones rolled on the floor by the anchor desk. Muffled voices from the studio control room argued back and forth but the cameraman seemed intent on keeping the camera trained on Jones. A wire under his shirt pulled taut as he flailed and his shirt-tail was yanked back, exposing the white flesh of his belly. Though he wore a suit jacket, behind the desk he had been wearing sweatpants with white fluorescent stripes down the side of each leg.

"Frank?" the woman from Idaho asked. "Tina, have we lost the feed — ?"

She held one hand to her ear and continued to speak, but her sound was muted. That was fine with Jaimie. She had a grating sound in her voice he hadn't noticed before, like metal on metal. He decided that in the confusion, the reporter had ceased to use her fake professional reporter's voice and had started speaking naturally.

Two men wearing headsets came forward, knelt and spoke to Jones. They all called him Frank, which sounded odd because Jaimie never thought of him as one short staccato sound. His sure, suntanned face had always been underlined with the three authoritative syllables of his name: Franklin Jones.

Franklin vomited on a big man in a white shirt. It looked like pea soup. Jaimie opened his dictionary and looked up *vomit, nausea* and *nauseous*. The small dictionary didn't list projectile vomiting, though later that's what his mother said it was. Jaimie also found the word *puke*.

The man who had been thrown up on ripped off his shirt. He ran off camera while Franklin Jones, now just Frank, asked for an ambulance. His mic was still working and Jaimie's sensitive ear was not necessary to detect how weariness and fear competed for supremacy.

A sharp-faced woman in jeans came on camera and knelt beside him, cradling his head carefully. She held a wet towel and wiped Frank's green chin. She had a headset, too. Though young, she seemed to be in charge.

Jaimie thought she was impressive, the way she spoke so calmly while others shouted in the background. She asked for three volunteers: a driver, a cameraperson and, as an afterthought, "C'mon, I need a sound tech."

There seemed to be a debate going on offstage and then she said, "If one of you doesn't step up, you're both out of a job. Now!" Apparently that worked because the off-camera voices settled and she gave someone off camera a curt nod.

"Ambulance," Frank said.

The woman told him all the ambulances were busy but she would make sure he got help. He nodded and began to throw up again. She turned him on his side, away from the eye of the camera.

"Oh, c'mon!" Anna said, her cookie still forgotten in her hand. "Don't spare us television history!"

The sharp-faced woman barked more orders and soon a fit young man with a stretcher appeared. From their exchange, it became clear her name was Beth. Beth grabbed Frank under the heels while the young man, named Chip, hauled Frank on the stretcher.

"He's burning up," Chip said in a high pink voice that felt like pencil erasers poking at the skin of Jaimie's forearms.

"Stay with us," Beth said, as they wheeled Frank off the set. It was strange seeing the television studio from this perspective. There was exposed lumber behind the façade of the stage where the news had been delivered. Jaimie realized the television news set was a theater. Seeing the man carried out through a long hallway reminded the boy of a Latin stage direction. *Exuent* means *They leave the stage. Exuent omnes. They all leave the stage.*

The camera bounced along behind Beth and, though they'd never heard her on camera before, she began narrating the race to the parking lot. She breathed heavily as she spoke. "To bring new viewers up to speed," she said, "news anchor Franklin Jones has collapsed on the set. Due to his symptoms, we're assuming this is the Sutr Flu which we've been reporting on almost exclusively. Franklin mentioned he wasn't feeling very well this morning and I asked him about it but he just said, 'The show must go on,' and so it did until he collapsed behind the CNN news desk just moments ago."

Chip backed up against a steel door and when they pushed through it a piercing alarm sounded. Someone said, "*Jesus!*"

"I bet that was the sound guy," Anna said.

"Sorry about that folks," Beth said smoothly as they emerged into sunlight. The sound of the door alarm retreated behind them. "We're taking the quickest route to the parking lot so we can load our colleague into a van from the pool and get him medical care as quickly as possible."

The cameraman tripped and gray pavement flashed across the screen before he could right himself. "Stay with us," Beth said, as if she expected the gaffe.

They stopped at a high steel gate and in the background a guard could be glimpsed talking with Chip. Beth turned, breathing hard and looking pale despite the calm assurance her voice conveyed. "We're going to follow Frank as far as we can into the nearest hospital. The coverage of the Sutr Flu crisis has taken a very personal turn with the CNN family today. If you were watching earlier, you saw CNN's own Dr. Karen Glass die in a treatment center in rural India. It seems this virus knows no borders and we'll of course continue to provide you with the latest news as this crisis unfolds."

"Holy shit!" Anna said.

"Language!" Theo called from the next room. They hadn't known his father was listening until he'd called from the dining room table.

"Uh-huh," Anna said, finally remembering the cookie in her hand. She shoved it into her mouth whole.

"I'm serious," Theo said. "When your brother does talk, I don't want his vocabulary to be limited to your swearing."

Anna looked back at Jaimie sitting cross-legged in the big leather recliner with the dictionary in his lap. "Yeah, that's a likely problem." She mouthed the word "shit", and several other words at Jaimie, before turning back to CNN.

"We know from authorities that no ambulances are available, as it is in most American cities at the moment. Paramedic crews have found themselves overwhelmed by demand and many have failed to report to work. We've been told that flu victims are arriving at treatment centers with the help of friends or family members. Bus services everywhere are cancelled for fear of spreading the virus through too much close contact with people who may be infected and not yet know it."

By his gestures, Chip seemed to be arguing with the anonymous security guard behind her. The camera shifted focus to Chip and the guard as Beth recounted Jones' collapse.

"Of course, if you do feel unwell, authorities are urging you to stay home. Tamiflu and Relenza stocks are currently depleted in North America though, as was reported earlier by our news team, Germany and France are said to be hoarding huge stocks of the anti-virus for their populations, ramping up tensions between these traditionally cooperative American allies."

The security guard ran offscreen. The camera followed the guard's retreat.

Someone said, "*Sonofabitch!*"

"Sound guy, again!" Anna said, spraying black cookie crumbs.

Beth glanced back at the camera, not missing a beat. "We're going to get a van here in a moment and make our way to the nearest hospital. We'll show you how the health care system is working for all of us from the inside."

Chip pulled out a cell phone. Beth's composure remained undented. "We'll cut away for a message from our sponsors and when we come back, we'll follow Franklin Jones as he meets with doctors and give you a front row seat. We'll be right back."

Things did not work out as quickly as Beth planned. Anna and Jaimie kept watching, but when a long string of commercials ended, an Asian woman they didn't recognize sat behind the anchor desk. They showed Jones collapse repeatedly and when they tired of that, they went back to showing Dr. Glass's demise in India.

Beth didn't return to the screen for two hours. This time when she appeared, she looked harried. She stood, mic in hand, in front of hurricane fencing. Print at the bottom of the screen now identified her as Elizabeth Harrison, CNN producer.

She recounted the story of the anchor's collapse at his desk, which by then had already been aired many times, including several times in slow motion. A vertical take-off jet lifted off a runway behind her.

"Our volunteer crew took Franklin to two different hospitals. There was a line outside of each emergency department and I saw no one admitted to either hospital. A spokesperson for one of the hospitals said they were only allowing people into the emergency room who were still ambulatory."

Theo, who listened from the kitchen while he prepared dinner, stepped into the living room. He frowned at the screen. "Did she say they were only allowing people in who could *walk* in? Isn't that…the opposite of what it should be?"

"Not if they've given up on the ones lying down," Jack said.

Theo gave his wife a sharp look. Jaimie sensed his irritation and her fear. They might have fought, but they couldn't take their eyes from Elizabeth Harrison.

Her sharp face looked gray, as if it had been several sleepless nights, not hours, since she'd been in the television studio. Her calm and control had evaporated. "I explained at each hospital that our colleague had collapsed but the *health official*," — she hit the words 'health official' extra hard — "said that even if they were to allow Frank in, there were no beds available."

Jaimie's right index finger hovered between *radness* (meaning *fear*) and *radoub* (referring to *preparing a ship for a voyage*.) Jaimie couldn't see the future, but watching the screen, this pair of words felt right together. It was as if the word wizards who wrote the dictionary were giving him a subtle hint of what was to come.

"It's worse than we've been told, isn't it?" Theo said to Jack, not so loud that Anna could hear.

"It's as bad as Cliff predicted."

"At least it's not here!" Anna said. "I bet all the celebrities are going to a secret bunker at the north and south pole or something."

Jack and Theo looked troubled but said nothing.

The camera zoomed in for a close-up on Beth. "At last, we were directed to a Sutr Flu Treatment Center in hangers at LAX. The National Guard is here, as is the Red Cross. I also saw several FEMA and Center for Disease Control vehicles by the gate. National Guard soldiers in gas masks took Franklin out of our news van and placed him on a stretcher. I asked to speak to someone in charge and was refused. I asked for a mask so I could stay with Franklin and that was also refused. When I insisted, a National Guardsman pointed his rifle in my face. He didn't say anything. He just waved me away. The last I saw Franklin...I'm...*concerned*."

"Why do media people talk like that?" Theo asked. "She's not 'concerned'. She's out-of-her-mind terrified."

Jack picked up the remote from the floor and turned off the television. "Let's give it a rest, shall we?"

"Mom! TV is what there is to do! What else is there?"

"You've got a pile of books up in your room and dinner is soon so stop with the snacking."

Anna went red-faced. "We can't all be like Ears, climbing inside a book and hiding there."

"Room!" Jack ordered.

Anna stomped up the stairs. Jack looked at Jaimie. Three lines formed on his mother's forehead. Anna slammed her bedroom door.

Jaimie moved his index finger down to the definition of "Ragnarok". It was a Norse myth that told of the destruction of gods and humankind in a battle with evil. He liked the soft edges of a Latin phrase he'd found better. Ancient sailors believed the end of the world waited only six hours' sail from Britain. They called it *ultima Thule. The end of the world.*

No Wine, No Roses, No Time To Play

Jaimie awoke to yelling downstairs. The lamp on the nightstand still shone and the Latin dictionary lay open by his head. The last phrase he had read was an interesting one: *ubi solitudenum faciunt pacem appellant. They create desolation and call it peace.* To the boy, the words tasted soft, as pleasing to his eye as they were black and dangerous.

He was afraid to move at first. He hadn't heard angry shouting like this since the day he sang his first words. He lay still until the banging started. There was a pause between each high metallic report, as if someone was winding up between each tinny crash.

"Let me go! Let me go!" That was Anna.

Jaimie leaped from his bed and ran to the top of the stairs, peering down into the well of light in the front hallway. His mother stood behind Anna, pinning her arms behind her back and pulling her toward the kitchen. He came down a few more steps, trying to understand what he saw.

"Stop! Stop it now!" His father's silhouette was framed in the open front door. The screen door was closed, but the thin metal square at its bottom had been mostly kicked in. Someone Jaimie could not see stood on the front step.

Bang!

"Stop it. This is already over. You just don't know it." His father's voice was even, but Jaimie could see his secret. He sounded like Beth, the woman on the television. Red streams of bright anger ran down his arms and out of his fingers, but a yellow ribbon of fear wrapped tight around his heart.

Jaimie crept down a few more stairs so he could see who was kicking the screen door. It was Trent Howser.

"Anna wants to be with me! You don't have the right to stop her!"

"She's my daughter and if you care for her the way you say you do, you'll leave," Dad said.

Bang! A hinge popped loose on the screen. Trent was eighteen, strong and on the wrestling team. If he had thought to grab the door and yank it, it would have flown into the front hedge. Instead, he kicked it again.

"I've already called the police, Trent!" Jack yelled. "You'd better go before they get here!" That was the third lie Jaimie had heard his mother tell, and so close on the heels of the last one.

Bang!

The bottom hinge floated out and free of the door frame and the flimsy screen's lock popped useless.

Trent caught the door before it fell and propped it against the porch wall. Then he stepped forward and delivered another vicious kick higher up the door, shattering the glass and ripping the screen. He could easily have charged in, but he seemed intent on destroying the door.

It came to Jaimie that this was a demonstration. Trent wasn't trying to break in. He was trying to convince Theo and Jack to let Anna out.

The boy walked unnoticed behind his mother and sister. The wooden block that held the big knives sat by the sink.

When Jaimie was three, he pulled a dining-room chair into the kitchen and climbed up on the counter by the sink. His mother was in the basement doing laundry. When she came to the top of the stairs and stepped into the kitchen, she found the little boy standing on the counter. He had pulled out all three paring knives and placed them in a row on the counter for counting. Jaimie knew the word *counter*. He thought counting must be what counters were for.

He pulled the long bread knife from the block and carefully placed it beside the paring knives. His mother stood in the middle of the kitchen, frozen and staring, still holding a basket of clean clothes in her arms. She told Theo later that it seemed to be happening in slow motion. She would never forget how Jaimie slowly drew out the meat cleaver from its wooden sheath and eyed the blade with naked curiosity.

"He hadn't noticed me and I didn't want to shout or jump forward at him," she said. "I was afraid that if I did, I'd startle him and he'd fall right to the floor and impale himself somehow."

She was shaking when she gently pulled her child from the counter. She held him tight in her arms. The boy liked the softness of her hair and tried to put his cheek against it. Instead, Jack took his chin and tried to force him to look in her eyes. The boy did not like that but, unable to resist, the three-year-old fixed his gaze on the little plane of skin separating her eyes. *G is for glabella.*

When he learned to read, the boy thought it odd that there is a name for the space between human eyes, but in English there isn't a single word for the place behind the knee.

"Promise me!" Jack had said. "Promise me you will never touch the knives again. Never!"

She moved her head close and side to side, trying to force the child to look in her eyes but Jaimie held his gaze on her glabella.

"He was looking at me with this crazy cross-eyed look," she told Theo that night. "I was crying and then I started laughing and then I couldn't stop so I took him to the living room and held him in the recliner and rocked him for a long time, like he was my quiet little baby again. He played with my hair the whole time. Though...you know...I wish to God he'd look me in the eyes, Theo." Then she cried some more.

Jaimie never forgot the promise his mother tried so desperately to extract. Still, he saw the solution to the violent man on his front porch. Trent had given them a demonstration of force. The family needed to give Anna's boyfriend a demonstration, too. Jaimie pulled the meat cleaver from the wooden block and walked back to the front hall.

77

"Ears! Get out of here!" Anna yelled.

"Jaimie!" Jack would have run to her son, but she was still struggling with Anna as the girl tried to twist out of her mother's grip.

Jaimie stood beside his father, looked at Trent and watched his aura change as he slipped the wooden handle to the cold, heavy steel into Theo's palm.

Trent's jaw went slack.

Theo looked at Jaimie in surprise but when he turned back to Trent his face was grim.

"Go cool off, Trent. Don't come back."

Trent backed away and hurried down the front steps.

Theo ignored the broken screen door and closed the front door, turning the deadbolt and sliding the chain in its slot. When he turned from the door, he looked at the cleaver like it was some new unfamiliar thing. He handed it back to Jaimie. "Thanks, son. Please put that back where it belongs."

Anna stopped struggling and her mother let go, reminding Jaimie of Chinese finger puzzles. She ran to the door to get a glimpse of Trent but he was gone. Anna did not cross the threshold. She leaned out, looked at the broken screen door and sighed heavily. "Trent, one; door, zero. Advantage: boyfriend."

"Okay, let's talk," Theo said.

"Ears, go upstairs," Anna said as he walked back from the kitchen empty-handed. The boy walked upstairs, but lay on his belly in the upstairs hall so he could listen.

"We're going to talk this out calmly," Theo said. "I thought your boyfriend was going to give me a heart attack.'

"What were you going to do with that meat cleaver?" Anna's voice climbed up, on the edge of hysteria. She began to sob.

"Jaimie just handed it to me. I had no idea what I would do, but I knew I wasn't letting Trent in here. What the hell is this all about? He's only been around for a few weeks. He took you to a movie and you talk to him on the phone all the time. Doesn't he know what's going on?"

"It's you who doesn't know what's going on. People die on TV and who knows when the flu will come here?"

"Under the circumstances, it's not too much to ask that you not see your boyfriend."

There was a pause Jaimie couldn't decipher. Then Jack said, "I didn't catch her trying to sneak out, Theo. I caught her trying to sneak back in."

"Oh, hell."

"Mom! Dad! You don't understand! Trent loves me and I love him."

Jaimie inched down the stairs a little, still on his belly, and peered around a banister post till he could see his family. They stood in the living room. His mother hugged herself. His father's hands were on his hips. Anna planted her legs wide and stiff, her upper lip was curled back in a snarl.

"Hormones," Jack said.

"We had them, too. I remember." Theo studied his daughter, searching for words that would not come.

"Don't do that!" Anna said. "I'm almost eighteen and I'll be out of this house next year, or dead tomorrow. Who knows? The point is, I need out of your cage! I've gotta live now because maybe I won't later. I don't want to die without seeing my friends!"

"Or your boyfriend of two weeks."

"We've been together longer than that, Dad," she said.

"Okay, so about a month."

"Dad!"

Jack flopped on the couch. "Two weeks, a month. That's when love fever runs highest."

Theo shrugged. "My dad used to say, 'Are you in love or are you in heat?'"

"Dad!"

"Jesus save us!" Jack ran her hands through her hair. Here and there she made fists and pulled on her scalp, as she did every time she felt a headache coming. "Anna, you make me wish I still smoked. You're not getting it. This isn't just about you and teen angst. Social distancing is necessary. It's not some elaborate plot to keep you from getting herpes from the local football hero."

"He on the wrestling team."

"I'll bet!"

"You're treating me like a dog!" Anna said through broken sobs.

"Honey," Theo said, "after the display of poor judgment Trent gave us tonight, I can't say I'm on puppy love's side. Your mom's right. This isn't about you and Trent. By going out with him tonight, you didn't just put yourself at risk. You risked me and your Mom and your brother."

Anna looked up and her mouth dropped open. "You think things are as bad as I do, don't you?"

"We all listen to the same radio and watch the same TV. It's hard to figure out what's going on between all the media hype and government understatement."

Jack started to cry in big blue and gray sobs. Jaimie slithered down the stairs another step, watching the trails of light. His stomach didn't feel right as he watched his mother weep.

Anna softened and went to the couch to hug her mother. "I'm sorry, but nobody's sick in Trent's family."

Theo moved to pat Anna on the back. "They think the virus has an incubation period that may last from a few hours to a few days. It's tricky. It's working away in its own little microscopic world, invading human cells, reproducing, unaware of all the hosts it kills. It's our job to contain any contagion, real or imagined, and stay away from people." He bent and kissed Anna on the top of her head. "In that spirit, go to your room. You're even more grounded. Goodnight."

Anna ran to the stairs. She spotted her little brother before he could retreat. "Ears! Go to your room!" she screamed, and threw her fist into his door as she passed.

Jaimie heard his father burble, "Don't worry! He won't tell anyone!" His parents shared a short burst of laughter before Jack shushed her husband.

Jaimie hadn't seen Anna like that before but he recognized the colors of a tantrum — a bad boy at school turned over desks in his classroom one day. He displayed a similar color pattern. Jaimie overheard one of the teachers say he was an "angry young man" but she said it like it was all one word. Another teacher replied he didn't know why the boy was incensed.

Jaimie took the word "incensed" literally. He had noticed that when people were very angry, sulphur and the smell of old leather shoes escaped their pores. A bitter taste he could not identify prickled his tongue.

The dictionary defined "incense" for Jaimie, but he didn't truly understand it. He'd never had any emotion that approached that state.

One afternoon, soon after the incident at school, Jaimie turned over the desk in his classroom to see if he could reproduce the same colors and tastes he'd witnessed. It didn't work. Some of his drawings fell to the floor and Jaimie became distracted putting them back in the order in which he'd drawn them.

Jaimie listened to Anna in the her room. She was, he was sure, screaming into a pillow and pounding her mattress with her fists. The boy went to his desk and sketched the cricket he'd seen in pencil, quickly and with precision. It was late, but he opened a drawer and retrieved a yellow crayon for the insect's eyes. Before he went back to bed, he planned to slip the drawing under Anna's door to make her feel better.

The previous summer, Anna took her brother on a bus downtown on a rainy afternoon. She bought the boy an ice cream and watched him eat it. Then she took him to a store that had a funny smell. She called the store "funky", or perhaps she was referring to the smell. Jaimie wasn't sure.

The boy had been content to watch people while Anna wandered the shop. Then he saw the word "incense". There were a dozen fat jars with sticks poking out of them. They didn't smell like angry people at all. Instead, they were mostly sickly sweet. One jar was labeled *pine*, which was pretty close to how pine trees smelled, only much stronger.

When they got home, Jaimie looked up incense again and realized he had breezed past another entry which explained the little sticks, which were for burning. He was unclear why people would do that.

Homonyms annoyed the boy. Why not have distinct words for everything instead of words that sound and look the same but mean different things? Jaimie would have known about the different definitions but he wandered around the dictionary the same way Anna shopped: aimlessly. When he picked up a dictionary, he wandered, touched words of interest here and there to understand their texture, and wandered on.

Before he had completed his drawing, the boy heard his sister clumping around her bedroom. A moment later, he recognized the sound of each shoe dropping to the hardwood floor, empty. A drawer opened and closed and he knew she was getting ready for bed.

Jaimie slipped out of his room and listened. His parents were still in the living room, on the couch.

"...if it's here, we'll deal with it," his father said, his voice low.

"What if we *both* get sick?"

"If we get sick, Anna will take care of Jaimie. Despite tonight, you know she can rise to the occasion."

"And if we all get sick and Jaimie doesn't?"

"What are the odds of that?" he said.

"The real world doesn't seem to affect him, Theo. It's like he's protected in his own world."

"You're talking crazy."

"Am I?" she said. "When's the last time Jaimie got sick? He's never missed a day of school."

"I don't know, Jack. That says to me that either he's got a great immune system and won't get sick...or he's got a crappy immune system because it hasn't had any test runs. It's probably because he doesn't interact with other kids. Kids are all petri dishes and he's— "

"Bubble boy. He's just in a bubble we can't see."

"Well, yeah. Unless he takes after his sister and suddenly develops an interest in chasing the opposite sex. He'll have to get over holding my hand whenever we go out in public first, I'm guessing."

"I'm serious, Theo. What if it's you, me and Anna who get it?"

"Even if we all got it, it's not like it kills everybody. People get over this thing, too. They get it like any other flu. They stay home and get miserable and feel sorry for themselves. They take a pill and watch too much TV and go through a box of tissues. Then they get over it and go back to work so they can't have as many sick days to play hooky when it's a sunny Friday afternoon in the summer."

"After Glass and Jones died, you can't con me with that. You saw how it can be. We all saw how fast it can happen."

"What's the value in hypotheticals?"

"Don't give me a politician's answer, Theo. I'm asking, what if?"

A long silence followed. The boy was about to get up when he heard his father mutter, "If it comes to that, we'll turn on the gas."

Jaimie didn't understand what his father meant. When he looked up each word, he still didn't understand.

Mourning What We Had

Things were quiet between Jaimie's parents and Anna for the next few days. Jack went out to gather supplies, staying away longer each time. No seeds were available in the city.

Theo paced, anxious for his wife's return. He forgot to make dinner so Anna heated some pasta noodles for herself and for her brother. Still angry, she made nothing for her father. When Jack finally came through the front door, it was dark.

Jaimie looked up from his seat on the recliner, his finger marking a passage in the Latin dictionary which read *major e longinquo reverentia* or *no man is a hero to his valet.* His mother had told him something similar from her Bible study. "No prophet has honor in his own country."

It seemed distance or absence made people love and respect each other more. This puzzled Jaimie. If he could will himself to speak, he would have asked about love first.

His mother's absence for the day seemed to increase his father's love for her. As she returned, he embraced her so roughly Jack dropped her bags. He pulled her surgical mask down and kissed her on the lips.

"I kept my phone off to preserve the battery in case I really needed it," she said.

When she took in his frown, Jack smiled, bent and retrieved one of the grocery bags. Through the white plastic, Jaimie could see the word *seeds* in big block letters.

"Everyone on the street is wearing a mask," she said.

"I was told masks don't work."

"Not so!" she said. "The radio said bank robberies are up seventy per cent. I guess they're good for something! What's the television say?"

"I've been watching the driveway," Theo said.

She looked to Anna, who sat on the living room floor. "I watched it earlier but I turned it off when they kept repeating the same things."

"Really no news at all about progress on a vaccine?"

"Elevated tensions in the Middle East," Anna mumbled around a red licorice stick.

"Still or again?"

"The news doesn't make any sense. First they said Sutr started in India. Now the CDC is saying it started in Pakistan and was a weaponized alteration of something that only sheep used to get. Then they say to stay away from bats, as if anyone was running to bats for love and comfort. Oh, and something's happened in England. Violent riots. No real details, though."

"Probably too many people ran out of food. Is that all they had to say?"

Anna shrugged. "Just the usual warnings about staying away from each other. Of course, *you* still went out. Way to go. Mom of the Year. When I went out, you guys pitched a hairy fit and — "

"I went out for seeds to feed us, Anna. Not to make out."

"*Mom!*"

Jack sighed. "Turn on the television again. I want to watch a movie or something. I want a story where everything works out well in the end."

"*SpongeBob Squarepants?*" Anna suggested as she touched the power button.

The sudden blast of an alarm from the television jarred them and hurt Jaimie's ears. A loud red and white tone filled the room and Jaimie jumped from his chair. His Latin dictionary fell to the floor, clapping shut. He tasted copper coming out of the television. He felt like his clothes were made of sandpaper.

Jack snatched the remote up and turned the volume down. "This is the Emergency Alert System," a man's voice said. It repeated that message three times.

"They've been testing that thing all my life," Theo said. "We know! We know! They used to call it the Emergency Broadcast System. About time we got our tax money's worth."

Jack and Anna went white and Theo's smile faded. Jaimie suspected he had tried to make a joke but no one laughed. Jaimie felt sorry for his father. Jaimie didn't understand jokes, either.

"The Office of Public Health and the Office of Public Safety, in coordination with the Emergency Services Bureau is declaring a health emergency in your area. The World Health Organization has declared the Sutr Virus a level six emergency. For public health and your safety, you are required to stay in your homes and avoid contact with others. Do not travel unless absolutely necessary."

The family sat and watched the screen, though it was just a red field with the same white words crawling across the bottom of the screen: Martial Law Declared.

There were a lot of new rules: a curfew of six o'clock in the evening was declared. No one was to gather in public groups for any reason. Trucks would come through the cities with supplies for people who needed them but they encouraged all citizens to "use what supplies you have on hand first."

Jaimie looked up the word *quarantine*. He thought the word beautiful. The *q* tasted sugary and *uaran* struck Jaimie as the essence of a ripe avocado. Best of all, the word ended with *–tine,* the sound of a little silver bell.

The message started to repeat so Anna switched channels. On a Canadian news network feed, three men and two women talked about nuclear missiles in Pakistan. In a small box at the bottom of the screen, a line of people seemed to be waiting for something but it wasn't clear for what. The family had seen similar pictures of people waiting in lines when they were covering the outbreak in India. However, these new pictures were mostly fat, white people.

The Weather Channel was working and predicting a rainstorm and unseasonably warm temperatures.

Unseasonably. So close to unreasonably, Jaimie thought.

All the other channels broadcast the same repeated message. Theo took the remote and switched to Netflix. He selected a black and white movie with an actor Jaimie recognized: Jimmy Stewart in *Mr. Smith Goes to Washington*. The credits said James but Jaimie knew everyone called him Jimmy. Theo watched his movies many times so Jaimie had seen them all. *Rear Window* and *Vertigo* were his favorites.

The family was still watching the movie when someone knocked on their front door. Theo answered and found Mrs. Bendham looking at the shattered screen door propped up on the porch.

Jaimie looked out from behind his mother. Jack pushed him behind her gently. Their neighbor had been crying. Her eyes were red and her face was gray.

"Could you come see Al?"

"What's going on?"

"I thought he was getting better. His fever broke and he was getting crankier, so I was sure he was getting better."

"What do you want me to do, exactly?" Theo asked.

"I don't know. Just look at him and tell me what you think I should do. I tried calling an ambulance last night, but the lines were so busy. Around five this morning, I got up and called again. I got a dispatcher and they said they'd send someone. That was this morning. Now it's dark."

The quaver in her voice was back. "The dispatcher said she'd put me on her list. I've waited all day. I don't know what to do."

Theo looked back at his family. Jack shook her head. He shrugged his shoulders and said he'd get his jacket. He grabbed a winter scarf from the front closet and wrapped it around his mouth and nose.

It was Jack's turn to pace, but she didn't have long to wait. Her husband returned in a few minutes, looking pale. Theo went straight to the kitchen sink and washed his hands with the bright yellow soap they used for washing dishes.

"She said he got quiet and fell asleep around ten last night. Before she went to bed, she put her hand on his forehead and decided his fever had broken."

His father washed his hands in a way Jaimie hadn't seen. Put the words *savage* and *urgent* together. That would define it well. *Somebody should make up one word for that idea*, he thought. *Savurgency, maybe.*

His father stood at the sink a long time, scrubbing his hands as the family watched and waited for him to say more. He flicked his wet hands at the sink instead of using a hand towel and turned to face them. "She thought his fever broke but I think that was when he started to go cold. Al's dead."

"Oh, Theo," Jack said.

"Yeah," he nodded, grim and gray, as if seeing Mr. Bendham's body had depleted him in some way. "I've mostly seen dead bodies at funerals. I never saw death like that before."

Anna shrank back. Jack stepped forward and gave her husband a hug.

"I've only seen a couple of dead bodies, when I was a little girl and that time in Paris," Jack said. "We've been lucky, haven't we?"

She moved to the coffeemaker. Despite the late hour, Jack pulled out the used filter and grind from that morning. Keeping her hands busy seemed to soothe her and allowed Jack to talk and remember.

"One Sunday, I was leaving a church service with my parents when I saw a man standing at the top of the stairs. That was the shortest route to the parking lot, but he was blocking the way. He asked us to go out through the front of the church. He stood there with his hands behind his back. I remember thinking that he was just another man from church, but the way he stood, made him seem official somehow. My father pulled me by the shoulder to spin me back toward the other exit, but not before I saw the old woman lying at the bottom of the stairs. I caught her in a single glance, but one peek is all it takes for something like that."

"What happened to her?" Anna asked.

"I don't know exactly, honey. I remember she was wearing a long dress, white with a purple design on it...you know, kind of an old lady dress. And she wore a hat. Must have been one of those deals where it was pinned to her hair because the hat was still on. She must have fallen down the stairs. God knows. Maybe she had a heart attack or a stroke on the stairs first, or maybe after she hit the landing. Funny, I can still see those white old lady stockings and the surprised look frozen on her face. *Frozen!* I could have done without that."

"Didn't they call an ambulance or something?" Anna said.

"That's kind of the weird thing. That poor, old woman was alone at the bottom of the stairs. That seemed really wrong to me — still does. We shouldn't die alone. My mother told me when I was little that people who die alone come back to haunt us. I know that surprised face still haunts me in odd moments."

Jack opened the coffee can. and The rich aroma of the brown beans wafted out. Jaimie thought he'd like to drink coffee when he grew old enough, but he wasn't sure how old he would have to be. His mother had never made coffee at night. Jaimie guessed that's what people do when the old man next door dies.

Jack ground the beans in an electric hand grinder and poured the brown mix into the top of the filter. "When I was a kid there was this little girl who came with her mother to pick up one of my friends from school. She was a little too young for the big kids' playground but she played on the monkey bars while they were waiting for my friend. When the bell rang, we came out and there was this circle of children standing around the girl. She wasn't moving, but lots of help came fast."

"What did they do?"

"Oh, nothing much. It turned out my friend's sister just got the wind knocked out of her. She was really okay. When she got her breath back, she started crying. They comforted her. I remember we formed a circle around her, everyone reaching with one hand stretched into the center to touch her head and let her know she was okay, not alone...loved. That's the way things are supposed to be. Somebody gets hurt or needs help and the more people standing close by, the better.

"But I remember thinking that here was this little old lady, surprised to be suddenly dead at the bottom of the stairs with her legs bent at crazy angles. There was no one near her, just this old guy giving us a smile and asking us to use the other way out. Sometimes when someone dies, no one is around. That's what God is for, so we're never alone."

"Sounds like God is an Orwellian voyeuristic dictator." As soon as he blurted it, Theo backed away a step, his lips bunched tight.

Regret tastes like a sour green apple, Jaimie thought.

Anna's eyes were wet and glassy.

Jack cleared her throat and did not look at her husband. "I asked my Mom what happened to the old lady and she said not to worry about it. It was a big church. Every month the pastor included death announcements about some elderly people."

"That was supposed to make it better? Did that make you feel better?" Anna asked. "That 'every month' thing bugs me, like the more numbers there were, each loss was, I don't know—"

"Diluted," Theo said.

Anna nodded. "Yeah, like, to God, we're mere statistics."

Jack poured water into the coffeemaker. She seemed to think a long time before answering. She pulled down the sugar bowl from the cupboard, some spoons out of a drawer and five mugs.

"The pastor never called it a death notice. He said Mrs. So-and-so went on to glory last week, or passed on to be with Jesus or was off to receive her eternal reward. Something like that."

"Sounds comforting. Too good to be true, in fact." Theo couldn't seem to restrain himself.

"Well," Jack smiled. "Comfort was where the focus was. Ought to be. God knows us each by name and He knows what He's doing. Look at the images we've seen from the Hubble telescope. Look at the symmetry in a flower. There's a plan and we're each God's child."

Anna turned to her father, who seemed to study the floor. "Where do you think we go when we die, Dad?"

"Down," he said. "About six feet...but I don't think about this stuff much, Anna. I was brought up in the church, too. We all were back then. I remember I was probably as old as Jaimie is now before I stopped worrying about burning in hell."

Anna's eyes were wide and her face serious. "How'd you stop worrying?"

"I just stopped thinking about it," he said. "I figured that if I spent my life worrying about death, I wouldn't have much of a life. That's worked out just fine."

"Till now," Jack said.

"Still."

Jaimie spotted a little electrical arc spark between them. His mother poured the coffee and handed Theo two mugs. "Go back. Ring Mrs. Bendham's bell, and leave the mug on her front step. I think we can spare a couple cupcakes, don't you?"

"It must be genetic," Theo said. "Anybody dies and, since there's nothing else to do, people bring food. Must be the comfort of the sugar and a dopamine reward for the brain to offset the grief."

An annoyed look swept over Jack's face. Jaimie did not read her facial expression. Such nuances often escaped him. However, he saw the scarlet flare of anger that reached her corona.

Theo shrugged and nodded his assent and took the coffee to Mrs. Bendham.

"If nobody comes by tomorrow...we'll dig a grave in her backyard."

"*Mom!*"

"Take it easy, Anna. It's supposed to be warm over the next few days. We can't just leave him in the house. That's not safe."

Anna looked shaky. "What about the police or a funeral home or...?"

"I'd say from what we know, the authorities are really busy right now. Don't worry about this. This is all going to blow over. In the meantime, we're going to have to take care of more things for ourselves. Just for a while."

That was Jack's mother's fourth lie, but Jaimie thought she believed that one.

For a moment, Jaimie thought Anna was going to cry but a rancid puce around the twist of her mouth told him it was repulsion that washed over her in waves.

His mother must have sensed it, too, because she seemed anxious to calm Anna, to act as if all this was normal. "Have a coffee, Anna. It's decaf. Relax a little and uh, gather your thoughts. Then I want you and Jaimie to gather up every bucket, pail, bowl and receptacle in the house. You guys have showers tonight and, after we're all done in there, we'll fill the bathtub."

"What are we doing? Are we getting ready for a tornado or the flu pandemic?"

"We'll wash every bucket and bowl really clean," she said. "It'll rain tonight. That's a couple of blessings. We'll save the water in case we need it later and...the ground will be soft in the morning, if we need it."

Theo returned and leaned forward to give his wife a kiss on the cheek. "All this time I thought you were wasting time praying. I guess you were using the time to think."

"You're confused, heathen. They're the same thing." She moved to her husband's side, wrapped an arm around him and gave him a squeeze. "Rough weather ahead, Theo. Things are changing fast. Maybe you'll rethink a few of these issues before things go back on smooth and easy autopilot."

"Highly doubtful," he said. "Pray all you want, but when it comes to it, I'm betting you'll take whatever vaccine the government has for us instead of a prayer."

"The first thing we have to assume under the circumstances is that the government is too busy to be of much help. Or they're somewhere else looking after their own families. If there's no vaccine to look forward to anytime soon, prayer may be all that we have left to rely on for now."

"Well, then God help us," Theo said, "...or the Buddha or Vishnu or whatever. I won't be too picky."

Jaimie turned back to the living room to look up the word *heathen*, but his mother told him to wait. "Have a bath after Anna's done her shower, Jaimie." She handed him the last mug of steaming coffee. His first.

He held the hot cup between his palms, enjoying the aroma. When he tasted it, he was disappointed. Its smell was nutty but the taste was acidic and he burned his tongue. He made a face and his mother laughed.

Jack's look of confidence and reassurance broke when the sound of air raid sirens rose in the far distance. The howl strengthened and ebbed, but did not stop, like a wolf that never ran out of breath.

Roast Together: Ugly, Good And Bad

The morning the Spencers were going to bury Al Bendham, an unexpected emissary arrived at dawn with terrible news. Douglas Oliver lived across the street from the Spencers with his dog, a German Shepherd named Steve. Though his two-storey house faced their own, the Spencers' interaction with him had been limited to exchanging waves as he drove his green Mercedes in and out of his garage.

Oliver's backyard was fenced in so they never saw him walking his big dog, either. Sometimes Steve barked late at night and they heard Oliver yelling the dog's name, swearing at him to be quiet.

Jaimie enjoyed listening to him. Born in Australia, Oliver sometimes did strange, unexpected things with vowels.

When they did see Oliver, it was in the warmer months when he practiced putting in his side yard. He said he wasn't welcome in his old church so golf was his new church. Jaimie thought golf was a strange religion, though no stranger than the others. Theo said Mr. Oliver tried to convert him once when he borrowed a crosscut saw from the old man.

"You interested in golf?" Oliver had asked.

Theo said no. Oliver told him about his golf game, anyway. Jaimie didn't understand the story. It started out with a ball you addressed and hit with a club. Then Oliver got a bird and Jaimie lost the thread entirely. Jaimie couldn't understand why anyone would chase a ball with a club when they could stay inside and read a dictionary.

When Oliver finished his story, he looked at Theo so expectantly, Jaimie guessed he was waiting for applause like they did with Show and Tell at school. Jaimie clapped, which made the old man laugh.

Theo grinned, thanked the neighbor for the saw and explained that he was an atheist when it came to golf (and just about everything else). "The only time I played, I got a hole-in-one, but that clown's mouth was pretty wide."

Jaimie didn't understand the mystery of the clown mouth, either. The discomfort of bafflement was small compared to the effort it took to speak. If people knew how much he didn't understand, Jaimie was certain they'd think he was stupid. Staying mute was the most intelligent course.

That cordial exchange between neighbors was the most anyone in the Spencer family had spoken to Douglas Oliver until he rapped on their front door to give them news of the plague.

The Spencer family was already up. Anna said it was all the coffee she drank the night before. "Decaffeinated doesn't mean no caffeine. It just means less, right? Besides, those sirens kept me up till three. What was the point of that?"

"I suspect," Theo said, "that they let the air raid sirens go to make sure everyone turned on a computer or TV or radio so they knew what was going on. When the National Guard starts arresting people out past curfew, they don't want to have to give the 'Ignorance of martial law is no excuse speech.'"

"Whatever. I'm getting used to this. No more school, no more books, no more teacher's judgmental eyes," she sang to herself. "I'm wired and electrified. And I want more coffee."

When the knock at the door came, Theo drew the meat cleaver from the knife block. Jack answered the door wearing a surgical mask.

Douglas Oliver swayed on his feet, looking gray. "The university hospital is a death house. Despite all the plans put in place for the flu pandemic, there aren't enough people to put those plans into action. Whatever you've been picturing, it's worse."

"How do you know?" Jack asked.

"I got sick and I went there. I've seen it from the inside…but don't worry. No fever and I'm past it. I'm not contagious anymore."

"How do you know for sure?" Anna asked, clinging to the door frame at the entrance to the kitchen.

"Because I ate the Sutr Virus for breakfast, young lady. It tried to eat me up and I ate it. I was horribly sick for days. I went to the hospital last week, though I'm not sure which day it was. I was too feverish. Lost track of the time. Just got back. My dog is gone."

"As in, dead?" Anna's eyebrows knit together.

"No, no! I assume not, anyway. He's doggone gone is all. I can see where he tried to get into the house — ripped the screen to my glass doors, poor, silly bugger. He must have had designs on his dog dish. Or maybe he planned to raid the fridge."

He gave Jaimie a wink. "Steve dug his way out under the fence. Must be off, nipping down to the market for a flan and a doggy bone. His favorite treats were those pigs ears. I wish I'd treated Steve with those more often. Maybe he'll come back for more."

"I'm sorry," Theo said. "We didn't even know you were sick. We'd have taken care of the dog had we known."

Jack gestured for Oliver to sit and he flopped down, beads of sweat on his forehead.

"Don't mind if I do," he said. "I kicked virus ass, but the fight went all twelve rounds. Damn near got me. I'm still weak as a kitten. I wouldn't have made the walk home except a kind young couple gave me a ride most of the way."

Jack left the room and returned a moment later with the cup of coffee she'd made for herself. Oliver nodded without saying thank you and asked for toast. "Just a bit of dry white or a rye if you've got it and I'll tell you what's really going on."

Theo and Jack looked at each other. Oliver surrendered an embarrassed smile. "*Quid pro quo* for the news of the world," he said. "I'm finding myself a bit too tired to make my own toast." Sensing the pause stretch out, he added, "And my bread got pretty moldy while I was incapacitated. Maybe you folks should eat it for the antibiotic boost, hm?"

Quid pro quo. It was a relief for Jaimie to hear someone speak such elegant words out loud. Jaimie wondered if he could have a conversation with Mr. Oliver. Maybe the old man could understand him better than others.

Mr. Oliver ate first, with one hand cupped under his plate to catch crumbs. He did not speak until he finished eating.

"Last week, I took my temperature. It was 102 degrees and I had no appetite after throwing up through the night. You know those dry heaves where there's nothing left to give and it comes up from, uh…your groin?"

Mrs. Bendham drove him to Emergency. There was no parking within blocks of the hospital. "We left the car in a convenience store parking lot. My beautiful Mercedes is gone. There was some broken glass where I left it. Mrs. Bendham helped me make it to the entrance at Emerge. I would never have made it without her."

Mr. Oliver's eyes took on a wet sheen. Jaimie watched him go grayer. His vibrancy faded. "I knocked on Mrs. Bendham's door before I knocked on yours. She told me about Al. Poor old, blind coot. If I'd gotten home last night, maybe I could have caught him in time to say goodbye."

He was quiet for a moment so Jaimie looked up the word *coot*. Good word, coot.

"Last week, I sure didn't think I'd be alive and he'd be the one laid out." Oliver wiped his eyes with the back of his big hands and pulled a handkerchief from his breast pocket. "Blind men make lousy golfers, but I tried to coach him at the driving range. Al always tried to muscle the drive. Never got into a smooth pendulum swing…a good friend, though. He said he'd take care of feeding Steve and I guess he did until he couldn't anymore."

"Tell us about the hospital," Jack said.

"Well, unusual doings. There weren't many doctors or nurses. I was one of the few patients who should have been there since I don't have family to take care of me. The original plan was isolation, but that takes personnel. Things stayed organized for a while, but without staff, they just opened the doors and told everybody to find a bed if they could. Most of the younger doctors and nurses stopped coming into work."

"How could they abandon people like that?" Anna said.

"Oh, don't be too hard on them. I think they were the smart ones, exercising the better part of valor. When the ship is sinking, you don't prove anything by going down with it. Suicide can be courageous, but the Sutr Virus doesn't need all those young people sacrificing themselves on the altar of misplaced duty."

"But all those sick people — " Anna said.

"All those sick people," Oliver raised his voice for the first time, "were going to be dead or not. We're so used to there being convenient solutions for everything and everyone dying in apple pie order, oldest first. Nature has other opinions."

He snuffled, blew his nose and gave Anna a soft look of apology. When he spoke again, it was in a low voice. "What I saw was families taking care of their own. I've seen the same in the Third World. People on cots in hallways, on roofs, anywhere there's a space for a body to lie down and die. Mothers and sisters and brothers and fathers camp out next to them and pray and wait because there is little or no medicine. That's what we've got for this. No medicine but water and caring looks. All we've got to rely on now is our individual immune systems."

"How long were you there?" Theo asked.

"Seven days, I think. This is Tuesday, right?"

"Wednesday."

Oliver went ashen. Jaimie thought, *I love the word ashen.*

"Wednesday. I guess the delirium lasted longer than I thought. It seemed like each time I came around there were different people in the beds beside me. We didn't talk much, except for Charlotte."

The old man looked from face to face and his tears came faster. Jaimie watched each tear track, slipping over the burst capillaries of Oliver's cheeks. Anna and Theo watched the living room carpet as Jack disappeared into the kitchen. She returned with the last of the coffee.

After a long silence, Oliver told the family about Charlotte. He had seen her when he first entered the Emergency department. Long lines of the sick snaked everywhere. Someone handed out masks at the door so everyone looked the same. "Charlotte stood out because she had the most amazing long, red hair. I saw her come and go. Lovely green eyes. She was tall. You couldn't miss her."

There wasn't a bed or a cot for Oliver at the hospital for the first day. "I'd have done better staying home on the couch. At least then I'd have the TV for company."

"Tell us more about the hospital," Theo said.

"Crowded. Charlotte told me that before things had gotten out of hand, there were more doctors and nurses and they could at least make people more comfortable. By the time I got there, they were running low on drugs. It's not just the epidemic. Everything else that hospitals do is shut down, too. Think of all those cancer clinics, the people who need dialysis. Right now their kidneys are killing them, blowing up and bursting or whatever they do when people don't get treatment that, last month, was a simple thing." He ran a hand through his thin white hair.

"Charlotte wasn't a nurse, you know. She was a massage therapist. She'd worked in a spa before everything went to hell."

"What was she doing there?" Anna asked.

"She was sent there. She told me The Powers That Be sent a truck around. When so many doctors and nurses refused to report for work, the government used all the addresses to anyone who could even remotely be considered a health care worker. Poor Charlotte. She didn't want to go, but they made her. She had a baby boy she left with her husband. She was a gopher, fetching this and that, moving bodies, helping people to the toilet and rinsing bedpans. She told me there were a couple optometrists who were telling her what to do but they weren't doing anything themselves."

"They sent a truck?" Theo said, incredulous.

"Government always does what it wants. In times like these, more of their dirty business meets the light, that's all. They kick in doors overseas and we don't blink. We shouldn't be so surprised they'll do it here, too, if it suits them."

"What happened to Charlotte?" Anna asked.

"Oh, I saw her at the beginning and the end. She got me a bed. I remember that. I was blubbering like a baby, asking her not to forget about me. I was on a cold tile floor when she found me. That felt kind of good at first but as time went on, I'd have sold my soul for a mattress to die on. She came back for me though. She remembered me and now all I can do is remember her."

Charlotte came back with a wheelchair and helped him to a bed. "The sheets were still warm and sweat-soaked, but I didn't care at that point," he said. "I thought I was lying down for the last time."

A harried nurse inserted an intravenous needle into his arm to remedy his dehydration. Oliver saw one doctor, once, in all the time he was in the hospital. He didn't see Charlotte for days and when he did see her again, she was a patient.

"It was bad, especially at night," he said. "The days were boring and I was in and out of consciousness. Nightmares teach that boring isn't so awful. I remember watching a digital clock and the numbers were fighting each other. It was this grand battle. I watched and it made perfect sense at the time. Fever cooked my brain a bit."

"But you got better and they discharged you?" Anna said.

"No one discharged me. I woke up last night and I decided I wasn't dying anymore. My sweat was cold and I felt hungry. I figured that had to be a good sign. When I sat up, I was the only person in the room still breathing. There were ten of us. Four were covered up. The rest just lay there, died in the night, I guess. The air smelled of shit and vomit and I figured I was alive, but if I wanted to stay that way, I'd better get the hell out of there. What we used to say in jest was never more true: the hospital is a terrible place for a sick person."

"*Everyone* was dead?" Anna shuddered.

"No, no. There were people moving around here and there. Looked like a horror movie. It was so quiet. I think it would almost be a comfort if someone had the energy for a good, full-throated scream and wail. Instead, the quiet was eerie. I think everybody went numb. Families carried their dead out if they had the gumption. If you could head to the exit, you did. A hospital without doctors and nurses and medicine is just a lot of brick and mortar with germs and viruses breeding."

Jaimie straightened. The word for hospital-bred infection is *nosocomial*. It made him think of viruses shooting up noses.

Oliver laughed a ragged cackle. "In the hallway outside my room there was a fellow on a gurney. He was propped up, reading a book of poetry and looking like an oblivious twit. The cover of his book read *Evil Poems for Everyday People.* Can you beat that? I looked around and I thought, who needs any more evil in their heads than what's all around us in the real world?"

"I offered to help him get out of there. The man said his back was bothering him and he was going to wait for someone to X-ray it. He refused to leave. I said maybe an optometrist would look at his back if he was lucky and I kept going. Moron."

"About Charlotte," Anna said. "Tell us."

He spotted Charlotte by her long red hair in the waiting room. There were people sitting around her, coughing into their masks or trying to sleep in chairs. "I chose to think a bunch were sleeping, but I knew mostly, they were dead or dying. No other reason to be there. I had to pick my way across the floor, stepping between bodies.

"When I spotted Charlotte, she had a carpenter's sawdust mask over her mouth and nose. She held her little blue baby in a blue blanket. She stared down into her baby's face. I spoke to her like she was still there. I told her how she had to take the baby and get out because she was better off at home." Oliver looked at the ceiling, as if studying the stucco for a pattern that gave him reasons and answers.

"The baby had a strip of cloth covering its mouth and nose. The boy stared back at his mother. They had the same beautiful green eyes."

Anna's face drained white.

"The germs are winning," Oliver said.

He began to cry and spoke through choked sobs. "I pulled their masks back. I-I'd n-never seen skin...so blue. I couldn't believe it. I c-couldn't understand it. Whoever the Powers That Be are, they murdered that poor girl and her baby."

101

Jaimie wanted to tell the old man the word he needed to understand was *cyanotic*. Of course, he didn't.

Pay The Piper's Cost

A far away bell banged to a steady beat as Douglas Oliver ate a second piece of toast on the Spencers' couch. Jaimie wasn't allowed to eat in the living room, though his sister broke the rule often. The word *impunity* sprung up in his mind, looking red and sharp around the edges of the *p* and *t*.

The bell rang louder as someone approached, a clear, happy jangle. The Spencers and Oliver walked outside, stood on the front step for a moment and moved to the lawn to get a better look. At last, a brightly painted red and yellow van turned the corner at the top of their street. The vehicle moved at a walking pace.

On the side of the truck body were the words: Burko's Knife Sharpening and Small Repairs. The bell was suspended from a side mirror and the driver pulled a rope and clapper to send out the merry peal.

Four men in coveralls, gas masks and gloves that reached to their elbows walked behind the truck, which stopped every 100 feet. The men split into pairs, each team headed for a house on opposite sides of the street. Behind the van, another truck idled. It looked like it was used for transporting livestock.

No one said anything. Everyone but Jaimie knew instinctively what purpose the procession served. Jack reached out and gently removed Jaimie's baseball cap from his head and gave it to him to hold.

In the back of the farm truck lay long, black bags. Piled atop them were long white plastic bags. On top of that, they could see two bodies, blank eyes watching an indifferent, blue sky.

Jaimie had never seen a dead body. He noticed something he had never seen in another person. The dead have no aura. Without breath, people are just things. Whatever they had been, they weren't that now. This was a spiritual realization in which to take comfort. The sight of the dead bothered him no more than would a truckload of coffee tables. The things that had once been people were just more inanimate objects throwing no interesting colors. Whatever spirit there might have been had gone elsewhere, fled to wherever it is energy goes.

Odd, he thought that there is no word for "one without an aura", but there is a word for "one without a shadow": *Ascian*. Perhaps that would do.

The driver rang his bell again and this time called out, "Bring out your dead! Bring out your dead!"

"He enjoying himself, you think?" Jack asked.

Theo shrugged.

"Gone a little crazy, maybe," Oliver said. "Perhaps it's early days for that, though. This isn't the end. This is the beginning."

As his family stood transfixed, Jaimie noticed a small anthill at his feet at the edge of the driveway. He bent to watch the ants scurry back and forth. Their movement looked random at first, but each ant had a purpose. He bent closer, squinting. He could just make out a tiny yellowish and dirty red aura around each ant.

He took a deep breath through his nose but, to his disappointment, the boy could detect no smell. He'd read that not only was there an odor trail each ant could lay down for others to follow, but each species, colony and nest had distinctive smells. Jaimie could detect nothing.

How much else, he wondered, was laid out before him but beyond his reach? Did ignorance bother people, or were they content to know less and live in tiny, narrow worlds? Everyone he knew could use their voices at will, but they didn't ask nearly as many questions as he would like to do.

The men knocked on doors, rung doorbells and called out to whoever might be in hiding. A young woman appeared at her front door clutching a wine bottle. She was a teacher who had moved in a few doors down on the opposite side of the street the previous fall. She wore a pink bathrobe and fuzzy bunny slippers. Before the men were halfway up the walk, she shook her head, waved them off and slammed her door.

The ringing continued, as if the van's driver were working at a faster pace than the plodding carriers of the dead.

"I'm getting déjà vu," Oliver said. "Bolivia, 1982. Toronto in 1988. In Bolivia, I was doing a diamond deal when a fever went through a little village. That took the babies and the old people. I didn't feel scared then. I was young and healthy and I didn't think anything could touch me. It was just sad and, to be honest, kind of an adventure. I told stories about dead bodies being carried out around me for years. Cocktail chatter."

He looked at his shoes. "Then in the late '80s, I lost many friends. So many beautiful young men with so much promise died all around me, wasting away, their immune systems blasted. Still, it didn't get me. And here I am in the middle of another epidemic. It almost killed me this time, but still, here I am. It's unfathomable."

Jack and Theo both reached out to put a hand on the old man's shoulders as they watched the men carry Al Bendham's body to the rear truck in a sheet. There was a moment of awkward jockeying as the men tossed the body on top of the pile and flopped it over. The sheet came away so they could see their neighbor's body. The men covered him with the same sheet they'd used to carry him.

A slender, bald man wearing a hospital mask stepped down from the van's driver's seat. Carrying a clipboard, he jogged to the Bendham house and walked in without knocking. A moment after he disappeared inside, a shriek went up and they watched as he back-peddled out. Mrs. Bendham, arms straight, pushed him with both hands. He, too, kept both arms straight. He held the clipboard between them like a shield.

"SD!" the man yelled. "SD! SD!"

The four men by the truck didn't move. They watched, a low chuckle betraying their amusement.

Oliver ran toward the Bendham house. His burst of speed surprised the onlookers, considering his age.

"Take it easy, Douglas!" Theo called. "You're still recovering!"

Heedless, Oliver pulled Mrs. Bendham back and held her by the shoulders.

"I just need a name, date of birth and when he died," the man with the clipboard said. "Official statistics!"

"Where are you taking him?" Mrs. Bendham yelled. "Where are you taking my husband?"

"We're taking all the bodies outside of town. North. There's a farm up there where we're…where they're all going. For public safety."

Mrs. Bendham looked up into Oliver's lined face, hesitated and, through gritted teeth, gave the man the information he wanted.

"Beware men with clipboards," Mr. Oliver said.

The man made a note and returned to the truck as two men stepped toward Oliver's house. "Never mind that one, you buggers. That's *my* house! You won't get me! I'm immortal!"

The other pair came up the Spencer's driveway. "Anything for us?" one asked quietly.

Jaimie stayed crouched over the ants but, as the newcomers approached, he looked up warily at the big strangers.

Anna, Theo and Jack shook their heads so the men turned to go.

"What's SD?" Jack asked.

"Social distancing," the bigger man of the two said. "Don't mind the boss, there," tossing a nod toward the man in the red truck. "He rings that bell real good but that's about it. Please excuse him. He's an idiot."

"But he's awesome at ringing that damn bell," the other man said.

The men followed the trucks as they slowly trundled down the street. At the intersection, four houses down, the Spencers watched as the men struggled another, apparently overweight, body into the back of the truck.

Mrs. Bendham had already retreated into her house alone and Mr. Oliver returned to retrieve his jacket. "Good thing she didn't see that abomination."

"Yeah," Anna said. "Imagine watching your husband's corpse get squashed under that fat load."

"Anna!" Jack and Theo said in unison.

"Hey, your daughter's right. And that's not the only thing that would drive her nuts. They aren't burying those bodies. They're off for burning."

"You sure?" Theo asked.

"I saw some other trucks like these last night as I was making my way back. For a little bit, I got a ride from one…in the front," he added. "The driver told me. Said there are big burning piles north of here. He had a full load in the back of the truck and he had a bottle of some god awful cologne spilled down the front of his shirt to drown out the smell."

When Theo said nothing, Oliver leaned in closer and added in a low voice, "I saw what the driver had seen when I looked in his eyes. Situations like this? The thin veneer of civilization that gives society its friendly, glossy sheen gets scratched off. I wasn't going to tell you this, but the truck I got a ride in last night that had a lot of bodies in back? It was a *garbage* truck."

Jack shuddered. "God help us."

The trucks pulled around the corner and out of sight. "I'll stay with Mrs. Bendham a bit," Mr. Oliver said, nodding toward her house.

"Anything we can do?" Jack said.

"I can't think what. We'll get out some old photo albums and she'll tell me all about how they met. I'll tell her about all the good times I had beating Al senseless at golf." He gave a pained smile. Tears came to his eyes again. "Al was the best friend I ever had. Besides Steve."

Jaimie watched Anna's face twist for a moment between a smile and a scowl. "It must be difficult, losing your dog and your golfing buddy all at once."

"Oh, no. I'm worried about my dog but…" Oliver strained for a smile through his tears. "I named the dog Steve, yes, but he came much later. My Steve died a long time ago. He's got a square in the AIDS quilt." The old man spread his big hands out, a bewildered gesture. "And here I am amid all this death again. Besides a touch of arthritis and Irritable Bowel Syndrome, I'm Superman. I guess my parents forgot to tell me I'm from Krypton."

Jaimie's head came up sharply from his study of the ant colony, his eyes bright. They hadn't thought he'd been listening. They jumped when the boy blurted, "Kal-El!"

Remember All You've Lost

Early on April 1st, Theo and Jack made jokes about how they wished the plague was a massive April Fool's prank. Somehow the curse would lift at noon and it would be just another day, like all the days before quarantine fell on them. Instead, it seemed some silent signal had passed through the city. By noon, it was obvious that many of the people in hiding had decided: it was time to run. They were off to seek out safer places, presumably far from the homes where viruses thrived.

They weren't just worried about Sutr anymore. They worried about the germs that sprang up around dead bodies. The man with the clipboard and his workers did not venture into homes where no one answered the door. In many of those homes, the healthy had taken care of the dying. Soon the dying were dead and it was their caregivers' turn.

Misericordia Drive fed an urban sprawl, a rabbit's warren of streets, courts and crescents of single family homes packed tightly together. The cars and trucks formed a slow line, "like a funeral procession," Theo said, as he stood at the window watching the exodus.

Jack punched him in the shoulder. "*Sh.*"

"Seriously, how does a panic start?"

"Dominoes, love. Dominoes. Somebody started packing up their car. Somebody else saw them packing," Jack said. "Panic's a virus, too. It spreads."

"They'd be safer clearing out the dead, watching out for each other and staying put," Theo said. "If everybody stayed and we dared to...dared to go into the quiet houses...everyone could stay."

"I don't think it's on anyone's mind to take care of anyone but themselves and their families now. It's not that kind of world anymore. I wonder if it ever was?"

The family had a front row seat because their house stood near the mouth of one of two exits spilling out on to Fanshawe Park Road. These names were a mystery to Jaimie because, as far as he knew, there was no Fanshawe Park, or least not one anywhere nearby.

Jaimie knew the name for the practice of naming places, cities, streets and rivers: *Onomastics*. But knowing the name of the work did not help him understand its mechanics. From what he'd observed, many places were named for what they no longer were. The new housing development to the west was called Fox Field. There used to be a field there, and presumably in the woods beyond there had been foxes. Now it was a sea of semi-detached homes.

One afternoon Jaimie became so stymied and obsessed about the ludicrous term "semi-detached", he bit his fingernails too short. It meant houses that were separate, but one, long board spanned the narrow space between them. Unfathomable.

From *onomastic's* dictionary entry, Jaimie glimpsed *Onanism*, the definition of which put him on to the definition of masturbation. That made no sense to him. The definition seemed oddly coy, meant to skirt understanding rather than to provide instruction. Jaimie turned the recliner to the window so he could watch the procession of cars and still explore his dictionary.

The parade carried on all day, as if the virus defied the Spencer's wish that the worst must surely be over. Each vehicle was fully loaded and low on the axles. Several cars towed pleasure boats.

"If you've got a cottage to hide out in, it might not be too bad if you've got lots of canned goods, or if maybe you're good with a deer rifle," Theo said. "Even better if you're on an island you can defend."

"Why's everybody leaving?" Anna asked.

"Not everybody, honey," Jack said. She stepped behind her daughter and wrapped her arms around her as they watched the procession.

"Look at that!" Theo said. A station wagon drove past their house slowly with bungee cords holding a huge cabinet to its roof. On top of that, a rocking chair lay on its side, secured with criss crosses of dirty, yellow rope.

"My God, it's like the Joads are escaping the Dust Bowl again," Jack said.

"Or maybe it's the Jews heading out into the desert," Theo said, "hoping for salvation in isolation."

"Or they're rats from a sinking ship," Anna said.

By late afternoon, they had tired of watching the cars creep by. Theo reached out and turned a dowel to close the blinds to the outside world. "C'mon guys," Theo said. "Let's do something else. We haven't played Monopoly in about five years and I think it's time for the anniversary game."

Anna groaned but didn't resist the distraction her parents offered. "What else am I going to do?"

"Onan?" Jaimie whispered.

Only Theo heard him. He had the grace to laugh.

The family spent their days inside the house, locked in or keeping the world out, none were sure. The flood had turned to a trickle and they rarely saw a car drive past. A few people walked, traveling in ones or twos, laden with backpacks. More trucks carried the dead away to be burned.

On the morning of April 7, Anna watched the body trucks roll by, the red and yellow van in the lead. She was jubilant. "Look! Look! They hardly have any bodies in the back of that farm truck! Like one or two, maybe. You know what that means? Maybe I'm not going to lose the whole school year after all. The virus is burning out! It's over!"

She immediately got on the phone to spread the good news to her friends. By noon she was deflated and lounged at the window, staring at nothing. The trucks returned and the pile atop the rear truck stood higher than before.

"They must have changed their route," Anna said. "And Jenna Simmons and Nattie Kilbourne are dead. I went to kindergarten and took music with them and they're dead." Anna wept and retreated to her room for the rest of the day.

The Spencers listened to the radio and waited for good news but there wasn't anything new except the government's repeated warnings that looters would be shot and intercity travel was dangerous and discouraged. The radio warned of barricades on all east-west roads. Travelers could spread disease, so if they tried to enter a city, interlopers could be shot.

Who would do the shooting was an open question. They hadn't seen a police cruiser for more than a week. The radio news mentioned National Guard deployment, but they'd seen no soldiers on patrol in their neighborhood. Eventually, even the radio news departments seemed to tire of relentless bad news and gave up several newscasts in a row, replacing useless words with music.

The news had taken on such a repetitive drumbeat that Anna started referring to it as "the olds". The music had changed on the radio, too. No rap or metal or thrash. Soothing blues, which Jaimie saw as a deep indigo, were ubiquitous, as was soft classical and somber hymns. It was as if all the businesspeople who managed radio stations got the idea at once that a mass funeral was going on and only classical violin would do.

"They're only playing music for the dead, not the people still listening," Anna complained. Quiet and subdued, Anna grew frustrated spinning the radio's dial. She switched to her iPod and listened for hours to her music.

"I don't miss the radio and TV ads," Jack said. "I just realized, there aren't any advertisements for anything."

"We never listened to the ads, anyway. We barely listened to the radio at all before the crisis," Theo said.

The only spoken word programs that had surged back across many radio stations were religious shows. Theo turned it off when they came on. Jack turned it back on, but low, bending close to catch the plethora of whispered warnings, I-told-you-sos and the many promises of a better world to come.

"This is just as has been foretold. This is a judgment, but it's not too late for redemption!" a preacher thundered. "It's not too late for glory. Give yourself over to Jesus Christ, let him into your heart, and reject the lives you have lived. All else is death and damnation everlasting!"

"Shut it off, please, Jack. You don't believe that stuff."

"I don't know what to believe," Jack said. "Sure, there are some crazy things being said here and there, but what about the underlying value? I want to fill up on some hope if you don't mind."

Theo crossed his arms. "If you'd grown up in Japan, that might be a Shinto priest yelling at you. Wherever you go, there are people trying to sell easy solutions. It would be nice if it were true. That doesn't make it true. Otherwise there'd be a Santa Claus."

Jaimie looked up from his Latin dictionary, his face pinched. At sixteen, he still believed in Santa. His parents and sister had spoken so earnestly about Santa Claus, and there'd been presents. How could it not be true? Now he'd spotted his father's aura as he'd spoken of Santa Claus as if he didn't exist. His mother spoke earnestly about God, but God left no presents each morning of December 25. He could detect no deceit from her.

The dictionary was no help. Santa Claus was the dutch name for Saint Nicholas, the patron saint of children. Santa was based in something real. But God? Jaimie wasn't sure. His mother referred to the deity as "merciful". God possessed omnipresence. Santa Claus produced presents. God, zero; Santa, one. As Anna would say, "Advantage: Santa."

Seeing Jaimie's troubled look, Jack took her husband's arm and they didn't speak again until they were out in the garden. "Let's not talk about these things in front of the kids."

"What do you want to talk about?"

She handed him a small packet of sunflower seeds. "Let's plant these around the perimeter of the yard," she said. People won't be able to see in our backyard so well. I love sunflowers. And their seeds."

Her garden plans had grown since her trip out of the city to find more seeds. She pointed to a bare patch of earth by their small shed. "I'm going to put pumpkins over there."

Theo was undeterred. "I don't want the kids hearing that religious crap on the radio, Jack. It has more potential to scare them than to give them any hope or solace."

"What about me?" Jack said. "People are dying all around us. I'm scared I'm going to lose my kids. When this started, it was slow and theoretical and now…"

"Now it feels like the house is on fire, I know. Now is the worst time to panic."

"I was listening to that preacher so I *wouldn't* panic. I haven't slept the night through in a week. I dreamt last night that the corpse handlers came back and piled Anna and me onto their truck and drove away laughing. My faith is kinda shaky right now. That's why I like to hear those preachers. They're a relief because they're so full of…"

"Crap?"

"Certainty."

Theo held his wife close, not knowing what to say. If he spoke, his voice might tremble and that might be enough reason for her to stop listening.

She pushed him away. "How do you do it, Theo? You're acting like you're on vacation."

"We're the parents, Jack. I'm afraid, but we don't have the luxury of looking afraid. Anna could lose it big time and I sure don't want her running off with that idiot boyfriend."

"Anna talked to him on the phone yesterday. His aunt and uncle died and Anna wanted to go over."

"You didn't tell me," he said.

"I know how you feel about Trent after the door incident. I didn't have the luxury of getting you all pissed off about it. Anna does well not showing it, but I think she's hanging on by her fingernails."

"At least he's just a few streets away. Remember our phone bills from when ours was a long-distance relationship?"

"I remember. It was hell."

"We thought it was at the time, sure. The plague wins first place in that competition."

Theo looked at the pack of seeds in his hand, scanning for instructions and finding none. "How far apart should we plant these things anyway?"

"I have no idea," she said.

He grinned. "Okay." He bent and pushed a thumb into the earth and dropped a seed in. A couple inches over, he made an identical hole and dropped in two seeds, wondering if that would ensure growth or make the seeds compete with each other and die. "I'll just have faith that it will work out," he said.

"What if it doesn't? What if it doesn't work out?"

"Then it doesn't," he said. "In the meantime, we have to watch what we say and," he looked at her meaningfully, "what we listen to. The radio isn't very helpful for much at all at the moment. Not for everybody."

Jack said nothing. Instead, they planted sunflower seeds together, each mulling their own thoughts.

Jaimie watched them work from the dining room window. They had their backs to each other, he noticed, and their energies did not intermingle the way they usually did. He didn't know what that meant, but he thought it was a good thing for his mother. Jaimie had watched the black specks in his father's aura grow in vibrancy for the last several days. Their ominous strength would soon make them wasps in his father's aura. That, he understood.

These Are The Lessons Of Despair's Cafe

Over the next few days the temperature climbed. The air conditioner had been on all day, which made it easier to stay inside and laze, reading books. Theo and Jack convinced Anna to get off the phone in her humid bedroom and join them for a game of Monopoly.

Jaimie watched them count out each denomination of fake money, "checking my math," his mother said. As soon as that was done, his eyes fixed once more on his dictionary and did not stray.

Theo peeked at the page and noticed his son seemed to be traipsing back and forth from the *Os* and the *Ms*. There was no pattern to the way Jaimie read the dictionary, or at least none that he could discern. Jaimie had been tested by experts, but his unwillingness or inability to communicate defeated most of the testing the doctors could muster. For instance, several doctors suspected selective mutism, while another few suggested he was merely "non-verbal" since selective mutism is an anxiety disorder.

It was getting dark when they finished their game and Jack announced that there was no way she was going to cook in the kitchen until the heat abated.

"I found treasure this morning," she said. "I was checking out what was in the freezer and found a bunch of steaks. Let's cook 'em up...or actually, you cook 'em up. We'd like some barbecue, please, Theo. Medium rare for me."

"Steak? Really?"

"I know everybody's skittish about cow but there's no connection between North American meat and the Sutr Virus."

"Maybe that's just the cattle industry talking," Anna said.

Jack rolled her eyes. "Let's enjoy it instead of being paranoid. That meat has been in the bottom of the freezer for months, long before Sutr cranked up. Let's eat it up before the cold burns it to a crisp."

Theo groaned and went into the backyard to pull the cover off the barbecue. They rarely used it, so the propane tank was full. "Hottest April on record."

"Look! Coming through the gate, walking across your patio! It's Superman!" Douglas Oliver announced as he strode up. He put his hands on his hips and struck a heroic pose, puffing out his chest. "How's your son, Theo? He pretty near knocked me on my ass the other day. I didn't know he could talk."

"He's a man of few words," Theo said.

"That's the best kind, though I never developed that knack myself. What's Jaimie's story, anyway? I always see him with a book but — "

"We really don't know," Theo broke in, speaking low. "When he's ready, he'll tell us." He looked back and nodded at the open kitchen window. "The thing is, Douglas, you never know when he'll be listening. I think he's always listening, very carefully."

The old man nodded and was quiet for some time before whispering, "Is he a genius in there?"

"He's Peter Pan. Jaimie is the boy who lives in Neverland and refuses to grow up. He's sixteen, but girls might as well be part of the landscape. To him, I think they're like trees from the window of a speeding train."

"That was true for me, too," Oliver joked.

Theo returned a strained smile.

"Really. What's wrong with him?"

"Wrong? Nothing's wrong with Jaimie. He's different. For a long time I was very concerned with diagnoses and labels. Aspergers? Autistic? Who cares if it doesn't help? Even the labels themselves change. They don't call it Aspergers anymore. They say a person is 'on the spectrum'. My son's somewhere in his own little rainbow. If anyone insists on a label, I tell them he's interesting. He is interesting, don't you think? Whenever we go anywhere, he still holds my hand like he did when he was a little boy. The day he stops holding my hand is the day I die a little more."

"Sorry," Oliver said, embarrassed. "Um…to be honest I wasn't coming over just to ask about my Superman fan. Did you hear the shots around dawn today?"

"Shots?" Theo shrugged.

"Gunshots, around five or so."

"Are you sure? I would think we'd have heard that."

"Well, it wasn't like a big shotgun or rifle blasts. This was more like *pop, pop, pop!* A handgun. I heard a yelp or something, too, but when I went to the window and listened, I didn't hear anything more."

"Sure you didn't dream it?"

"I'm sure. Besides, I wasn't the only one who heard. Everything stopped, like the birds were listening along with me. It reminded me of the jungle. People don't realize how loud the jungle can be. Get a couple howler monkeys screaming at each other and some birds chattering over tea and it's bedlam. Then you fire off a few shots, everything stops to listen and wonder."

"Where was that?"

"Bolivia, among other places, on business. I used to be a jewel broker."

"S'cuse me for asking," said Theo, "but how old are you anyway?"

"Seventy-three, next month."

"You look closer to 60."

"Good genes."

Theo flipped a steak and the flame leapt up. "That looks good," Oliver said. "Could I interest you in a little quid pro quo? The smell of barbecue lifted me out of my chair from across the street." He nodded at the steaks sizzling on the grill. "That smells good and looks even better. I can feel the craving for meat in my eye teeth."

Theo looked at the grill, taking his time to answer.

"I'm sick of canned beans and I'm running low. I've been out trading. All my silverware is gone, but I've got a few precious stones left or a diamond ring your wife might like, unless you're into art. Honestly, that's hard to trade this side of the south of France."

Theo gaped at him. "A diamond? For a steak? Are you crazy?"

Oliver smiled, but not unkindly. "You are a lousy negotiator, friend."

Theo moved his hands in a seesaw gesture. "Lousy negotiator maybe, trying to be a decent human being, maybe. How about I split my steak with you? They're huge. This would be more protein than any Third World family would see in a month."

Oliver nodded his agreement and patted his stomach. "All this sitting around is no good for my girlish figure, anyway."

"You've been out trading? That hadn't occurred to me. Tell me about that."

"As a Sutr survivor who enjoys this lovely immunity, I feel some freedom I imagine others don't. There's little to do at home, so I go walking and see who I come across and what they've got of interest. All the stores are closed and the damn golf courses are too far away. Have you been watching TV? It's as execrable as ever."

"Not much. A bit of news and old reruns. I find *The Mary Tyler Moore Show* quite soothing in times like these."

"Don't blame you. There hasn't been much new to talk about. I keep waiting for that old guy anchor on CNN to collapse. I'm not sure they give him time to take a pee. Catheter under the desk, you think?" The old man brayed. Theo joined his laughter.

"There was some news that's actually new," Oliver said. "A young actor in Hollywood — I didn't actually recognize or remember the name — shot six paparazzi over a two-day period."

"Wait, the paparazzi were still *covering* him?"

"No, no. He hunted them down."

"Interesting."

"That may not be the worst part in the grand scheme of things. He hasn't been arrested. It seems the police have bigger fish to fry than a celebrity serial killer."

It took a moment for Theo to digest this fact. "When the world changes this much, you wonder how long it will take for it to change back."

"Dunno," Oliver replied. "How long did the Dark Ages last?"

"We've been pretty much on a media fast to avoid questions like that. I'm worried about my daughter especially. With the TV off, there's less to worry about. What else have you heard?"

"Oh, you know, more talk about escalating tensions between Pakistan and India and Israel is on high alert. Britain is still blacked out."

"Nothing new there."

"Yes, except President Obama is pulling all troops home where they're needed. They're leaving Afghanistan, South Korea, Europe, Japan. Everybody's called home. *Everybody.* Over nine-hundred bases around the world and they're all rushing back."

Theo picked up a set of tongs and piled the steaks on a big plate. "They've had those bases forever."

Oliver leaned over and twisted the knob on the top of the propane tank closed. The barbecue let out a little pop as the last of the gas burned out. "I appreciate the steak, but I'd save the propane if I were you. You may want it later."

While Theo and their neighbor spoke in the living room, Jack and Anna got out the fine china and wine glasses from the cabinet and put them on the dining room table.

As she set the table with the good silver, Anna asked why they were using the fancy plates.

"Because we never do. The last time we all sat together at the table like this was Christmas, I think," Jack said.

"We didn't use the china even then," Anna said.

Most evenings, while Theo worked at the library, the big dining room table was covered with Jaimie's dictionaries and Anna's homework. They rarely sat to eat together as a family. The kids ate when they were hungry. Jaimie ate while he read. Anna pored over her homework or alone in her room, eating sporadically.

"We got this china when we were married," Jack said. "We didn't really need it. Nobody really does. Still…it's fancy. If we're going to be holed up here, we might as well make things as comfortable and nice as possible."

Even as she laid out the gold-ringed plates, Anna said, "I'm not sure I like this. It feels like bad luck."

"What do you mean?"

"I don't know, exactly. It feels like a goodbye dinner." Her eyes were wet.

"Sweetie, at your age, everything seems significant. Don't be superstitious."

Anna rolled her eyes. "Like you listening to the guy on the radio talking about how Sutr is punishment for our sins? You're the queen of superstition. I feel like I should curtsy in your presence."

Smiling, Jack said, "This is what I get for marrying an atheist. Eighteen and your father's still got his hooks in your brain."

"We're not very evil, but I'd like to take this opportunity to point out that any time I disagree with you, you bring up my age. I'm supposed to be going to college next year!"

"I'll try to cut back on the condescension if you'll give me fifty percent less eye-rolling whenever I speak."

"Deal. I can do that. Your condescension and my eye-rolling are directly related."

"Sometimes I look at you and I think, yep, that's Theo's daughter. But am I really your mother?"

Mother and daughter laughed together. "Shall I get the young prince whom we all serve faithfully and who never has to set the table? Jaimie is perfect. He never rolls his eyes at anything his sainted mother says."

"Yes," Jack said. "Call the prince to dinner. Thank you."

"Mrs. Bendham is doing quite fine, though sometimes I think she misinterprets my intentions," Oliver said.

"Oh?" Jack said. "How so?"

"I'm not trying to move in now that poor Al's gone. I'm entirely chaste, in fact," he said.

"Doesn't she know you're gay?" Anna said.

Jack shot her daughter a look as Mr. Oliver chortled. "Actually, I think she believes her charms are powerful and, in these desperate times, how could I resist her lure? I wouldn't be the first guy to succumb to loneliness. Any port in a storm."

Anna shuddered. "Mrs. Bendham, no offense, is like a thousand years old."

Jack rapped her fork against her wine glass, ringing it hard. "Weren't you just lecturing me about not using your age against you just a few minutes ago?"

"It's alright, Jacqueline," Oliver said. "Mrs. Bendham *is* a thousand years old. But she's not dead yet and whatever happens, we're all young on the inside." He smiled at Anna. "Hard to believe at this stage, I know."

"Tell us about the outside world," Anna said. "I've been staring at these walls so much I'm thinking weird thoughts, like how I'll never live in a house with beige walls again. I'll never live inside a house ever again when this is over. I want to go live in an open field so I can watch the clouds all day and not worry about what might be on the wind."

Oliver said he'd been as far as the mall to the west and it had been looted and rifled. "There's not an unbroken piece of glass in the place."

"What were they looking for?" Anna said.

"Nothing very useful now, I don't suppose. Some extra clothes maybe. If they're thinking they'll steal something now and sell it later they might have something there. Otherwise, clothes, would be the most useful thing they could stock up on that I can think of."

"I did want a new cell phone," Anna said.

"You spend enough time talking to him as it is," Jack said.

"Him who?" Oliver said.

"The boyfriend."

"Ah, well, it must be difficult for you to be away from him," Oliver said.

"Thank you," Anna said. "Thank you very much for saying that. It is. I'm not allowed to say so around here, but it is very difficult."

Oliver looked at his plate and focused on cutting his steak into small pieces. He glanced at Jaimie, who was chewing a wad of steak while fingering a phrase in his book: *facta non verba. (Actions speak louder than words.)*

The boy read the words like Braille. This Latin phrase felt like sandpaper under his fingers. Jaimie understood the words were a warning that demanded work. Some ancient man might be sending a message with this Latin phrase, telling innocents to beware liars.

"Slow down, young man. You want to take little bites. If you choke or fall down or break a leg, the EMS is not showing up with an ambulance any time soon."

Oliver told the Spencers about the day before. He had walked east. "I saw the Ginger Gas Man. He's a freckled, red-haired man at the nearest garage. Said he was waiting for a new gasoline tanker to arrive.

"The Ginger Gas Man said the truck was supposed to come any day now. It was supposed to come 'any day now' a couple weeks ago. People keep driving in and driving out cursing the Ginger Gas Man. There's no line, but they still expect he's got gas in the tanks? People are nuts.

"He just sits there on a rocker all day and night, living off candy bars and chips and pop from the vending machines," Oliver said. He flips people the bird as soon as they pull across the hose that rings the bell. Hard to figure, considering the TV is still working. People make their own entertainment wherever they can find it, I guess."

Oliver found The Home Depot, grocery store and pharmacy had all been looted. "There was a young family digging through the garbage in the aisles at the drugstore, looking for whatever crumbs were left," he said. "I think when it started, people were raiding these stores at night. Now, it's clear no one is coming. Day or night makes no difference."

"What about the military?" Anna asked.

Theo jumped in before his neighbor could deliver more bad news. "Mr. Oliver said all of them are coming home. They'll be here soon, I'm sure."

Oliver shook his head and cleared his throat. "I didn't say that exactly."

Theo gestured for the old man to continue.

"As soon as they're here, I think the same thing that happened with the police, firefighters, EMS, doctors, nurses…it just…" He seemed sad and gathered his thoughts. "Everyone has a family and they'll all want to be together. Everybody talks country first, but it's really either family first, or maybe just me first, in times like these."

"But they'll get shot if they desert."

"Maybe. Maybe not. Whoever does show up, I suspect they'll be rather thin on the ground. This is America. That's a lot of ground to cover. The government, whatever's left of it, would do better to shrink wrap Texas and start again from there. That would be plenty ambitious given the area versus the manpower."

The family sat quiet for a time, weighing the old man's words.

"It could be even worse than no army, in fact."

"How's that?" Theo asked.

"Warlords. Nobody thinks it could happen here, but I was a jewel trader in Bolivia and several African countries. No one is so different that it can't happen here. People are the same everywhere."

"So…you're picturing rebellion?"

"If I were a general, I'd set myself up in a small city or maybe even a large one if I was ambitious. I just wouldn't call it a rebellion. I'd set up a city-state that never quite got around to setting up a democracy while I was alive. Whatever I did, no matter how horrible, I'd say it was for everyone's safety and security. Not so different than it's been lately in many ways."

"That's a dark, worst-case scenario," Jack said. "I don't think that would happen here."

"Nobody ever does until it's already happened. Kent State, 9/11…the Sutr Virus wasn't supposed to happen, either, except every virologist and epidemiologist and historian agreed we were overdue for a massive plague." Oliver glanced up at Jack and saw she looked stricken. "I'm sorry, Jacqueline. How much more should I say?"

"Tell us everything," Jack said. "We can't hide it from the kids and I think we've been hiding it from ourselves. We've been insulated so far, thanks to Theo's brother."

"I walked east and south to a group of low rent apartments. A young man was selling drugs for gold rings. I don't know what sort of quality it is, but I gave him a couple rings and he gave me some weed and some ecstasy."

"You've got X?" Anna was wide eyed.

"Medicinal reasons. You never know when some cat might need tranquilizing and I might be that cat. The thing you need to understand about the new economics is, the banks are shut down now. We're on our own again. The system has collapsed while you've been hiding. I'm surprised the television, phones, power and water still work, but some intrepid souls are still on the job somewhere, keeping a skeleton crew working. When things well and truly fall apart, it will take the turbine a while to get up to speed again, but no worries. You've got lots to trade, right? Trade is the new economy. What's old is new again. We're pioneers again. We might even get back to covered wagons, depending how bad it gets."

All but Jaimie stared at the old man, dumbfounded. "You folks really did have a media ban here, eh? When things change — and at some point everything always changes — it happens quickly."

"I'm still getting over you going to a drug dealer," Anna said.

"I did say the pharmacy is cleared out, didn't I? If I break a leg one morning or get a toothache or just can't stand the horror of it all, I do have a fallback position. Suffering should always be optional."

Theo recovered faster than his wife. "How are the roads?"

"Still passable as far as I could see. Either everyone pulled over to the right when they abandoned their car or, more likely, someone from the city is hauling cars and trucks out of the way, probably to keep up the free flow of the trucks carrying the dead out of town."

Oliver looked from face to face. "I'm sorry if I've spoiled anyone's dinner. That was a fine steak."

They ate in silence for some time before Anna pushed her plate back. "I can't eat. I've lost my appetite."

With the speed of a hawk scooping up salmon from a lake, Jaimie stuck a fork in what remained of Anna's steak and plopped it on his own plate. He immediately returned to where his right index finger marked his latest Latin phrase: *Fronti nulla fides. Appearances are deceiving.*

Everyone else burst out laughing. They laughed until there were fresh tears on their cheeks and they had to gasp for breath. Jaimie chewed and read, oblivious.

Insistent rapping at the glass at the dining room window silenced them instantly.

Pray All You Want In Our Final Days

The thin, disheveled man peered in at them, looking left and right. Long, greasy hair obscured half his face. He pounded on the glass.

Theo leapt up. "Hey! You're going to break my window!"

The man stopped, looked at him and waved for him to come outside.

"Careful," Oliver said.

Theo ignored the man's gestures and instead spoke to him through the glass.

"What do you want?"

"Food!" the man said. "I'm all out and my kids are starving. Please give me some food!"

Oliver stood and moved from window to window on the first floor, checking outside.

"I could smell that meat cooking down the block!" the man said.

"How many in your family?" Jack shouted out to the man.

"Three. I mean, four including me," he said. "We've run out of food. We've been scrounging, but people are hoarding and I don't want to go in any dead people's houses." He eyed each face, as if to memorize them.

Jaimie glanced up from his Latin dictionary entry: *e pluribus unum. One out of many* was famously the motto of the United States, of course. However, looking at the man in the window, Jaimie thought the new meaning might now shift to something darker. The man was one survivor from many dead. The plague had divided the nation again. The country was becoming merely land, where names and boundaries were useless. To Jaimie, the man in the window seemed more angry than hungry.

"Please, the baby won't stop crying."

He was lying about his family. Jaimie was sure. There was no baby.

"We can spare some tins. I'm sick of the peaches and there's some soups we got that we didn't really want in the first place," Jack said.

"This is a really bad idea," Oliver said.

Jaimie couldn't tell whether Oliver believed the man about his hungry family or not. He wasn't sure that mattered to the old man.

Theo nodded to Jack and gave Oliver a helpless shrug. His wife jogged from the table and soon returned with a plastic bag filled with several tins of food. Jack walked to the door but Theo stopped her.

"I'll take it out and talk to him," Theo said.

Oliver came with him. The man waited by the window. When the intruder's eyes fell on Anna, he licked his lips and stared. He kept watching Anna until she moved from her seat and out of sight.

Outside, Theo extended his hand to the stranger but Oliver put a hand on his arm to stop him. "Got a name?"

"Bently," the man said. He pointed at Theo. "I think I recognize your kid, the one who never speaks. I've seen him at the mall before, walking with you."

"Where do you live?" Oliver said.

"The other side of the drive. I'm a tax attorney."

Oliver smiled. "The tax deadline will come and go with no one noticing. Not for a long time, I think."

"Yeah, they'll just have to print up the money this year. They'll get back to us once this all blows over." Bently eyed the bag of groceries.

"What have you got to trade?" Oliver said.

"Nothing."

"Everybody's got something."

Theo looked at Oliver but said nothing.

"Look," the old man said, "That was the last of our meat tonight. We don't have anything more to spare."

"I smelled steak," Bently said. "Your barbecue is still warm."

"That tells me you were poking around instead of just ringing the front door like a normal person. You a raccoon or are you a man?"

"Look, grandpa," Bently said, "I'm hungry. My family's hungry."

"You left them alone?"

"Safer for them," he said.

"Not if you bring home the bug. Why aren't you wearing a mask?"

Anger flashed across Bently's face, but he said nothing and shrugged his shoulders in a helpless gesture.

"If you don't have anything on you, at least tell us what you've heard," Oliver said.

"Where have you been out looking for…donations?" Theo asked.

"I've been all over the neighborhood. A lot of people have cleared out. I don't know where they think they're going."

"Know anything about that?" Oliver said, pointing his chin at a gyre of three hawks circling over a property behind a high hedge. The Spencers' view of the crescent that snaked behind their house was blocked, but the birds must have been circling something dead or dying.

"There's a couple bodies in the driveway one street over, on the crescent behind you."

"What'd they die of?" Theo asked.

"Wasn't the flu. There was blood all over both of them."

"Did you see a weapon?"

"No…but that doesn't mean anything. I've seen a few ugly scenes of murder/suicide. Somebody could have come along and taken a gun from them after it happened. Before I came along, I mean. There are still some people around, you know. You watch some of these houses long enough, you'll catch a curtain moving. It's what makes going from house to house so dangerous. I've heard shots and even seen a couple of boobytraps where the people left, but somebody came before me and the scavenger was on the wrong end of a shotgun blast. Kinda discourages further exploration, in case there are more traps."

"What else?" Oliver said.

"What do you mean, what else?"

"Who have you talked to? What's the word out there?"

The man thought for a moment. "There's talk that there's a gang going around to houses at night. I haven't seen them myself, but I came across a house behind the mall last week that was wrecked."

"Seen any police?"

"Nope. I called the police station a couple times and at first the line was always busy. Call 'em now and it just rings and rings. Voicemail is full."

"What were you calling the police about?" Theo said.

"Wild dogs," Bently said. "They almost chased me down a couple times now." The man gave an ingratiating smile. "You know, you oughta be careful with that propane grill. The smell might bring the dogs instead of a guy like me."

"I'm still trying to figure out which I'd prefer," Oliver said. "You saw these dogs?"

"Yeah. Haven't you heard them howl at night? There's a pack of them."

"One of them a big German Shepherd?"

"I don't know. Maybe. I was a bit busy running for my life. They chased me into an empty house and I had to stay there all night. You missing a German Shepherd?"

"Yeah, but I got another couple to keep me company," Oliver said.

The color change fascinated Jaimie. He recognized the lie by Oliver's aura, gray and white and blue went to a rustier shade around the edges. The old man's voice and face betrayed nothing.

"What did you find in the house?" Theo said.

"Nothing. The people who left took everything useful they could carry."

"Oh, c'mon," said Theo. "You're starving and you were holed up in an empty house all night with dogs howling for your skin and you didn't take a hard look around? There must have been something."

"I'm just saying I'm no looter," Bently said.

"The man didn't say you were," Oliver said. "It's not looting if you leave a nice note saying you'll pay it back. That's the new rule. That, or trade."

"Look, fellas, I appreciate the food but I need to get back to my family."

"We're just looking for a little quid pro quo," Oliver said.

"A what?" Bently said.

Oliver seized the bag of groceries from Theo's hands and whipped it across the man's face, opening a gash over Bently's right eye. The plastic bag burst and the cans rolled around the patio with a tin and liquid clatter.

Bently did not fall down but staggered back, holding the wound over his eye. In shock, his mouth hung agape with one hand to his forehead. He held his head like a man who had just experienced a terrifying epiphany. After a moment's hesitation, he bent and picked up the cans of food.

"Doug!" Jack yelled from her seat at the table. "What are you doing?"

Bently scurried, wary of Oliver but picking up the groceries as fast as he could.

"There's nothing more here for you, raccoon! Don't come back! Don't *ever* come back!"

His arms full, Bently ran for the gate. "You shouldn't have done that! I know where you live! I know where you live!"

"Raccoon!"

Theo and Oliver followed him out to the front yard. Bently walked away as quickly as he could manage. He retreated up the street toward the intersection with Fanshawe Park Road. Soon he disappeared out of sight.

Jack met them on the front lawn. Anna followed, pulling Jaimie behind her. He was still chewing some steak but, for once, he was not carrying any kind of dictionary in his free hand.

"Why did you do that?" Jack Spencer looked pale. Her lower lip trembled.

Theo patted Oliver on the shoulder. "A tax attorney who doesn't know the phrase quid pro quo?"

"Not bloody likely," the old man said.

"He recognized Jaimie!" Anna interjected. "He may not be who he says he is, but he's from around here."

"Don't worry about that too much, honey," Theo said. "We're quite memorable when I walk around the mall holding the hand of my sixteen-year-old. I've had a lot of ugly sneers directed my way. They don't ease up unless they notice Jaimie's — " he struggled for the right word.

"Distracted retard look?" Anna said.

Jack swatted her lightly across the back of the head. "Your father was probably going to say something about Jaimie's other-worldly manner."

"Yes," Anna said, rubbing the back of her head dramatically. "Ears is positively *ethereal*."

"Actually, I think that's exactly the right word," Oliver said. The old man turned to Jack and held out the big gold ring that had been on the third finger of his left hand. "For your hospitality," he said.

Jack put her hands up. "No, Doug. No."

He held it out to her, waiting. "Barter is the new currency and I have to distinguish myself from that, that — "

"Raccoon?" Anna said.

"Yes," Oliver said. "Bandits and vermin, rifling the trash cans with small, clever hands. If the new economy is going to work so things don't descend into chaos, we've got to work with what we've got. I was going to offer you some of my weed but I don't have it on me at the moment."

"I have another idea," Theo said.

"What?" Oliver said.

"Let us move into your house. I don't feel like my family is safe at home."

"Theo! Don't you think we should discuss this? I don't think Douglas — "

But the old man was already nodding. "That's not a bad idea. He thinks I live here, too. Prolly thinks I'm the mean old grandpa. Since

I opened the bugger's head, he might decide to come back and do something uncivilized. Like he said. He knows where you live. Besides," Oliver shrugged, "I'm shacked up with the Widow Bendham most of the time, keeping her company. There's room at my house. I bluffed about having another couple dogs in reserve, but I don't know if he bought it. It sounds kind of silly now that I think about it, though in the heat of the moment...you know. Best lie I could come up with since I didn't have advanced notice."

Jaimie watched their neighbor's aura, curious. The old man *did* have advanced notice.

Theo ignored his wife's protests. "It's for the best. It's not like we have a machine gun nest on the roof if he does come back. And we don't have so many food supplies that we can make deadly weapons out of grocery bags full of cans, though that was surprisingly effective on that guy."

"He's right, Mom," Anna said. "I don't like the way he looked at us. I *really* don't like the way he looked at me."

At that, Jack relented. She turned to Oliver. "What does rent go for in apocalyptic times?"

For the first time, Oliver looked down, at a loss. Finally, he said, "I don't know. What do you think is fair? Make me an offer."

"We share our food with you," Theo said.

The old man didn't hesitate. "That's a grand idea! Don't worry. I'm an old man, so I just take a senior's portion...but I must agree with one caveat."

Caveat, Jaimie thought. Why wasn't there one English word that was that succinct for the idea behind it?

"Yes?" Jack said.

"Well, no offense, but you folks haven't exactly been much in survival mode. You loaded up on lots of canned groceries but I bet you're eating through the supply fast. In our conversations, I've had the distinct impression that you are all waiting for the cavalry to come over the hill any moment. As we discussed, I don't think that cavalry is coming."

Deus ex machina, Jaimie thought. Another succinct phrase that English couldn't match.

Oliver balled his fists and shook his head at the same time, looking like a man who needed something to hit. "This isn't a fire drill. This is the real thing!"

Jack sputtered. "I call it having faith and hope that things are going to work out soon."

"That's good. I wish I had the comfort in faith that you seem to have. I'd sleep better at night. However, when God sends the flood he expects you to have your ark packed and ready."

"What exactly are you proposing?" Theo said.

"For your safety, strict rationing and beefed up security of some kind," he answered. "Don't get me wrong, Jacqueline. I think you've done a marvelous job so far, thanks to having the good sense to heed that warning from your brother-in-law early on. However, we can't assume your stocks are going to last as long as the crisis."

"Theo's brother said The World Health Organization's recommendation was for two to three *months* worth of stocked food. We've got that and we're putting in a garden."

"I wonder if the WHO even exists anymore? And what if the seeds don't take or the weather's bad? One bad crop and we're out risking our lives, scrambling for old cans of tuna in booby-trapped houses...or homes full of bodies and viruses and bacteria. I've survived Sutr, but cholera comes next. We're going to have to secure a clean water source and really make sure it's filtered. It'll be hard but we do need to band together against looters. I believed Bently's story about the wild dogs, too. That might become an issue. If my dog is with the pack, I hope he remembers his old master."

"Of course, you're right," Jack relented. "We should move in to your house. Bently might come back. From your house, we can watch our house and stay safe."

"If he comes back, maybe I'll get a chance to sneak up behind him and smack him on the head with a shovel," Theo said. "Or my wife could hit him with a purse full of soup cans."

Jack noticed her daughter shaking and gave Anna a hug. "Screw that," Jack said. "I'll use the meat cleaver."

Jack and Theo shook hands with their old neighbor. Oliver threw Anna and Jaimie a friendly smile as he put his gold ring back on.

Jaimie had watched the rusty edges around the old man's words as they rolled out. He had the distinct impression that Oliver had planned this all along. He had somehow led his parents to this conclusion. They thought moving across the street was their idea and to their benefit.

The boy was sure his mother and father were wrong. Jaimie watched the old man. He thought Plautus, the ancient playwright, might have sent him a warning about Mr. Douglas Oliver from 200 years before Christ: *lupus est homo homini. Man is a wolf to man.*

An Army Rises And The Dead Will Have Their Way.

In a converted industrial building off Riding House Street, Pete Grimsby had a fever. He told his family about the woman in red biting him. His sister-in-law cleaned the wound and bandaged his neck. The children were fascinated with the injury at first. As he told and retold the story (leaving out the part about kissing the beautiful woman's neck) the kids shrank away, clutching their toys, their stuffed animals and each other.

His older brother, Leland, insisted he take to his bed. However, as soon as Pete agreed, Leland locked the door behind him and taped the crack at the base of the door closed. A moment later, Pete heard the rustle of plastic as his big brother secured the sheeting to the door frame. "Just in case!" he called.

"I'll suffocate, Lee!"

"Breathe out the window all you want, you fool. I just don't want you breathing our way. Settle down and we'll get you some soup to ride this thing out. People get sick of this thing. They get well, too. Don't be a git about it."

He peed in a bucket and his piss was hot. An hour later, the thirst hit him. It was an overpowering thirst and he clamped his mouth on a bathroom faucet. Pete drank and drank but couldn't seem to slake the dryness. He went back and forth from the sink to the toilet, drinking and pissing for so long he got bored of it. He yelled through the door, "I think that biter gave me diabetes!"

"Piss off and get some sleep! You'll be alright in the morning!" Leland yelled. "This is embarrassing. You're being a baby!"

The fever took Pete down until he became too weak to get up from the toilet. He slumped there, pants around his ankles and slipping into a dream. He saw the woman in red again. She had long fangs. He thought she must be a vampire, but somehow he knew she didn't just want blood. She wanted *meat*.

In the dream, he called out to her for help. She knew something he needed to know. At the pub, she'd said something about no more worries. He held to that idea now, worrying at it but coming no closer to understanding.

The woman in red called back to him, inviting him to dinner.

"But I hate you," he told her. Even in sleep, his empty stomach answered her with a rumbling, gnawing hunger.

"You won't care about anything soon. You worried about money and your job and your health and what made you sad and what might someday make you happy. No more...just take one bite. One bite is best for now."

When Pete Grimsby awoke, he wasn't Pete Grimsby anymore. He did not worry about money and comforts. The torn flesh at his neck was nothing more than an annoyance. He didn't have a coherent thought in his head. His only concern was feeding himself. Nothing was left of Pete Grimsby but overwhelming hunger. He had no more conscience than wolves. Perhaps, much less.

The rooms next door were full of children. A thin door and bits of plastic sheeting and tape were no match for that ravenous hunger.

Across London, in a fourth-floor room with a view of Buckingham Palace, the woman in red waited in the dark for her legions to assemble. She knew her emissaries were out in the night somewhere, recruiting. Her army would soon outnumber the many at her feet.

The baby kicked and she placed a hand to her abdomen. A shoulder passed beneath her palm. She felt it roll over in her womb.

"Still here? That's a surprise, baby girl, but that's okay. By the time you arrive, Mama's going to make it a brave new world for you. No more bankers...no rich or poor. No undeserved pain."

She stared out the window at the brightly lit palace grounds. Silhouettes and shadows of security men patrolled the perimeter. "No more queens and kings…unless you count me, of course."

The next mutation of the Sutr plague claimed London as the infection spread: man to child; child to woman; woman to man. Wolf to wolves.

No, she thought. *Sutr-X was a sad infection, a failed experiment. Sutr-Z is an infestation, a brilliant invasion.*

Only Shiva knew why.

The woman in red smiled wider. She wondered how Corgis might taste. A delicate little appetizer before the royal feast to come? She toasted the moon with a glass of red wine and waited for the big show to begin.

Season 1, Episode 3

I am the zombie queen!

~ Notes from The Last Café

Zombies Are The New World Disorder

The Tube's automated command to "Mind the Gap" still worked. It was a tiny reminder of the normalcy London had lost.

Aadi Vermer walked to work from Knightsbridge station, limping a little in worn shoes. Officially, the Tube was closed. However, Aadi's manager had procured a pass so Aadi could keep his job. Most of the other people who traveled the Underground were police or military. Passengers stayed away from each other and breathed shallowly, as if that would protect them.

His cheap, black shoes cut at his heels. He stuffed newspaper around his socks for comfort in the long hours ahead. Aadi had to put off buying new shoes for another month or so. His two girls, Aastha and Aasa, were six and seven and growing fast. If there was extra money to be spent on shoes, his daughters came first.

His wife, Riya, died in the early days of the plague, but with the help of some neighbors, the girls were cared for while he put in a shift to protect Harrods.

Before the Sutr-X virus, Aadi reported for work just before ten in the morning and got home by nine to kiss the girls goodnight. The huge department store was closed, of course, but his manager called him each day to say the disease would abate soon and the store would open again. Aadi didn't know what to believe, but he was glad to have the job.

When currency wasn't useful anymore, Aadi's manager, Mr. Richardson, paid the security staff with food supplied from the store.

"Everything will get back to normal," he affirmed. "This is London. We've seen worse than this."

Riya's death made the young security officer bold. "How could you have possibly seen worse, sir?"

"We suffer, but we have to take the long view. People used to say, 'Think globally, act locally.' I say, 'Learn from the past, think of the future and act in the present. London has seen fire, war, the Blitz and another, very notable, plague. God and the Devil can get together and do their worst. London is the one city that will stand forever.'"

Aadi pulled the keyring from the clip at his belt and opened the glass door to Harrods, waving at the security camera. He assumed Dayo was watching from the back office, but he knew that could be hit or miss.

Dayo had been a calm and steady security officer before the plague. Now, she shook when she talked. She admitted to Aadi that sometimes she fell asleep on duty for ten or even twenty minutes at a time. She couldn't sleep when she was supposed to, but when wakefulness was required, she fought to stay awake. He couldn't blame her. He had difficulty sleeping. "You're anxious and I'm depressed," he told Dayo. "But who wouldn't be messed up somehow?"

Before the plague, Aadi watched people from his station at Door 2 by the men's tailoring department. He smiled and welcomed shoppers and asked tourists to take off their backpacks before allowing them to browse the world's most famous department store.

Aadi's name meant *first*, as in *important*. His job didn't make him feel that way. When Riya was alive, his importance definitely came last. With his wife's passing, he was promoted to second, with his daughters tying for first place.

He was about to lock the door behind him when his jaw went slack in shock. A small, naked woman walked down the middle of the street toward him. Aadi squinted. She looked about age sixty, perhaps more. The woman walked in a wide *S* pattern, as if leading an invisible conga line. A small dog — a cute, little brown mutt — trotted ahead of her and she seemed eager to catch up to it.

As she came closer, Aadi could make out multiple bite marks, like bloody half moons, covering her shoulders, torso and legs.

He opened the door and called to her. "Lady? Lady! Come here! You will be safe in here! Get out of the street! I'll get you help!"

She wandered his way, but seemed too confused to focus on him. She acted like she'd been in a car accident and suffered a concussion.

Aadi stepped into the street, turned his radio on and keyed the mic. "Dayo! There's a woman in the street! She's been attacked!" Then, he called again, "Lady? Come here! I can help you!"

The radio crackled a moment. "Door 2? Check in?" Dayo was awake.

"Stand by, Dayo. We've got a weird one."

Aadi started toward her, waving his arms. "Lady? Who did this to you?"

The woman straightened her course and dove on the dog. It yelped and barked and tried to get away as she gathered the small animal in her arms. The dog struggled as she crushed it to her breasts. It nipped the tip of her nose and barked twice more.

The woman grabbed the dog's snout and forced its head back. It had a second to whimper and void its bowels down her body as she buried her face in the little dog's throat and ripped through its flesh. When she raised her head, blood dripped from her gore-spattered teeth and jaws. She chewed thoughtfully as she stared at the security guard with cruel, milky eyes. She smiled.

But it wasn't the ghoulish smile that made Aadi's knees weak and his heart race. It wasn't even the careless way she threw the dog to the side and ran at him that made him cold with fear. It was the mob of ghouls up Brompton Road, racing to join her.

Aadi managed to get inside. The key clattered against the lock plate at the top of the door. He locked the door behind him just in time.

The woman threw herself against the heavy door, heedless, like a bird flying into a window. He recoiled and fell on his back. She fell to the side, her forehead open and smearing an arc of streaked blood down the door.

When the others arrived, they paid her no attention. They trod over her to smear the glass with saliva and blood, pounding on the glass, desperate to get in.

No, he thought. *Desperate to get at me.* The world's rules had changed more than Aadi, or anyone else, could have imagined. Amid the mob, he saw the young and the old. Middle-aged mothers and graying fathers and young and fit yobs alike head-butted the thick glass. He saw a beautiful young girl break her teeth on the door handle in her hunger for him.

Aadi had seen poverty and desperation and tragedy in India. He'd endured great loss in his adopted country. He'd never seen ordinary people behave like rabid wolves.

Aadi got his feet under him and keyed his radio mic as he ran. "Dayo, check the doors again to make sure they're all locked."

"Already, done, mate."

"Do it again, or we're brown bread!"

"I did the rounds, I assure you," she replied coolly. "Where's the woman you —"

He burst into the office before she stopped speaking into her radio.

"Look at the Door 2 cameras! Help me double check the perimeter or we're brown bread!"

Dayo gaped at him as if he'd gone mad.

"Dead! Dead Dayo! Dead Aadi! Move your arse out of that chair and check the damn doors again or we're the running dead!"

As soon as he could escape, he would run to his daughters. He would find them and protect them, if he could. Aastha's name meant *faith and trust.* Aasa's name translated to *hope.* If he lost his daughters to such monsters, he would lose the past, the future, his heart and his mind.

Making History And The Future Poorer

The family worked through the night to gather their things. Anna cried off and on. Jack was stone-faced but her movements were harried.

"We'll be right across the street," Theo said, trying to soothe them.

His words seemed to placate the women the first time but, after he repeated it several times, Jack blew up at him. "Damn it, Theodore! I know! I know! We'll be right across the street. Across from our home. Away from the marks on the doorframe where I marked the kids' heights as they grew. Away from all our things. It's the safe thing to do, to move into Doug's house, but that doesn't mean I'm happy about running out of my home. We're packing up here like we're never coming back!"

"We have to prepare like we aren't," Theo said evenly.

She threw a sweater she'd been holding into a laundry hamper full of folded blankets. "I'm just sick of this. I'm sorry but this really sucks and...and...I want our life back. I want to wander around the mall and take the kids out for a movie and an ice cream." She sat on the bed, defeat disfiguring her lovely face.

"I know," Theo said. He sat beside her and rubbed her back. "You've got cabin fever and switching cabins isn't helping."

"That guy pounding on the window freaked me out," she said. "We *should* go."

"I know. When you call me Theodore, you must be freaked out."

Jack melted a little. "Your hands are really warm." She looked into his troubled eyes. "Did you load the van all by yourself?"

"Jaimie helped. Doug said we should park it in his garage so, if that guy comes back, he won't be tempted to give us the gift of four flat tires in the morning."

"You should have asked for more help packing up, Theo. You're sweating something awful."

"I have cabin fever," Theo said.

"Are you okay? Really?" But she already suspected.

"I'm very tired. That's all. After we're moved in across the street, I'm going to bed and I'm going to sleep until this is all over."

"How much longer do you think this can go on?" Jack said.

"There's no way to know."

"You could lie. You could tell me it'll be over soon. A well-placed lie would be great right now, actually."

"You always know when I lie."

She smiled and leaned her head against his shoulder and then sprang back. "You're too hot." She put the back of her hand against his forehead.

"I got a lot of exercise hauling stuff across the street. Let's not try to take everything. We don't have to empty out the house because of one nut. Douglas has a kitchen sink, so we can leave ours here. Let's just call it a night."

Jaimie stood at the door, waiting for his mother to tell him to take a hamper full of clothes across the street. He watched his parents for a moment, observing the intermingling of their energies. He stepped forward and pulled his father away from Jack.

"What's wrong?" Theo asked.

Jaimie shook his head. He clapped his hands together and then, mimed difficulty, as if his fingers were glued together. He then pulled his hands apart. Then he held his hands spread wide and shook his head more.

"I don't get it," Jack said.

Theo put a hand on his son's shoulder and tried to smile. "Okay, buddy. Let's get out of here. Take that basket, please. We'll be right along." Jaimie shook his head but Theo nudged him out the door. "I understand. It'll be okay."

Theo turned to his wife. "He means I'm sick." At the door he turned to look at her. "I never told you this, but you're really bad at figuring out when I'm lying. Fortunately, it's not something that's come up much."

"I thought I knew."

"Maybe it was denial, but I don't like that fish casserole of yours. I never liked your mom any more than I liked mine and all this perspiration is not exercise-related."

Jack gathered herself and slowly stood. "I wish you'd just spoken up about the casserole. I don't like it, either, but I thought you did, you lying idiot." Her eyes were wet.

She moved to go to him but he shook his head and put his hands out to ward her off. He stepped backward, out through the bedroom door and into the hallway. "It'll be okay. But we need you healthy. Doug's got a nice leather couch. I'll sleep there tonight. Maybe this is just regular flu. Sutr isn't the only game in town."

She followed him, but as if there was a wall between them.

"Regular flu has a low chance of killing me and if it's Sutr, I-I'll make it."

Despite his claims she couldn't tell when he was lying, Theo seemed certain that, if it was Sutr, he was dying. "You...bastard! Don't even think you're getting away from me."

Theo gave her a brave smile. He'd rehearsed this smile earlier that afternoon, as he felt the sickness slowly close him in a fist. "Well, thanks for making it easier to let go and go to the light."

"You don't believe there's a light to go to."

"Whenever there's a light at the end of a tunnel, experience tells me it's probably an oncoming train."

Jaimie returned from his errand to Oliver's house. The boy stood at the bottom of the stairs behind his father. He watched the spots of black energy crawl over his father's lungs, shiny at the edges, moving slightly in and out, a boiling soup of Sutr. His mother smiled at him, but a tear tracked down one cheek. Jaimie tasted chalk mixed with vinegar: hers was truly a bitter smile.

147

Jaimie knew bees and birds and dogs and chameleons all have unique visions of the world: infrared, black and white, stereoscopic. Still, no one really knows how anyone else sees the world. The color-blind think they know what red is until they're told that they aren't in on the common agreement everyone else is party to. Jaimie pushed the thought away because with it came an unfamiliar feeling. Something shifted over his heart.

That night, lying awake in Mr. Oliver's bed, Jaimie pulled the covers over his head and flicked on the flashlight his mother had given him.

"Don't go near the window at the front," she told him. "If you have to get up in the night, use the flashlight and be quick."

Under the yellow beam, Jaimie let his hand slowly caress the dictionary's pages. The sensuous texture ran under his hand as if he had put his hand out the window of a moving car, the subtleties of the air winding through his fingers, whispering through the Ls, alive and instructive, past "ligan" and "ligate".

Soon his hand fell on "lonely." A tingle of recognition swept through him. This was the word he was. With so few people around, he was no longer diluted with what was accepted as normal. A survivor among so many hiding, missing, silenced and dead, the boy was finally less alien. With no bullies, no judging eyes, no whispers and rude remarks, Jaimie felt more calm and less self-conscious then he ever had. He hadn't been aware how self-conscious he had been until the Sutr virus killed his tormentors.

The boy might even have been grateful for the plague, except the fever had his father now.

Howls rose in the distance, as if the dogs were telling him they were lonely, too. Out in the cold without masters, they understood this feeling. It was the first he'd identified in himself. Jaimie knew he was different, sick in the way the one-eyed king is sick in the Kingdom of the Blind. The boy wasn't a king, though. He knew what "retard" meant, though the bad words had not hurt him like the ones he found for himself in the dangerous pages of his dictionary. *L* had lonely and loneliness. Tonight, he discovered that these words had the power to open himself to the feelings they described.

The other dangerous word — a word that had made him feel — he'd found in a medical dictionary. "Aspergers" hit him like a hammer out of the dark.

Jaimie knew. He had recognized himself in that moment just as he recognized the feeling behind the definition of loneliness. For so long, the boy had been comfortably numb. His emotions had been as slow and dull, as an artificial limb. Had the Sutr virus lit that part of him on fire? Was it responsible for these feelings bubbling up?

Why not? He'd already seen the seeds of black specks growing in the aura of the truck driver at the grocery store. He'd then seen its black claws sinking into the head librarian. He'd seen the virus boiling through his father's etheric, settling down deeper, closer to the skin, arriving as sure as anything is sure.

The dogs howled again, but there was something else that was closer. Gunshots, spaced minutes apart, but coming in batches. The reports came in a chorus, two bass, one alto and another pop, pop, pop staccato that had a grating, soprano whistle at its edge. Jaimie had heard these sounds many times while his father watched old movies. There was a western with Mr. Clint Eastwood that had featured a weapon that made that high-pitched shriek with each shot: *The Good, the Bad and the Ugly.* He couldn't tell how far away the sounds were. They seemed to move in a circle through the night. *Gunfire,* he thought. *Such a poetic image for the chemical discharge and flame at the end of a weapon.*

Soon another sound arrived that made Jaimie feel the loneliness more deeply. It was closer than the howls of the dogs. It was even closer than the circling gunfire. It came from downstairs, like a short bark. Jaimie got out of bed, thinking perhaps Steve, Mr. Oliver's German Shepherd, had returned home. He found his way to the staircase in the dark, navigating around the unfamiliar shapes of a chair and a small couch as he walked through Mr. Oliver's study toward the stairs.

Doug. They were calling him Doug now, like he was family, as if moving into his house had somehow made them the old man's kin. Maybe family isn't just blood, but geography, the boy reasoned, though he was sure the dictionary would say that was wrong.

The boy crept down the stairs, not bothering with the flashlight in his hand. It wasn't barking. It was his father, on the couch in the living room, coughing.

Jaimie pulled a rocker out of a corner and sat beside his father's dark form. He was propped up, a large pillow underneath him. The glow of a streetlight outside illuminated the room enough that Jaimie could see his father glowing red, burning with fever. He reached out and touched his forehead, which roused his father from his fitful sleep.

"Hi," Theo said. "You probably shouldn't be near me right now, son."

Jaimie rose from his seat immediately but returned a few minutes later with a cold, wet cloth. His father began to protest but fell back on his pillow and broke into a series of short, ragged coughs again, rumbling from deep in his lungs.

After the episode passed, Theo settled back and gave his son his thanks. "Your mom fixed the curtains for me so I could watch TV. *Key Largo* was on. I love Bogart movies, but a movie about people trapped in a hotel by a storm and bad guys with guns...seemed a poor choice. I watched it anyway. Hadn't seen it in years.

"It would have been great to see *Some Like It Hot* again. That's one of the best comedies of all time. Two guys dress up as women and Marilyn Monroe's in it. Tony Curtis was pissed off because the director used all the takes that were good for her but weren't necessarily the best for him." Another coughing fit came and went.

"After *Key Largo*, I opened the curtains. I've been watching the house. Doug went out late and still hasn't come back. What the old guy is up to at three in the morning, I have no clue. I think Mrs. Bendham is worried. She's waiting up for him, too. I saw her outside in the garden looking up and down the street. She was wearing a mask."

Jaimie hadn't seen Mrs. Bendham since her husband died. He turned and looked through the big bay window at his own house. Beside it, in the Bendham house, a light was on. He saw a shadow move back and forth. He squinted and could just make out the silhouette of the old woman's high pile of hair. She sat in a chair in front of her window. Jaimie wondered if she could see him. He waved but she did not wave back.

"Too dark in here for her to see in," Theo said. "Doug's got a pretty fancy place here. The windows are tinted, so it's hard for anyone to see in, anyway."

Jaimie examined the glass before returning to the seat beside his father.

"I tried calling dad — Papa — again. Even at two and three in the morning, it's the same." At this he attempted to mimic an automated voice. "All circuits are busy, please try again later..." and then fell into another coughing fit. When he recovered he said, "I think there's plenty of room for hope left, you know. It's just a flu. All societies through the ages... They have all had epidemics."

And most of them are dead civilizations, Jaimie thought. The boy kept watch on his own house, its dark face looking blank and abandoned. He'd read in stories that houses were lonely sometimes, too. He could see his bedroom window, like a black eye. The last time he slept there he wasn't bothered by this new knowledge of loneliness. He knew thousands of words and their definitions, but only two had weighed him down so far. The sharp slice of the words "Aspergers Syndrome" had left him cut with self-recognition. The word *loneliness* settled on him like a lead apron.

And now they were living in Mr. Oliver's house, giving him their food and not allowed to eat as much as they wanted. He had overheard his mother say to Anna, "This will be hard on Jaimie. He's not good with change."

Anna had replied, "This is harder on me. Jaimie doesn't get what's going on."

His sister was wrong. He wished he could bring himself to tell her so. People made assumptions about him. They were always wrong.

"Look at that streetlight," Theo said. "Despite all this, that streetlight is still coming on and going off when it's supposed to. Somewhere there's someone keeping things going. It's only the flu. Things look like they're jumping the rails here, but — " he broke into another quick series of coughs that produced nothing — "things aren't so bad. We still have water. People underestimate what a triumph that is. Without the wonder of plumbing, our lives would be much more complicated."

The boy reached out and felt the wet cloth on his father's forehead. The fever had already heated through. He turned the cloth over, got up again and, after a moment's banging search in the kitchen, returned with a cereal bowl full of cold water. He'd seen his mother do this, once or twice a year. When Anna took over the couch and the remote control to the television, she often missed a week of school because of flu (regular flu they called it now).

Jaimie watched his father carefully as Theo coughed, reached down to a box of tissues, blew his nose and cleared his throat. He seemed more animated now, so Jaimie settled back. He rocked and watched the dark square of his bedroom window across the street.

His father talked to him until dawn, and through the night, as his father's fever peaked and pushed him into delirium, Theo Spencer spoke of the Gateway to the Spirit World.

Let Go Of What You Know

"The gateway is hidden on the East coast," Theo told his son. "It doesn't look like much, but at night, in the right spot, it feels like you're floating in space. The sky's so clear, the Milky Way seems much closer to Earth there."

Jaimie couldn't understand how this could be true. He went back and forth in the rocking chair, watching his house across the street and listening to his father do battle with slippery ideas in a boiling brain.

"I want to tell you something. It's a confession," his father said. "Just in case."

Jaimie tapped his temple, meaning that he'd remember.

The boy wondered if that was why it was called "the temple". Since the brain was the church of memory, perhaps some forgotten poet had likened the power of memory to a temple. Was that how that couple of square inches of each person's head got the name temple? Later, someone applied the term to anatomy. Jaimie did not approve of homonyms, but he liked the anatomist's whimsicality.

"When things get bad, Jaimie, we'll have to run," his father told him. "We'll escape to Papa Spence's farm. It's a long way and it will be dangerous. It's most of the way across the country, but we'll make it. You're going to love Maine. All those little towns with a view of the sea…that's a food supply, too, son. It's not just about the view."

Jaimie nodded to show he was listening.

"When I was a boy, there were a couple of towns nearby Poeticule Bay where I'd go play baseball sometimes…well, villages, really. Your grandfather used to call them 'not so much villages but wide spots in the road.' There was this chant we'd do at little league games. All these little towns had baseball teams and, somehow, the rhymes caught on. The one I remember wasn't about my hometown, Poeticule Bay. Strange. I remember the chant for those wide spots, up the road." Theo chanted, in a voice that started out surprisingly strong.

"Squirrel Town Squirrels!
Mink Cove Minks!
And nobody goes to Sandy Cove 'cause
Sandy Cove stinks!"

Theo Spencer's voice was a rasp at the end, but he was determined to continue to speak, as if afraid that if he slept, he would not return from the empty dark. Through his fever, he told Jaimie how to find the stone. "The gateway," he called it.

"You'll need a compass. From your grandfather's house, at the back step, walk southeast from the back door. There's a special place. The gateway is the only safe place I know. We'll go there together or I'll meet you there." He gave his son the instructions twice, even though he suspected Jaimie was incapable of forgetting anything.

When his father laughed, Jaimie tried a smile. His was an awkward attempt that only showed his top teeth. His smiles caused his classmates to ridicule him.

As the sky bled from black to gray to blue, Theo told his son stories of Poeticule Bay. Jaimie's grandfather had first worked for a grocer at a groceteria. "It was really a sort of general store. Papa liked the word 'groceteria' better. It's like a grocery store except each customer tells you what they want and you go get it for them from shelves behind the counter. A generation before that, people would have called it a mercantile."

Groceteria. Jaimie approved of that word. All those vowels made it musical.

"I think Papa Spence would have stayed in the grocery business forever. The original owner was a butcher so he learned how to cut meat, too, but mostly, it was a really social job. I'm sure that's what he liked best, talking to the customers all day about the weather and whose cow got loose on the road the night before."

Jaimie took the washcloth from his father's forehead, noted that it had heated through again, and wet it in the cold water in the bowl at his feet. He wrung it out and put the cool cloth back over Theo's forehead and eyes.

"Better," Theo said. "Thank you."

Jaimie nodded and his father continued. "The groceteria was in Shell Cove, before the move to Poeticule Bay. I grew up in Shell Cove until I was ten. We didn't do any moving around until my father's business burned down. There was a garage next door. They were doing some welding on a wooden floor and poof. Everything was gone. Your grandfather lay in a snowbank and cried because all that he'd managed to rescue from the groceteria fire was the record book full of debts he owed."

"Later, Papa Spence became an insurance salesman but that didn't last too long. Papa still thinks insurance is a big scam. The way things are working out, I guess he was right about that.

"Anyway, we moved a few more times until he got a job as a lumberjack outside of Poeticule Bay. Our new home was another wide spot in the road called the Corners. They called it that because two country roads met out there to form an intersection and that's where the general store was. Your grandfather was better with numbers than he was with an axe and saw, so the owner put him to work in the office.

"Eventually Papa owned his own sawmill. Papa has a way with people. He made the owner a friend and then the owner became his business partner. He's social in a way I never was." Theo lifted the washcloth to peer at Jaimie. "I guess you take after me a bit too much in that way. We both prefer books to people." He sighed and repositioned his cold compress.

"I always stuck close to the family. Your Uncle Cliff, well...he was always off doing other things. Cliff is my older brother by five minutes, but he may as well be ten years older. Identical twins aren't really identical. While I stayed with Papa and Nana, my brother went off to boarding school, Christian summer camps and later, science camps. I don't remember him going to the Corners much. Thanksgivings, probably."

Jaimie shrugged and focused on the outline of his father's chin moving up and down in the dim light. He couldn't see any of the Sutr virus blackness through his father's aura, but he guessed that was because it was too dark. Jaimie felt more comfortable not knowing how the disease was progressing.

"We moved into Poeticule Bay, but Papa bought a farmhouse in The Corners. It was a very old house then, but I was quite a bit younger than you are now, so I guess it's right to call the farmhouse ancient. A hole in the middle of the kitchen floor could drop you to the shallow basement when your grandfather took over the old place. He paid a couple yahoo lumberjacks to live there one summer and work on fixing it up as a cottage. The family went there every weekend and that's how I got best friend I ever had. That's how I started in on my greatest regret.

"That boy I befriended? We found the Gateway together, but only he went through it."

That night, Theo Spencer told his son the secret of the Gateway. The way his father spoke, Jaimie thought of it as *arcanum arcanorum, the secret of secrets*. In Latin it referred to Nature's secret, the knowledge that held the key to everything else there was to know.

To Theo, it was his first and last confession about the boy he killed.

Secrets Hide Where Ghosts Go

"D'Arcy sounds fruity," he said when anyone called him by his given name. He preferred "Kenny", short for his last name. Kennigan.

Kenny had three older brothers who had earned a reputation for being bad from The Corners to Poeticule Bay. They bragged that even the cops in Bangor were scared when they came to town. Of the three, it seemed two were often in jail for some petty crime. Mostly, they broke into the cottages of summer people.

The Corners had a population of just a couple of hundred in winter. When the summer people came, they roared up and down Black Water Lake in motorboats. That left many vulnerable cottages the rest of the year. Kenny's older brothers often enjoyed the luxuries of rich strangers' cottages for days at a time.

Two of them were caught (twice) by the sheriff because they left tracks in the snow all the way back to their shack on the ass-end of The Corners. After that, whenever there was a break in anywhere near Black Water, the sheriff came knocking on the Kennigans' door first.

Kenny's father drank. His brothers, whenever they were home from the detention center, enjoyed beating their little brother. Kenny stayed away from home as much as possible. He had a pellet gun, so he walked the old logging roads looking for things to shoot: birds, squirrels and snakes. Kenny wished his targets were his brothers. He imagined it wasn't just a little pellet gun for plinking in his hands.

Kenny was headed home in the late afternoon one Saturday when he saw a boy about his age with a bow and arrow. The boy had set up a fancy straw target. It was pretty big, but the boy missed consistently. Kenny watched him from behind some trees before he stepped out into the field and waved hello.

"Maybe you should start with the side of a barn," Kenny suggested.

Theo Spencer smiled and pulled back the bowstring, intent on showing the townie boy his archery skill. He let a white target arrow fly. It missed, flew well past it and was lost in the field's high grass. "For your information," Theo said, "I'm trying to hit the grass behind that big circle thing."

"Can I try?" Kenny said.

"Can I try that?" Theo asked, indicating the pellet gun in the boy's hand.

They exchanged weapons. They didn't talk much. They just enjoyed playing with the gun and the bow and arrows, experimenting with the unfamiliar. After some time passed, Kenny said, "No wonder the Indians lost all that land."

"It was taken, not lost," Theo said.

"Well, no wonder," Kenny said.

They spent the next hour shooting the target with the pellet gun. The gun was less frustrating to master. They only stopped because it was suppertime and they heard Theo's mother calling from the back step of the family's cottage.

The next Saturday, Theo was back and Kenny was waiting, already firing at glass bottles and cans he had set up on a rock.

"Glass bottles aren't so good as targets for arrows," Theo said.

Kenny handed him another pellet gun. "Belongs to my older brother, Jimmy," Kenny said. "Figured you'd be along. Don't ever tell him he lent you his pellet rifle. He don't know how generous he is. Wouldn't want him to get a big head."

That night Kenny had dinner with Theo's family. The following weekend, Theo told him to come over after dark on Saturday night. Theo brought a telescope out into the backyard.

Impressed, Kenny let out a low whistle. Kenny called Theo "Moneybags" after that, and later, simply "Bags."

Theo could name all the constellations. Theo taught Kenny what he knew about the moon, stars and planets. "The country's so dark and the air's so clear, it's like the stars are closer out here than they are in Poeticule Bay."

In return, Kenny told Theo about girls from school he liked. He was convinced several of them were very close to going to third base, though the meaning of the expression was hazy to both young boys. "Damn teases always chicken out just short of third base," he complained. "I get a few kisses and they get too girly about it."

Theo was shy around girls, so he was doubly impressed with Kenny's progress. It never occurred to him that Kenny was lying, or that his feigned worldliness was an amalgam of boasts he'd heard from his older brothers.

When challenged, Kenny replied that it didn't matter if it was a lie. "Just don't let me bore you. It's about a good story. A good story keeps us from looking at the shit."

That fall, a couple of weeks before Theo's family was to close up the cottage for the winter, Kenny brought a sleeping bag and the boys stayed in the backyard through the night to watch a meteor shower.

"They're falling at four or five a minute," Kenny said at the shower's peak. "This is better than fireworks. I mean, you have to keep your eyes open and really look for them. It's like hunting, but the payoffs come faster."

The boys should have stuck with hunting shooting stars.

The next day, a Sunday, Kenny left early but soon returned. He found his friend in the wood house chopping lengths for the wood stove. In his hands, Kenny held two shotguns. "Don't tell my brother Brian that you borrowed his .20 gauge. He don't know how generous he is."

Theo hesitated. "I don't have a license or anything."

"That's why I took the .20 gauges. The .12 has too much kick for a little girl like you."

"Then how come you don't have a .12 gauge for yourself?"

He shrugged. "Eh, makes too much mess of the rabbit."

Kenny held out the shotgun and Theo grasped it. He liked the weight of the weapon in his hands. The closest he'd gotten to a shotgun was watching criminals use them on TV.

Theo handed it back his friend and told Kenny to wait behind the outhouse. Theo raced into the house. He made two ham sandwiches and grabbed a couple of cold bottles of Coke from the refrigerator.

"I'm going for some target practice with Kenny in the woods!" he yelled up to his parents, who were both still in bed.

"Okay, honey. Be careful!" his mother yelled back.

The boys walked the logging roads that led deep into the forest. "My dad says there are goldmines around here somewhere," Theo said.

"Gold?"

"Well, all the gold's mined out now probably."

"So, there are big holes and tunnels around here somewhere?"

"Somewhere," Theo said.

"Cool. Didn't know that. We should find one and make a fort."

They saw no rabbits but satisfied their lust to try out the guns by shooting their cartridges at the Coke bottles they'd brought. The bottles shattered, each boy hitting his target the first time.

"Good shot, Bags. You're ready to move up from hitting the broadside of a barn."

"You know what we should do next time?" Theo said. "We shouldn't drink from the bottles first. Think what it would look like if we'd shot at them when they were full!"

"That would be ten times cool," Kenny replied, "but wasteful. There's an old logging truck in the woods behind the mill. It's a wreck, but there's still some glass left in it."

"Twenty times cool," Theo said.

"We better wait till next summer, though," Kenny said. "We're far back here, but the woods by the mill is right up close to civilization. I wouldn't want to be caught with a couple shotguns. Take the course and get a license this winter, will you?"

"Sure," said Theo, not sure he was old enough to get a license, but he'd be eleven soon.

"Good. You gotta man up, Bags. If my brothers knew I was running around with a summer kid who can't even shoot, they'd beat me senseless and make me marry you. But we have to get married, anyway. You're pregnant."

"It'll be a tasteful ceremony, but you can't wear white."

"Yeah, I'm a big ol' slut," Kenny said.

That was the last time Theo ever truly *giggled*. They had laughed as boys laugh, giving themselves over to it with abandon. For the last time on a cool autumn afternoon under falling blood-red maple leaves, the boys' laughter rang through the listening trees.

When they recovered, Kenny flicked his head in a come-along gesture. "Bags, it's long past time we went to the moon."

"You aren't going to show me your bum, are you? I was just kidding about the whole marriage thing. I can't marry you. You're a slut."

"I can't marry *you*," Kenny replied. "I want a bride with long blonde hair."

The boys followed a logging road back to the mill. It was Sunday afternoon and no one was around. Before them stood a huge mountain of sawdust, four stories tall. "Welcome to the moon," Kenny said.

They hid the shotguns in the bushes and climbed the sawdust mountain. It was made of discarded sawdust, wood chips and small pieces of wood. It was hard climbing, but the fun was in hopping back down. They bounced down in spongy, springing lunges.

"Told you! No gravity! We're on the moon!" Kenny yelled.

They raced up and jumped down, over and over. When they tired of that, Kenny showed Theo the top of the mountain. Long narrow chasms cut deep into the surface. Some reached a depth of seven to ten feet. "Frost did that," Kenny said.

"Looks like those pictures of ice caverns in the Arctic," Theo said.

"Looks like it could swallow you up, doesn't it?"

At that, Theo jumped into one. Kenny went white. "Jesus! Get *out* of there! If it collapses, you'll smother or burn or die smothering and burning!"

"You're full of it."

"No, *seriously*, Bags! Get the hell out of there!"

Finding traction on the side of the steep chasm was harder than Theo expected. Wood chips and sawdust gave way under his feet. Kenny lay on his stomach and reached down. Theo grasped his hand and climbed. Kenny pulled, rescuing his friend from the narrow cut. When Theo finally did throw a leg over the lip of the hole, he managed to roll out onto his back. Both boys gasped for air and coughed on the rising dust.

Kenny fell back, breathing hard. "Don't do that again!"

"And you call *me* a girl."

His friend sat up, took Theo's bare hand and thrust it under the surface of the sawdust.

"*Ow! Agh!*" Theo yanked his hand back out into the open air and shook it.

"Yeah, it gets pretty hot, huh? On a summer day, you could cook a chicken in there in a few minutes."

"Sorry," Theo said.

"Hey, I wasn't doing it for you. What if you up and died in there? I'd have to carry two shotguns all the way back on my own."

Theo punched Kenny in the chest and they chased each other around the surface of the moon.

Then Theo stopped short and took in the view of the Corners below them.

"Yeah, we're up pretty high. There's the Mersey River. In the spring, they have the eel traps down there. The traps look like wooden boxes."

"Are you kidding? Eels?"

"Somebody eats 'em. They pay a lot of money to eat that snaky fish." Both boys shuddered. "The traps go all the way across the river. It's kind of neat to see as long as you don't think too long what it's for, you know, with all the wriggling of those things in there."

"People are crazy," Theo said.

"Yep."

They bounced on the sawdust mountain. Before they were done, the boys ran up five more times, each time telling each other, "Just one more time!"

When they were sweaty and covered in wood chips, they retrieved the shotguns from their hiding place in the bushes and headed back to Theo's cottage.

"I'm tired, Bags. Let's cut through the field. I know a shortcut. This way."

The boys left the logging road and walked through the forest amid patches of ferns and sorrel. The green moss felt softer and deeper than any carpet.

"When will you be back to your farmhouse?" Kenny asked.

"It's just a cottage now. My dad talks about making it a real farm again, with goats."

"Cottage? Still bigger than my house."

"We'll open it up again in the spring, though dad has some friends who want to come out in November for deer season. We won't be here that much till the end of black fly season. Mom gets claustrophobia. She says the black flies are like walls closing in. And the ticks freak her out."

"I don't blame her," Kenny said. "I'd love to be anywhere else, but especially in the heat of July. It's not as bad with the wind off the lake. Black flies and ticks. I hate the ticks!"

"You ever get down to Poeticule Bay? It's not far and with the wind off the ocean, you don't have to worry about black flies. "

"We never go anywhere, except Waterville sometimes to visit my brothers."

"They got a place there?"

"They got a *cell* there, yeah. They call it the Kennigan hotel because one of them always has a suite reserved at the detention center. They act like it's no big thing, but I've seen all of them cry at sentencing hearings every time they go to court. Even Brian, and he's the toughest of my brothers."

"How come they don't just stop doing things that get them sent to jail?"

"They figure they'll never get caught. Then they do. They don't know nothing else."

"You're not like them," Theo said.

"Nah. I got high hopes. Maybe I'll make it as far as Bangor." He shrugged. "Big deal. Guy like you, you'll call me up one day from some fancy office in New York with hot and cold running secretaries and you'll say 'Remember that great day we spent doing nothing?'"

"Yeah," Theo replied. "And you'll say, 'Who the hell is this?'"

Both boys were quiet for a time, walking slower the closer they got to their destination. It was almost dusk when they came to a rusted barbed wire fence, twisted and sporadic, that ringed one edge of the field behind the Spencer family cottage.

"There's a rock fence up the side of the field," Theo said. "Dad says it's all the rocks they pulled from this field when they farmed it. He's talking about putting in Christmas trees next year. He's thinking of filling up this field with them, to make it pay."

"That's why you're Moneybags, dude. Your dad's always thinkin' and mine's always drinkin.'" Kenny put his shotgun on the other side of the fence and climbed over. "Pull your balls up," he said as he pulled down on the barbed wire to give Theo room to swing a leg over.

"Oh," Kenny said, stepping forward to stop Theo. "Wait, don't climb over wi—"

Boom!

The shotgun blast tore through Kenny's chest and left shoulder, knocking him off his feet and into the tall, soft grass.

Theo dropped the gun. The trigger had caught on a sharp tine of wire. The echo of the shotgun blast rolled back to him, freezing him for a moment, one leg still on the ground, the other still up, his pant leg caught in the fence wire.

He tore his pants to break free, threw himself flat and scurried under the wire. Theo ran to Kenny, who had landed on one side, twisted in mid-air as the pellets had ripped through his left lung.

"I'm sorry! I'm sorry!" Theo cried.

Kenny blinked wide blue eyes at him. He winced and coughed up blood. Theo dared a look. He saw the white flash of Kenny's bared ribs and looked away.

Shotguns forgotten, Theo grabbed the shoulders of his friend's jacket and dragged him toward the house, shouting for help as he went. After forty feet, he felt so weak he doubted he could go on.

At the top of the rise sat the lone tree, a twisted oak, in the center of the fallow field. He made that his destination. From there he'd be able to see the cottage and then maybe his parents would see him or hear his screams for help. The nearest doctor was in Poeticule Bay. Theo pulled Kenny again, in desperate lunging spurts.

How much blood does one person have to spare? The boy didn't know. His brain drained of any thought but the pulling.

The light was dim as Theo pulled Kenny under the big tree. He stood and looked down the field. The car was gone. His parents were out, probably picking up the farewell dinner. They'd talked about getting Chicken Burger take-out. The boy didn't know how long it would take them to return.

Theo looked down at his friend in the grass. A long bloody trail had followed him up the rise to where Kenny lay. Kenny waved him to come closer. He was breathing in short gasps, but he managed to whisper in Theo's ear.

"Say I did it," Kenny said. "Say I did it."

"That doesn't matter now," Theo said.

"They'll kill you," Kenny gasped. "I did it. Brian will kill you."

"I'll go get help!" Theo said, but Kenny grabbed his sleeve and held on.

"Stay…don't leave me alone…stay…not much longer."

Theo held his friend in his arms and cried. After another moment, he pulled some moss away from the base of the tree behind them and put it over the gaping wound. He put pressure on the wound like they said to do in movies. Theo leaned heavily on the moss.

After some time passed, Kenny spoke again in a high voice. "Doesn't hurt anymore."

The ground beneath them was soaked black in the dull light.

"Cold."

Theo gave up on pushing on the moss and hugged his friend. He held him and cried and rocked and shouted for help.

The light abandoned them to the creeping dark and stars arrived to welcome the dying boy. Soon the night took over and the Milky Way unfurled overhead.

"Shooting stars?" Kenny murmured.

"I don't know, man. We'll watch and see. There must be a few more left over from last night. Must be. We'll wish on one. My parents will be home soon. We'll wish and we'll get help."

Some time passed. Theo was never sure how long.

Headlights from his father's car swept the field, but Kenny had already left through the Gateway.

Theo lay beside him, staring up into space, wondering where Kenny went. In church, they sang a hymn called *"I'll Fly Away"*. Theo tried to remember the words, not to sing to his friend, but for clues. It was so quiet and clear, Theo could make out every cold star, every indifferent constellation.

His parents went into the cottage, each carrying a bag. In a moment they were outside calling his name.

"If Kenny's gone somewhere…if he's not just gone…give me a sign."

His father had bolted back inside the house and returned with a flashlight. They were headed his way, heading toward the field where he and Kenny usually played with the bow and arrow and shot targets.

"They're coming," Theo whispered an urgent prayer. "Give me a sign, God, please!"

No loon called. No warm breeze caressed his cheek. Not a single shooting star shot across the sky.

Theo opened his eyes and regarded the outline of his silent son in cool morning light. "People make a big deal about lots of things, but time moves on. People change and move. I moved away as soon as I could. I escaped to a boarding school. I went to university. I reinvented myself. No one knew I killed Kenny in a careless moment. Nobody knew I lied about how it happened. I got away with it."

His chest spasmed and he coughed hard for a few minutes, bringing up green sputum and spitting it into a tissue. Jaimie didn't move. Theo expected no reaction from his son. It was as if he was making his confession to a stone.

After another wave of coughing ebbed, he looked at the ceiling. He relaxed talking to Jaimie, his secret as safe as talking to himself. "After all's said and done, guilt is just geographical. Something bad happens, and if you move far away, the artificial borders we put on places is enough."

Jaimie detected the empty sound in his father's voice. He thought it likely that was the first lie his father had spoken to him. But is it a lie if you don't know it's a lie?

"Eventually, we'll have to go to Papa's farm. Out under that old oak tree, by the stone, that's where you'll find it. Southeast from the back step, hidden amongst the stand of Christmas trees my father planted the year after I shot Kenny. That's the Gateway to the Spirit World. It's where I go. There would be a symmetry to that. We'll go there, or maybe I'll meet you there. Or maybe you'll have to carry me there. That's where I should go. I should leave Earth from where D'Arcy Kennigan left."

Theo turned on his side toward Jaimie, his eyes haunted. "When he died out there, something died in me, too. I already died once, with my friend. I was only ten…but it didn't hurt that much and it was over quick. I just…it's the place I'm not afraid to die. I'm afraid to die here, but out there, it'll be okay. That's where I should be when I'm ready to let go and see what happens next. Out under the stars."

Jaimie nodded. He wanted to say, "I'll make sure," but, of course, he couldn't bring himself to say the words.

The Chain Of Food Is Upside Down

Jaimie had seen his father cry once before, on the phone in the kitchen, when he got the news of Nana Spence's death. Nana Spence had been Jaimie's grandmother. She was divorced from Papa Spence and Jaimie had never met her.

The boy watched and wondered about death, a word that seemed to have much more weight than the dictionary conveyed. The dictionary entries were short and clinical, but held no answers. The wizards who had devised language were painters without enough paint on their brushes when it came to the real meaning of death.

Jaimie had examined his father for clues as he received the news of his mother's demise. Theo held the phone in one hand and in the other he held a bright red apple. As tears crept down his cheeks, Theo listened to Papa Spence describe how she died. He listened a long time, silent and nodding. When Theo looked at the apple, he didn't know what to do with it. He rubbed his eyes roughly with the back of his hand and stood awkwardly, saying, "Uh-huh…uh-huh…uh-huh…" into the phone.

Jaimie took the apple from his father's palm gently and watched a tear stream to his father's chin and hang there, ripe, until it fell to his shirt.

Animals move through the world with more purpose than people do, he thought. *Perhaps because they don't see their ends coming and so, are less distracted from their needs: food, water, shelter, love.*

"Love" was a word strangely like death. Countless words had been written about love, but it was no better understood. In that case, Jaimie surmised that the wizards had too much paint on their palette and so their thick illustrations came out black and indecipherable. People said love was like this or like that, but Jaimie was still unclear what it was. People love babies and each other and TV shows and hamburgers. Surely, the word was too flexible.

Why had Theo ruffled Jaimie's hair while he was on the phone? Jaimie was confused. He guessed at the warmth of his father's gesture. That looked like love between a father and son. It felt good, but the love his father felt for Nana Spence now? It looked painful. That sort of love did not appear to serve Theo.

As his father recounted D'Arcy Kennigan's death, had Theo told him a story about boyhood love? Or was it only guilt over an accident that brought on his father's tears? Had he loved his friend Kenny? Or was it his father's love of the boy he'd been, before the accident, which gave him such pain now?

Jaimie watched as his father finally cried himself to sleep. Jaimie had seen Anna do that often two years before when she broke up with her first boyfriend. Jack said she was too young to have a serious boyfriend, but Jaimie thought it must matter to Anna very much. For months, she either did not speak or spoke of little else. Jaimie didn't understand tears, but he understood how something could occupy your mind so much you couldn't think of anything else.

Obsession is a kind of love, he decided. Jaimie loved dictionaries.

Anna's first obsession had been a new boy in her class named Thomas. Her first love had lasted three weeks. Then Thomas called Jaimie a retard and Anna got angry and all the kissing stopped. The fighting started. Thomas, who'd been a daily staple, disappeared. Anna seemed furious with Jaimie and he couldn't understand what he had done wrong. Then she was furious at Thomas again. Later, Anna flew into a rage because Thomas had another girlfriend too soon. Jaimie searched his dictionaries, but he couldn't find a rule about that.

Jaimie's obsession with words and their easy confusions irritated and puzzled him, too. *Puzzle*. There was another annoying homonym: puzzle, the verb; puzzle, the noun. But these were trifles compared to his sister's mood swings. Anna's rapid changes in temperament, especially her anger, bewildered him. Anna's love for Thomas turned to anger in a tornado mix of colors that Jaimie took some pleasure in observing, so rich and deep were the passing hues of her moods. Anna's aura was most vivid, like moving impressionistic paintings that raged in surprise storms.

"Teenage hormones," Jack had said.

Love, Jaimie decided, could be understood only in the abstract, the way people understood that the number pi kept on going, but past a thousand places, it became another meaningless word, like "death", or "mind" or the curious demand to pair "forgive and forget".

Forgiveness and forgetting do not equate in the dictionary, but Mrs. White, Jaimie's special teacher at school, frequently told him the words were equal and he should think them so when bad boys called him names.

Around seven in the morning, Jaimie heard a familiar rattle of metal outside. After a moment, Douglas Oliver appeared with a shopping cart full of red gas cans. The old man walked quickly, but he moved like his feet hurt. He leaned heavily on the cart's handle. The gray colors of exhaustion wrapped around him like an old, wool blanket.

As Jaimie watched, the old man tried the handle on the Bendham's garage door. It lifted a few inches and then fell back. Oliver tried again twice and then stalked to the end of the driveway and waved to someone down the street to join him.

A thin bearded man on a battered bicycle wheeled up to him. The bicycle was fitted with a large woven basket, secured haphazardly with silver and green duct tape. The basket was filled with things. Some kind of rifle stood high in the basket. It reminded Jaimie of a painting he'd seen of a man on a bicycle with a large basket of bread. The rifle could be like the tall stick of French bread in the painting. (Why *French* bread? They had American bread, but his family just called it bread.)

When the man on the bicycle turned to look at Mr. Oliver's house, Jaimie saw who it was. It was Bently, the man Oliver had hit with a bag of cans. Bently seemed to be no danger now.

Oliver spoke quickly, urgently. He pointed to each house on the block, apparently giving instructions. The old man pointed to every house except his own. Oliver pulled the thin little man toward the garage. Together they lifted the door and emptied the bicycle basket of plastic bags. When they were done, only the rifle stayed in the basket.

Jaimie couldn't see what it was they moved in the garage. When Bently stepped back, he looped a long necklace twice around his neck. Anxious for Bently to leave, Oliver pushed the bicycle at him and shooed him away. Bently shrugged and pedaled slowly down the sidewalk.

Douglas Oliver spun toward the Bendham house. Bently looked back over his shoulder. He did something Jaimie had seen often, but couldn't find in his dictionary. He put up the middle finger of one hand and pumped it at Mr. Oliver's back. Anna called it "flipping the bird." Jaimie wondered if he needed another dictionary so he could discover the secret signals everyone else somehow seemed to know. Where did people go to learn these things?

Theo Spencer rumbled and rasped in his sleep, shifting back and forth on the couch as if pinned under a heavy weight. The washcloth had fallen to his father's chest. Just as his mother did when Anna was sick, Jaimie gently placed the back of his hand on Theo's forehead. (No one term for the back of the hand. Why not? He'd have to write his own dictionary and remedy that oversight.)

Jaimie plucked the washcloth from Theo, rinsed it in the bowl of water on the floor and wrung it out before placing it carefully on his father's forehead again. His father stirred and shifted and then settled back down into a snore.

The boy thought about his father's friend. Kenny was a dead boy who sounded very much alive to his father. His memory had made his father so sad. Memory could be dangerous and, Jaimie thought uncomfortably, his own memory was excellent.

As the boy climbed the stairs to bed, he wondered if ghosts were made real through the power of memory. He thought about the definition of *haunted*. The feel of the word on the page matched the feeling he got when he had touched his father's forehead. D'Arcy Kennigan was still alive somehow. His father had the power to make the long dead live.

Jaimie had read Halloween stories about ghosts and curses. When his mother noticed him reading one of those books, she often said, "You know none of those stories are real, right?" But the boy knew his father tended to remember bad things very well while his mother seemed to remember only things that pleased her.

When they argued, his mother sometimes asked Anna, "Do you wanna be right or do you wanna be happy?" That binary choice seemed to sum up his parents. Theo chose being right. Jack chose to forget.

Haunts and curses and ghosts. These things seemed to be coming back to life as the world that was, real and regular, slowly ground to a halt. Jaimie climbed into bed, content as he fell asleep, because sleep was the only time he wasn't bombarded with flashes of light and disturbing colors and more information than he wanted.

Like a vampire in sleep, the boy closed a lid on a box, blocking out insistent perception. He did not suffer dreams. Sleep brought the relief of darkness. Everyone worried so much about the end of things. Jaimie didn't understand their concern. He thought death would be black and empty. *The fancy word for death is so stark and beautiful*, he thought, as he slipped into darkness: *oblivion. Such a beautiful word.*

But living without his father's presence, his protection and his hand to hold? That worry chased the boy into a fitful sleep.

If he could have seen the disaster unfolding in London, the boy would not have slept at all.

Now Rabid Wolves Wear The Crown

Bored, the woman in red traipsed around the fourth-floor office of the building on Birdcage Walk. The man who owned the office stared up at her from the floor by the photocopier. The hole in his forehead was small and neat. The hole at the back of his head was not.

"Poor wage ape. I'll call you Allen," Shiva mused. "You're going to miss the party, Allen."

As if she'd voiced a magic spell, she heard the first screams rise. Her wolves were loose. "Ha! Ha! They're playing my tune, Allen! Sutr-Z has come to call! I wish you could see this, Allen, but you can't seem to take your eyes off me. Can't blame you, though. I look great in red. I am the Red Death."

She went to the window and watched the guards at Buckingham Palace's outer perimeter. They cocked their heads, turning this way and that to divine the direction of the climbing terror headed their way. Screams bounced and echoed off towers and through the concrete and stone canyons of London's streets.

"My army is coming, boys. And so many of them. And so hungry. And so angry."

The screams grew. Many voices answered and became one choir, united in fear.

"Like Genghis Khan, I drive the innocent before me." She laughed and poured herself another glass of Chardonnay.

To her left, she saw the civilians trying to outrun her army. Precious few were fast enough. A few athletes who looked like they'd be at home on the soccer field ran by fast, wisely not daring to look back.

After them came security men running for their lives like rabbits from a relentless predator. The hunters had become game. The police officers, most dressed in riot gear, cast off their armour as they ran, trying to gain speed. They headed for the fortress that was Buckingham Palace.

Shiva toasted their efforts. "Allen, I think this is an excellent time to quote Lewis Carroll. My father wanted me to become an English teacher instead of a virologist. Imagine what would have happened if I'd let him have his way? Today would be just another boring day of slavery."

Men, women and children, young and old, were driven before the horde. Any who fell were set upon with teeth. The slowest were swallowed into the crowd and, with one bite, added to Shiva's army.

Shiva cleared her throat. "Pay attention, Allen. I recited this in school and haven't lost a line, I'm sure! 'Beware the Jabberwock, my son! The jaws that bite, the claws that catch! Callooh-effin'-Callay!' She chortled in her joy!' Well...I skipped over a lot to get to the meat of the issue."

The woman in red took another sip of wine and pulled her chair up to the window to watch her army's rampage. Below her, a man — well, what had once been a man — launched himself at the legs of a woman carrying a child. He sunk his teeth into her calf before she hit the pavement. Two women, dressed as nurses, went for the child, each pulling an arm as if in a tug-of-war. The dispute was settled when another ghoul ripped the child away.

"Allen, this is getting distasteful. I think it's time I let the authorities know they aren't the authorities anymore."

She opened her purse and took out her cell phone. She put the battery back in and sat back to wait. Before she took two breaths, her phone purred and vibrated.

* * *

Dr. Craig Sinjin-Smythe ran from the thunder. The pounding of thousands of feet came first. Then a shout followed by screams. Then more screams until the shrieks built to an unholy din.

The doctor broke into an office building off Maiden Lane. He noted there was a North Face store nearby. If all went according to plan, that could prove useful. Alarms sounded, but security forces were spread far too thinly for him to worry about the police. But Interpol did worry Sinjin-Smythe. Since the compromise of the isolation unit at Cambridge, undoubtedly he would shoulder the blame.

His dentist, Dr. Neil McInerney, operated a clinic in a second floor suite of the building. From his vantage point, the running crowds below were far too close. The uninfected were driven from their homes by the infected and run to ground, rabid hounds on timid foxes.

Sinjin-Smythe's cell battery flashed low and he was grateful to find that the power was still on. He'd grabbed his charger in his rush out of his office, but he hadn't dared to put his phone's battery back in place until he was miles away from the explosion.

He also had a memory stick with all the research files he had on the Sutr Virus. If Interpol showed up, he might have to bargain with that to live. He reasoned he was too valuable to jail. But it wasn't beyond the authorities to put him back to work, jailed in a lab.

He'd been trying to call his fiancée for hours, always on the move and far from the ruins of his laboratory and not daring to go home. If Interpol had Ava, they would answer and tell him to give himself up for questioning. It was reasonable to assume the love of his life, Ava Keres, was dead of the virus.

He tried calling her again from the dentist's phone. He hadn't had much hope since the landlines were usually clogged. Not so, now. It rang.

The landline worked, but he got Ava's voicemail: "I'm not available to take your call right now. I'm probably in the loo or handling some desperately dangerous chemicals so if you could leave a message, that would be brilliant. Or, if you're calling to sell me something, please do kill yourself. Cheers!"

As the mob careened by below him, he put one hand over his other ear to block out the screams.

Sinjin-Smythe left a voice message on her phone: "Darling, if you get this message, I want you to know that I still love you and whatever is going on, we can work it out somehow. I'm sorry if I did something which would make you...which would make this happen. The lab's gone red, Ava. You and I are the only ones who got out. The powers that be will have questions.

"I'm going to turn my phone on and off sporadically because I want to talk to you before I talk to Interpol. If you can get this message, you can call me. Call me, Ava. I love you and I think I have a way for us to get away from this mess and work out some answers. Call me, please. I need to know you're okay."

He would have cried, but there wasn't time. In case Ava was alive, he had to arrange the escape route he hoped for. He looked to the wall. Opposite the dental chair where he'd received his last cleaning, Sinjin-Smythe gazed at the framed photo of Dr. Neil McInerney standing proudly at the helm of his 24-foot sailboat.

The virologist stabbed a button on the office phone marked "home" and called his dentist for an emergency appointment.

Human Jaws Become Monsters' Maws

Jaimie wandered downstairs, ravenously hungry. It was 11 a.m. His mother gave him a nod and a bowl of canned stew.

Anna was reading a book called *Murders Among Dead Trees* at the kitchen counter. She glanced up at her brother and smiled. "Siddown, sleepyhead. There are fires downtown. There's nothing on the radio about it, but you can see plumes of smoke from the backyard."

Jaimie spooned the stew into his mouth in a hurry and returned to the stove for more.

"No, Jaimie," Jack said. "You can't have more."

Jaimie stood still, holding the bowl out to his mother.

"We're rationing." She was stern. "Go look that up. *Rationing.*"

Anna got up and took the bowl from her brother. "Easy, mom. He can have my share. I can't eat, anyway."

Jack put her hand to her daughter's cheek. "Are you feeling okay?"

"Sure," said Anna. "I felt a bit queasy this morning but I'm okay now."

Her mother stared at her, weighing her daughter's words.

"I'm fine," Anna said. "No fever."

"You look flushed."

"That's just healthy. You're too pale, Mom. Please just let Jaimie have my stew. I can't even look at it. If he has my share, what's the difference?"

"You're sure? We have to make the food last. We've been slow about this, but you understand Mr. Oliver is right about saving the food, making it last until things get back to normal?"

"That might be a long wait."

"It's a flu. The flu comes every year. This is worse than normal, but it's still just a flu. Someday we'll look back on this — "

"And laugh?"

Jack heaved a sigh and stared at her daughter. Jaimie could see a new thought forming as the colors of her aura changed. His mother's energy field charged up, from green to a sickly yellow that quickly slid into an angry crimson.

"Anna! I'm worried about you getting sick, but…is there a chance you're pregnant?"

"Mom!"

"Because there really couldn't be a worse time!"

"Mom. Stop talking." Anna said. She handed Jaimie her bowl.

Jaimie sat at the table, opened his dictionary and paged through to the *R*s. His mother hovered a moment, unsure whether to attack or retreat.

"Dad was so hot when I checked on him, he started taking his clothes off. He was mumbling and shivering," Anna said.

His sister's face pointed at him as she spoke, but it was her mother she was speaking to. Jack's heels struck the hardwood floor hard up the hallway as she stalked away, toward her husband.

Jaimie wondered if his mother had noticed Anna had not answered her question. When he finished the stew, he picked up his dictionary and went to the front room. He sat in the doorway and listened while Mr. Oliver and his mother spoke in hushed tones by his sleeping father.

Douglas Oliver knelt beside Theo, his eyebrows knit together above his sharp blue eyes. "Comes in and out of it," he said to Jack, "but your husband will be okay. Just give it time and watch the kids for any sign they've caught it. We should be keeping them away from him."

"They seem fine," Jack said, "although this thing seems to have quite a variable incubation period."

"Yes. That's one of the reasons it has spread so well. We fly all over the world picking up bugs here and there and transporting them back home. Sometimes these strains jump species, getting stronger with each jump. Now it's come for us. We've been overconfident."

The old man looked up and caught Jack's annoyed look. "Sorry. I should be taking care of Theo. No one else. I'm immune. In fact, if I'd thought of it sooner, I would have put up some plastic over the door or kept your husband over at your house instead of bringing him here. We have to keep the kids away from him. It's especially important for your daughter to stay away from him."

"Especially Anna? Why?"

The old man felt for Theo's pulse and stared at his watch, perhaps taking a count, perhaps playing for time to choose his words carefully. "Pardon me for asking, but uh...were you planning on having any more children?"

"What? No! I'm done having kids. I'm past that."

"Sorry," Oliver said, "but Anna is not past child-bearing age. In the near future...well..." He shrugged.

"What are you saying? That's it's up to my daughter to repopulate the Earth? This is absurd."

"I don't think it's absurd at all. It's not like I expect her to be a baby factory all on her own. It's just, I look around and I think of Kurt Vonnegut."

"What the hell are you talking about?"

"Things come apart. Vonnegut saw how Dresden fell in one night to Allied bombs. He was surrounded by carnage. We're surrounded by carnage, but the houses are still standing, so you don't see it yet. This is a stealth Apocalypse. You wander around the neighborhood and it feels like everything's pretty much the same except it seems especially quiet. I've seen more wildlife lately. Deer, cats...a lot of rats."

Jack watched the old man speak, but she wasn't sure she was processing what he meant to convey.

Oliver cleared his throat. "When Vonnegut got back from the war, he remarked on how many fine young men and women had died. Some of those people might have done important things had they lived. Maybe we'd have had jetpacks by now. Maybe there would have been a cure for cancer. One of them could even have found a cure for the Sutr virus when it was just an idea in some mad scientist's brain...if you believe the conspiracy theory about Sutr being of military origin."

"What does all that have to do with my daughter?"

"Jacqueline," Oliver addressed her gently. "The geniuses that make and run things? They only come along once in a long while. There aren't enough geniuses to go around. We've had a population explosion on Earth for the last 100 years. Nature is now containing that explosion. You might even say fighting back to preserve her resources. But we need a lot of babies to get enough geniuses capable of putting us back on track. We still have the books. The information is out there so we can have progress again. That will only work if we have enough people who can really figure out smelting, solar panels and water purification. I'm worried. Monsanto made almost everybody use seeds that are only good for one year. That's the *opposite* of what we need to survive this. I mean, for humanity to survive this."

"Sutr isn't going to kill so many people that we're headed for the Dark Ages. We'll recover," she said.

"How do we know how many people Sutr has killed? Are we going to rely on statistics from governments? You don't seriously expect real numbers of dead from them, do you?"

Jack sat and watched her husband's chest rise and fall for some time before speaking. "You talk about Sutr like it's intelligent and evil and out to kill us. Viruses are the dumbest things around. Some scientists say viruses aren't even really alive by many standards: no DNA of its own, and if it's really successful, it kills its host so it dies, too."

"So much for Intelligent Design," Theo said, making both Jack and Oliver jump.

"You scared me," the old man said. "Thought you were in La-La Land."

"I was," Theo said, his voice hoarse. "Then I heard the familiar sound of my wife getting pissed off and thought I better wake up and apologize. If she's angry, it's probably me. Did I do something I shouldn't have, Jack?"

She knelt beside the couch and looked into her husband's eyes. "Yeah, we were just saying how you better hurry up and get better. We don't know how long this vacation is going to last and I have a lot of things for you to do around the house."

"Vacation," Theo said. "Heh, yeah. Any news?"

"Good news in that you're fighting off the virus."

"Really. I feel like I'm the hotel room and Sutr is a coked up rock star. He's trashing me."

"The bad news is that there are fires south of us," Oliver said. "Not sure how far, though I'm sure there aren't any firefighters on the job."

"How do you know?" Theo said.

"I went out on a reconnaissance mission last night to see what I could find out. The local radio station is still going, but it's a lot of canned repeats. I get the feeling there are a bunch of reporters holing up at home and phoning in. There's probably one or two guys at the station trying to keep things going."

"What's it like out there?"

"I heard some gunshots, but far off."

"I heard those, too," Jack said. "Around midnight."

"I thought I saw my dog," Oliver added. "But he didn't come when I called him so that couldn't be Steve. First I saw the one dog following me, the one I thought was Steve. Then I saw more dogs and realized they were all following me."

"What did you do?" Jack asked.

"I threw rocks at the leader and that turned their tails. I ducked into a house and they moved on. It was a bit hairy for a minute or two there. I'm not much for running anymore and I don't think anybody could outrun a pack of really hungry dogs."

"Bear spray," Theo said hoarsely. "I've got some in our gear in the van."

"Excellent," Oliver said. "I wish I'd known about that last night before I met up with the dogs."

"While you're up — " Jack began.

"While I'm still conscious, you mean," Theo said.

"Shut up," Oliver said. He reached for a bowl of stew on the floor and handed it to Jack so she could feed her husband. "Eat, Theo. It'll keep your strength up." He gave an encouraging nod. "Please continue Jacqueline. About the proposition."

"Mrs. Bendham has asked to come with us if we have to leave."

"I've been collecting some food and things to trade," Oliver said. "Between that and what canned goods Mrs. Bendham has stored up, we'd have enough to get away if the fires come north." He considered his words carefully, "The wind is blowing our way and if it's as big as it looks from here, the flames could easily be jumping streets. All it takes is a roof to light a tree to light some leaves that blow over to the next property and before you know it, we have a firestorm."

"That's troubling." Theo swallowed some stew with difficulty and began coughing again. It seemed to hurt him more to cough now. "And things were going so swell."

Oliver allowed a grim laugh. "I've been working on our exit strategy. We're smart and, with your van, we'd be fine."

"Roads?" Theo asked.

"As far as I've seen, the roads are down to one lane but someone's keeping them clear. I imagine that's either the city or the military at work."

"You don't know?"

"I still haven't seen anyone clear the road myself, though I haven't gone farther than a few blocks lately. There's no one around to ask, but the body trucks are still running."

None of them had seen the man in the red and yellow van with the bell for several days. However, a farm truck had gone by once. The truck body now had a canvas cover so they couldn't tell if it was full of bodies or not.

"I had hoped we could hunker down and wait this out, but that fire worries me. I think we should seriously consider her offer. Mrs. Bendham is quite a canner. She's got lots of goodies stored up for a rainy day. What is it about jams and jellies and little old ladies?"

"We need her rainy day supplies," Jack said. "It's not just raining. We're in a flood."

Theo nodded wearily. "If Mrs. Bendham comes with us, the kids will learn a lot about opera."

"Oh, don't tell Anna that," Jack said. "She'll — "

"Listening to everything you say!" Anna called from the kitchen.

"Wash a plate, Anna!" Jack yelled back.

"Vaccine?" Theo managed.

Oliver shook his head. "They said at the beginning of this — remember when they said this was all a tempest in a chamber pot? They said they had 90,000 doses of Tami flu. That all went to politicians and their families and maybe trickled down to some frontline hospital staff. Pandemics come in waves, and, from what the short wave says, there won't be any vaccine coming for this thing until a while after we go through the third wave. Even if there was a vaccine, there'd have to be more organization up and working to deliver it. I've seen no evidence of that."

"I was happier having fever nightmares," Theo said. He managed to eat half a bowl of stew. Oliver finished it for him. "No worries about backwash," he told Jack. "I'm still super! Sutr will never get me. When you're well, it'll never bother you again, either."

"This feels so bad," Theo Spencer rasped, "I wish it would either get it over with, whatever it's going to do."

There was no self-pity in his voice. Only exhaustion.

"There's no cavalry coming over the hill, is there?" said Jack.

Deus ex machina, Jaimie thought. He'd read somewhere that it made for bad stories. Since God was not showing up to rescue his family, their lives must be a good story.

"Whoever could come to the rescue," Oliver said, "has the same problems we do. We're going to have to rely on ourselves for some time yet. Don't ask how long, but don't worry. I have things well in hand. With all the food and supplies you've gathered, we'll be set up well if we have to run. And we can take Mrs. Bendham with us."

Jaimie thought of ancient Roman wisdom. *Donec eris felix, multos numerabis amicos*. Roughly translated, it meant that with a van full of supplies during a plague, you'll suddenly have lots of friends.

The Ungrateful Living Face New Laws

Jack and Oliver stepped out into his backyard to let Theo sleep and to avoid Anna's eavesdropping.

The grass had grown long in his absence and Oliver absentmindedly bounced a tennis ball off the concrete patio deck. At the rear of the property, along the base of the tall wooden fence, they could still see where Oliver's big German Shepherd had scratched and pawed at the dirt until he escaped.

"Ordinarily I'd come out here and play a little fetch with Steve."

"Thanks," said Jack, "but I don't think I'm up to it at the moment."

The old man smiled. "I'm glad you are willing to take Mrs. Bendham along. In the spirit of the new economy, I've got a good-sized bag of trinkets to pay for my ticket on the Spencer Express."

Jack began to protest. "You've already taken us into your home— "

"No, no. This is just enlightened self-interest at work. I've got some good jewelry. I've got an eye for it, of course. In my business, I know cheap costume stuff from the real thing. Mrs. Bendham has food to contribute and I've got loot. And my startling good looks, of course."

"How soon can she be ready to leave...you know, if we have to?"

As if on some unconscious signal, they both turned to look up. Plumes of dark smoke gathered so the sky looked like a black thunderhead hung low over the city.

Jack put a finger in her mouth to wet it and held it up to the wind. "If the wind doesn't shift soon, we may be leaving faster than we thought."

"I miss firefighters, and not just for their calendars." Oliver looked at his house and yard, as if already saying goodbye.

"So Mrs. Bendham is ready to go when necessary?" she asked.

"Jacqueline, that old woman started packing up as soon as her husband died. She's been holed up over there, rocking back and forth and praying and she never takes her mask off so her glasses are always steamed up. She's driving me batty. She's over there boiling and listening to the radio and praying to Jesus. When we look back on this, we'll think of those who died. When she looks back on it, she'll say the cabin fever was worse. For the next apocalypse, everyone will be better prepared, and they'll all have decks of cards and Scrabble games ready. "

"Has she gone crazy?"

"No, just grieving. Mostly she's doing it quietly so I approve. She's stopped singing. That's really a shame, too, since I've never liked her that much — Al was more my friend than she ever was — but she does have a beautiful voice."

"That just leaves the big question," Jack said. "If we have to go, what's the route?"

"Can't go south. Too many people and I've heard of trouble around the state border."

"From whom?"

"TV. Radio. Around."

"What kinds of problems?"

"Too many people with too many guns. It's the old west, but without the helpful sheriffs to keep the towns clean. Times like these, nobody wants a stranger coming to their door."

Jack nodded. "So…?"

"We could go north," Oliver ventured, "but that's too few people for my taste, and food might be a problem."

"I've heard Mormons have to have a year's supply of food stashed away," Jack said. "Maybe we could head farther west, find some Mormons and they'd share."

"Iffy. They might feel that's presumptuous. Also...you might be thinking of Seventh Day Adventists or Amish. I'm not sure who the religious hoarders are. I was a Presbyterian so I'm sure it's not them."

"And we'd definitely have to convert," she said. "If it's the Mormons and things go into a slide, Theo might take it into his head to get a harem going."

"I think I'm too old to really enjoy a harem much, although having a bunch of young fellas around to paint the house and do the landscaping sure would be sweet."

They laughed together. Despite his Australian accent, the old man's easy laughter somehow reminded her of her grandfather. He was a take charge kind of man, but with a lighthearted demeanour that pulled her toward him.

With Oliver and Mrs. Bendham stuffed in the back of the van — two somewhat crazy surrogate grandparents — the kids would have a taste of what family used to be. It would be a nuclear family, together instead of spread across the country. She wondered if all families would be cobbled-together and close again now that the world had slowed to survival mode.

Oliver threw the tennis ball with surprising force against the back fence. It bounced just a foot from the hole his dog escaped through. "It's a long ways to run, but young Anna has told me about Theo's father's farm in Maine. That could be..."

"Sustainable?"

Oliver shrugged. "Salvation."

Jack thought a moment. "Spence — my father-in-law, I mean...he would take us in. He never wanted us to leave the east coast."

"You lived out there, too?"

"I'm originally from Poeticule Bay," she said.

"*Where?*"

She smiled. "A little place no one's ever heard of on Maine's coast. We've got a really nice postcard."

"I'm guessing it's a scene with a lighthouse," he said.

"Exactly!" she laughed. "With lobster traps at the bottom."

"That how you met Theo? High school sweethearts?"

She shook her head. "Freshman sweethearts. We met in the cafeteria at Stanford. Theo's a little older than me and he went away to boarding school so we had to meet all the way across the country to find each other. Poeticule Bay's so small, it's a miracle we didn't know of each other. He never liked it enough to even visit home."

"It's an awful long ways to run to not to be welcomed. You sure it would be good with your father-in-law, taking in a couple of old strangers like Mrs. Bendham and me?"

"Oh, it'll be fine with Spence," Jack said. "It's Theo, I'm worried about. He swore he'd never go back to that farm."

"Bad blood?"

Jack shrugged. "Theo didn't get along with his mother and never wanted to darken that door again. I've tried to talk to him about it. Theo just says it brings up too many bad memories. He said they wanted him to stay and work in the family business. That wasn't for him. You know how some families can be."

"Is Theo's mother still alive?" Oliver asked.

"No. Helen died a couple of years ago. She divorced Papa Spence and they never reconciled. Suicide. She was bi-polar and sick, as well, so she might have chosen lots of pills over another round of chemo. That's another family secret rarely uttered. Sometimes talking to Theo or his dad, it feels like they work at the Pentagon or something. When Helen died, Theo was broken up, but for the wrong reasons. He got depressed because he and his mom never worked out their differences. When she died, he cried a little because he thought he should cry a lot. Theo didn't have it in him to mourn her much. I'm sure it's his greatest regret."

"I'm sorry to hear of Theo's loss, though...now that his mother's gone, there's really no reason *not* to make the run to salvation when the time comes, is there?"

She nodded her assent.

"That's good," Oliver said. "Because if Helen was still there, we'd have had to kill her, wouldn't we, Jacqueline?" He caught her shocked look and patted her arm and waggled his eyebrows at her. "In the spirit of mutual benefit and enlightened self-interest."

He moved on briskly. "The weather's warming up. Should turn on the air conditioner and enjoy it while we can. Let's get back inside. Seems like there's no point to having a backyard now, not unless you've got kids or a dog." He let out a long sigh. "I miss Steve."

"I'll make some coffee," Jack said as she stepped into the kitchen.

Anna was still sitting across the kitchen table from Jaimie. She'd switched to reading a book about girls in love with the vampires who would inevitably kill them. "Coffee is mom's solution for everything," Anna said.

"What? Are you taking over for your Dad?" Jack said irritably.

"Just filling in," Anna said. "He's not feeling up to tormenting you." Jack gave her a reproachful look and Anna added, "For now. He'll be up and yanking *you* again in no time."

Oliver went up on his toes and peered over Jaimie's shoulder. The boy was studying a dictionary page that went from "reveal" to "reverse", but he couldn't discern what could hold a sixteen-year-old's attention so fast.

"Where's your coffee, Oliver?" Jack asked.

"Jacqueline, I do not dabble in that inferior ground up stuff in a big can. That's for commoners. If you're going to live in my house, you'll have to elevate the tone. The grinder is on the counter and you'll find a bag of rich, delicious and not so reasonably fresh coffee beans at the back of the fridge. That's the way to make hot bean juice, the way God intended."

"Sorry," Jack said. "I didn't know your stance on coffee was a religious one, but it's a view I happen to share."

She opened the refrigerator door and stared.

"Find it?" Oliver said. "Look to the back. We're out of milk of course, but there's that awful powder that impersonates cow cream."

"The refrigerator light is out."

Oliver reached out and flicked a light switch with no effect. The old man cursed. He looked at Anna, suddenly embarrassed at swearing in front of the girl. He shrugged. "Excuse my Polynesian. It's rusty. I thought we'd have more time."

Anna put down her book and got up from the table. "That's okay, Mr. Oliver. I speak fluent Polynesian, in fact." She breezed past him and stepped out to the living room. "Tell me it's just a fuse." She flicked three light switches in the foyer but no lights came on.

Anna cursed heavily.

"She *does* speak Polynesian," Oliver said.

Jack's face fell. "Anyone want the rest of the stew in the pot while it's still hot?" Jaimie held his bowl high with his left hand, his right index finger still pinned to the word "revelator".

Theo woke early the following morning. He gave a hoarse cry for his wife and Jack ran to him first. Anna, Jaimie and Oliver came to the living room in a rush to find him staring out the bay window.

People walked past the house and up the street toward Misericordia Drive's exit. The loss of power was a signal and the second exodus had begun. It wasn't quite a parade but it was more than a trickle.

A family of three were just disappearing from view. A young woman pushed a too-pale woman in a wheelchair as her father trailed behind, wearing a crammed backpack and carrying a cardboard file box. Grocery bags, a sleeping bag and a fishing pole lay across the lap of the woman in the wheelchair. She was obviously dead.

"I wonder how long that fool thinks he's going to carry that box?" Oliver said. "And where are they going with the dead woman?" He went to the front closet, dug around the rear of the top shelf, and quickly left carrying a small leather bag that fit in his palm. He followed the sad trio up the street, calling after them.

Three small cars roared past, racing. Each one was packed full of young people. Their horns blasted as they swerved crazily around Oliver.

Next came a tall man with a wheelbarrow. The wheelbarrow carried a pile of firewood and an axe. He was wearing a red dress and he wore a long blonde wig.

Precarious and *askew*, Jaimie thought as he watched the wig. *Good words, rarely used.*

"You think he chopped up that wood off some neighbor's tree?" Anna asked.

"Nah," Jack said. "Must have stolen it from a neighbor's wood pile. I'd never try to chop firewood in spike heels."

Theo's laughter had a coarse edge that was rough to their ears. "Too bad," Theo said. "That would be pretty sexy."

"Dad!" Anna said. "*Sh!* You're too sick to make jokes like that."

"Never...never too sick..." Theo said, gasping a little to catch his breath.

"Okay, you'll make me sick with sick jokes," Anna replied.

"The power outage has made people crazy," Jack said. "We've had brownouts before — "

"It's a *signal*, Mom," Anna said.

They all looked to her. Anna shrugged. "It's the signal we didn't know we were waiting for. Civil defense sirens are scary but they're far off."

"She's right," Theo said. "Things have been falling apart...but this? This tells us...something."

Jack knelt by her husband and patted his shoulder, quieting him. "Utilities are gone." She looked at Anna and Jaimie and added, "At least for now."

"No fire department, no police and now no power."

Oliver appeared at the window. He carried a fishing pole. He stalked through the front door and leaned into the living room. "Somebody put this aside. I got it from those people with the wheelchair."

"How'd you convince them to give that up?" Anna asked.

"They were carrying too much. A couple little ruby rings are much lighter. Fakes, actually."

"Teach a man to fish — " Theo said.

"Don't feel too bad for them. I wanted to give them one real pearl from a necklace but the kid was quite a negotiator. Put the rod and reel in the front closet. "I'm going to go check on Mrs. Bendham, get her packed up and situated."

"You want to leave now?" Jack said. "I think we should wait. Stay still and sit this out."

"I hope we can, but we've got to be ready. The wind is still blowing north and the smoke looks much closer. I'm not saying now is the time. I'm saying, just in case." He ducked back out, quick for his age. Jack began to follow but he was already out the front door with a slam.

She turned to her husband but Theo had fallen asleep, his shirt soaked with sweat.

Anna didn't say anything but her eyes told Jack she was afraid. She moved to her daughter and held her, hugging tight.

Through Anna's long hair, Jack looked at her son, almost as tall as she. He was sixteen going on seventeen in August. Where would they be and how much more would things change by his birthday?

Jaimie sat on the floor in front of the window. He looked so content scanning his Latin dictionary, it was as if her son existed on another plane, a ghost who travelled with them but otherwise kept to himself.

Jack pulled Anna to her even tighter, still gazing at her son. She wished he would think to stand and hug her. Even as a baby, he had never cuddled like his sister had. Once he had discovered books, words were all he wanted besides a steady supply of food and oxygen. She ached for him to need her more.

Jack would have put all her attention to embracing her daughter if she'd known how close she was to losing Anna.

Return To The Beginning, Man To Animal

At three in the afternoon, a car horn blasted from the street. Anna's boyfriend pounded on the Spencers' front door. Trent's father and mother sat in the front seat of their black SUV.

Theo woke and slowly hauled himself upright from the couch. "That boy has something against our front door." He managed to struggle up and steadied himself against the walls as he staggered to Oliver's front door.

"Anna! Anna!" Trent yelled. The screen door he had destroyed stood beside him on the Spencers' front step. The front door shook under his fists.

Jack emerged from Oliver's kitchen, tying the strings of a hospital mask behind her head. She slipped under her husband's arm to help him walk into the sunshine.

Trent's father, Jake Howser, punched his car horn again. Gina, Trent's mother, spotted the Spencers slowly making their way down Douglas Oliver's front walk.

Jaimie wandered out behind them. Jack threw a glance over her shoulder. "Your bare face is hanging out, young man. You aren't wearing a mask."

Jaimie ignored her, sat on Mr. Oliver's front step and opened his Latin dictionary. A wasp buzzed in and landed on the white page. Jaimie paused to take in its delicate wings and squinted at the insect's stinger. He wondered what the insect saw when it looked up at him. He wondered if the wasp saw people at all. Maybe it only saw food and threats.

Jaimie gazed at the wasp, admiring the beauty of its construction for a moment. Then he clapped the book shut. He reopened it, found the same page and picked up the tiny broken body carefully, weighing it in his palm.

"Trent! Trent!" Jack called. "We're over here!"

The boy looked over his shoulder. When he spotted Theo, Trent's face was fear. He turned and pounded on the Spencer's front door even harder. "Anna! Anna!"

"Idiot," Theo spoke in a low voice only his wife and Jaimie could hear.

"We're *all* over here!" Jack called, struggling under the weight her husband put on her shoulder with each small step.

Trent spun around. "You *moved*?"

Theo smiled and gave a weak wave. "Moron. If it looks like I'm going to throw up on him, stand back."

Theo's obviously frail condition startled Trent's parents. Jake and Gina stayed in the car, rolled up their windows and locked their doors. "Don't come any closer!" Jake shouted. "Stay back!"

The Spencers stopped. Jack pulled a white and blue carpenter's mask out of her back pocket and handed it to her husband.

"Great," Theo whispered. "Now they can't read my lips when I call them names."

Trent rushed to Theo and Jack. "Where's Anna? Is she okay?"

"Stay away from them!" his mother commanded. Gina Howser unlocked her door and stepped out of the car on the far side, looking wary.

She was a strikingly exotic woman with big dark eyes and long, curly hair. She stayed by the car, watching the Spencers with such intensity that Theo suspected she had, in fact, read his lips.

Her husband Jake rocked side to side in his seat. "Gina! Get back in here! They are *infected*, for God's sake!"

"Shut up, Jake. You're talking about our outlaws."

Jake froze and stared straight ahead, gripping the wheel, knuckles white. He hadn't turned off the engine. He looked like he was driving along a particularly narrow road at the edge of a cliff.

Trent ignored his parents and stepped closer to Jack and Theo. "Answer me! Is Anna okay?"

"She's — " Jack said.

"I'm better now that you're here!" Anna ran out of Oliver's front door and into Trent's arms. "I was sleeping. I heard the car horn." Trent hugged her. She kissed him on the mouth. Theo and Jack looked away.

"I had a dream. You were in it." She glanced at her parents and smiled. "And now you're here."

"Oh, crap," Jack said.

Trent spoke in anxious bursts. "Buddy's dead. We just went by his house and there was a big orange X painted across the door. There are a bunch of those same Xs up the street."

"What's that mean?" Anna asked.

"I think it means quarantine. Like don't come near this house or you'll drop from Sutr Flu before your next underwear change. Like everybody's dead inside."

"Oh, God!" Jack said.

"God had nothing to do with it," Theo said.

"Trent! Say what you've got to say. We are burning daylight here," Gina Howser called.

"Have you heard from Benny or Sharon?" Anna asked.

Trent shook his head.

"Jenna?"

The boy shrugged. "My cell's dead. I can't even text them." Trent said the last person he spoke to on the phone was his brother Bob four nights previous.

Bob, two years older than Trent, had a part-time job downtown. "His boss made him stay overnight, keeping an eye on his lousy garage. They didn't even have any gas but he was supposed to stay there and watch for looters. When Bob asked what he was supposed to do if looters showed up, his boss gave him a big wrench and told him to use his imagination."

"You haven't heard *anything* more from him?"

Trent's face went red. "If he was okay, he could have crawled home by now. We're driving down there to see if we can find him. Then we're headed up to our cottage up north. You can come with us."

"Oh, no," Jack said. "That's not happening. You are not going downtown and you *certainly* aren't going anywhere with the Howsers."

Anna held Trent tighter, her face in his neck.

"It's in the woods," Trent said, "not far from a big lake. There's a wood stove for cooking. Dad was a boy scout. We'll be fine up there, at least until things settle down. You'll love it. We can go fishing and canoeing. It'll be great! It'll be safe. There are too many people around here. Have you heard the gunshots at night?"

Jack Spencer shook her head emphatically but a lump in her throat seemed to be getting in the way of her voice.

"Can my family come?" Anna said.

"No, no," Gina called, shaking her head harder than Jack, as if they'd entered into a competition to see whose head would fall off first.

"*Mom!* We have room for them!"

"It's a cottage, not an ark, Trent! If you're coming, we have to go now." Gina focussed on Jack and Theo. "My other son may be bleeding somewhere and we can probably make it to the cottage by dark if we hurry."

Theo coughed and struggled to maintain his balance, pushing his voice past the razors in his throat. "You're not taking my daughter on some fool's errand. Downtown is where the fires are."

Anna looked at Theo. "Daddy — "

"I'm sorry for your loss," Jack said to Gina, "but there's an excellent chance your other son is dead. If he's not, he'll find you. I don't mean to sound heartless, but you've probably already lost Bob. I'm not going to risk losing my daughter while you go look for him. Look at the sky. The city to the south is on fire!"

"You wouldn't let me go downtown alone on the bus when everything was peachy," Anna said.

"I didn't. You're right. So you're sure as hell not going anywhere now," Jack replied.

"I'm going to find my son and we'll make it to the cottage. We spend every weekend of the summer up there. We've got lots of friends there. It'll be fine," Gina said. "Staying *here* is the dangerous thing to do."

"I could come," Anna said to Trent. She looked to her mother. "Just until things blow over."

"No," Theo managed and then bent over, his hands on his knees, coughing hard. The coughing continued until he pulled his mask off and gasped, taking in fresh air.

"Jesus!" Jake Howser came to life, clawing at his door lock and bursting from the SUV. "Get away!" he yelled. "Get *away!*"

Jake grabbed his son by the neck and pulled him back across the street toward their car. Gina grabbed something from her seat and rushed forward to join her husband. As she ran forward she tied a winter scarf around her face. She joined her husband in pulling Trent toward the car. Trent couldn't decide whether to resist or let them take him. He reached toward Anna uselessly.

Theo collapsed to his knees, coughing more but bringing nothing up.

"Daddy!" Anna cried. She froze in a moment of indecision and then moved toward Trent.

"Sonofabitch!" Jack cried and sprang forward, leaving her husband to grab Anna's arm.

"No! No!" Anna shouted. "Wait!" She almost squirmed away when Jaimie appeared behind her. The boy clamped his arms around his sister's waist. She leaned back, pushing hard at Jaimie's shoulders, surprised at his strength.

Anna's mouth dropped open. Jaimie gazed straight into her eyes. She stopped struggling. He had never looked into her eyes. What she saw there made her a statue. Anna nodded at her brother, her mouth still hanging open. "O-oh," she said.

Trent broke free of his parents but Gina and Jake immediately fell on him again. His father grabbed Trent's arm. His mother wrapped both of her legs around one of her son's legs.

"Enough!" Anna yelled. "Family is family. Your family needs you and mine needs me. When they don't, I'll come back. Just wait. Everything is going to work out." Her voice had a new strength and authority she had never shown.

Jack went back to Theo's side and helped him to his feet. The spasms in his chest passed.

"G-good," Theo said. "Plan B was I hose 'em all down with vomit."

"Jaimie, c'mon," Jack said. "Help me with your father." She looked at her daughter a moment more, trying to decide if she'd run now that the way was clear to escape with her boyfriend. The look on Anna's face told her she shouldn't have worried. Mother mouthed to daughter, "I'm sorry."

Anna gave a firm nod.

Trent broke free and gave Anna one last, long kiss as his parents climbed back in the SUV.

"C'mon! C'mon!" his father yelled and blasted the horn.

As far as Oliver's front door, they could hear Gina tell her husband to shut up.

"That's what happens when your wife is a ten and you're a balding idiot, Jaimie," Theo muttered. "Beware marrying a girl who's out of your league. They'll run your life and you'll be grateful when they spit on you."

"Oh, shut up," Jack said.

Theo managed a smile at his son. "See? It's a wonder we don't all run away."

Jaimie noted the similarity between the words "run" and "ruin" and wondered if they shared a common language root.

Anna stood on the sidewalk. She watched Trent drive away. When the car barrelled out of sight, she turned and walked back into Douglas Oliver's house. Her head was full of what might have been. She wouldn't let her parents see her cry. She was determined to hold back the floodgates until she got to her bed.

Anna closed the door behind her and pulled the covers over her head. For weeks she had done this. Each night, Anna had prayed to disappear. All she wanted to do was disappear into a world without the Sutr virus.

But now something she couldn't name had shifted within her. The set of her jaw was defiant and commanding. Anna mourned her boyfriend's absence to be sure, but she felt different somehow. She was no longer a little girl lost to circumstance. She'd made a choice and she knew it was the correct one. She was stuck in Sutr World and if she was to see Trent again, she'd have to take her world back. She'd have to make a stand and fight for it.

"One day," she promised herself, "I'll find Trent again." When he saw Anna, she wouldn't be tied to her family, helping to protect her brother, mother and father. She'd be stronger. He might hardly recognize her, but he'd love what he saw.

Anna looked out over Misericordia Drive and surveyed a few stragglers on three-wheeled bicycles pedalling up the street. She studied the sky. The wind had shifted away from them. The dark cloud reflected a red glow from the flames of the city beneath, but the roads east would soon be engulfed in flame. A wall of flame was not coming to take her home at the moment, but the Spencers would have to head north beyond the fires before they could begin the trek east.

"They haven't needed me, but they will," she said. Anna spoke to herself for a long time, plotting the journey in her mind. "It's time to be Batgirl or Tomb Raider or something." Tears slipped down her smooth cheeks, but the set of her jaw was still grim and defiant.

The girl didn't see the curtain move in the front window of the Bendham house. None of the Spencers knew they were being watched from behind lace curtains by anxious, prying eyes.

It wasn't just old Mrs. Bendham who spied on them. It was Bently, too. He sat in the old lady's rocker and watched the girl stand at the upstairs window.

Bently stared and rocked, waiting for the signal, with a big yellow-toothed grin.

Human Sacrifice And Bloody Ritual

When Douglas Oliver came through Mrs. Bendham's front door, Bently straightened at his post in the rocking chair. "Spencer is still up and moving around I see. Too bad you still have an extra mouth to feed over there."

"Go out the back and over the fence behind the pool," Oliver said. "Don't come back until after dark and bring me more gas. I'm worried about the wind shift. In case the wind shifts again, we're going to need a lot of fuel to get where we're going."

Bently stood, his legs braced straight. "If we bug out, where are we going?"

"I'll tell you when the time comes. Now get to work! Can't you smell the smoke? If we have to leave, that changes the variables. Go be useful."

Bently stalked out. Oliver caught his angry look but let it pass. He needed Bently and men like him, at least for now.

When he turned, Mrs. Bendham stood in her bedroom doorway. Pale, she leaned against the doorframe listlessly. The old woman had lost enough weight that her second chin was gone.

"Marjorie. Have a seat. You look tired."

"I don't know why. I've been sleeping for hours. Before the plague, I never slept enough. Now I feel like I'm catching up on the sleep debt of a lifetime, but I never feel rested. When I wake up, the sheets are twisted around me and I'm soaked in sweat."

"Dark in here. Maybe we need to make it cheerier." Oliver turned the dowel on the Venetian blinds, lighting the living room.

"Your man couldn't keep watch like that so we kept the blind closed."

"I know."

"How is it he's your man, anyway?"

Oliver sat on her couch. A chunk of salty cured meat sat on her glass coffee table, leaving a stain of grease. Flats of bottled water lay before him on the floor. He pulled a TV tray closer and propped one leg up on a short stack of water bottles.

Oliver pulled a leather bag and a small sheet of black felt from his jacket pocket. He turned the bag over to reveal jewels of many colors. He examined each one and sorted them carefully.

"That's a good question, Marjorie. If Bently were smarter, maybe he wouldn't work for me. However, he's still caught up in the remnants of the old economy. Pieces of fancy paper don't matter anymore. People are still attached to the values of a month ago." He gestured to the rings, earrings and necklaces and began sorting each piece by type: gold, diamonds, and other gems.

He reached down and chewed the meat slowly as he pondered the gems. She couldn't tell if he was savoring the taste of the meat or admiring his collection, but he looked satisfied in a way that made her uncomfortable.

Oliver caught her look. He didn't miss much. "Marjorie, people should value what they can use and what they can eat. However, I convinced Bently that the principles of the old economy still have value. Well, the ancient economy, really. Trading really hasn't changed in thousands of years, whether it's Spanish gold, Indian spices or animal pelts. For years, hucksters have been selling bars of silver and urging people to stash gold away in case the government collapsed. Heh. They still think they can eat gold, maybe. Jewels are portable, but soon? I think a lot of people will give up every piece of gold they have for one goat. The trouble will come when the guy with the goat asks himself why he needs another gold ring."

"So why do you have all these gold rings, then?"

He smiled. "Because not everybody wises up at the same time. If they did, there'd be no commerce at all." Oliver pointed at the boxes of water bottles. "I'm preparing for the shift in values. The next economy will be trading cans of food that aren't expired yet. The next economy after that? Finding someone who is still alive who is a blacksmith. Carpenters are going to be rich again after being devalued for years. The richest man in any town won't be a politician or somebody who wants to be a boss. It's the dentists and doctors who will become really wealthy."

Oliver surprised her by pulling a pack of cigarettes from his jacket and fishing a lighter out of his pants pocket.

"I didn't know you smoked. I've never seen you smoke. Please don't smoke in my house."

Oliver ignored her and pulled a cigarette from the pack. He flicked the lighter's wheel a couple of times and a tiny flame sprouted. He lit his cigarette and took a long drag. "I did quit. I quit for years. I was worried about my health. I was so worried these things would be the death of me someday. But I'm old and I survived the Sutr virus. It feels like it's reasonable to relax some old standards of behavior, don't you think? Live a little. Take more risks. The rules have changed. Our life expectancy isn't so good, anyway, especially the fewer of us there are. Time to stop and smell the deadly nicotine and cancer-causing chemical agents once in a while. What do you say? Nobody lives forever. Spit in the devil's eye, Marjorie." He held the cigarette pack out to her.

The old woman ignored the offer and gathered her housecoat around her, hugging herself. "I heard Bently say we still have another mouth to feed over there. What did he mean by that?"

"What do you mean 'we'?" He looked up at her as he tore another hunk of the meat with his teeth. He reached for a bright yellow, nylon rope and wound it between his shoulder and his elbow in a neat oval. "I'm the one building the tribe so as many of us as possible get to live. Don't pay attention to Bently. Bently shouldn't talk at all."

Mrs. Bendham looked at the floor and hugged herself harder. "I'm sure you'll save as many of us as possible." *But especially you,* she thought. She walked to the kitchen.

She opened the refrigerator door. The old woman had lost track of the number of times she had opened and closed that door. Was it twelve or thirteen times since the power went off? Each time she looked in, she found the same few rectangles of stale cheese and some expired packets of plum sauce and catsup from a forgotten take-out order.

A fat bottle of green relish still squatted on the top shelf — "hot dog-slop," Al had called it. It was still cool to the touch. Her husband had loved it.

"Be sure to gimme that hot dog-slop, Margie," he'd always say when they ate the soy frankfurters that were supposed to be better for you but tasted like cardboard. He'd say, "I loves me my Marge and hot dog-slop and the Mets." Then he'd add, "And when the Mets crap out on me, I'll always have my Margie and the hot dog-slop and the Yankees! I love 'em all with relish!"

Her dead husband would laugh his grinding cornball laugh that reminded her of her father's awful jokes. How she had loved her dead husband and his stupid jokes. How easy things had been, to live with someone for forty years who was so easily amused, so ready with a smile even when there wasn't anything much to smile about.

Marjorie knew she shouldn't open and close the fridge door so much now that the power was off. She was wasting what cold was still left in the ice box — Jerry had always called them that long after there were no more ice boxes.

Checking the fridge was her small rebellion, a tiny defiance against Douglas Oliver. He'd taken over her house. His invasion had seemed a friendly gesture at first. Then he said it was too dangerous for her to be alone, so he became a fixture, coming and going at all hours without knocking. Oliver filled her home with supplies but warned her not to touch any of his inventory. He said any inconvenience she suffered was for her own good. He acted like he was the only one with all the answers, if only everyone would simply do as he ordered.

She reached in and touched the plastic bottle again, as if to reassure herself that yes, it was there; yes, it had weight. She'd gotten it for Al. His bottle of relish, old photographs and the smell of his clothes closet was all she had left of her husband. "We never took enough pictures," she told the empty kitchen.

She didn't look forward to eating the relish, but it was growing more tempting as the days stretched on. She had never had hunger pangs, not like this. She realized now that, before the plague, she had never waited long enough for hunger pangs to even begin to gnaw. She had run ahead of them to the fridge or the kitchen cupboard, never allowing herself to feel discomfort.

She stared at the bottle of relish. "I wish I'd gone with you, Al. What have I got to look forward to?"

People who knew hunger before the plague knew how to be hungry, subsisting on scraps. Mrs. Bendham now understood how wonderful a fully stocked grocery store really was. She had not been alone in this arrogance and advantage, but there was still some shame in this new knowledge.

Oliver regarded her with disdain, begrudging her needs. "Wait until the *real* famine hits," he said. He allowed her a tiny portion of the meat now fouling her coffee table with grease. Oliver picked up an old paring knife and examined the circle of meat. He measured her worth and finally cut her a measly quarter of it. He held it out to her. His eyes told her she wasn't worth a quarter slice of sausage.

"You can have this much. Chew slowly and maybe you'll lose another chin. It'll do you good. Plenty of protein in that."

She'd eaten it in a rush, trying to slow down, knowing she should try to make it last, but failing. She'd swallowed it down, barely chewing. Then Marjorie Bendham hated herself for the gratitude she felt to the old man for that puny scrap. The hunk of meat slid down into her stomach, thick and hard to digest, feeling cold and heavy in her shrunken gut. It melted away. The hunger remained.

Her self-hatred moved on to something else: hating Douglas Oliver. He sat there, winding another length of rope and eyeing her like a dog begging at his table.

Marjorie knew there was canned food in her garage. She didn't know how much, but she knew that, with all of Oliver's nocturnal foraging and dealing, the boxes must hold many treasures. Sometimes she hoped someone would shoot him for looting.

She snuck out to the garage when Oliver was out on his midnight runs. Each dawn, he returned with more supplies, usually with Bently doing the heavy lifting. Oliver was stocking up for a rainy day, as if it wasn't pouring torrentially right now.

She didn't know what all the supplies were. He wouldn't tell her, though Bently had a clipboard and tallied everything up for Oliver. Then the old man double-checked.

At first, Oliver had placated her with talk about his love for Al and how it was now his duty to see that she was safe through this crisis. Her husband had hit golf balls with Oliver, but she hadn't thought they were as close as her old neighbor claimed. How much fun was hitting a golf ball to a blind man, really?

Marjorie returned to the kitchen to rummage through her cupboards again, finding nothing. Oliver put her canned preserves in a box, sealed it with duct tape and recorded the entry on his clipboard. Oliver warned her to stay away from *his* supplies. "We're going to have to leave soon. If you want to be with us when we go, you'll mind my druthers."

His warning infuriated her. The old queen, usually so charming, had moved in, lectured her, raged at her, and finally threatened her in her own home. "Touch any of that reserve and we all die! But you first. Do you understand?"

"Yes," she'd said in a little girl voice she had forgotten, and backed away. He told her the supplies would keep her alive, but only when the time came. She began to think she was a pawn to his king in a chess game where only he could see the larger board.

Citing her safety from the Sutr virus, Oliver had forbidden her from visiting the neighbors, even when she thought she'd go crazy if she didn't walk outside and look at the blue sky. Oliver hadn't allowed her to step outside her own door, even after Oliver had let the Spencers move into his own home across the street.

It galled her. She'd lived next door to the family for years. She knew the Spencers better than Oliver did. Not well, but they'd shared the same fence and talked amiably, always friendly, though not friends. She'd marched over with cupcakes the day they moved in years ago, the first and the only person in the neighborhood to attempt to make the young family feel welcome.

Mrs. Bendham had watched the Spencer kids grow up: the pretty girl growing to a young woman; that odd little boy growing up into an awkward, somewhat spooky teen who never looked her in the eye.

She searched her cupboards and found only tea. Then inspiration struck. The old woman got on all fours. Her knees creaked and ached and she had to cling to the cabinet to lower herself carefully.

All that was left in the cabinet with the Lazy Susan were an assortment of teas and spices. She pushed her head in further. The kitchen was too dark and she didn't have a flashlight. Marjorie reached to the back and groped until her hand closed on a smooth, cool tin can. It had fallen to the back of the cabinet from the rotating shelf.

When she brought it out into the light, she found it was an expired can of seafood chowder. It was the white, New England stuff, not that awful, red New York chowder. The thought of it made her mouth water.

If Al were alive, he wouldn't stand for Oliver's demands and threats. But Al was dead, burned to a crisp somewhere, his ashes anonymous and in the wind. She resented him for that. He should have lived for her. If he'd loved her more, maybe he would have fought harder to survive. They'd dealt with his blindness and the cancer and his affair with a nurse when they were newly married. But they'd stuck for forty years. Then Al let the flu take him away from her.

She needed her dead husband to tell her what she should do. Instead, she was alone with Oliver and, as angry with him as she was, she was also afraid to tell him to go. If Douglas Oliver left without her, she would truly be alone. She'd be an old woman with no one to help her, no one with whom to talk, worry with and work through the problems of surviving.

Instead, she hid behind her curtains, staring out at the world and only daring sometimes to step out into the backyard at night when Oliver was out. She stared at the stars and wondered what Al would say now that she was a scared old woman, an old widow, ordered around by an old, cranky queen. And was Al now sighted and dancing with that slut of a nurse in some strange heaven?

The electric can opener would have made too much noise and alerted Oliver to what she was doing. Without power, making too much noise had become a non-issue. She dug a manual opener out of the back of a kitchen drawer and hurriedly cranked the tin. It was months past its best before date, but she was too hungry to worry about food poisoning.

Marjorie Bendham sat on the cold kitchen tile as the darkness gathered. She spooned the soup in cold. The chowder was a slimy gel that slid down her throat thickly. This time, she ate slowly.

When she was a little girl she'd sung in the church choir. Long after she lost interest in the church, she'd stayed so she could sing for an audience. A dimly remembered memory surfaced. She remembered the lavender and lace the old women around her wore, in much the same style as she wore now.

"In prayer," her old preacher had said, "God doesn't give you the right answer until you ask the right question."

She prayed now, more to Al than to God. Looking for answers felt very much like groping for something lost in the dark. Then her mind closed around something cold and she thought, *Aha. I've finally asked the right question.*

Knees cracking and clinging to the kitchen counter, the old woman pulled herself up. Once she was on her feet and steady, Marjorie opened the fridge door again and stared at the relish bottle.

Something clicked over in her mind, like a lever switch closing, completing a circuit. Soon she'd be hungry enough to eat that relish right out of the bottle, smearing her lips green as she greedily sucked it down.

When she became that hungry, she would have to eat Al's "hot dog-slop". When that was gone and the hunger pangs returned, Marjorie Bendham resolved to slip a steak knife from her kitchen drawer and, while he slept, she imagined the great satisfaction she would feel when she slit Douglas Oliver's throat wide. When his blood pumped out in spurting arcs, she would smile again. She might even grab a teacup and drink the old bastard's blood for good measure. Plenty of protein in that.

The Virus Spreads, Making Evil Minds

Jack knelt beside Theo. Her husband lay sweating on Douglas Oliver's living room couch. She thought of a freshly caught fish on a dock, gasping and bewildered, its gills working uselessly. Theo sweated so much, he hadn't urinated all day. The trip down the front walk had exhausted him.

"You've got to drink more. You aren't getting enough fluids."

Her husband gave a weak nod and pulled his head up to take a small swig from the bottle of water she offered.

The carpenter's mask she wore annoyed her, steaming her glasses and making her face uncomfortably hot. When she went outside to take it off, the air felt so fresh and cool, it was a release from choking claustrophobia. Jack wanted desperately to stay out in the backyard until this was over, but when would this be over? They couldn't hide forever behind masks.

With little else to do, Jack had made it her mission to find a bendy straw to make it easier for Theo to drink. Oliver didn't have a bendy straw in the whole house. She had searched until she was certain.

She continued to search in unlikely places until she had to admit defeat. Besides, a woman looking for bendy straws in the back of a clothes closet wasn't really searching for bendy straws anymore. She was looking for distraction.

"I've been a good sport, God. Now let me off this ride. I want to get off."

Anna was locked in her room. When Jack checked in on her, she was either crying, sleeping or pretending to sleep. Her daughter needed time.

Jack remembered the desperate need that soaked through her skin and surrounded her heart when she was a teenage girl in the throes of love.

Theo hadn't been her first love, but theirs was a love built on a powerful foundation. Theo had taken her in his arms at the end of their first date, maddeningly sure of himself. "Let's have our first kiss, and savor it and take it really slow. This is dangerous business," he'd said, his lips almost touching hers, but not quite.

"Why dangerous?"

"Because this will be the last, first kiss for both of us," he said.

"You sound awfully sure you're my prince and we're going to have a happily ever after."

"I don't believe in that. There's no happily ever after in the end. This is our happily ever after right now."

"You better shut up and give me my last, first kiss before you talk your way out of the deal."

"These days, at the beginning, are the best." And they shared the kiss that had delivered them here and now instead of making other choices that would have led them into a different mystery.

Jack pushed the memory aside. That seemed like eons ago, something that happened to someone else. That was long before she started coloring her hair black. That was before she started wondering how long she could keep that up before her face and gravity would expose the pretense of hair dye. She was forty-eight. The Sutr virus had broken up young lovers and made her feel old.

But at least she'd had her time. She had been to Paris, Mexico, Bermuda and had seen the country. She'd gotten married and had her children. She'd studied and had jobs and made it half-way through a normal life span. Or...maybe she had been middle-aged at twenty-four and hadn't known it. If she had known she would die this year, would she have made different choices?

Of course, all that she had already accomplished in life wasn't a salve at all. She thought it *should* be, but it *wasn't*.

"Don't confuse an ought with an is," Theo would say.

Jack Spencer wanted *more* time. She needed Theo to live. Her husband had to live to help get the family back to safety in Maine. She needed him to live to see his children grow up. She needed his help to deal with Jaimie. If Theo died, she might just give up. If everything was reduced to surviving, there'd be no more room for living. Without Theo, she'd have to do it all herself and she knew she wasn't ready to face that.

Thank God for Douglas Oliver to get her through, at least until Theo recovered, she thought.

Jack had seen plenty of disaster movies. Theo was a movie buff and had drawn her into his obsession. Those movies always hit the same highlights: Riots and looting and the solemn president's address to his nation and the world. Mass destruction and lots of film of brave young pilots and rescuers and saviors taking off in jets and helicopters. None of the movies had anything to say about the crushing boredom of waiting for whatever came next.

In real life, she knew most of the action was taking place in living rooms that looked very much like every other beige suburban living room. People, each a potential victim, waited for whatever would come next, battling depression and eyeing the pills in the medicine cabinet.

In movies, you could be sure that things would work out fine for whomever the camera followed. The biggest movie star on the screen would always survive to somehow forge a new civilization out of the rubble. You could safely enjoy any disaster movie as long as you identified with the one star the camera loved the most.

Those movies always followed the people who were at the center of the action: Center for Disease Control bureaucrats arguing over strategic plans; executive orders from the president; gas-masked troops in the streets scaring the hell out of civilians; and, of course, the last honest man who knows the secrets of the cause of massive death and who to blame. Add one extremely unlikely love interest who worked her way through her biochemistry PhD by swimsuit modelling in her spare time and you had a summer hit.

Wouldn't it be great if there were enough troops to give us some sense of order, that someone was in charge? She'd love to see soldiers sworn to protect her wandering around her neighborhood about now. Trucks full of food supplies and Army engineers swarming over the power grid to get it running again would be most welcome. However, when the disaster is *everywhere*, the help has nowhere to come *from*.

What would a movie of a real global disaster look like? A collage of her pacing and praying? Should she conform to the demands of a more dramatic script and pound on Anna's door, giving her daughter an inspiring speech about how all we have is each other and if we're going to survive…?

No.

Anna wasn't sent over from Central Casting. If she tried to lecture her daughter about fleeting love and how Trent wasn't really so important, there was a chance Anna would run off after him. Young love is rigid steel and a girl with romantic ideas in her head might not stand the test of familial loyalty. Jack was frightened she'd lose her daughter. She knew someday it was inevitable, but today, she couldn't do without her. Not now.

She didn't want to risk talking to Anna yet and she didn't want to put her mask back on to check on Theo. If Oliver was right, they'd all already been exposed and there was no point taking extraordinary measures to isolate themselves from her husband. Jack walked downstairs aimlessly.

Jaimie, her ghost son, sat on the back step, reading — no, *analyzing* — a dictionary. He clapped the book closed and immediately reached for his Latin dictionary, as if something in one reference book had piqued his curiosity and led him to the other.

Jack bent beside him, put a light hand on his shoulder. Jaimie ignored her. "What do you see in there that's so interesting?"

No answer, of course.

"Or are you just hiding?" she wondered aloud.

His eyes slid sideways and he shifted his weight, shrugging slightly, turning away.

She watched his reaction. Had she hit the mark? If she someday happened across asking Jaimie the right question, would he suddenly turn to her and say, "Finally!"

If she caught her son at just the right moment, would a dammed up torrent come flooding out? She longed to swim in his words the way he swam through his dictionaries. Her son was as remote as the moon, only occasionally sending a brief, garbled telegraphic message back to Earth.

Theo seemed to have a better handle on Jaimie's intent, somehow intuiting their son's rare, cryptic utterances. To her, Jaimie's occasional messages seemed to boil down to one thing: "Still here."

Jaimie was her strongest reason for needing her husband to recover. He was his father's son and, as far as Jack could tell, Jaimie merely regarded her as someone he lived with. Or maybe she was wallpaper or a potted plant to him.

Jack watched Jaimie read, wondering what intrigued him so. For a selective mute to be so fascinated with words was beyond the land of irony and deep into cruelty. On some level, she was pleased and impressed. At least he was a reader.

Jaimie's teachers suspected he was some kind of savant, albeit not a sort they had ever encountered. She knew the official term used to be "idiot savant" and that annoyed her. She took little pleasure in the knowledge that Jaimie was somehow on the same mysterious spectrum as autistic math wizards or great pianists. Beyond those esoteric skills, they lived in their own world that only occasionally touched the world she knew.

Sometimes she wished Jaimie's talent — "special interest" the doctors called it — was one of the more expressive sorts so she could at least hear him play a piece of music or do long division at tax time.

Once, she had asked him why he loved to study reference books. He had perked up unexpectedly, like a scuba diver popping out of a hot tub. Jaimie had opened a dictionary, flipped pages, heading toward the front of the book. He pointed out a word to her: *Assiduously.*

She sighed and walked away, crying silently. Was this the way it would always be? Long periods of silence interspersed with odd scraps of words, some brief moments of light in long darkness?

"Jaimie has conversations by approximation," Theo told her.

Jack put her mask back on and headed to the living room. Her husband lay where she had left him, looking gray. She listened to his labored breathing. Would he turn blue next? Was this the worst of it? *If you're planning a remarkable recovery*, Jack thought, *now would be an excellent time to turn things around.*

"Hey," he said, eyes open. "Wouldn't it be easier if it was just me who wore the mask instead of making everyone else wear one?"

"Sure," she said, "but you'll breathe easier this way."

Could he even suck air through the paper of a mask? She guessed Theo would be thinking the same thing. The question hung unspoken between them. Married people, through long practice, had conversations by approximation, too, she supposed.

She sat on the floor against the couch, her back to her husband. "I've been talking to Oliver."

"Yeah?"

"The last thing we want to do is leave. We're better off just staying put. The wind has shifted away, at least for now, so the fire's headed off to ruin a bunch of other people's lives instead of ours."

"So...yay."

"Uh-huh." Jack somehow found the energy to smile. "I know you're worried about your dad — "

"If Dad hasn't got the flu, he's in better shape than we are," Theo said. His voice was weak but he was coughing less. Jack thought that must be a very good sign or a very dire one.

"But," she continued, "if we do have to bug out—"

"Bug out?"

"That's what Oliver calls it."

"As opposed to simply leave?"

"Bugging out means we're running out of here with our hair on fire," she said. "Metaphorically."

"I get the nuance now."

"He keeps going through his stuff and our stuff and Mrs. Bendham's stuff and trying to figure out what to take. I think he's packed and repacked the van a few times now."

"Tough job," Theo said. "No matter how you pack, it's never really enough. We need an 18-wheeler for the hardware supplies, a few 18-wheelers for the food, one just for movies — "

"Several for books," she said. "I know, I know. I turned the house upside down looking for a damn bendy straw for you. Who would have thought *that* was a survival tool?"

"I'm surviving," he said.

"I just really wanted to make you more comfortable," Jack said, her eyes welling.

"When there's no medicine, you have to rely on time to heal you," he said. "Have you given any thought to what things will be like after all this is over?"

Her lips became a thin line. "What else is there to think about? Once we're through this, it will be the same, except with fewer people and we'll have some long stories to bore our grandchildren with."

"I don't think so," he said. He sat up a little and she moved to help him, pulling on one arm and moving his pillow farther down his back to prop him up. "I think we're headed to the Dark Ages again, like after the Black Plague."

"We keep better records now. We won't lose so much knowledge. This is a blip. History keeps repeating itself and it's awful, but it's all a blip for the next generation."

Theo shook his head. "Dunno. You could be right. There's an argument that Hitler influenced his century more than any other person because all that evil spurred so much invention, leading to technological developments we're still benefiting from."

"Funny," Jack said. "Douglas was quoting Kurt Vonnegut, saying that a lot of talent died in World War II and that was a loss of progress for generations. Maybe we would have had iPhones by 1970, instead."

Theo shrugged. "When you talk about Kurt Vonnegut, it makes me think you're trying to distract me from other things."

She picked up the water bottle at her feet and offered it to him. He refused it and stared at his wife.

"Your dad's place is still the best bet."

"What about taking over a farm that's closer?" he said.

"You just said yourself, Theo. If Papa Spence hasn't got the flu, he's in better shape than we are. What if this drags on into the fall or gets worse?"

"It can't last that long. Things are messed up on the ground right now, but there are people somewhere who know what they're doing. They are working to beat this thing. There's some guy or some woman who's bent on being the world's savior. They're falling asleep looking at test tubes in a centrifuge right now," he said.

"I'm just saying, what if?"

"Then we'll deal with it here," he said. "The fire will stay away. The whole damn city can't burn down."

"Fall through that bridge when we come to it?" she said. "You might be overestimating your sheer force of will, baby."

"The last thing we want to do is leave. We need to just stay put and stay calm," he said.

"I'm calm," she said. "That's why I can talk about this stuff."

"I don't want to go back there," Theo said, "and I'm not calm. I'm scared. Almost scared to death. But I'm feeling a little better. You didn't think I'd let a little thing like untimely death stop me, did you?"

"You remember our last first kiss?"

"On the front steps of your dorm. Of course."

"Good. Get better quick. We have a lot to do and I need you to hold Jaimie's hand all the way to Maine when the time comes."

"I promise."

Big Brother Lies And Denies

Jack slipped a fresh mask over her face. She wished she really thought the mask would make a difference. Hospital workers she'd seen on the television news took a variety of precautions, from hair nets and double masks to Hazmat suits and N95 respirators. On YouTube, she'd seen police officers wearing gas masks. Some people with new gas masks had suffocated because they didn't know they had to take the plastic cap off the filter. Many nurses wore hospital masks with plastic shields that covered their eyes.

If those protective measures had worked correctly, she didn't think she'd be scanning an empty street now. The home across the street from which her family had fled — *her* home — was a standing invitation.

"I know where you live! I know where you live!" that ragged little man had said. For the first time, she wondered if they had overreacted moving in with Douglas Oliver. Still, if Bently showed up, there were no police to haul him away.

Growing up in Maine, she had often hunted ducks with her father. She wished she had that double barrel over and under shotgun. It would have allowed them to stay in their home. That gun was no doubt still in a gun cabinet in Maine, though without postal service or airplanes, that gun cabinet may as well sit on the surface of Mars.

Jack wanted to go home, if only for a few minutes. She hesitated at the road, checking left and right, not for cars, but for observers.

Seeing none, she dashed across Misericordia Drive and up her driveway, running as fast as she could to the front door.

As soon as she unlocked the door and burst inside, she felt foolish. She was a superstitious little girl sure that mommy would catch her crossing the dangerous street on her own. Or maybe that cretin Bently had the power to appear from nowhere and hurt her.

The door had a solid deadbolt but, as Oliver pointed out when they moved to his house, the old door was too light and thin to withstand anyone really determined to enter. If Trent had been serious about busting down the door, he could have.

"Locks are for friends," Oliver had said, "and doors and frames like that are to keep out ten-year-olds." Now she wished that in all his supply-gathering, she had asked Oliver to return with a heavy metal door and something to reinforce the frame. A bazooka would be nice, too. She'd sleep better with a bazooka under her bed.

As Jack slipped inside, the smell of her home comforted her. The air was a bit stale, but every family home has its unique aroma and only now did she realize how much she'd missed theirs. It was as if she had been away a long time though it had only been a few days.

Everything was as they'd left it. Family pictures still hung on the walls. A laundry basket of unneeded things still lay on its side where she had knocked it over in her rush to pack. The beds were made, hospital corners.

It was the kitchen that was a wreck. Cupboards stood empty, their doors yawning open. They had been in such a rush to flee that dirty little man's threats, that awful runt of a man — "*I know where you live! I know where you live!*" — they'd grabbed it all in a near panic as Theo fell ill.

She kicked the empty recycling bin under the kitchen table. "Terrified like rabbits," Jack said aloud, disgusted.

Jack grabbed the long cloth bag from its hook. It held all their plastic grocery bags. She would take them all with her. Plastic bags had all kinds of uses. She assumed she would carry things in them, of course, but she might need them for other things: Keeping feet dry by putting them over socks or shoes. Plastic bags could contain human waste in a pinch. When it got cold, maybe she'd have to stuff the bags between layers of clothes and the plastic would serve as insulation to keep her family warm.

She rummaged through a cabinet. There was little detritus to rummage through: an egg separator, a potato masher, some corn cob holders and picks to dig out lobster meat from claws. She couldn't remember the last time she ate lobster. Growing up in Maine, it had been a holiday staple. Then she moved west and learned from one of Jaimie's books that lobsters were in the lice family. She hadn't craved lobster since.

In another cabinet, she found the old dishes from her college days. They did not use them now, but Jack had kept them for Anna's college years. She thought of those cheap plates and chipped bowls as Anna's "first apartment dishes." Jack let out a sniffle, thinking of what Anna would now miss. How long would her daughter have to wait before there was such a thing as a university again?

Jack looked through another drawer: Still no bendy straws. She let out a savage curse that shimmered an echo off the walls. Wiping a tear away, she felt like she was running scared, chased by something big, but not really seeing it as she raced away for her life.

Sutr was too big to see all at once. It was as if hurricanes had hit everywhere at once and she couldn't pull back far enough from the world to take in all the devastation.

What was the government doing? Was a vaccine or a cure even close, or was Sutr going to be a virus that hung in the world, always there and waiting for its next opportunity to strike?

Those questions had no answers she could provide, so her mind turned to the little man who had threatened her family. Bently had run from an old man who'd drawn his blood with a bag of groceries. She'd moved her family into that same old man's house, throwing in with a stranger, and shared her family's food. She'd thanked Douglas Oliver for the privilege. She'd listened to the old man's lectures on survival strategies and tolerated his rants that they were eating too many of their rations too fast.

Instead of threatening Bently, perhaps they could have made him an ally. She suddenly felt that, as a concession to emergency, she had given up too much far too easily. The man had been hungry and frightened and someone had to break the cycle of fear and the problem of me-first. If survivors worked together, everyone had a better chance to live.

She put a hand to her head. Her palm came away slick, but she did not feel unwell. She decided the sweat was a combination of worrying and exertion.

"Careful, Jacky," she told herself. "Don't talk yourself into getting sick." People could make themselves sick by thinking too hard about being sick. It was the nocebo effect, the opposite of the powerful and helpful placebo.

She took deep breaths and looked around her kitchen, taking the search slower so she could be more methodical. Still no bendy straws. Theo wasn't drinking enough. He'd told her he felt better, but she wasn't sure she should believe him. Jack wondered if her husband was drinking less because of the virus, or was it because he thought he'd be dead soon, anyway?

She glanced up at the late afternoon sky. To the east, the sky glowed orange, but what she saw much closer made her jaw drop and her pulse race.

Birds, columns of them, filled the sky in circling hordes. Many looked like vultures. Black turkey vultures, maybe.

The fires must have blown past the city's edges. Wildlife would be driven before the walls of flames, but scores of birds rose from the wooded land and come to the city to search for the dead under ominous, widening gyres.

The city had emptied of the living. Flights of carrion eaters were coming to claim their prize.

Despite herself, she pictured vultures clawing at her family's faces and eyes. That was the moment Jack was sure they really would leave. To live, they would become strangers in a terrible land that had once been so familiar.

That was the real horror of this plague: the everyday and familiar turned to blood, rot and ruin. In this new world, *innocence* was a sound and an undecipherable code. It had become an alien word without meaning on Earth.

This wasn't her home anymore. This was an open grave. Waiting.

But The Zombie Queen Claims Her Prize.

Gunfire rattled and boomed across the grounds of Buckingham Palace. The siege was well under way. Superior firepower was no match for masses of human wolves with no thought for their safety. For every one-hundred killed, ten got through the line of military and police. The savagery was primeval. The ghouls' hunger knew no bounds.

Shiva watched, smirking from her high window on Birdcage Walk. The gathering inhuman maelstrom had no strategy, only hunger. The infected did not corral the uninfected. They simply overwhelmed their terrified prey with ferocity and greater numbers from all directions.

"A conversation, Agent Perdue, is where you speak and I speak. This is not a conversation. This is an ultimatum."

The man on the phone began to object.

"Do you want me to hang up or do you want to figure out where I'm calling from?" she asked.

Her question was met with stunned silence.

"Good, now be quiet and I'll tell you a story while you figure out where I am. Just let me know when the sniper is in place to kill me. Understood?"

"Very well," the perplexed Interpol agent replied.

"Do you know what a rat king is? Oh, excuse me. I told you to shut up. Never mind. I'll tell you." She took another sip of wine.

She'd switched to red and she was feeling relaxed despite the baby's incessant kicking.

"A rat king," she explained, "is a ball of rats held together by their twisted tails. The nest intertwines in an obscene knot, as if the rat colony becomes one disgusting organism. They can't get away from each other. It's a curious fluke of nature. It's not seen often, but a ball of rats can be thirty or more. Some say they've seen a mass of the vermin with as many as 100. Imagine *that* in your bedroom, broiling and fighting and feeding on your bare feet, Agent Perdue."

She heard him swallow hard.

"They end up feeding on each other. They strip their brothers and sisters clean to the bone. Imagine your brothers and sisters, neighbors and sons and daughters, all in a tangle, ripping flesh from bone and sucking the juice from each other's eyeballs to live. Well, look outside at those poor civilian plague victims. I don't suppose you have to use your imagination at all."

"I hope there is a point to this story."

"Is the sniper really in place? Were you surprised how close I was to your command center? Did your superiors argue with the Queen and beg her to leave for the relative safety of Balmoral? Good of her to think staying was a noble statement to the doomed populace. Stiff upper lip and all that. Tonight she can get a real taste of the commoner's life."

"We know where you are. The snipers are ready."

"Doubtful," she said, though she stepped away from the window. "That would be awfully quick of you and I daresay you would have shot me already. Or are your personnel far too busy, shooting into the crowd, killing their daughters and fathers, brothers and sisters, sons and mothers? Ripping flesh from bone, as it were?"

"You're mad."

"I'm angry," she replied. "You shouldn't tell the crazy lady she's crazy, even if it's true. I bet that's not in your hostage negotiation handbook."

"You have a hostage?" Perdue asked.

"You might say you are the hostage, silly man. You just don't see it yet. In a way, I'm the hostage since you have to save me at all costs. And I'm not really mad, by the way. Let's be clear. I am very focussed. A thousand years from now, the historians will say I *saved* the human race. And believe it or not, that will be true. Of course, history is written by the victors."

He cursed. "If you're going to talk my ear off, I may as well have you shot and go join the fight outside. Say something that makes sense or I'll know you're stalling."

"Your machine guns are so loud and scary, but those barrels must get awfully hot. How much more ammunition could you possibly have on hand? And Sutr-X must have softened you up and depleted your forces devilishly, of course."

"The sniper is in place, Miss Keres. And with our technology, it doesn't matter if you step away from the window. He sees you just fine."

"Oh, lovely." She raised a glass and toasted her would-be assassin. "Thermal imaging scope or do you have something even newer and fancier? Were you really planning on a sniper or are you calling in a helicopter gunship to wipe out everyone, from me to the Queen's front door?"

"Miss Keres," Perdue said, "I am giving you one chance to surrender."

"Counteroffer. I'll give you one chance at a small chance to save what's left of the world."

There was a pause and she sensed the Interpol agent muted the phone to speak with someone standing beside him. When he came back on the line, his breathing was shallow.

"Tell me, Agent Perdue. Do you want to be the one who takes responsibility for say, destroying the Internet or burning down the library at Alexandria or killing the one person who holds the key to the survival of the human race? If you saw Jonas Salk walking down the street with the polio vaccine still an idea in his head, you wouldn't kill him would you? You'd take a bullet for him, the needs of the many and all that. You'd do *anything* you could, wouldn't you? Edward Jenner discovered the key to ending smallpox. You'd sacrifice yourself and a few others just for the hope of winning the long game, right?"

"What are you talking about, woman? Speak plain."

"Try to follow me here. This is very important. The way to deal with a rat king is to poison it. I have poisoned the rat king."

She moved back to the window and sipped her red wine. "Hello, Mr. Sniper! Please stand by a moment more."

Below her, the gathering darkness transformed the mass of bodies into a silhouetted orgy, a blood sacrifice to Shiva's ambitions. Only muzzle flashes illuminated the horror in strobes of human debasement: a ghoul tore at the throat of a policeman in riot gear here. Small children gnawed at the calves of a palace guardsman there. Another guard was on the ground, screaming for help under a riot shield. Seven women pinned him fast and crawled over each other to claw at his face and rip and chew his bare feet.

"I have poisoned your rat king, but there is an antidote."

"There's an antidote to the Sutr-X virus?"

"Oh, no. That was a failure. Sutr-X was an unfortunate miscalculation. But there is an antidote for what you see in the street below."

"How do I know you're telling the truth?"

"Because I'm alive. I injected the one vial of vaccine in Britain before I allowed a lab rat named Bogart to bite me."

Perdue turned from the phone again, consulting someone.

Shiva took another sip and turned to her iPod. The screen lit her face as she selected the song she wanted to hear. "Agent Perdue? Are you still there? Don't be rude."

"I'm here."

"The vaccine is coursing through my veins, fighting off the infection so I don't turn into one of those zombies. Is that a cliche? Should I really call them that? Does that sound too silly?"

"What do you want?"

"An excellent question. I am the Zombie Queen. I demand tribute."

"What do you want, Miss Keres?"

"Don't storm the building or attempt any useless heroics. All the stairways are wired to explode. If you try it, your last best hope for humanity — that would be me — will perish with the knowledge that could save the future."

"I see. And how do I know you're telling the truth?"

"You already know about Bogart and you can't imagine I accomplished all this on my own. A helicopter is coming for me. It will come to the roof and I will go unharassed."

Someone whispered something in Perdue's ear that Shiva couldn't quite catch, but his defeated tone reassured her she remained in control.

"Okay," Perdue said.

"In the meantime, I have three more demands. No helicopter is to leave Buckingham Palace. She's quite a fit old woman, I'm sure, but if you try to make her run for her life, I shall be quite...displeased."

Perdue sighed.

"You are to tell her my name. Names matter. Tell her Shiva says hello and that there can only be *one* queen. Open your gates. Throw open your doors. Cry havoc and let slip the dogs of war!"

Perdue gave a nervous laugh. "Why would I do such a thing?"

"Because you have to keep me alive to have any hope for the human race. Comply and there's a future. Defy me and I set off the bombs. I'll disappear in a flash of light, painless and smug. You'll still die screaming, but all the progeny from here to the last of those things will become the once-humans. Monsters will roam the Earth. If I die, Hope dies."

"You like the sound of your own voice too much."

"Tell your sniper the bombs will go off if I so much as trip and fall down."

"I think you're bluffing," the Interpol agent replied.

"I think you're very brave, Mr. Perdue. But I don't think you're so brave that you will be reckless. You believe you are a noble man and your cause is just. That's why you won't take the risk that I'm a liar. All of humanity is too much for a good man to gamble. If it makes you feel better, the zombies are winning. Open your gates and you welcome the inevitable and maybe you'll even save the future you imagined for the human race. Be a coward and all is lost and you'll die anyway."

She hung up, plugged her earbuds in her ears and touched the screen. Her selection came on: *We Want Your Soul* by Adam Freeland.

From ninety yards away, Staff Sergeant Tom Clayworth lay on his belly on a roof. He watched the pregnant woman through his rifle scope. Through his lens, she appeared in bright yellow and he could make out the cell phone and the wire to the iPod. Either one could harbor a gyroscope trigger to the bomb she claimed to have.

He keyed his radio mic. "I still have eyes on, sir. Permission to engage."

A long pause. "She told me names matter. My name..." The agent's voice shook. "My name means 'lost'. Perhaps everything really is pre-ordained."

"Sir? The target?"

"Negative on the target. Move to concentrate your fire on the riot, Staff Sergeant."

"But, sir. I have a clean shot."

"We're about to open the front doors, Clayworth. Buy us a few minutes if you can, please."

"Repeat, sir?" Clayworth put the ball of his index finger on the trigger, lining up a head shot.

"We're letting those things in, Staff Sergeant. Do not engage the target."

Clayworth hesitated a second more before following the order. He wondered how long he could stay on the roof before those rabid animals found their way up? He reached into his belt and put one round in his shirt pocket, sure to save one bullet for himself.

"But, sir...the Queen."

"I'll make sure she won't suffer," Perdue said. "God save our tomorrows because the Devil owns us tonight."

Clayworth took one last glance at the target through his scope.

The Queen of the Zombies danced.

Season 1, Episode 4

**You have forgotten you are meat.
You will be reminded.**

*

**We're pretty smug, thinking we're at the top of the food chain.
Worms are the all-time champs.**

~ Notes from The Last Café

Run Fast From The Zombie Horde

"Hello?" The woman sounded like she had just been roused from a deep sleep.

"I need to talk to Dr. Neil McInerney, please. I'm one of his patients and this is urgent."

"Uh...um...is this about a dental emergency? With the flu, the office is closed. He's not seeing any patients. You might find some help at the hospital."

"I'm calling from his office."

"What? You can't be at the office. It's closed."

Sinjin-Smythe closed his eyes and took a deep breath. "I smashed through the front door. It's open now." He heard rustling on the other end of the line as screams and running feet pounded one story below.

"Who the hell is this and what's this about breaking into my surgery?" He recognized the voice of his dentist.

"This is Craig Sinjin-Smythe."

"The...volleyball player?"

"Dr. Craig Sinjin-Smythe. I'm overdue for a cleaning."

"What?"

"I'm not calling about my teeth, Neil. I'm a virologist. London is falling. There's been a new flu mutation and it looks very much like rabies among the new victims."

"Oh, my god! Is it airborne?"

"Hopefully not yet. But I'm sure it spreads through bites."

"If what you say is true, we should bar the doors and wait it out. If it's human rabies, better we stay off the streets."

"And then what? This is our chance to slip away. By tomorrow, there will be too many. When you try to get away because you're hungry, the streets will be full of them."

"I don't like the sound of this at all."

"You don't have to like it. You have to move. Now. You've forgotten that you are meat. You're part of the food chain. If you wait, you will be reminded. This is a matter of life and death, Craig. *Your* life and death and from what I've seen, we don't have much time."

"Where will we go?"

"First, anywhere but London. After that? I'll tell you when we're under sail."

He couldn't convince McInerney to come to the office. Since his dentist lived in St. Mary's Gardens, south of the Thames, they agreed to meet at his boat. It wasn't far. Only hundreds, perhaps thousands, of rage-filled victims of the new Sutr-X variant blocked their way to St. Katherine's Docks.

Dr. Jianjun Seong reached out and pulled Shiva aboard the helicopter. She greeted him with a warm smile and embraced him. "My sweet little brother-in-arms!"

As soon as she belted in and put the big headphones on her head, Seong ordered the pilot to take off. Two more passengers — an Asian man and a swarthy woman wearing a hijab — sat in the helicopter's cabin. All were dressed as if ready for a hike, except each wore a sidearm and automatic rifles sat on top of packs at their feet.

They all bowed their heads in Shiva's direction and then craned to watch the bloody carnage below in fascination.

"My queen," Seong said, bowing lower than the rest. "History and a new future are made!"

She laughed. "Now, now, Brother Seong. There'll be none of that in the new world order, thank you very much. That's the sort of nonsense we're getting away from. We are pioneers, not the rich descendants of ancient warlords like those parasites." Shiva pointed at the Buckingham Palace grounds below. *"That's* what we're getting away from, Brother Seong." The battle was a boiling mass of dark shapes.

"It's impossible to tell who's infected and who isn't from here," Seong said. "Your new variant is impressive. It spreads so rapidly."

"I call it Sutr-Z. The CDC told me you were dead, Brother."

"They were supposed to think that. They still don't know."

"So? What's the progress report? Give me your good news."

Seong took his time answering. "Sadly, the course correction is not as large as we'd hoped." He pulled out an iPad and flipped through screens until he came to the document he needed. "Hong Kong went down easily, as I predicted. With all the commerce and flights in and out, the first stage of Sutr spread satisfactorily in the first attack. However, Sutr-X was contained better than we anticipated on the mainland. It seems the Chinese government learned much from the 2002-2003 SARS outbreak, Sister."

"What are you saying?"

Even over the din of the rotors, Seong heard the hardness come into her voice. "The secondary attacks were very fruitful." He pointed to statistics on a bar graph that showed the extermination numbers for farm animal populations. "I'm particularly pleased with the reductions in the cattle population."

Shiva did not look as pleased. "I expected that we'd have a greater reduction in China's chief product, Jianjun. How many Chinese were killed by the Sutr virus?"

"Millions by Sutr-X itself, Sister."

She huffed. "Details."

"Shenyang, Wenzhou, Ningbo, Baotou and, of course, my home city of Nanjing is gone. There were eight million in Nanjing alone."

"Show me a graph, Brother Seong. Perhaps that will get us to the point faster."

The doctor switched screens and handed the iPad to her.

"Baotou is in Inner Mongolia with barely three million people. The fact that you even mention it shows how far from the mark you've missed."

"The Party took drastic action to contain the outbreaks, but that also helped the cause. The good news I've been holding back, Sister, is that the Chinese government used *nuclear* weapons to contain the outbreaks. Nuclear weapons on our own land! Amazing, isn't it? I didn't expect them to be so sweeping and decisive."

"This is disappointing. Your target was our prime concern. If you'd isolated Sutr-Z as I did, China's surviving populace would be crawling over each other by now. I didn't even control the whole lab, but I didn't fail!"

"I apologize, Sister."

"You know what this means, don't you? We have to take some of the infected from here and take them all the way back to bloody China for a fresh attack. I'd planned to take America with you by my side, Seong. Now we have to go back and do the job right the *second* time."

"Yes. I am sorry I won't be able to join you, Sister, but I can do as you ask and this time I will succeed. The infected will carry Sutr-Z to every corner of China."

"You can do that? You're sure?"

"I can do that."

"I know you can, Jianjun. The community gave you your name because it means, *He who builds an army.*"

Seong nodded his appreciation and smiled.

Shiva pointed at one of the other passengers. "But can *he* do the job right the first time?"

The Asian man's head snapped around. He gave a crisp nod. "We make history and a new future, Sister. I can do as you ask."

Shiva slipped a long dirk from her sleeve and plunged the three-sided blade between Dr. Seong's ninth and tenth ribs. His jaw dropped open as he tried to gasp. He could not. She gave the handle a ruthless twist and he stiffened. Blood gushed over her hands as she hit the release on Seong's seatbelt and tipped him to the floor."Tell the pilot to swing back around, hover low and open the door. We should feed my children a sweet little dessert."

Seong still clung to life as she kicked him out of the helicopter and into the teeth of the madding crowd.

Pack Your Memories, Grab A Sword

Jacqueline Spencer tore her gaze from the widening gyres of vultures that filled the sky and climbed the stairs to her room. The Spencers had emptied their home of everything they felt was essential. Was this what it was gong to be like from now on? Empty city? Empty house? Empty life?

She scanned her bedroom. Of course, Theo shared it with her, but there could be no doubt it was hers and she just let him sleep there, allowing him a little closet space. The wallpaper had been her choice, as had the bed and furniture.

In sleep, Jack liked to spread out, allowing Theo just a quarter of the bed. Theo joked that in bed she made him feel like a woman. "You rip the covers away from me and push me to the edge. Thanks for letting me keep one butt cheek on the mattress, Jack."

When the opportunity arose, he toasted Jack with, "One cheek!" without explanation to the kids and gave his wife a kiss. Theo's toast to her: A tiny, happy ritual.

She wished he were sleeping with her now, but there was the issue of contagion. If they slept together, the virus might slip into her mouth and nose and throat and lungs as they slept. Of course, that may already have happened. Part of the virus' power was that it seemed to have a long incubation period, infecting others while the carrier was still unaware they were sick.

Jack slept differently now, lighter and fitfully. She did not spread out her arms and legs to take over the bed. Instead, she curled up, alone and fetal, often awake and listening, straining, to hear any sounds of danger in the night.

They watched their house carefully. Now that Theo was sick on the couch in Oliver's front room, he felt useless. Watching his own house whenever he was awake was the only thing he could do. Still, Jack worried that Bently would come back, perhaps sneaking in the back of the house to destroy their garden out of spite.

She thought again how Bently had looked at Anna, ogling her and unashamed to do so in front of her family. That was the crux of it, she decided. He was a short, grimy little man, but he was not afraid. There was no law and order any more, no common conventions. Bently was dangerous simply because he didn't care about those conventions. He'd openly broke the unspoken agreement everyone has. You don't look at somebody's daughter like that. He did and, despite running from an old man, Bently still stayed long enough to collect the cans of food, rolling on the ground. Hitting him had been like shooing away a vulture who wouldn't leave a corpse alone. Even though threatened with superior force and numbers, he'd be back. He wouldn't stay away if there was anything left he could take.

Jack hadn't known mental exhaustion could cut her this deep. *Stressed out too long,* she thought. Even a lab rat forced to run in a maze gets to rest. She lay on her own bed in her own house and let out a deep sigh. The bed was stripped and the quilt she'd bought from a Mennonite woman at a farmer's market was now across the street in Oliver's house.

She bet those farm women were set up nicely now. Fresh vegetables, horses and buggies for travel and root cellars full of everything they'd need. And a large group to protect them. The Mennonites and the Amish were ready for primitive conditions because their lives were always simple. Their community would work together. With so little contact with the regular world and its technology, they would barely notice the ravages of the world flu pandemic beyond what deaths might sweep through their community. Armed with their religion, they'd be better prepared to deal with funerals, too.

The Native American communities had some of the same advantages, but the reserves had been the dead canary in the coal mine in the early days as the Sutr virus spread. Already unhealthy in many ways, flu had killed many more of them than whites, perhaps because contaminated water sources on reservations had weakened their immune systems.

Jack recalled from early news coverage, the Swine Flu pandemic had infected many more Indians on reserves than anywhere else. History had repeated itself, but nothing was done to protect the indigenous population from the contagion. Lessons paid for at great cost had not been learned. She supposed the politicians responsible were probably safe in a bunker somewhere, though perhaps, they weren't safe from their own decisions anymore.

But even the highest-ranking politicians had family members they couldn't take into a secure bunker. When the enemy is a virus, was there any such thing as "secure"? She supposed there could be, in some rarified circumstances, an army outpost under a mountain or a remote Center for Disease Control facility where everyone was jailed in plastic suits breathing artificial air all the time. The price of admission to that illusion of safety sounded too high.

What good was it to be a president or a senator or a prime minister if there was no one left to follow your orders? Were there still people taking orders, people so committed to duty that they'd carry on as if their families weren't in danger? She supposed there must be. She hoped they existed. Whoever they might be, they would be as alien to her as any little-known exotic plant from Madagascar. She asked God to bless the research scientists and doctors and to provide an answer soon.

On Jack's bedroom wall above the dresser hung a painting she'd created while she was pregnant with Jaimie. She preferred to paint in oils, but she was concerned about the toxins in oil paints and the elaborate cleanup the paint required. She'd switched to acrylic because she could simply clean her brushes with soap and water. It seemed a silly thing to have been overly cautious about now.

The small painting was a seascape. Smooth black rocks poked out of green water at low tide in Poeticule Bay. As an afterthought, she had stuck in a whale's blue barnacled tail sticking out of the waves close to the shore. She'd grown up not far from that beach but had never once seen a whale there. However, the painting had asked for a whale tail. The process of creation, wherever that came from, *required* it. It was the whale's tail that made her fall in love with that painting. It was her only painting that she had bothered to frame.

She had rushed out of the house with survival and Bently the Vulture on her mind. In the midst of panic, there was no room for art. "Scared widdle bunny wabbit," she said to herself.

She took the picture from the wall. A rectangle of dust and unfaded paint told her exactly where it had hung. How could she have left without this? She had been afraid of Bently — she still was very much afraid of what he might do — but, except for Jaimie, they had all rabbited about in a panic.

Bently's threat, the first of her life since schoolyard tiffs to be sure, had sent her running. How would her family deal with the challenges ahead if they couldn't face down one scrawny man? The house was not on fire when they'd run across the street to Douglas Oliver's house. She hadn't thought to take her painting, or even a couple photo albums. Even people fleeing houses on fire thought to grab their kids' baby pictures.

How deep would Sutr reach down into the fabric of what had been and tear with unforgiving teeth? How resilient was that fabric? Was civilization just a thin sheen of varnish over shiny, black claws of primal aggression? She knew Theo thought so, but she hoped her husband was wrong.

Perhaps that hope led her to the back of the closet in Jaimie's bedroom. She knew it was the one place where her memory box would be safe from Anna's prying eyes. The letters were still there in a large round cookie tin marked "Personal." It was taped shut and it took Jack a few minutes of working with her thumbnail to pry up the yellowed, gummy tape. She hadn't looked at any of these letters since before the kids were born...no, before she and Theo had even moved in together.

All the letters were from Theo to Jack. He'd always called her Jack, from the moment she'd introduced herself as Jacqueline. She had tied the envelopes in small bundles with lengths of red ribbon. It made her feel like she had been a silly girl. There was something Victorian and stupid about squirrelling this bit of their history away.

"In case of emergency, dig out tin and remind yourself you were young once," she announced to the empty room.

Jaimie's room was remarkably empty except for books stacked in neat piles on his desk. The room wasn't big enough for an echo, but there was a definite ring of emptiness off the bare walls. Unlike every other teenage boy she'd ever met, there wasn't a single poster. On her knees by Jaimie's bed, she spread the love letters out before her in little piles arranged by date. The collection now seemed far more sad than she had anticipated when she'd dug them out from the rear of the closet's top shelf.

Theo had written her long letters every day detailing how unhappy he was without her. He'd been planting trees in Oregon while she waitressed at Poeticule Bay's Seafarer's Pub.

All the letters were about missing her, professing love. Her then-boyfriend wrote about the physical pleasures they'd shared at Stanford. She supposed Anna felt those needs now when she thought of that dolt, Trent Howser.

Theo and Jack were apart all that summer and the next. He got a summer job as a house painter in Illinois from a college buddy and she stayed with an aunt in Bangor and temped in secretarial jobs.

The separation had been hard on them both, each worrying about the other's summer temptations, wondering if their young romance could bear the weight of time between the beginning of April and the end of August. Each September when they reunited at Stanford, they found their love had survived the time apart.

She paged through a few letters at random: One from June (depressed at their separation); another from July (an angry rant that his father had gotten him the painting job and how low the pay was.) The letters leading up to the end of August became more giddy. (Only 15 days left! was written on one envelope.) Theo wrote the number of days until their reunion on the same spot in small script under each stamp.

Some of the letters were, of course, pornographic, all in Theo's rushed, slashing handwriting. She had given as good as she got, but when she asked him once where her letters to him went, he shrugged and said he'd thrown them away so no one else could read them. She'd been silent for two days after he told her that and he hadn't understood how his lack of sentimentality could make her so angry.

Everyone older than e-mail, she supposed, must have letters they don't want their children to read. No worries with Jaimie, there. She knew handwriting was as opaque to him as the printed word was hypnotic.

But what teenage girl, no matter how virtuous, wouldn't read the letters from her father as a young man to her mother? Jack was afraid that, at best, Anna would invade her privacy and rationalize it by getting all gooey over how romantic her parents had been. Then, at an inopportune time — during an argument over Trent, for example— Anna would throw the letters in her face, reminding her mother that she was trying to deny her daughter the exquisite sex life she had enjoyed until Theo fell ill.

Jack reached for another letter at random. On the back, Theo had written S.W.A.K. "Sealed with a Kiss." She kissed the back of the envelope now and began to cry. She couldn't kiss her husband now, not without fear of inviting infection. Now that this simple pleasure was denied her, it seemed more important than ever that she be allowed the indulgence.

She threw the letters back in the tin, still sobbing with great heaving gasps. It wasn't because she couldn't kiss Theo that she cried now. It was because going through these old sweet and sexy letters now seemed like a morbid act, nostalgia transformed into something ugly. She felt like an old widow pouring over a dead husband's correspondence.

It was then that she felt she wasn't alone. There was a creak at the top of the stairs that she knew well. Whenever either of the kids got up at night to go to the bathroom, that floorboard creaked.

A month ago, Jack had stopped Theo in the middle of urgent but quiet lovemaking because she had detected a noise, so attuned were they to the squeaks and creaks of hallway floorboards. Anna, in a rare post-midnight bathroom trip, had gotten up to pee. Theo and Jack giggled and whispered, unwilling to continue until they could be reasonably sure Anna had returned to her room, oblivious to incriminating sounds from her parents' room.

Another creak.

Had she locked the back door? She wasn't sure. No, probably not, she decided. She was only going to be a moment but when she glanced at her watch she wasn't sure how much time had elapsed since she'd entered the house. It must be at least twenty-five minutes.

"Hello? Is anyone there?" She already knew the answer. For a moment she thought about hiding under the bed, but if the intruder hadn't heard her crying already, he certainly knew she was in there now.

She cast about, but could see nothing that could be used as a weapon.

Creak!

"I've got a gun here!" she said. She'd have been delighted to at least have a long sharp stick. The heat rose in her cheeks. She was still on her knees by the bed, frozen. Her legs and buttocks ached from tensing.

Wouldn't that old over-under from her childhood home be great to have now? That would change the entire equation. *I used to be such a liberal,* she thought. A crazed laugh burst from her lips.

Jaimie stood at the door holding his Latin dictionary. He peered into his room. He didn't look right at her, but instead appeared to be looking to her left, as if a ghost stood behind her only the boy could see.

"Jaimie! You scared the hell out of me! If I'd had a shotgun I would have blown your head off."

He seemed unperturbed, but he usually looked that way. His cold detachment unnerved her.

"Nothing personal." Her hands were ice as she put them to her hot cheeks. "I'm shocky." She went to her son and held him. As usual, he let her, infuriating her anew with his indifference.

"Sorry," she said absently and squeezed him tighter to her chest.

He put a hand on her elbow and began guiding her out of his room and down the stairs, pulling her.

"Wait," she said, and went back for her whale painting. He followed her and pulled again on her arm, at first timidly and then he got behind her and pushed. She ran ahead, downstairs to the book case in the living room to grab her wedding album and another book of baby pictures.

She tucked the painting awkwardly under her arm, cut through the dining room into the kitchen with her son on her heels. She scooped up the big bag full of smaller plastic bags. She took a moment to stuff the albums in one of the bags.

Jaimie pushed her again, urging her to go, but she slipped around him and back upstairs. An afterthought, she ran to Jaimie's bedroom and hurriedly piled the letters back into the tin. The circle of the cookie can stretched the mouth of the biggest bag, but she managed to stuff it in and headed downstairs.

Jaimie kept pushing even as she was passing through the back door.

"Okay! Okay!"

Her shoes clapped on the concrete of the deck in an angry rush. Now Jaimie pulled her back and held her fast. Jack rounded on her son. "What? What? This strong silent type thing is really getting on my nerves."

He waved at her in an impatient "c'mere" gesture and headed toward the fence at the rear of their property.

Mrs. Bendham's house was to their right. Jaimie cut left, looking back just long enough to confirm his mother followed. With surprising grace, Jaimie put one hand on the top of the fence and climbed over, never dropping his dictionary.

Jack handed him the bags and leaned over to carefully put her painting in the tall grass on the far side. With less grace, she climbed over. They stood at the rear of their other neighbor's property.

The bungalow belonged to Mr. Sotherby, an aging, divorced pilot who seemed to use his house as a quick pitstop to change clothes and head off again. A lawn care company took care of the property, at least until recently. Jack had never glimpsed the pilot out of uniform. Whenever they had seen him, he was rushing somewhere.

It occurred to Jack in that moment how he was so much like Douglas Oliver, as if they were the only family in The Neighborhood of Mysterious Old Bachelors.

There was something different about Jaimie now. His was not the usual dreamy, distracted stare. He was looking for something. His head was often cocked to one side (his bewildered cockatoo look, she called it.) Now he moved with purpose, his back straight. He gripped her forearm tightly, the same way she held him in pressing crowds. Now it was her son's turn to lead her.

Then Jack heard something: A bicycle's gear shift. Someone was out front of the house in the street. She peeked around the front corner of her empty house.

Bently steered in a circle, staring at the Spencer house. She pulled back quickly and prayed he missed her. In a blink, she'd had taken in all the information she needed. The rifle stood high in the bicycle's handlebar basket. She had also spotted a red gas can stuffed in beside the rifle.

In trying to push a thought away, an idea is given more power and it comes for you, stronger and scarier. The image that popped up was of her children, on fire and screaming.

"Get out of here!" she heard. It was Oliver, yelling from his front lawn. "Go! Get away!"

She risked another look and saw that Bently now stood beside Oliver in the Bendham's driveway. Bently dismounted, looking relaxed. Oliver whispered something, his gestures urgent. Bently nodded, got on his bike and pedaled away slowly, defiantly.

When Bently was out of sight, she leaned out to make sure the vulture was gone. She thought the old man had retreated back into Mrs. Bendham's house but she was wrong. Douglas Oliver stared at her. Was he startled because he thought she'd done something wrong? Or had she seen something she was not supposed to see?

Oliver paused a moment and then steamed toward Jack and her son across the grass. She stood her ground, arms crossed in front of her chest. "What was *that*?"

"I told him to go away," Oliver said. "I don't know how long that will last." His eyes searched hers. "I was right to get you to move into my house. That thug was casing your place."

"He didn't seem particularly mad at you," Jack said.

"He wants me dead," Oliver said. "He had the rifle."

"He didn't do anything."

"He was here to check us out."

Us? she thought. *Is there really an us?*

"He was here to intimidate. Bently wants us to know he hasn't forgotten."

"Are you playing us?" Jack asked, watching the old man's eyes.

"Of course not!"

"I'm trusting you, not because I'm sure I can but because I have no other choice."

"I let you move into my house so you'd be safe! I am protecting you."

"That better be true, Douglas."

Jaimie pulled his mother away. Oliver stared after them, hands on hips.

The boy looked back at the old man, staring back, directly into Oliver's eyes. Something wormed and wriggled in the old man's bowels and he felt the sudden urge to urinate. His heart skipped a beat. Oliver felt a moment's disorientation, like not quite enough oxygen could find its way to his brain.

Jaimie's eyes were black stones from a cold alien planet. The old man felt a touch of fear.

When They Come For Us, Hungry And Red

"We have to go out on a mission," Oliver announced.

Jack and Theo looked up together, surprised to find the old man standing at the entry to the living room.

"Still my house," he said. Then, suddenly embarrassed by his own forthrightness, added, "Sorry if I intruded. I shoulda knocked."

Theo gestured for Oliver to sit but the old man paced instead. "There's more smoke to the southwest," he said. "New smoke."

"We've been discussing possibilities," Jack said coolly.

The old man stopped and smiled. "It's a bugger to figure out what we should take and how much of what. I mean, can we find gas along the way or should we just take as many gas cans as we can pack into and onto the van and just go with that?"

Theo shrugged. "I hope it doesn't come to that...where we have to decide to abandon our home. Leaving it to go across the street has been enough of a hassle. I'm feeling a bit better and Jack and I were just discussing moving back home." He looked to his wife. Jack had already told him about spotting Oliver talking with Bently. The old man, it seemed, was trying to proceed as if that hadn't happened.

"I hope we don't have to leave, either," Oliver said. "I'm no farmer, but your farm might be the best option, Theo. Still, there's an awful lot of smoke in the city, and dry woods and lots of wood houses between here and Maine for that matter..."

"Pray for rain," Theo said. "And it's my *father's* farm. It's been a long time since I was there. I don't know what kind of shape it's in."

"But it's remote, right?"

"As much as anything can be, I suppose..." Theo ended with a hacking cough and brought up something green and red and black into a rag. They had run out of tissues days ago.

Oliver continued, ignoring the interruption. "Remote is good. There are other farms that are much closer, no doubt, but with so many people pouring out of the cities, they'll be headed to the rural areas. I don't imagine whoever is left will be welcoming."

"We could find a farm close by." Jack squeezed Theo's hand as he struggled to sit up and clear his lungs.

"I don't think so. The farms will be overrun with gangs of city-dwellers looking for a safe place and taking what they want by force. I wonder how many little wars are going on as we speak, surviving farmers on one side, hungry refugees on the other?" Oliver allowed the enormity of his suggestion sink in. He looked shocked when Jack Spencer shook her head.

"Are we going to talk about Bently?" she asked.

"What is there to talk about?"

"The way you were talking to him...you looked casual about it."

"I told him to go away."

"He had a rifle in his bicycle basket but he didn't use it on you."

"Maybe he didn't have any bullets. Maybe he realized I'm an old alpha dog and he shouldn't fuss with me."

Jack turned to her husband on the couch. "That's a lot of maybes in a short space of time."

"Jacqueline, what have I done that is so suspicious? The last we met Bently, I socked him in the face with cans of food to make him go away. The next time you see him, I'm telling him to go away. What else is there?"

"I don't know what to think."

"I think I've taken you into my home to protect you from him. Your family is safe here. I've done nothing but care for you people. If we're going to survive this thing, we have to work together. Don't you agree?"

Theo cleared his throat and spit into his rag again. "We're grateful, Douglas. And yes, we will have to work together. Just so we all understand each other, everybody has to work together, right? Us with you…and you with us."

"Of course. Which brings us to pressing business. I'm thinking of a proactive venture to solidify our alliance and get us a better chance of getting out of here. We need to go on a trip to the mall. A foraging mission. We should see what's salvageable. You asked about bendy straws, for instance."

Jack laughed in a climbing trill. "It's kind of a risk just to get some straws, don't you think? Besides, I thought the hordes had already cleaned out the mall."

"Not everything is gone and it's not about the straws specifically." His guard slipped then and his irritation showed. "This is a *survival* situation. We need to do more reconnaissance and see what's out there. We may find something we didn't know we needed until we find it."

He rearranged his face, aiming for reasonable and relaxed and not quite making it. "Besides, it's only a few blocks and it's for our tribe," he said.

Jack and Theo looked at each other. "Tribe?"

"Look," he said, "if we were suddenly transported to Gilligan's Island with limited resources and hostile cannibals lurking around, you'd rearrange your priorities faster. You'd be thinking water, food, shelter, clothing. But we're not marooned on an island. We're in familiar houses while the ground changes beneath us. The worst that's happened to you *personally* is a scary guy was rude to you, you moved in here and the power's off.

"I've been fighting your inertia, trying to wake you up. If not for me, you'd be at the mercy of that hungry kook or you'd have burned through all your food by now. You've got to get out of your suburban self-satisfaction and get into survival mode, 'cause this is the rainy day everyone warns you about."

"He's right," Anna descended the stairs, sat on the bottom step and hugged the bannister post. "Let's go shopping. I can't stay up in that room another minute. It's time to take action and get more control over our situation."

"I wouldn't call it shopping, exactly, young lady," Oliver said.

"Shopping. Looting. Whatever. Any excuse to go to the mall. Maybe we'll find out what's going on. Aren't you just dying to find out what the hell's going on? When I played soccer, the coach was always screaming that we had to assert, engage and attack to win. So let's go win something."

Jack stood. "Okay. Everybody who can carry something goes. Everyone else stays here and holds down the fort." She looked at her husband meaningfully. "That's you and Jaimie holding the fort."

Anna shook her head. "Jaimie's stronger than me and Mom put together."

"Ah, fair youth," Oliver said. "I was naturally strong when I was his age, too. We didn't have gyms but for some reason we didn't need them then."

"He can carry heavy things just fine," Anna assured her mother. "It's the dictionaries that gives him those muscles."

Anna pulled her mother aside. "I listened to the wind up radio early this morning."

"Really? I gave up on it. When I first wound it up I thought it was kind of cool. Then winding it so often became too much of a bother."

Anna gripped her arm harder. "Mom! Listen! I caught the end of a scary news report. It's like London's gone crazy."

"We heard there were food riots. Supply lines to cities will be cut off — "

"No! Worse than food riots. People attacking each other. The reporter said people were *eating* each other, Mom!"

"It's hard to believe things could go that sour. Look, we've heard all kinds of rumors since this thing started. Who reported this?"

"I don't know. The signal went in and out."

"Those are called skips. It's a trick of the atmosphere bouncing radio signals around." Jack put an arm around her daughter's shoulder. "When I lived in Poeticule Bay as a girl, sometimes we caught skips of the Boston police radio on the stereo. If the atmosphere is just right, you can get anybody saying anything into a microphone. What you heard couldn't have been from England, though. It was just a report of a report. The news has turned into an echo chamber. They sensationalize so much, we shouldn't take what we hear too seriously."

"This was real." Anna looked as haunted as an old, broken house.

"Sweetie, on 9/11, rumors were reported as fact. First they said the attack on the Pentagon was a helicopter explosion. Everybody believed it. Then they said it was one of the planes. Then someone said it was a missile. Then we didn't know what or who to believe anymore. Ever."

"So, believe no one?"

"Believe me, Anna. We're going to be okay. You know why? Because we're going to assert, engage and attack our problems."

Anna smiled. "Okay."

Jack leaned closer and whispered, "But since you bring it up, don't trust Mr. Oliver."

"Why?"

"I don't have real evidence, I suppose, but your dad and I have changed our minds about the old guy. We've decided to watch him more carefully. After this trip to the mall, and if the city's fire burns itself out, I think we'll move back home."

Anna smiled wider. "I'm good with that. I want to sleep in my own bed. The one I'm in is lumpy."

"Good. It's decided then. And don't worry. We'll go to the mall and see what supplies we can find. If the old guy steps out of line, I'll find some sweet and sour sauce packets in the food court and I'll eat him myself, starting with his lying face."

Don't Bother Hiding Under The Bed

Oliver, Jack, Anna and Jaimie left at five in the afternoon. "It's only a few blocks, Theo," Jack told him. "Have a nap and we'll be right back."

"Isn't that what they say in every horror movie before something terrible happens?"

"Shut up, love. Sleep."

Theo Spencer looked up at his wife, weary, but his eyes were brighter. "I love you, too."

Jaimie tried to take his huge English dictionary but his sister took it from him gently. She held up his little paperback of Latin phrases and put it in the bottom of his school backpack. Jack and Anna's backpacks remained empty. They hoped they would be able to pack them full of useful finds for the trip home.

The old man carried a long walking stick in one hand and the can of bear spray in the other. The spray was a short, fat yellow can fitted with a bright red nozzle and a trigger. A strap circled Oliver's wrist so he couldn't drop it. "Works on humans, too," he said. "Like squeezing a skunk in their eyes. Very discouraging."

The mall was only four blocks away. Jack and her children came to a halt at once as they came to the top of Misericordia Drive where it spilled onto the thoroughfare that was Fanshawe Park Road.

A fire engine lay on its side up the street. It was a ladder truck and the longest ladder with a basket atop it splayed out in two lengths

248

along the pavement. The forgotten machine looked like a broken dinosaur carcass.

"The '40s and '50s had the mushroom cloud. The '60s had flower power and the rocket to the moon. The '70s had disco, the '80s and '90s were run by a stock ticker, and the 2000s had the World Trade Center attack." Oliver pointed with his chin toward the wreck. "There's the new symbol of our time. Of course, it's like the Bachman, Turner, Overdrive song title, 'You ain't seen nothin' yet'."

"Who?" Anna asked.

"Don't blaspheme, girl," Oliver replied.

They walked on. But for the wreckage in the street, it was a lovely late spring day filled with birdsong. Tall, gray slab walls bordered the road on both sides. They were built to shield suburban homes from traffic noise. Fanshawe Park Road was a major east-west conduit along the north end of the city, but now there were no cars or trucks barreling through. Except for the abandoned emergency vehicle, the street stood empty.

The sound barrier walls, normally a long expanse of gray concrete, had become a riot of paint. Anna paused to admire an artful copy of the Christ on the cross marred by several illegible gang symbols. Another graffito was scrawled at regular intervals: Stay out of the X! Beside that was scrawled in another hand: Beware the Wolves!

The writing was a complete mystery to Jaimie. He saw no words. The writing was not uniform enough in its cursive and italic loops and lines for him to decipher. Each writer's intent and character was too varied for him to read. Where the others saw messages sprayed on the walls, he saw only abstract pictures, ciphers impossible to decode.

His sister, mother and neighbor could read the messages, however, and he could tell by their auras that their moods were plummeting the farther they walked along the wall.

Anna chewed her lip and held Jaimie's hand tighter. Repent! read one message in day-glo green. Someone else had written over that in blood red: Lord have mercy! and a third tagger had written below that, Obviously, God don't care.

A little further on stood several memorials. "Olivia, you were a good wife," read one. That was in white and, unlike the others, written large to fill the height of the wall for several concrete panels. The tribute had been painted with a wide brush by a tall man.

Another simply read: Andrea. Why?

Another, more hopeful message told them: The Brickyard's a safe refugee camp. Protected by good military. If you're unarmed, you get in and get medical help.

Here and there, fading pictures of missing loved ones dotted the wall and fluttered in the breeze. A phone number was listed below a picture of a stunning redheaded woman wearing cat's eye sunglasses. Heather Pritch, 29, separated at hospital. Came back for you. Will wait at train station. Tara.

The flyer, fixed to the wall with a scrap of twisted duct tape, looked like it would lose its tentative hold with the next breath of wind.

There were also a few with directions and warnings:

Todd, Meet Us At Deb's, Love Beth.

Go around Chicago!

Detroit's Burnt DOWN!

Army's taken over Tahoe. They shoot all who approach.

Another read: Michigan has militia! but it wasn't clear if that was a warning or a hopeful sign that somewhere there was order.

A more informative message read: Refugee Camps at NIAGRA FALLS has gone X. Many dead. Stay home and indoors. God bless.

Just before a gap in the wall ahead, a green winking ghoul admonished them with a pointing finger. 'We want you!' was scrawled over its grotesque head. Below a smeared wagging finger were the words: Not to Litter! Burn Your Evil Dead! It was signed, The Ungrateful Living.

At another spot, a column of numbers from one to 24 stood, each number exed out. The next number in the series jumped to 26. Beside the column were the words: Tally of Looters shot.

Jack and Anna and Oliver read each message with curiosity, growing more anxious with each step, but no one spoke.

The one that bothered Jack most was a large caricature in chalk, well-executed, of a smug-looking Edgar G. Robinson with a cigar stuck between thick lips. Jaimie recognized the face as an actor who played a gangster in movies his father loved.

The figure had a huge head atop a tiny body wearing a toga. It would have been comical except the words below it in neat purple sidewalk chalk read: Where's your deliverer now, see? Where's your deliverer now?!

Jack Spencer wanted to cry. Instead, she looked to the clear sky. She couldn't look at the messages anymore. She forced a smile and surveyed the empty road to their right. "At least all those people who left got pretty far away. I was worried the road would be jammed."

"The traffic snarls are farther south," Oliver called over his shoulder. "I haven't gone very far, but I did find a bicycle yesterday and got south as far as Oxford Street. The road is down to one narrow lane in some places but it was passable."

"I wonder where all those people went?"

"I'm betting a bunch went up north. If you want to get away from people, you go to the trees. Lots of people own cottages, or know someone who owns one. And if you live in a tiny apartment, you didn't have any room or money for building up a supply. They had to get out earlier, get somewhere where there was food. I'm sure a lot of 'em moved back in with their parents and hoped there were lots of cans of soup in the basement."

"We were so lucky to have more warning about the Sutr virus," Jack said. If not for her brother-in-law's letter, the Spencers might have been like so many others and trusted that, whatever the challenge, the established system would grind on through trouble. As they watched people spend wildly as Sutr hit, the bankers must have thought they'd get rich off the disaster and be paid later. She wondered where those bankers were now that every city was devastated by Sutr. Could the survivors start over and get back to that happy, ignorant and arrogant place? At the time, the transition seemed slow. Now piles of bodies were being burned — Jack assumed someone was still burning them, anyway. Funeral homes had been overwhelmed early, conceding they could handle no more only after their services were scheduled late into the night.

The truth was, everyone had had enough warning, but the signs were much easier to see in retrospect. It wasn't just the growth of the Sutr virus on other continents before it spread here that should have been sufficient warning. It was the obvious incompetence of those in charge, no matter how well-intentioned.

Images of the World Trade Center attack swirled through her mind. The Bush administration had been warned about Osama bin Laden, but took no steps to protect their citizens before the attack. The FBI had received warnings from flight schools of weird behavior from pilot trainees. When dangers are that clear in hindsight, somebody should have had some foresight.

The horrors of Hurricane Katrina, Hurricane Sandy and the devastation of New Orleans had delivered a strong message that was largely unheeded: when the human waste hits the ceiling fan, we're all splattered.

Only Jaimie looked back at the twisted ladder truck. He wanted to go for a ride in one of those fire trucks. He hoped they'd find one that wasn't damaged.

Broken fire trucks make everyone sad, he thought.

They came to a break in the wall. A large house stood back from the road to their left. It looked out of place, a ramshackle three-story surrounded by neighborhoods of single family dwellings. Some properties in the city's north end occupied larger, irregular lots. This area had, not so long ago, been farmland on the city's outskirts. Suburban sprawl swallowed these oversized properties. Most cornfields and orchards had been sold off to developers and divided up into a patchwork of tiny tracts for housing land. Subdivisions packed houses so tightly neighbors could hold hands across the space between the homes.

"Look at that," Douglas Oliver said.

A screen door, ripped from its hinges, lay in the yard. The large, ornate front door stood ajar. Even from their vantage point on the sidewalk, it was clear the dark wood around the frame and the doorknob had been splintered white.

"Your boyfriend take up breaking and entering as a hobby you think?" Jack said.

"Mom!" Anna elbowed her mother in the ribs.

"Look closer," the old man said. He pointed with his walking stick. Farther back on the circular driveway, a line of rats crossed the open ground from the hedge rimming the property, headed toward the house. Dozens ran across open ground in waves.

Anna's hand, already so tight around his hand, squeezed even tighter and Jaimie pulled away to loosen her grip.

She looked his way and whispered "Sorry, Ears."

He watched as an orange-yellow wave of revulsion moved up and down her spine. Anna shivered. "Gross!"

"Sutr isn't our only problem," Oliver said. He glanced at the others, "Looters, hunger, fire and packs of feral dogs and the current abominable lack of access to *Downton Abbey...*"

"Yeah, we got 99 problems," Anna agreed.

"A good thick, steak would be nice, too," Jack said.

"You're thinking of more to worry about?" Anna couldn't take her gaze off the rats.

"I was thinking what comes next," Oliver said.

"Not all the dead are getting burned or buried. And nature is...well...nature. There are other, older plagues that tend to follow untended corpses."

Yet another wave of rats followed their brothers and sisters toward the house.

They stood transfixed as another group of long brown rats scurried across the yard.

"They are the armies of the night," Oliver said, "only it's daylight and they are feeling bold."

"All our food that isn't in a can is stored in plastic," Jack said.

"The fridge and freezer are empty and warm now, but maybe we should put the food in there as an added precaution, just so we don't attract any vermin by the smell," Anna suggested.

Oliver nodded. "And maybe we'll scrounge up some rat traps or poison bait somewhere. At the mall, I'm hoping."

"That's something else that should have been on the list," Jack said, "but I never would have thought of that in a million years. Should have thought of it. After 9/11, New York had rat traps everywhere. There was a burst in the rodent population with the increased food supply. First all the abandoned restaurants, then the rubble."

"Mom! Enough!"

"I-I'm sorry," Jack wiped her brow with her forearm. "I just should have thought these worst-case scenarios through. Everything's so clear now."

"I'm old," Oliver said. "I understand. You get to a stage in life where you look backwards and you think it was pretty much inevitable that you'd wind up where you're at." He shrugged. "It's always a surprise, anyway. It's the curse of the Law of Unintended Consequences."

"That's how I feel right now," Anna said, "like we're all God's unintended consequence."

"You feel that way now," her mother said, "but someday you'll be telling your grandchildren about this trip to the mall. We're all going to get through this and it'll make a great story."

"Moving on," Anna said, taking the lead. She pulled Jaimie close to her side. "Disasters aren't adventures when you're in the middle of them," she told her brother. "People add the romance to it later so they can rationalize away the crap-your-pants scared part."

Two blocks behind them was home. Two blocks ahead was the mall.

"When I get to lie down tonight, I'm so tired, I don't care if I wake up," Oliver said.

"I want to go find Trent," Anna said.

"And I just want to sit with my husband and nurse him back to health," Jack added.

Jaimie longed for his big dictionary. He was curious to feel the sharp edges of the *i* and the soft black loops of the *bs* in the word *bubonic*. *Bubonic* was powerful. It smelled of a heavy organic rot that was sickly sweet, but the vowels felt gentle and pleasant as he formed the word in his mind.

They trudged on, ignoring the omens. They pushed their revulsion at the horrors of the wall away. They tried to forget the disgust and fear they felt at seeing hordes of greasy rats.

Each step felt like a bad investment they could not abandon. Each step felt heavier.

God's An Absent Father To A Quiet Son

The blackened mouth of the theater entrance showed there had been a fire. Empty spaces stood where glass doors had been shattered. It looked like a skull with empty eye sockets.

They thought they'd need flashlights, but there was enough light leaking through the skylights that the mall was cast in the weak slanted light of early evening.

"Shoulda come at noon," Oliver said. "It'd be brighter."

"Should have," Anna said as she stepped through an empty door frame, pulling Jaimie behind her. "At noon the advantage is with the mortals. Less sunlight? Advantage: vampires."

"Shoulda, woulda, coulda stayed home," Jack said. "Let's just get in and out quick. Oliver, you've got the bear spray. You go first, fearless leader." Jack stepped in front of her children and pointed the old man toward the mall's gloom.

Shattered glass, discarded merchandise and garbage formed the edges of a broad path through the corridors. Looting had been the aim of the first wave of invaders. As they made their way through the eerie quiet, it seemed thieves had turned to destruction.

"What do you think is left for us to steal?" Jack asked Oliver.

He shrugged. "Under these circumstances, it's never stealing. We're on a treasure hunt. Treasure doesn't always look like treasure."

The gloom deepened here and there where the skylights deserted them, but it was clear the jewellery store had been robbed clean. The gem cases were all smashed. The food court had also been sacked thoroughly.

"That's a shame," Anna said. "I could really go for a coconut smoothie right about now. Or a latte."

"I'm feeling hungry enough, some of those little plum sauce packets might do," Jack added.

Far off, there came a sound on the edge of hearing. They all stopped, heads cocked, ears straining.

We're like deer on the Discovery Channel, Jaimie thought, *just before some animal with big fangs and claws runs them down.*

They listened for a full minute before anyone broke the silence. "It's the wind," Oliver said.

Jack looked at him. "How do you figure that?"

"There must be a window broken somewhere, that's all. It's wind soughing through trees," Oliver said.

Jack shook her head and turned to Anna. "Your ears are younger. What do you hear?"

"Angel song. It's far off," she said, shivering. "They're singing a song of welcome."

"Give me a break," Oliver said.

"That's what I hear."

"Let's just go a little bit farther in," Oliver said. "It's a big mall. There's bound to be other explorers here."

"Looters," Anna said.

Oliver waved his walking stick, urging them to follow. "We'll leave a grateful note."

Glass crunched under their shoes. Twenty paces farther, they stopped and listened, hearing nothing. Then, just as they moved forward again, the sound came louder. Far off, someone sang a light tuneless song, like a harp plucked randomly, occasionally falling into running scales.

Jaimie's pant's leg caught a wire hanger which was hooked into other hangers. The discarded clothes hangers scraped together like metal strings, clattering. The echo bounced down the corridor. All went silent, as if now someone was listening for them. Jaimie was sorry the music had disappeared. It was beautiful and familiar.

Jack spotted a bookstore ahead and signalled for everyone to wait while she entered its dark mouth. She was a few feet in before she pulled a flashlight from her pocket. She wished she'd opted for the long, heavy Maglite with the line of batteries in it. It could be used as a club, but she hadn't wanted to carry more weight than was necessary.

As she played the beam up and down the bookstore shelves, she began to feel more calm. The store was largely untouched. The shelves seemed emptier than usual, but the store hadn't suffered near the damage that other mall stores had.

"Everything okay, Mom?" Anna called. Jack looked back. The corridor was well lit by an overhead skylight. She could plainly see Oliver gesticulating madly for her daughter to be quiet. Watching the old man's commanding self-possession desert him made her smile a little.

Theo would have called her feeling *schadenfreude*. She wished he was here now to help them through this expedition. Theo felt stocking up on books was just as important as laying in cans of food and bottles of water. Jack preferred to think the lack of destruction in the bookstore indicated the looters had shown the merchandise some respect. For her husband, the lack of looting here would be an ugly metaphor confirming the human race was irredeemable and largely illiterate.

"Mom?" Anna called again, pointedly ignoring Oliver.

"It's all good," she said loudly.

"Don't try to be hip, Mom. That's so old."

"I'm fine, thank you," she yelled.

She searched for maps, but that shelf stood bare. She started back toward the store entrance, thought better of it and went to the far wall. It didn't take her long to find what she was looking for.

"Turn around, guys," Jack told her children when she emerged from the blackness. She unzipped their backpacks. "Graduation presents," she said. "It's time Jaimie read *Catcher* and Anna, for you, I think you're old enough to read *Portnoy's Complaint*."

"I read *Catcher in the Rye* already," Anna said, "but *Portnoy's Complaint*? Isn't that an old person's book?"

"It's the funniest book you'll ever read," Jack said flatly. "Your father will be pleased."

"I'm probably way past the time when I should have been introduced to it then," Anna said in her wry, I-am-not-a-child tone.

An image of her daughter with Trent came up unbidden. *She's a healthy, pretty18 and Trent's a good-looking idiot,* Jack thought. *Yes, she'd probably been protecting Anna too long.*

Two of Anna's schoolmates had unplanned pregnancies. They'd had the condom talk when her daughter had turned fifteen, but Jack had hoped fervently that Anna had not used any of the box of condoms she handed her. Anna had uttered a disgusted, comforting "*Ew!*", which pleased Jack. She promised her daughter she would never count the number of condoms in the box.

Such conventions and passages seemed a trite, almost silly thing now. The new world was born with the Sutr virus and safe, prolonged childhoods were at an end.

"If the book club is finished its meeting, could we get on with the fight for survival and all that?" Oliver said. "If it's not too inconvenient?"

"Somebody needs to read a funny book," Jack said.

"Sorry. Almost dying of Sutr must have made me cranky."

They picked their way forward. The glass displays were all broken but someone had gone at the mess with a push broom. Farther on, the shards of glass had been pushed to the side and piled out of the way.

Most stores were empty. Racks and shelving littered the floor. At each empty doorway, they peered in and shone their lights to see if there was anything worth daring the dark.

"It's worse than when I was here the last time," Oliver whispered to Jack. "We should leave soon. Feels like a shrine to conspicuous consumption has become a tomb."

The quartet doubled back, Anna still holding Jaimie's hand and pulling him along at the rear. Several times they stopped to listen. The rise and fall of the voice did not come again.

Oliver motioned for them to move faster. However, Jack darted into a kitchen supply store. They heard her shift something out of the way. A crash and a clang.

"Mom!' Anna called. "Is everything okay?"

"Fine!" A moment later, Jack emerged from the store holding a frying pan in each hand. One was small and light. The other was a heavy iron skillet. "Found it under a display," she said. "Almost missed it, but the handle was sticking out."

They moved forward again, passing a dead fountain. The clothing stores had been sacked. Jack turned Anna around and put the small pan in her backpack. The big skillet wouldn't fit easily. Jack felt its heft and opted to keep it as a weapon.

They came upon another dark store. Jack motioned for the group to stay at the storefront and disappeared. While Oliver kept a wary eye on the corridor ahead and behind them, Anna watched the bobbing circle of light play over the store's debris.

The shop was narrow and deep. Before she walked more than ten feet, Jack's feet slipped out from under her and she was on her back. The flashlight rolled and spun away to her right. She had a firm grasp of the iron skillet and it made a formidable clang against the floor as she went down. She arched her back and looked toward the entry point again.

Anna, Jaimie and Oliver stood, upside down and far away. The breath had been knocked from her, but only for a moment.

"Mom? Mom!"

When she caught her breath, Jack assured them she was well. She leaned on an empty display as she got to her feet. "Hell of a lot of trouble to find a good sweater or two."

"I shopped here not long ago," Anna said.

"Things change," Oliver said, looking away, searching for...what?

Jack realized the old man had not moved, or even looked in her direction, when she'd fallen. Instead, he had kept watch. Jack knew the old man was nervous, but even Jaimie had looked her way when the skillet banged on the floor. Jaw tight, she recovered the flashlight.

Despite all he'd said and done, Douglas Oliver didn't care enough about her. This little expedition had taught her that. When they got back, she'd sit down with Theo and discuss whether they could risk taking their old neighbor along with them if they had to run.

"I slipped on a plastic shopping bag," she announced.

"Grab it," Oliver said.

She found a pile of them behind the counter. She stuffed a few in a pocket and, when that proved inadequate, tucked the rest under her belt. She played the light over the floor. There must have been a fight. There were shreds of fabric here and there, as if looters had actually had a tug of war and T-shirts were the rope.

Jack wanted to turn around and return to the light, but she thought she might find something in a change room. Fallen shelving made the floor uneven. She almost lost her footing again a couple of times.

Jack directed the flashlight beam at her feet, not comprehending what she was seeing at first. Jack turned her light upward and understood. "People ripped out the ceiling tiles!"

"Why would anyone waste energy doing that?" Anna called back.

"Because they could," Oliver said.

Jack looked back, feeling foolish for staying so long. In a store where even the ceiling tiles were ripped out, she was lucky to find discarded plastic bags for salvage. She was about to back out when the smell hit her. She sniffed the air like an animal, searching not just to identify the smell, but to find a direction. It was coming from the back of the store.

She moved deeper into the darkness. She knew it would be better just to turn around now, but what if someone had a cache of food? Among maggot-riddled and stinking waste, there might be a useful can of tuna or salmon.

The closer she got, the less likely that seemed, but she had come this far, so what was a few more steps? Perhaps that same smell would have repelled other searchers, so they missed something she would not. However, the closer she got to the source of the stench, the less it was about finding food. Curiosity took over. She needed to *know*.

A bank of change rooms lined the rear wall. A steel door that must lead to a storage room or an office stood to her right. She knocked twice and, suddenly feeling silly at the pre-pandemic gesture, put the end of the flashlight in her mouth and yanked on the handle several times. Locked.

There might be useful things in the office, but she moved on. A cross bar from a coat rack might give her the leverage she needed to crank that steel door open.

There was no one in there waiting to be rescued. She was sure there was at least one decaying body behind that door. Maybe more.

Jack thought of Sigourney Weaver's character, Ripley, from *Aliens*. By some unlikely Hollywood miracle, the hero of the movie discovered a little girl who had survived a massacre by evil, rampaging monster aliens.

There must be heroes in every disaster. There must be children who survive while everyone else around them dies horribly. Real life is not so mercifully scripted, she knew. She thought of Nature's wrath leaving dead children in trees after a mile-wide tornado ripped through Oklahoma.

After she spoke with her husband about Douglas Oliver and made sure everyone was fed, she planned to curl up with her Bible and study by the light of her flashlight. Maybe there was no making sense of the Sutr plague, but Jack needed to try again. She still hoped for solace.

Jack checked the change rooms for discarded clothes. Something that hadn't fit someone else might fit Anna or herself. Jack smiled at her own naiveté, at how hard old habits died. She was in the wreck of a women's clothing store and she was still thinking that what she found there could only serve Anna or herself. On a cold night this winter, sitting around a fire, neither Jaimie nor Theo would object to the warmth gained from another sweater, even if it had big girly flowers on it.

The first change room was empty. The second booth was not. She kicked the flimsy door back with a bang and the stench hit her in the nose, as if the disturbed air currents mixed and stirred risen death.

Advantage: vampires, Anna had said.

Jack reflexively held her mask tighter to her mouth with the hand that held the skillet, lightly conking herself in the temple. *Ripley wouldn't do that,* she thought.

Heat rose to her cheeks. She felt incredibly stupid banging around the back of a deserted store with bodies in the back. Plastic bags couldn't be worth this.

After this, Jack knew she'd never return to the hulk of a mall. The new place to shop would be the homes of the dead. They'd undoubtedly passed hundreds of empty homes behind the wall. In each home, there were plenty of closets with more clothes than they could wear in a lifetime, let alone carry. This trip had been Douglas Oliver's idea and now she realized how stupid an errand it was.

The thing on the floor (*this corpse, this poor, abandoned husk,* Jack thought) had been a woman who favored wearing red pumps to a looting. The skirt was long and matronly. Jack thought she spotted a clot of varicose veins where the skirt rode up high on a blue-gray thigh. It could be one of her neighbors or the mother of someone at her kids' school.

Curiosity pulled again. She let the flashlight beam play up the body slowly, steeling herself for what she might see. This had been someone once. How had she died? Who was she?

In the next moment she was to learn the lesson again: pre-pandemic thinking did not apply anymore. How this woman had died, her identity, were heavy concerns in the old world. Now it was knowledge to be avoided. The lesson came hard: Jack saw the pool of crusted blood. *So much blood.*

Then she thought she saw the head move.

The thing's eyes opened. Bright yellow, wild eyes.

Nowhere To Hide, Few Places To Run

They heard a bang and a short shout from within the clothing store.

"Mom!"

Anna let go of Jaimie's hand and searched for her flashlight, cursing herself. She should have had it out and ready. She should have gone in with her mother.

Before she could pull the flashlight out of her front pocket — her jeans were too tight — Jack burst out of the darkness with her hand over her mask. She was gasping for air as if she had just risen from deep water. She leaned against Anna.

"It's okay! I'm alright!" She pulled her mask away from her mouth to pull in fresh air. After a few more long drags to fill her lungs, she readjusted the mask over her mouth again. "At first, I thought someone had taken a dump in a change room," she said. "There's a body in there."

"That's awful," Anna said.

Jack shook her head vigorously and swallowed hard. "— and a cat!"

Her mother's eyes told all Anna needed to know. Her eyes widened as she guessed what her mother had seen. "That's much worse," Anna said.

"Was it Sutr?" Oliver asked.

"I don't think so...but I hope cats get the virus. Every one of them."

They were silent for a time after that and surveyed each store more quickly. The carnage seemed complete. Overturned kiosks littered the centre of the corridors.

"I guess people really thought they'd need skin lotion from the dead sea," Anna said, pointing at a sacked kiosk.

A scatter of cell phones littered the floor. "And people finally got some vengeance on their cell providers," Oliver added, poking a pile of the phones with the end of his walking stick.

"Couldn't those phones be useful? I mean, the network isn't working now, but it might later, right?" Anna asked.

Kind silence met her naive suggestion.

Douglas Oliver bent to look under a Cookie Hut kiosk. He found nothing in a sealed package and sighed. "Anna, the only central service that's still intact, the one that requires the least maintenance in the short run, is water. I'd guess we're a long way from having cell phone service back up. Whatever services that might return are no doubt prioritized by the government. They don't want us talking to each other on cell phones, I'll bet."

"What government would *that* be?" a young man's voice came from above. "You see any government here?"

The search party craned their necks but saw no one. Someone on the second floor moved around, sneakers squeaking on the tile, but they couldn't spot him.

"Who's there?" Oliver said, his hand tensing on his canister of bear spray. He held it up in a gesture of defense and then let it go slack at his side, feeling foolish. The spray was no use at this distance. If he tried to spray up at such a steep angle, he'd give himself a dose of the stuff.

Jack waved her children back toward the wall, out from under the second-floor balcony. They were slow to comply, still searching for a face to go with the voice. Frustrated, Jack jumped up and down to draw their attention. "In case he decides to drop a couch from Sears on top of us, *move!*"

"Who is that?" Anna called.

"Mallrats!" the man replied. "The only government here, baby!"

There was a rustling and more footsteps. Jaimie glimpsed a beautiful young black girl, maybe aged five, with a fall of curly hair framing her sweet, oval face. She looked afraid. Unseen hands pulled her away from the balcony railing and it grew quiet again.

"Hello?" Jack called. "We're not looking for trouble!"

There came a murmur from above. The high arched ceilings above acted as a whispering gallery. "If you're taking things from the mall, you're taking something from us and that's trouble!"

Someone stomped their feet to a beat. Others joined in. The beat started slow but quickly built to a crescendo. It sounded like an angry platoon of crazed soldiers.

"I think we should run before I pee my pants," Anna said.

Jack stepped out from the wall to show herself. Oliver waved her back but she held up a hand.

The drumbeat of heels on tile suddenly stopped. "I'm unarmed!" Jack called up.

Oliver gritted his teeth and backed away, headed for the exit. Jack signalled for the old man to wait.

"How many are you?" the young man's voice came again from a different spot, a little farther away.

"Four!"

Oliver frowned at Jack's honesty.

Another murmur hummed, followed by sounds of running feet receding from the upper balcony. A moment later, the pounding feet and shouting returned, this time on the ground floor. They came in a rush, five from in front, two cutting off the way to the exit. None of the Mallrats wore masks.

Most carried weapons fashioned from sticks. One crept from behind holding a bow, the arrow poised to fly. All were teenagers. Above them, a young man appeared with the little black girl in his arms.

Oliver held up the can of bear retardant, though the kid with the bow and arrow was outside the range of the canister's spray. The kid's weapon was a large compound bow, which could be very effective in putting an arrow through Oliver's chest or brain, if the kid was steady and practiced. The old man's eyes locked on those of the archer. The kid had the bowstring pulled all the way back, yet he didn't appear to shake at all under the strain. Oliver stepped behind Jaimie, using him as a human shield.

The archer grinned and said, "That's cold, dawg, but my arrow will go through you *both*!"

Jack put her hands up in an openhanded, please-sherriff-don't-shoot gesture. She stepped in front of her son.

Oliver scowled and barked, "Jacquelin — "

"Shut up, Oliver!" Jack said.

"Yeah, shut up, Oliver!" the man standing above them said. "This is Mallrat territory. You shouldn'ta come here."

"Is your mom okay?" Jack called up to the young man.

"Wha — ?"

"I haven't seen you since you were much younger, but occasionally I see your Mom around...at school."

His eyes narrowing. "I don't know you!"

"I've got a girl about your age," Jack said. "If you're from the neighborhood, we've probably met at the same playgrounds. Have I seen you in a school play? Or at church maybe?"

He put the girl down and stepped close to the railing to look closely at Jack. He was a handsome fellow, though he wore microdermal implanted silver studs over his left eye and a Chinese tattoo on his neck. "Do I look like I was in a school play, bitch?"

"Every kid is in the school play when they're in elementary school," Jack said evenly. "You go to Jefferson? Or Ginsberg Private?"

"Ha!" he said. "You're bluffing."

Jack shrugged helplessly. "I don't know your name. I'm going to guess either Chad or Spider. How should I know? You do look familiar, though."

"It's David. My name is David. And you're starting to really piss me off." He squinted down at her.

She cursed herself. Chad? Spider? She could at least have tried a common name, like Joe, for instance, though no one his age was called Joe anymore, either. In a moment, she was going to tell the kids to run. Oliver would be the slowest moving target, but he was the one with the bear spray. He was the one so willing to sacrifice her son. She would sacrifice the old man. Jack was ready to gamble that the gang wouldn't be so organized as to catch her or her kids with the old man drawing fire.

"What's my mother's name then?"

Jack shrugged again. She glanced at the others. Many held hockey sticks, but she took in each face, looking from one to another. Most looked almost as scared as she was. Almost. Some looked happy and excited.

"Are you bluffing me, old lady?"

"Who are you talking to? I'm not old!"

The group grinned and a couple laughed out loud.

"Just a sec. I'm coming down." The sound of wheels on tile whizzed away and after a couple of minutes, he was coming to them. The little girl stayed by the balcony rail staring down at Jack.

The young man rolled up on a skateboard. At first, Jack thought David was going to knock her over. At the last moment, he jumped off the board and jabbed at the back end with his forefoot. The skateboard popped up into his arms. He held it up like he was about to bash her in the face.

David scowled. "I don't know you, and more important, you don't know me or my moms. You tried to play me! You think I'm stupid?"

"Are you sure you don't know me?" Jack offered. "I know a lot of people…and you lost your glasses, didn't you?"

A girl in the closing circle tittered. She carried a large mahogany piano leg with nails sticking out of it.

"Don't mess with me, lady."

"Watch out," the boy with the bow called, taking a step closer. "She might turn you over her knee and spank you." The group laughed again.

Oliver stepped away from Jaimie, closer to Jack and the group's leader. Seeing his movement, the Mallrats moved closer still, holding their weapons higher.

"Step back!" Oliver yelled. He held his walking stick out like a lance, warning them, sweeping it back and forth. Two larger boys moved left and right to get the old man between them.

Anna dashed forward to her mother's side and Jaimie followed slowly, looking up at the glass in the high ceiling. By the slant of the light, he thought it would be dinner time soon. He was getting hungry.

The archer ran forward, making sure he wouldn't miss.

"Stop it!"

Everyone froze at the clear, high voice. It was the little black girl.

"Stop!" she repeated and pointed at Jaimie. "I know him! He goes to my school! He goes to my school!"

"You *sure*, baby girl? He's too old to go to your school," David said. His hands were tight on his skateboard. He still looked as ready as ever to attack. "What's that kid's name, Baby Girl?"

In her strange high voice, the girl answered, "Retard,"

Except for Jack, Anna, Jaimie and David, the group laughed. Some nearly collapsed in laughter.

"Baby, you know Daddy doesn't like that word."

"I didn't say it," she said. "The other kids said it. They're mean to him." She pointed at Jaimie. "He's nice. He never hurt nobody."

"You mean he never hurt anybody," David corrected the girl.

"That's what I said."

"Lots of people are mean that way," Jack said. "Your little girl is very cute."

"Yeah."

"I'm sure you wouldn't want her to see you bash me in the face."

David's grip on his skateboard relaxed, though the boys circling Oliver weren't letting their guard down. Sensing his distraction, the young archer moved up behind Oliver and placed the tip of his arrow at the base of his neck. "My arm is getting tired, old man. Put that stick down. And that other thing, too."

The bear spray canister hit the tile with a clang and, rather than drop his walking stick, Oliver leaned heavily on it and he put his free hand to his chest, breathing hard.

"Oh, great," he grimaced. "One way or another, you bunch will be murderers when I drop dead." Oliver began to pant.

Two boys with hockey sticks stepped away from him and even the steely-eyed archer faltered, giving the bowstring slack and letting the arrowhead slip from the old man's neck to point to the floor.

David gave the archer an encouraging nod of approval and turned to look up at his daughter. "How is Ret — um...how is that boy nice, Baby?"

"He's never been mean to me. The same kids who are mean to him are mean t'me."

"They're mean because they're jealous," Anna said. Everyone turned to her. She stepped in front of her mother, close to David. "I never knew her name, but I know who she is. I pick up my brother from his school. He takes special classes from a teacher who works with kids like him," Anna said. "I pick my brother up every day. All the moms who pick up their kids at the playground call her the singing girl."

David nodded. "Yeah, my Baby Girl sings all the time. She's going to be a star some day. When this is all over, I'm going to be able to finance her career and no record company will own us and we'll go on tour. She'll remind the world what beauty is. She'll be our opening act." His face took on a dreamy look. "It's gonna be sweet to be a rich man. The toilets are backed up now, but after plague days are done? It's going to be sweet. Fewer people, fewer hassles."

Oliver's face was red and he was beginning to shake. "Excuse me..." he gasped. "Dying here." He pointed at his chest. His jaw worked up and down but no sound came out.

The archer stepped around him, looked in his face and kicked the walking stick out from under him. Oliver collapsed to the ground, landing on his face. "Ouch!" he cried out.

"Give it up, old man," the archer said. "Nobody's buying it."

Oliver looked up at him and a lopsided grin crawled across his face. "Worth a try," he said. "Not long ago that act would have gotten me an ambulance."

A tough-looking girl of about fifteen with purple streaks through her long hair stepped forward. She held two uneven lengths of rebar. "So you know Baby and Baby recognizes your retard brother from school. So what? Trespassers will be prosecuted. We said that, remember? This is Mallrat territory! What's it worth if we don't defend it?"

"Shut up, Sonya!' David said. "Everybody just chill. Brass-balled momma here is right. I'm not going to scar Baby for life by, y'know, scarring anybody for life. What's wrong with you?"

Sonya retreated to the edge of the group in disgust and dug out a cigarette pack from her pocket.

David turned back to Jack, squinting at her again. "You really tried to bluff me. That's funny."

"It worked once when some kids were about to throw water balloons at me. They were a lot younger than you, though," Jack said.

David laughed and nodded. "Okay, Brassy. I hereby grant you a pass. Get out of here, and tell everyone you meet to stay out of the mall. Tell them it's Mallrat territory."

Anna stepped closer to the gang's leader. "We'll tell everybody we meet there are at least a hundred of you in here if you want — "

"That would be good."

"For a price," Anna said. "We're not leaving with just a bunch of plastic bags. If you want fewer intruders, you should put up a sign. Seems to me you need someone to go out there and say how badass you are so the legend spreads. The name Mallrats is nothing but a movie unless somebody spreads your word, David."

Jack and David looked at her with new respect. "Your daughter, huh?" He looked Anna up and down and gave her a friendly smile. "It's cool. I got a soft spot for hotness."

He turned to Jaimie, stepping close to study his face. He stepped back almost immediately. It felt like he'd walked into a forcefield. "Uh...okay...I got an idea. Follow me."

Zombified, Carrier Or In The Ground?

Dusk closed the day quickly as birds searched out their nests for the night. The Mallrats leader escorted Douglas Oliver and the Spencers out of the mall. Baby Girl's angelic voice followed them out, echoing after them until they reached the door to the parking lot.

The fires to the south seemed much closer in the encroaching dark. Fires threw orange light to the sky, mimicking city shine.

Jack, Anna and Jaimie each wore new hiking boots. David had refused to give Oliver anything and the gang confiscated his bear spray.

There'd been so little of value where Jack had searched because anything useful or edible had been moved to the mall's second floor and was guarded by the Mallrats. They squeezed everything they wanted into Target. The store was their warehouse and their fortress.

For all the danger, the hiking boots seemed a small prize. David had decided their public relations efforts were worth three pairs of hiking boots, or maybe it was just a demonstration of good will for Baby Girl's sake.

David put a gentle hand on Jack's shoulder. "Hey, Brass Momma. I have to tell you something. We've heard stuff. We hear there are looters, like gangs of them in the 'burbs. They might look military, but they're looters. Have you seen them out there in the wilds?"

"Gangs? No. We have heard gunshots at night sometimes."

"Watch out," the young man said. "A lot of people are dead, but everybody who *ought* to be dead isn't yet."

David gave them an elaborate bow and paused to endow Anna with a smile and a wink. "You're welcome to come back, by the way. Hotness is always welcome."

He backed up, and, before he turned away and disappeared into the mall, he nodded to Jaimie.

Jaimie nodded back.

Oliver had been silent since his heart attack ruse had failed. He could contain himself no longer. "That wasn't smart! That wasn't brave! That was lucky! You never tell an enemy you are unarmed."

Jack shouldered her pack. "You're right."

"My god! I — " Oliver began.

"I said, you're right. What more do you want?"

"I want my bear spray back! It was the only weapon I had that worked at any distance."

"It was our can to lose, not yours."

"We've got a deal. You share everything with me and I help keep you alive," Oliver said.

"Okay, so you just lost one-fifth of a can of bear repellant. Nobody likes a whiner, Douglas. You seem to already have forgotten that you used my son as a shield. You've forgotten. I won't. When we get back to the house, we have some things to work out."

Oliver started to reply. Jack cut him off. "And if I hadn't tried to make friends, we'd be dead. How many of them did you think you could get with the bear spray before they killed all of us?"

The old man did not answer her question. He moved on quickly to his plans. "The only reason he let you have the hiking boots was they couldn't possibly wear every pair they had. We should get some guns and come back and take this place. That's exactly what we should do. They're just a bunch of kids."

"Right!" Anna said. "They're just a bunch of kids trying to survive, so leave them alone."

"We made a deal with them, Douglas," Jack added. "I got this peachy bunch of plastic bags, too, so quid pro quo and yay, me." She nodded to her children to follow her and began the trek home.

"Shopping is much more complicated than it used to be," Anna said.

"Someday there will be more to life than this." Jack hoped she sounded more sure than she felt.

"And we'll be able to say we knew Baby Girl before she was a star," Anna said.

"When her father threatened to bash in our heads to protect his looted stash," Oliver added. "It's a sweet, inspiring story. Makes me glad to be alive."

As they walked back down Fanshawe Park Road, the hulk of the abandoned ladder truck loomed up, now black in the deepening darkness.

"It shouldn't get this dark so fast."

"It's the smoke," Jack said.

"I can smell it now," Anna said. "It's blocking out the sun."

"The wind shifted again. It was bound to happen," Oliver said. "We might have to bug out tonight."

"Yeah, well, we'll see about the 'we' part, Douglas. I'll talk to Theo about your place in our matrix."

Jack made an unconscious decision and led them closer to the fire engine's wreck this time. They made their way down the middle of the street rather than walk past the graffitied wall. They couldn't read the messages without using their flashlights, but none of the expedition felt the urge to look at the wall again. The messages to and from the dead seemed a curse and an omen.

None of them said anything as they neared the broken truck.

Every ruin is a warning of what's to come for everything, Jack thought. That sounded like something her husband would say. It was as if Theo's ghost walked beside her, whispering his obsessive thoughts about entropy.

She answered his thought: *We've been married too long, sweetie. We know each other so well, we don't even need to speak anymore.*

Though they knew the truck's color in daylight, the darkness was so deep now they couldn't see the engine's red paint. They had forgotten how dark the world was without xenon gas streetlights and the ambient glow of a million burning bulbs.

Jack touched the truck's cool metal with her palm as she passed. "If we could find these guys...if we could get one company of firefighters together, we'd all be okay, you know that? Touch the truck for luck." *Like a talisman from an ancient world,* she thought.

"Like the opposite of walking under a ladder, huh?" Anna suggested.

A Latin phrase came to Jaimie. He'd studied it that afternoon. It was: *anguis in herba,* meaning *hidden danger.*

It was only four blocks, but it seemed much farther in the dark. They moved slowly, following Jack's bobbing circle of light.

A dozen pairs of eyes followed their progress — wary and fierce — unseen and circling, closer and closer. The ragged creatures, drooling and impatient, ached with hunger. Only meat could slake them now.

Wolves Howl Louder When Food's Around

Misericordia Drive awaited them like a dark maw. The wind picked up and pushed them back, as if warning them away from home.

As they rounded the corner to the drive, Jaimie broke away from Anna, shot forward and grabbed the old man's walking stick, pulling hard. Oliver instinctively resisted. Jack wrapped her arms around her son's shoulders, pulling him back.

"What is it, Jaimie?"

"Yeah," Oliver said. "What is it, Lassie? Did Timmy fall down the well?"

The boy pointed, not to Douglas Oliver's house, but to his own. Flashlight beams moved back and forth through the Spencer's windows. Strangers were in their home.

The salvage party had almost walked into the middle of their street. They moved to the side, sticking close to the shadow of a high hedge, to get a closer look. The Spencer's couch was stuck half way out the living room's shattered window.

"They didn't see us." Jack touched her son's head and thanked him. The boy ignored her, peering instead toward the darkness behind them.

Anna crept forward, touched her mother's shoulder and pointed beyond their house to the Bendham house. Marjorie Bendham stood in her front yard. She carried a large flashlight and paced. Bently stood in the Spencer's driveway, talking to the old woman. They couldn't hear their exchange.

A moment later, a man hooted and laughed as another began to howl like a wolf baying at the moon. Jack was reminded of the westerns her husband was so fond of, the ones where, at the beginning of the movie, the sheriff has been shot dead and chaos reigns at the local saloon. "Bently's finally come back with friends."

Friends and fiends and one little r, Jaimie thought. *Funny how close those words are. Could that be someone's etymological joke? A little nod to how easy it is for one thing to become another thing entirely?* When he got back to Oliver's house, he intended to go look up the word origins of *friends* and *fiends*.

The man who bayed like a wolf howled again, louder and crazier this time.

There were, the boy thought, many examples of language quirks in English. Irony, for instance, means that what one says is the opposite of what one means. The idea was ludicrous to Jaimie, and much more alarming than strange men wandering his home.

"What are they *doing*?" Anna asked.

"So far, stealing stuff that can be replaced, I suppose. Your Dad must be going crazy with worry. Thank God he's safe on Oliver's couch," Jack said. *Well, I assume he's safe, the ugly thought came unbidden.*

"We have to get back to Oliver's house and let Dad know we're okay. We'll go through the backyards," Anna said.

"Assert, engage, attack," Jack agreed. She covered her flashlight with her fingers. In the faint glow, Jack could just make out the faces of her children. Anna looked terrified. She saw Jaimie's face in profile and envied him. He had no anger or dismay. His mind was busy elsewhere, wrestling with what mysteries she could not guess.

No. That was unfair. He'd heard the men from half a block away, seen the flashlights and he'd known it meant danger. He'd warned them. Her son was still a mystery to her. However, under the stress of plague days, she'd seen more glimmers of what might be going on in her son's head than she had through all the mundanity of their lives before Sutr came to town. Jaimie's wiring might be pathological from a clinical perspective, but he was more functional than she'd ever expected in this crisis. That was good because, with home invaders threatening their safety, she needed Jaimie to be more than the strange, distracted kid with a book in his hand.

Jack inhaled deeply to quell her growing fear and anger. She turned off the flashlight so she could take her children's hands in hers. "Stick close behind me."

Oliver rose from a crouch and shook his head. "I'm too old to be running around climbing fences," he said. "I'm going to have a chat with these fellows," he said.

"That's crazy!" Anna said. "Bently is with them. They'll kill you."

Before Oliver could answer, Jack flashed her light into his face, making him turn away squinting. "I don't think they will," she said. "They're his friends."

"Not friends!" Oliver said.

"But?"

"They work for me," he said.

"Knew it," Jack said.

Anna was stuck halfway over a fence and pushing through shrubbery. They couldn't see her face but they could hear her voice tremble. "What's going on, Mom?"

"Jaimie and I saw Oliver talking to that guy."

"This doesn't make sense," Anna said.

"It might," Jack said.

"When were you going to tell me?" Anna asked her mother. The girl's voice was an edged weapon.

"When I knew for sure what it might mean." Jack kept her flashlight beam in the old man's eyes. "What about it, Oliver?"

"In that hooligan David's parlance, you might think I'm 'playing' you. I'm playing them. This isn't a game. It's about survival."

"Ours or just yours?"

The old man paused a moment too long before answering.

"I think I have my answer," Jack said. She took Jaimie's hand and pulled him toward the fence. "We've got to go, kids."

"I've got a deal with them," Oliver said. "I'm using *them*. I've got this under control. Don't be such a child! This is good news for you."

"If it was good news for us," Jack replied, "you would have told us before you had to."

"They're gathering stuff for me. I pay them from my jewelry stash. You think you're going to survive the winter here without dealing with the black market? You think that little garden of yours is going to provide for all of us through the winter? The black market is the only market there is! Jacqueline, don't be an idiot! I'm the ground floor. I'm Macy's! I'm Sears! I'm the new Wal-Mart. By spring, if you want to get anything, it's going to be through me. The people who survive this are going to be the ones who adapt early. I am *it!*"

"You lied to us, Oliver." Jack groped for the fence and moved to Anna's dark outline, pushing her over the top. She didn't want to risk the flashlight anymore.

"I was going to tell you once things settled down," Oliver said. "I haven't met all of Bently's group yet, but they need a leader. I can organize things so it's better for everybody."

They couldn't see his face but his voice sounded wounded, desperate.

"If Bently's on your side, why get us to move into your house?"

"Because you're my family. Everybody needs one and I needed— I *need* you on my side! Loners don't make it in a disaster. No one who tries to get through this alone will survive. I've seen disasters before! Jacqueline, don't do this!"

Anna was over the fence. She pulled back cedar branches so Jack and Jaimie could climb over easily. Jaimie paused to smell the sweet cedar and Jack nudged him forward. When he moved, she swung her leg over the wooden fence. A splinter dug into her palm as she tumbled after her son.

"You want a family, Oliver? There they are down the street, looting my house. You lied to me so I can't trust you. Show me I can trust you, Oliver. Go prove we're your tribe and not those screaming idiots."

Jack pulled her children across the dark backyard toward the old man's house. Theo would be worried. It occurred to her that her husband might even try to stop the looters, which wouldn't be smart even if he weren't so sick.

Oliver called after them. He was saying something to her, calling her name, but all she heard was the blood pounding in her ears as she ran blind, as fast as she dared.

A high fence marked the perimeter of the next yard but there was a gate and it was unlocked. Anna began to speak but Jack shushed her daughter. They were just three houses and across the street from the men rifling their house. A hundred miles would have been too close. Jack began to pant as her heart slammed against her breastbone. She hurried her children, holding hands, moving three abreast. *As if we're all kids,* Jack thought, *like we should be skipping.*

It was Jaimie who jerked his mother back, narrowly avoiding a fall into the pool at their feet. They skirted the edge of a large piano-shaped pool and, as one, stopped to listen.

A man yelled at someone, though the words weren't clear. The wind was stronger now, pushing away the words and swallowing them before the message could reach the trio.

"Is that Douglas?" Jack asked in a whisper.

"No," said Anna.

The wind pushed clouds back from the moon. It emerged at their feet first, a white globe reflected in the pool. They looked up at the full moon, born from columns of smoke. Jack cursed under her breath. The moonless night had been to their advantage. Advantage: vampires.

Light from the full moon bathed them white. Advantage: werewolves.

Jack could see her children's faces easily. Jaimie's gaze was fixated, up and away, on the racing clouds, or perhaps, on the moonscape. With a stab of annoyance, Jack wished Anna's boyfriend was here. Trent was a football player, and strong. Who was on her side but her girl, a very ill husband and the mostly mute son she loved but couldn't reach? Maybe Douglas Oliver would be of help, but probably not. The old man might be selling them out, pointing to his house and saying to the wolfmen, "Take your prisoners and do what you want."

Fresh moonlight made Anna's face luminous, reminding Jack how much her daughter resembled her. Anna had Theo's mouth but her eyes were her mother's. In this light, it was easy to imagine she was looking at her younger self, shivering and terrified.

Maybe that was why she was so much closer to Anna than Jaimie. Her daughter was easier to read. She wasn't thinking about their furniture and broken things. She remembered the lust and animal danger in Bently's gaze when he'd ogled Anna. Jack was sure Anna contemplated that now, too.

Dark clouds obscured the moon again and Jack went cold. The man across the street yelled in short, unintelligible barks.

"Did you catch any of that?" Jack asked.

Anna shook her head. "But the tone — "

"What?"

"Whoever it is, it sounds like he's giving orders."

"And it's not Oliver," Jack said.

Theo was just two houses away, but she forced her children to slow down, to move carefully and stay unseen. Jack had to know the way was clear. She had to make sure the marauders hadn't gotten to Oliver's house, and to Theo, first.

They were in the backyard next to Oliver's house when another howl rose. It was close and it made them freeze again, searching for the source as if they could see in the dark by sheer force of will. It could have been a wolf, but Jack was almost sure it was a man. Or a crazed man who had become a wolf. The thought sucked the energy out of her. If she hadn't been holding her children so close, she might have fallen down.

Until now, Jack hadn't realized that Jaimie had Douglas Oliver's walking stick. Jaimie pointed at the sky and the white moon emerged again from the roiling cloud cover as if called. It was as if her son held a magic wand.

The howl came again from the direction of their ravaged home. It was a man, but he sounded more animal with each gleeful bay.

"Advantage: maniacs," Anna said.

"Sh!" Jack searched the dark, but she couldn't see an enemy.

Jaimie looked into the darkness behind them. He watched creeping energies beyond a chain-link fence. The auras connoted hunger, but on a scale he'd never seen.

Jack touched her son's shoulder, wondering if he saw something behind them she did not.

Animals followed them, but Jaimie felt curiosity, not fear, and so the predators kept their distance. The animals were wary. They sensed he was different from the other humans and, since his kind was unknown, they took him for something dangerous.

Another long howl from the crazed man broke clear on the crisp air. Jaimie thought of the book in his backpack. The Latin for what he heard was: *lupus est homo homini. Man is a wolf to man.*

Jack shook Jaimie's shoulder, urging him to move.

The boy turned his head toward his mother, but he did not search out her eyes. She followed his gaze to the moon again. "Lyconic," he said dreamily.

Under different circumstances, Jack would praise her son for speaking. Instead, she said, "Oh, for God's sake, shut up, Jaimie!"

Take Your Reward For The Struggle Of Life

Oliver walked up to the Spencer house wishing the Mallrats hadn't taken the bear spray from him. Jaimie had taken his walking stick and he missed the feel of that in his hand, too. Bently wasn't supposed to show his hand yet, but the man was stupid. Oliver was confident he could talk the little rat man back under his thumb again and Bently would thank him for the privilege.

Though the old man didn't know these new men with Bently, in a crisis, people need leadership. Oliver was sure he was the man to claim that leadership and keep it. He'd told lesser men what to do his whole life. Tonight would be no different. The key was to show them they were joining him, not the other way around. That was the way to stay in the driver's seat.

This was a negotiation and the dynamics of civilization weren't an ancient lost memory. He was dealing with people who had been shopping at a grocery store (instead of the houses of the dead) just a few, short weeks ago.

As the old man stepped closer, the headlights of two Jeeps, both military-issue, flared on. They were parked on the lawn, pointed at the Spencer house. A third vehicle sat idling in the driveway. Oliver's vision was poor at long distances at night. He cursed his age. Still, he strode forward, looking jaunty and confident.

A young guy in a white T-shirt and Bermuda shorts sat on the half of the Spencer's couch on the outside of the window casement. "Hey, Bently!" he called. "Your boyfriend's here!"

As he got closer, Oliver slowed. A police car, with a box trailer attached to it, was backed up to Marjorie Bendham's garage. The trailer was red and yellow and adorned with a fancy calligraphic font that read: *Mere Entertainments.*

Marjorie Bendham looked lost. Her vision must have been worse than his own because she hadn't spotted him yet. A young man in a muscle shirt loaded the back of the trailer. They were stealing Douglas Oliver's inventory from Mrs. Bendham's garage.

"Hey!" Oliver yelled. "Hey! What do you think you're doing with all my food?"

Bently walked up to him, a rifle in his hands. Oliver had dealt with the little man many times. He had no fear of him. The old man had even talked him into taking a shot in the jaw with a bag of canned soup to gain the Spencers' trust. He was confident he could deal with the man right up until Bently slugged him in the gut with the butt of the rifle.

Oliver collapsed, gasping for breath. Something felt very wrong in his rib cage, like there was too much movement there. A burn spread around his back as he gasped for air.

Marjorie Bendham stepped closer, but did not cross her property line, as if an invisible fence kept her back.

His eyes wide, Oliver gaped up at Bently. Bently stared back as if the old man was an entirely new and particularly ugly species of bug.

He looked past Bently to Marjorie Bendham. The old woman smiled.

The anger Douglas Oliver felt at seeing his cache of negotiables stolen evaporated. He'd long thought of anger as a secret source of strength, but now all he felt was terror. He was afraid Bently might hit him again and kill him.

The man in the Bermuda shorts sat up straighter to get a good look and let out a hyena laugh.

"Sully! Get the lieutenant," Bently called to the man on the couch.

The lieutenant? What was this?

The guy in Bermuda shorts, hauled himself up off the couch and jumped to the ground with a grunt. He shouldered his shotgun and disappeared into the Spencer's front door.

In a moment, Sully returned with a fat man in green camouflage. The lieutenant didn't look at all surprised to find Oliver lying at his feet. "Is this the man you've been telling me about, Mr. Bently?"

"Yes, sir," Bently said.

The lieutenant sat on his heels and looked into the old man's eyes. "Douglas Oliver. You are charged with black marketeering," he said. "How do you plead?"

"How do I plead?"

"We'll skip the formalities," the lieutenant said, pulling out a cigarette pack from one of his many pockets. "Mr. Bently here has infiltrated your organization and has told me all about your activities. Looting each night, dealing in stolen jewelry, illegal drugs, etcetera."

Through the pain, Oliver nodded toward the Bendham's garage. "You mean the jewelry and supplies you're stealing from my garage right now?"

"That isn't even your garage. The old woman says all those spoils are your doing." The lieutenant paused to light his cigarette. "Admit your looting and I won't have the old woman shot alongside you." The lieutenant smiled and puffed a cloud of smoke into the old man's face.

It hurt Oliver very much to cough. He managed to say, "There is no 'organization'. Bently works for me. And it's not looting. It's salvage and survival."

"No, old man," the military man replied. "He works for *me*. He works for the Provisional Militia. I am Lieutenant Francis Carron and you are my prisoner, soon to be executed for high crimes against the state under martial law."

Oliver's chest pounded with pain and his breath was short. He was sure at least one rib was broken. Or maybe the heart attack he'd feigned a short time ago had arrived for real. He winced and gasped and gripped his chest, his hand a claw.

Carron laughed at him and bent closer. "All this time, you thought Mr. Bently was working for you? Not so, old man. *You* have been working for *me*. Bently says you know gems. That's good. Your stuff will be useful. I don't want to try buying food from nearby municipalities and negotiate using costume jewelry. That's the sort of thing that can lead to hard feelings. I don't want my men to get shot. It's important that, in negotiations, that everyone be made happy. That's something you did not seem to understand when you used Mr. Bently so harshly."

"I can negotiate for you. I'm still an expert on gems. Without me, you could get faux pearls made of glass or plastic and never know the difference. Keep me around and…everybody will be happy."

"I already have another jeweller, Mr. Oliver. She's a pretty thing. I have a position for her in the militia. I don't need you." He puffed a stream of cigarette smoke that hung in the cold air and turned to slow, yellow milk in the cast of the Jeeps' headlights.

Before Oliver could say more, Bently stepped forward and kicked the old man in the ribs. Oliver began to cry and cursed himself for allowing himself to sob aloud.

Carron stood and gazed across the street at the dark outline of Oliver's house. "Mr. Bently is not very happy with you, Douglas. Bently, did you really let this man hit you in the face with a bag of groceries?"

Bently scowled but said nothing.

"It was a play that got out of hand."

"No. A *ploy*, I think," Carron said. "I don't see any of that family here so I guess you didn't gain their trust, after all, huh? You underestimated poor Mr. Bently's irritation and his loyalty to me, of course. Do you know we were just discussing you this morning? Mr. Bently reminded me that looters are to be shot." The fat man smiled, baring long, yellow teeth.

Oliver wheezed, "You thieving scum — "

"Said the thief." The lieutenant's laugh was a metallic bark. "It's a new world, Mr. Oliver. There isn't a place in it for those who fail to adapt quickly."

Oh, God, Oliver thought. *My own words!*

"The end of the world is a tough situation for an old man, I imagine. I'm not old yet, but I am determined to get that way."

Bently grabbed Oliver and hauled him up. The nerves running along his ribs screamed in protest.

Lieutenant Carron threw Bently a careless salute and headed toward the Bendham house. He yelled unnecessarily loud, so all his men could hear, "Finish searching the house and move on. Oh, and do what you want with the prisoner. Your reward for excellent undercover work is to use your own judgment."

Carron almost strode past Marjorie Bendham as if she wasn't even there, but he paused to ask her a single question. The old woman was too afraid not to answer. Unfortunately for the Spencers, she was so guileless, it didn't occur to her to risk an easy lie.

Death By Disease Or Salvation By The Knife?

If Dr. Craig Sinjin-Smythe could have observed the infected objectively, he would have noted their excess production of saliva mimicked the familiar cardinal sign of rabies: foaming at the mouth. He would have noted their elevated skin temperature and their milky eyes.

He would have noted these things, but he was busy running for his life. Sinjin-Smythe preferred tennis, but he jogged around the Cambridge campus a few times a week to keep fit. No mere jog could keep these predators from bringing him down. Three of them were on his heels and gaining.

The monsters' vision seemed dim. However, when the virologist knocked over some garbage cans in the street, the clatter got him more attention. Two more Sutr-Z casualties joined the chase. Perhaps sound attracted them to the hunt. Sinjin-Smythe was sure he'd never have a chance to share those findings. The predators were gaining.

There was indeed a resemblance to fictional zombies: Bite marks, blood, torn flesh and hanging skin. But these were not the familiar and slow undead of fiction. These mindless animals ran for their dinner.

Behind him came a thin black man in a hotel doorman's uniform, three barefoot women who appeared to be dressed for a formal dance and, bringing up the rear, a snarling boy of perhaps twelve.

St. Katherine's docks were just ahead, but the doctor was almost out of breath. He swung his arms harder, vaguely remembering a track coach bellowing that arms and legs working together was one of the secret keys to winning races. His briefcase bounced at his hip. In another moment, he was sure one of the infected would manage to grab that case by its long shoulder strap.

"Help! Help me! Oh, dear God!" Should he scream or was he wasting breath and energy? It didn't matter. The doctor couldn't stop screaming.

They would drag him down and begin to feed. If it was like a nature documentary, they'd tear his throat out first and huddle around him in a circle, their teeth clamping on his hands and face and genitals. He'd be conscious for the first part and glad to slip away from blood loss quickly.

Or were the infected out to make more like them? Would they rip chunks from his body and then leave him to succumb to the new virus variant? If so, maybe he'd have time to find some way to kill himself. The infected numbers had grown exponentially in such a short span of time, he didn't know how long he would have. Hours or one hour? Perhaps just minutes.

One of the women grabbed the strap to his briefcase and he spun away. Some memory fired and he remembered another nature lesson: under stress, people fight, flee or freeze. If he froze he was dead. He was losing this footrace. The doctor had to turn and fight.

Sinjin-Smythe ran down a narrow alley. The woman who'd been closest smacked her head into a brick wall as he ducked left.

"Four!" he said.

The monsters ignored the fallen woman and continued to give chase.

The alley was too narrow for him to be surrounded. He stopped short and threw himself at his pursuers' legs, rolling into a ball. All but the child ran into him and fell like bowling pins.

The boy came at him, snarling, as the doctor staggered up to run back the way he'd come. Sinjin-Smythe hadn't struck a twelve-year-old since he was a twelve-year-old. What Sinjin-Smythe lacked in fighting expertise, he made up for in greater weight, height and strength. He balled a fist and whipped the back of his hand at the child's temple with all the force he could muster.

He missed the temple and hit the boy in the cheekbone. The zygomatic arch was crushed from the blow, but it was the force of the child's skull slamming against the alley's wall that saved the doctor from a bite.

Sinjin-Smythe ran on, not daring to look back. "Three!" he screamed.

The woman who ran into the wall was getting to her feet and finding her focus.

"Oh, shite! Four!" The doctor leapt at her and planted the heel of his shoe in the middle of her chest. She flew back against the wall and a satisfying streak of blood smeared the brick behind her skull.

"Three!" he said, but his heart was hammering and he was out of breath. He looked back as he reached the mouth of the alley and the three infected ghouls were closer than he expected. He only had one last burst of speed born of terror left in him, but after that? What?

He guessed the best he could do was to try to make it to the marina and jump in the water. Then he'd find out if zombies could swim as well as they could run.

Sinjin-Smythe looked forward just in time. It was a wonder he managed to avoid getting hit by the speeding truck. He threw himself sideways and rolled, scraping his knees and elbows raw and bloody.

The truck rolled over the man in the doorman's uniform first. The van's rear wheels tore the coat and pants off the infected man and left him dead and nearly naked. The van's grill hit Sinjin-Smythe's remaining two pursuers. They flew back and van's tires screeched and skidded as the vehicle rocked to a stop. In the moonlight, he made out the insignia on the side of the truck. His rescuer drove a delivery van from Harrods.

Sinjin-Smythe fell back, too bruised and exhausted to stand. *Should have run more and done less tennis,* he thought.

When he looked up, a small, brown man held a sledgehammer high, poised to bring it down on his head. Sinjin-Smythe tucked into a fetal position and screamed. *"Don't!"*

The moment passed.

"You're a surprise."

The doctor looked up cautiously.

"Sorry, mate. Thought you were one of them."

The man held out his hand. Sinjin-Smythe took it and allowed himself to be pulled to his feet. "I almost killed you twice," the man said. "Where are you headed?"

"That way," Sinjin-Smythe pointed. "To St. Katherine's docks. There's a boat waiting."

"Then it's good I almost killed you, mate." The man pointed in the opposite direction. "St. Kat's marina is that way."

"Then I think you could say you saved my life three times over. I'm Craig." They shook hands.

"I am Aadi."

"Do you usually run over crazed infected people in your lorry, Aadi?"

"It's a new hobby, but I had to clear the area before I dared to get out of the truck. It's worse uptown. You should have seen the masses and mobs around Knightsbridge this morning."

"Glad I didn't." The doctor glanced at the man's jacket. It was a dark blue and he made out the words Harrods Security in white stitching. "Why were you 'clearing the area' exactly?"

Aadi smiled. "I stand for safety and security. Gotta get a boat, man. My friend and me and my daughters — "

A scream rose from behind them. A zombie, one of the women Aadi hit with his delivery van, was not dead enough.

Aadi ran forward with his sledge, but before he could get there, the truck lurched forward and slammed into the infected woman. Whoever was driving the van kept their foot on the accelerator, crushing the monster against the brick wall. The zombie's compressed lungs didn't allow it to scream. Instead, it pushed uselessly at the truck's hood.

The infected woman looked up. Aadi moved to put her out of her misery with his weapon. She looked toward the stars and, in a grisly display under the van's bright headlights, her eyeballs burst from her sockets. When the dead woman collapsed forward, her head bounced and rang off the metal.

The large black woman sitting at the wheel rolled down the driver's window as Sinjin-Smythe ran up. She was crying. Aadi reached through the window and patted her shoulder. "Craig, this is Dayo. Dayo saved your life, too. My daughters are in the back."

Two young girls cried in the rear of the truck.

"You all have my thanks," Sinjin-Smythe said.

"Your thanks is nice, mate, but what we need is your bloody boat."

"Of course. Come with me. I need a security force and you're it. If I don't get across the Atlantic with this" — Sinjin-Smythe slapped his briefcase — "we're all zombies."

Dayo frowned and wiped her tears with the back of her sleeve. "That sounds mad, but after today…"

"The situation is mad. I'm not. From the last reports I saw, Sutr-X is killing about 60% of the world's population. If I don't get to America, the remaining 40 percent will turn into crazed cannibals like that."

An involuntary reflex made the pinned corpse shudder and Dayo, Aadi and the doctor shrieked in unison. The zombie's mouth opened in a riot of jagged teeth.

Season 1, Episode 5

**Beware wolves at the door.
History shows they huff, puff and blow your house down two-thirds of the time.**

~ Notes from The Last Café

Here We Sit In Death's Cafe

The dentist wasn't waiting at the dock where he was supposed to be. Worse, his 24-foot sailboat wasn't there, either. Sinjin-Smythe cursed. "The bastard left without me." He glanced down at Aadi's children, embarrassed. The girls, Aastha and Aasa, were six and seven. They had been left behind in a city crawling with the infected, as well. Sinjin-Smythe looked to the girls' father. "Sorry, Aadi."

"Don't be sorry, doctor. Fix it."

Sinjin-Smythe shrugged. "I don't know how to sail, either. Even if I knew how to steal a ship, I'd run us aground before we cleared the river."

Dayo scanned the shoreline, shifting her weight from side to side. "We have to get out of here before sunrise. If those things find us, we'll be torn apart. Let's figure out how to steal a boat. I don't care if it's a paddleboat." She glanced at the little girls. "If it comes down to it, I'd rather drown."

Aasa, the seven-year-old, tugged on her father's sleeve. "You want to go to America, Daddy?"

Aadi frowned. "Yes, darling. That's what we're trying to work out."

"Don't people take an airplane if they want to fly there? I want to go in an airplane."

Dayo and Aadi looked to Sinjin-Smythe, but he shook his head.

"It's a great idea but for two problems. I'd be a worse pilot than I am a sailor and we're officially in a red zone. All flights have been

295

grounded except for military jets. Any planes leaving British airspace will be shot down. I don't have the clearance to get us out."

"How can they do that? We're rats in a trap." Dayo paced and her voice shook. "This can't be happening. I thought the regular plague was quite bad enough."

"I'm sorry. I begged my CDC contact not to go from green to red, but the protocol is, as soon as a new Level One outbreak variant is declared, that's the way it is. As far as the World Health Organization is concerned, the British Isles are gangrenous and you have to lose the arm to save the body. In a small boat, we'll have a chance to escape, but my understanding is, any plane caught on radar will be blown out of the sky."

"It's monstrous," Dayo said. "They condemn the uninfected and the infected alike."

Sinjin-Smythe scanned the Thames up and down, hoping to spot another boat that would suit their needs. He didn't think houseboats would fair well in the North Atlantic's high swells. "I remember being in a meeting in Atlanta. Some military men came in and it was all very hush hush. They talked about all kinds of scenaria. This was one of those projections. I didn't give it a moment's thought. I just dismissed it with confidence that it would never come to this. Now there are nineteen or twenty ships out there, trying to keep the infection in, trying to stop the red from bleeding all over the map."

Dayo held a length of lumber. Sinjin-Smythe wanted to take it from her and go bash some zombie heads. He'd die, but he'd feel more useful.

"What if we got a plane and headed north or south?"

"Same problem. If British jets didn't get us, the French would. Getting hold of a boat was enough of a long shot."

Aadi stepped close. "Craig. You're sounding very defeatist and I've got two scared little girls here. I don't have time for your tone. I told you to fix this and you will. You're the smart insider. How does a fellow with a name like Sinjin-Smythe not know how to bloody sail?"

The doctor took in a deep breath and let it out slowly. "I was never a joiner, I guess. The other kids were in sailing clubs. I played with a microscope and a chemistry set. I'm out of ideas."

A man's voice whispered from the darkness. "I have an idea."

Dayo whirled, lumber at the ready. "Who's there?"

"It's Neil McInerney. Keep calm and please do shut up."

"Easy, everyone. It's my dentist."

An older, balding man in glasses stepped out of the shadows carrying a long boathook. "Those things are very sensitive to sound. If they hear you, they'll come for us. We had some trouble on the way here. Whatever this is, it's like mass psychosis. I've never seen its like."

"I'm sorry, Dr. McInerney. Your boat isn't in its slip," the virologist said miserably. "I assume someone stole it."

"They did. No matter. It's catch-as-catch-can. My wife and I stole a better one."

"Excuse me. What's your name, Miss?"

The young woman looked up slowly from her iPad. At first glance the man was dressed casually, but his shoes alone were worth more than all her possessions. She knew this from years of serving men like him. "My name is Lijon, sir."

"I've never known a Lijon. Where are you from?" His smile revealed perfectly even teeth that gleamed white. His accent said he'd been educated at Eton and Oxford.

"The Marshall Islands."

"Marshall Islands? I think I've been just about everywhere but I've never heard of them. Where's that?"

"You've probably heard of the Bikini Atoll where the United States government performed sixty-seven nuclear tests in the atmosphere. There. Everyone has seen the atmosphere detonation tests on film. My mother and father saw them in person."

"Wow. You're a long way from home." He glanced at his watch. It was platinum with diamonds set in its face at twelve, three, six and nine.

"It was better for me to leave, sir. I do love Dublin, but I emigrated here as a little girl in the hope that I wouldn't get stomach cancer like my parents did, from the radiation."

"I'm sorry to hear that," he said, but his charming mask did not change. "Listen, Dijon — "

"Excuse me. *Lijon*, sir."

"Yes, *Lijon*. Very well. Do you know who *I* am?"

She tapped the identity card clipped to the lanyard around his neck with her scanner. The machine let out a sharp beep and she read the liquid crystal display. She looked for his name on the list on her iPad. "Yes, sir. Edwin George Stanhope. You're in the correct boarding area. I'll let you know when we're ready for you and your family."

Stanhope cleared his throat and stiffened. "Here's the thing, Lijon. I received an evacuation call. A bunch of executives from our company did, in fact. The ones who lived in central London haven't arrived."

"Sadly, I'm sure they won't be joining you. You were very lucky, sir."

"Luck's not something I believe in. I've been hiding out in a concrete bunker waiting for Sutr to pass and now the whole country has gone crazy. We thought it would be economic collapse or race riots. I can't believe we ended up in hiding from this sort of madness." He pulled back his suede jacket to reveal an oil company emblem over his breast pocket. His shirt was a fine, white linen. "The thing is, we all paid a lot of money in advance on the chance we'd need to be evacuated in this situation. My family and I are anxious to get aboard the big ship. That's what we paid for with all those heaping sums."

"Yes, I'm sure permanent residency on the *Mars* will be very exciting for you," she said. "Until then, this container ship is the *Gaian Commander*."

"After some things I've heard, we want you to put us aboard this thing now. Also, we couldn't help but notice this is a container ship. Where is the bloody ship I paid for? Where is the *Mars*?"

"Don't worry, sir. The *Mars* is the world's most expensive condominium cruise ship. It's safe in international waters. This is merely the evacuation ship to accommodate people like you. We have to get outside the military barricade first."

"I paid handsomely for clearance to get us on that ship. Isn't there another ship to take us faster and more comfortably? No offence, but this ship looks like a rusty scow to me."

Coming in low out of the night sky, a jet helicopter swung in fast to land on the *Gaian Commander's* helipad. Lijon had to raise her voice to be heard above the rotors' din.

"We will rendezvous with the *Mars* in Reykjavik!"

"Reykjavik?"

"I'm sorry, Mr. Stanhope!" Lijon put a soft hand on his arm and leaned close to his ear. "We do it this way for your security. You'll find your transport ship is quite deceptive. The comforts aboard aren't what you imagine. Soon you'll see what all that money bought you, I promise."

The moment passed and the man relented as the big helicopter's rotors wound down. "Alright, then. But can't you at least get us on the bloody scow so we can pick out a good bunk?"

Lijon glanced at her iPad. "I'll call you in order, sir."

"Excuse me, but what's the order?"

"We're waiting on a bus full of investment bankers, actually. The bankers must board first. They get the first choice and best cabin assignments. Passengers board in order of priority and you are not our first priority...*sir*."

"Lijon, before this is over, I'm going to make sure you stay right here for that remark." Stanhope leaned closer. She thought the man might strike her. "I hope you love Dublin as much when it's overrun by those psychotic cannibals."

He stalked back to a cluster of executives and stood glaring at her as he spoke to his fellows.

Lijon turned back to her post. Her eyes widened as she spotted a beautiful pregnant woman in a blood-red dress, high above her and standing at the rail. A moment later, she heard that same woman's voice on the radio receiver tucked in her ear.

"Do you have a report on our investors, Sister Lijon?"

"Two-hundred, twenty-six accounted for with a bus of fifteen more on the way from the Shannon airport. The piggies are restless but well-behaved, Dear Sister."

"Good. I like my piggies anxious for the slaughter," Shiva replied.

We Are The Zombie's Reluctant Buffet

Bently pushed Oliver forward. The old man stumbled as they walked into the Spencers' house. A drunk man lurched past them. He wore a ripped white wedding dress. "Liquor's under the sink." He pointed vaguely with a shaky hand that held an opened bottle of red wine. The drunk wandered to the front step, looked up at the moon and howled.

The living room was surprisingly bright. Three gas lanterns threw circles of white light across the long room. Bently used his rifle as a prod to slam his prisoner against a wall. A picture of Theo, Jack, Anna and Jaimie rattled by Oliver's head. Bently shoved the old man against the wall again and the picture fell. Shattered glass from the portrait's frame skittered across the floor.

"That glass will never come out of that area rug, dude," Bently said. "Now, to business. Where you keeping that sweet, young thing?"

Oliver smelled the little rat man's hot breath and recoiled.

"Where is she? You can introduce us, right?"

"I don't know where she is," Oliver said.

Bently hit him just above the kidneys with the edge of the rifle butt. Oliver would have sunk to his knees but Bently used the rifle again, this time pushing him up by the back of the skull. He forced the old man to stand, pinning him to the wall.

"Where are you hiding her? *Which* house? You might as well give her up. We're doing this whole neighborhood tonight and I'm sure you didn't hide her far away. She's too pretty to be far away."

Bently leaned in close, whispering in Oliver's ear. "We checked the old lady's house. She's not there. You keeping that family over at your house still? I'm *sure* you are. You could have moved them farther. Should have. But that's where they are, aren't they?"

Oliver turned his head to try to look Bently in the eye. "You already know where they are. You're asking me questions just so you can hit me. Is this foreplay? You aren't my type."

Bently punched Oliver in the kidney and the old man cried out. Bently leaned in close again. His breath smelled of rot. "No, not just so I can hit you. I could do that, anyway. I want you to tell me. I want you to give them up. I want you to betray them, old man. Then maybe we'll get some cans of soup and bash your face in. That was a good con. That family trusted you. Now I get to play. Just for fun."

Tears ran down Oliver's cheeks. He wondered if, when he eventually died, he would suffer enough that he'd see heaven. Would his old lover, Steve, be waiting for him with consoling words in a peaceful place that never knew disease or cruelty?

Someone cackled behind them. Bently turned Oliver around, now holding the rifle's muzzle under the old man's throat. Two large, middle-aged men in green camouflage jackets, blue jeans and new, white tennis sneakers stood across the living room, each holding a bottle of beer. It wasn't just that they wore the same clothes that marked their resemblance. They were twins. "The front door was locked," said one. He held up his rifle. "But this key opens all locks. Where's this pretty girl Bently's been telling us about?"

"Slow down and save me some beer!" Bently said.

"You're so little," one of the men said, "you won't need much."

Bently pushed Oliver toward the top of the basement stairs. "Jackson! Jackson!"

A shirtless teenager appeared. Jackson was covered in tattoos and his head was shaved. He held a long crowbar, the tips painted yellow.

Too many of them, Oliver thought. *I'm dead. No way out.*

"Anybody downstairs?"

"Nah," Jackson shrugged. "The master bedroom is always where the best stuff is." The boy looked to the twins, preening. "This isn't my first B&E."

"You check downstairs yourself?"

"Sure," Jackson said. "It's one of them splits. Lower level with like an office. Lots of books. Farther down is the basement."

"The people who lived here had good taste in beer," added one of the twins. "Heineken."

The other reached for a wine bottle on the floor. "They had good taste in wine, too."

"How would you know good wine, Carl?"

"Price tags, dumbass. Not a bottle in the house is worth less than eighteen dollars." He began opening a bottle, working a corkscrew he'd pulled from a hook on his belt. "What goes with an occasion like this?"

"Definitely red," his brother replied.

"Too bad, this is white. Champagne, actually. Probably left over from New Year's Eve. Now, every night can be New Year's Eve if we say so, huh, Earl?"

Carl loosened the cork quickly and used both thumbs to shoot it at Oliver with a loud pop. The cork barely missed his eye and stung his cheek. Champagne shot across the rug.

"Easy! You're wasting it! They aren't making more of that, you know!" Bently said.

In answer, the man raised the bottle in a toast, brought it to his lips and tipped it back.

Jackson leaned against a wall by the stairs and snickered, watching as the twins riled Bently.

Carl smirked at Bently, and raised his voice to play to his audience. "You suck at math, huh, Bently? We can waste as much as we want. We'll have a lifetime supply of everything. You'll never get through all the champagne there is with the few survivors left. Drink all you want, and never pay the bill and toast the dead, dumbass."

Earl drank to catch up with his brother. "We haven't done a thorough inventory of the basement yet. There's a lot of stuff down there. You should have been more careful stocking the basement, Bently. Bad job! Bad dog! Imagine letting the old man run you like that."

Carl wiped his mouth with his sleeve. "I hate it when people are disorganized."

"Lieutenant's orders are to do inventory first," Bently said.

"You talk like we're boneheads working retail," Jackson said.

"I'm in charge here!" Bently said.

The boy shrugged. "Whatever. Just sayin', what's the point of not getting the plague if it's business as usual?"

Bently pointed his rifle at Jackson.

Jackson crossed his arms. If he was at all bothered, he didn't show it. "Whatever."

"Cheer up, Bently," Earl said good-naturedly.

"Yeah! We're on a break," Carl said. "I'm new to the militia but I've been a union man all my life. Some things are sacred. Taking breaks is part of the job."

Bently's face burned. He turned on Jackson. "This old man is a black marketeer. *You* guard him."

The tattooed boy sneered at Bently but gave a slow nod of assent. He reached out with his crowbar, prodded Oliver toward the stairs and pushed him roughly. If he hadn't grabbed the railing, Oliver would have fallen down seven steps head first.

The back door was to his right but before he could try to run, Jackson stepped close, holding his lantern high, swinging it back and forth. "Don't even think about it."

Oliver turned, his hands up. He looked around. They stood in Theo's rec room lined with books. There was nothing he could use as a weapon that would outdo the crowbar in the young man's hands. He also knew he couldn't match the boy's strength in a fight. His breath was still coming in gasps.

Oliver wished the archer at the mall had shot that arrow through his head. At least he would have died quickly. That was just this afternoon, but the ordeal now seemed a remote and friendly encounter by comparison. "Just books down here, huh? Nothing *you* could use."

"Don't be stupid, old man," Jackson said. "We'll be needing lots of kindling for cooking fires."

Oliver rolled his eyes and the boy swung at him, slamming the knuckles of the hand that held the crowbar into the side of his head above his left ear. "Don't do that. Don't roll your eyes at me."

The old man held his hands in front of his face. He cowered, expecting the next blow to be with the crowbar. The terror rose in him and he moaned as liquid warmth spread across the front of his pants and ran down his legs. His urine came not in little spurts but in a long uninterrupted stream. The ripe, yellow puddle spread out toward the boy.

Jackson cursed, long, loud and creatively. The boy stepped back to avoid the pool of urine at Oliver's feet. Just as quickly as he was to anger, the boy tittered at his prisoner's humiliation. "Get back! *Pathetic* old man!"

He pushed Oliver with the tip of his crowbar, forcing him back toward the next set of stairs that led to the sub-basement. Without slowing so Oliver could turn and find his footing at the top step, the tattooed boy shoved the blunt end into his ribs so he tumbled backward down another seven steps. Douglas Oliver landed hard on the concrete floor.

Oliver gasped and cried out in pain. The boy slammed the door after him, pitching him into blackness. "Useless, disgusting old man!" Jackson yelled through the door. Oliver cried, the snot spreading across his face. The warm wet mess dribbled down his chin as he slowly rolled onto his belly.

Slowly, with great difficulty, he rocked back and forth, reaching into his front pants pocket. Hampered by pain and the wet cling of the thin fabric, Oliver pulled out what he needed. He took as deep a breath as his sore ribs would allow, closed his eyes and triggered the wheel on his small, silver cigarette lighter.

This step of his plan was very dangerous. However, if he was to survive the night, no part of his plan was safer than any other. *When everything's an emergency*, he thought, *then nothing is.* The lighter flashed twice and lit on the third try.

Through his tears, he crawled forward on his elbows, saving what strength he had for a very risky idea. He stank of urine, but he had peed himself on purpose.

Despite the pain, he allowed himself a hint of a grim smile. His anger returned to take over from the fear. He hoped the pumping adrenaline would fuel his strength for what he had to do.

The Deepest Wounds Are Those Unseen

Jack threw herself at the high, wooden fence and, with a push from Anna, dropped into Oliver's backyard. She landed roughly and, she thought, too loudly. She looked around. From what she could make out by moonlight, she was alone. Someone howled again from the street, but everything appeared as she had left it.

Jaimie climbed the fence next, then Anna. He looked amused. A novelty, she supposed. Anna still looked as terrified as Jack felt.

The back door to Douglas Oliver's house was unlocked. That was also as they'd left it and, she thought, amazingly stupid. There were a lot fewer people around now, but the survivors could be more dangerous. Jack was in too much of a hurry to enter cautiously. She sprang through the door, desperate to find her husband.

When Jack rushed in, she almost knocked Theo over in the darkness. The truck in Mrs. Bendham's driveway was parked at an angle to make room for the long U-Haul trailer. Its headlights shone into Oliver's front room. If anyone had been looking, they'd have spotted her silhouette immediately, even through the slightly tinted windows.

Theo gripped her arm and pulled her back from the window. She pulled her mask away and pressed her lips to his neck.

Theo looked at her with a wan smile. "I'm glad you're back. I-I'm sorry. I didn't know what to do."

"Doing nothing was the right thing to do. We're fine."

Theo pointed across the street to their abandoned home. "No, we're not."

The Jeep parked on their front lawn was equipped with a spotlight. The man in the wedding dress, *Jack's* wedding dress, laughed and howled to the man in Bermuda shorts. The other man howled back as soon as the man in the dress ran out of breath.

"*Oh...*," Jack said. She took a half-step toward the window. Theo held her close so she wouldn't be caught in the light.

Anna and Jaimie walked in holding hands. Even in the dim light, Theo caught his son's wave of Oliver's walking stick. It meant, *Look what I've got, Dad!*

Jaimie broke from his sister and held his father's hand. Theo straightened as if he'd received a small burst of energy or was refreshed from a power nap. "They've got Oliver."

"Got him? I thought they *worked* for him," Jack said.

"What do you mean?"

She shook her head. "He can't be trusted. He's been using us to build his little black market empire."

"Empire?" Theo said, incredulous.

"I don't know. That might be overstating it. It's just...Oliver only cares about himself. He wanted us out of our house so we'd take care of him if he needed help. When did he ever talk to us before his trip to the hospital? I think he wanted a tribe and he chose us. But he's selfish."

"He's a bad burrito," Anna agreed.

Theo turned back to the window. "From what I saw, there are worse men than him. And they have him now."

The man in the dress was back on the front step, still howling back and forth at the man in the Bermuda shorts.

"Those guys choose one song and play it to death," Theo said.

The screen door Anna's boyfriend had destroyed lay cast aside on the grass, like a small insult forgotten because of deeper wounds.

The man in Jack's wedding dress shook a can of something. He stretched his arm up and sprayed paint back and forth in broad strokes. When he stepped back, a thick orange phosphorescent 'X' was visible across their front door.

"Wolf Pack!" the man in white yelled in triumph.

"Wolf Pack!" the man in Bermuda shorts answered. They howled at each other again. The sound rose, up and up, a terrifying animal sound.

Jack began to cry. She put a hand to her head and Anna moved forward to catch her in case she fainted. Jack stumbled forward into her husband and lay her head on his chest.

The curtains moved against the window pane under the steady eye of white light. The guard in Bermuda shorts caught the movement from the edge of his vision. Was that a trick of the light, or was someone watching them? He'd been watching that window and wondering.

He stood, dug a white hospital mask out of his back pocket and grabbed his shotgun.

Between What We Were And Where We've Been

Oliver pulled himself up by the rough, wooden workbench. He tried to disregard the sharp pain across his back and chest, but his breath was ragged.

How many ribs had Bently cracked? That could be nothing in the long run, if a jagged rib didn't pop one of his lungs first. If the end of a broken rib did rip through the lining of a lung, deflating his balloon and pressing on his old heart, he'd die. He doubted Jackson had the skills or inclination to perform a thoracotomy to save him.

In the flickering light of his old lighter, his cold hands shook as he searched in vain for a weapon. Years of accumulated junk littered the workbench: Discarded training wheels for a bicycle; old rolls and scraps of wallpaper; coffee cans full of screws and nails. A forgotten flower pot lay on its side.

Oliver would have preferred a long, flat screwdriver but all he could find were smaller ones. Perhaps Bently had already gone through the workbench, taking what he thought useful for their cache. Oliver almost fell reaching for a tiny Robinson screwdriver from a plastic rack.

At the top of the small flight of stairs, the tattooed boy was still cursing him, laughing at him and making gagging sounds through the door. Terrified Jackson would rush in and swing his crowbar any second, Oliver grabbed the small screwdriver. It was so small, the tool disappeared in his palm, but he would have to make do.

He fumbled and gasped as he knocked a can of screws over. The screws and nails scattered and clattered across the concrete floor towards the washer and dryer by the far wall. To his despair, the sound had carried to Jackson's ears.

"What you doin' down there, old man?"

Oliver snatched up the empty flower pot and, despite his pain, pushed off the workbench and launched himself back toward the stairs and off into the darkness to the left, going by feel and memory. He'd hidden his treasure by the furnace.

The red plastic gas cans lay under a tarp. This was the inventory he'd told Bently to store in the Spencer's house. The fuel was meant to power their escape to the promised haven of Theo's father's farm. It might save him now.

The old man felt the cool plastic under his hands in the dark. He could save himself if he had enough time, but time was slipping away.

His hope didn't last long. His captor pounded down the stairs.

Oliver was fit, but he was still an old man. Even without a broken rib, he wouldn't have tried attacking Jackson on his best day. However, there was another, long-shot option.

Jackson headed toward the laundry room. His lantern held high and swinging wildly, Oliver caught just enough thrown light in his corner of the basement to help him close on what he needed with a sure hand.

That moment saved Oliver from immolating himself. In his rush and desperation, he'd come close to using the lighter. Instead, he stabbed at a gas can with the screwdriver point. He had meant to stab it low, close to the floor, but as he stooped, pain shot through his chest and he heard something crack and shift.

The screwdriver, with all his lurching weight behind it, plunged through the thin plastic easier than he expected. Gas slopped out. Oliver gasped and dropped the flower pot. His hands on his knees, the old man bent farther, each breath a misery. He shifted the flower pot with his foot till he heard gasoline splash into it.

The boy heard him. Jackson rushed forward but was hampered by a pile of cardboard boxes. He wound through the mess, holding the lantern and the crowbar higher, searching the basement.

Oliver straightened as best he could and leaned against the furnace. "I'm here."

The boy slowed, cautious now. He saw Oliver bend down and heard his pained gasp. The boy smiled and came closer, bold and sure, raising the long crowbar.

The old man straightened again and held up something silver in the light.

Jackson faltered for a second, thinking his prisoner had a knife or a gun, but it was far too small for that.

"Time to die, old man."

"Alright."

The clay flower pot had a hole in its bottom. There wasn't much gas in it, but Douglas Oliver swung it up from his knee and the fuel hit the teenager in the face.

Be Killed Or Kill In Days Like These

"Somebody's over there," the man in Bermuda shorts said, pointing at the house across the street.

"Nah," said the man in the white dress. "Your imagination. And the wine."

He howled his wolf howl again but this time his fellow guard ignored him. "I'm almost sure I saw something." He pointed again to Douglas Oliver's house, at the living room window.

Jack stood behind that window, the horror building as she peered through a narrow gap in the curtains. It was as if the lens of a powerful microscope had been turned on her. The man in the white dress — *her wedding dress* — shrugged and gestured with a wine bottle, urging the other guard to have another drink.

No. Not a microscope. A *rifle* scope. The crosshairs would be aimed between her eyes. She could feel it like a real pressure between her eyes. "Oh, please. Oh, please..."

The guards argued. It was a soundless pantomime, but their gestures were clear. Jaimie began twirling the walking stick as he had seen Oliver do. Anna grabbed it and, in a hoarse whisper, told her brother to be still.

The man in Bermuda shorts put his shotgun down, sat back on the Spencer's couch and adjusted his surgical mask so it now sat on top of his head. Anna, Theo and Jack let out a long sigh. Only then did they realize they had been holding their breath.

The man in Bermuda shorts stood and pulled his mask down. The man in Jack's wedding dress sprang forward and picked up his shotgun from the ground by the front step. The guards hurried toward the Spencers.

A wide-brimmed hat stuffed on her head and a winter scarf across her face, Marjorie Bendham crossed the street carrying a small, black suitcase and an umbrella in one hand. In her other hand she carried a large cooler that banged against her knee. The old woman made a beeline toward Douglas Oliver's house.

"We're Anne Frank and the neighbor's an idiot," Anna said.

"Head for the garage!" Theo ordered, "If we don't get out of here, they'll kill us."

"Or *worse*," Jack said.

Jaimie thought Mrs. Bendham looked like an older version of Mary Poppins. He loved that movie, especially the song about the very long word. He wished he could say it loud so he could sound precocious. All language was multidimensional music to Jaimie. Mary Poppins' voice made it prettier.

If Mary Poppins were here, she would take the bull by the horns, or, as the Romans put it more elegantly: *Tenere lupum auribus. Hold the wolf by the ears.*

Pray For God's Mercy Or The Red Queen's Disease

Though the gas burned the tattooed boy's eyes, he kept coming at Oliver. Gagging, spitting, cursing — but still coming. He hadn't dropped the lantern or the crowbar.

Douglas Oliver retreated until his back was to the furnace. Gas spilled at his heels. The old man thought Jackson would run as soon as the gas hit him. At worst, he thought his guard would pause long enough for Oliver to hold up his silver lighter and threaten him. He thought he'd have a moment to relish the look of terror in the boy's burning eyes. It had been the perfect plan.

Half-blind, Jackson swung out with the crowbar. Vicious after-images followed the arc of metal. It clanged against a thick furnace pipe by Oliver's head.

"Get back or I'll burn you alive!"

When angry, Jackson was not a listener. Instead, he swung again and barely missed.

Too stupid and mean to live, thought Oliver.

Jackson, one eye squeezed shut and spitting gasoline, stepped close to his captive, too close to miss with his next swing. The boy raised his weapon over his head. In his left hand he was still gripping the lantern. That's what saved Oliver. Despite his age and his pain, he had another hand free to fight.

Pulsing with adrenaline, the old man grabbed Jackson's crowbar. Expecting a tug of war, Jackson yanked back to free the weapon. Oliver was no match for the younger man's strength and couldn't resist the pull. Instead he fell forward. His greater weight fell on the boy as he toppled backward. More by luck than design, Oliver brought up an elbow to fend off blows to his injured ribcage. The meat and bone and blade of his forearm smashed across his attacker's throat.

The savage blow shocked and choked Jackson. The lantern dropped to the floor, its light a small circle. They were shadows moving in dim light, both wracked with pain and gasping for air. Oliver used all his weight, pushing through the burning, spreading pain. The crowbar clunked to the floor. The boy pushed away, got up and tripped over Oliver's legs. He spun and twisted and tripped and fell into the pile of gas cans.

Oliver's first instinct was to run, but when the boy gathered himself up, he'd be on him again before he made it to the stairs. He knew he was lucky Bently and the twins upstairs hadn't been drawn to the noise yet. More likely, the men were content to drink and listen to what they presumed was his brutal beating and slow murder.

Oliver ignored his pain and groped through the dark to find the crowbar. His need for time left no room for pain.

Or so he thought.

The next moment proved what an arrogant idea that had been. As Oliver bent for the weapon, something hitched in his breathing. His back and ribs gave another horrendous crack.

Oliver couldn't simply push the pain away. Pain pushes back. He fell to his knees, too heavily. The bare, cold concrete felt like knives driving into his old kneecaps. Pain rocketed up through his bones. It made him shriek, gasp and cry out again. Dropping so heavily to his knees felt almost as horrific as the pain through his chest.

He'd heard getting gut shot was bad, but few things could compare to knee pain. He was too old for this fight. He was sure he wouldn't have the chance to get any older.

Oliver could hear Jackson moving, finding his feet, scattering the gas cans. In a just world, the kid would have been knocked out in his fall. In a movie, the boy would be out cold on the concrete and Oliver would have time to plot something clever for the men upstairs.

Instead, the boy would pounce on him again and this time, Jackson would finish him. As he sought the crowbar, he imagined the sickening sound and the burst of pain if Jackson found the weapon first and brought it down with both hands, with all his strength, on the back of his neck.

Yes. His captor would paralyze him first. Somehow Oliver was sure of that. It was cruel, so he was sure the boy would do it. Then the boy would take his time.

Jackson was up, scrambling against the plastic drums. Thumping. Liquid sloshing. Scrambling in the dark, eyes still burning from the gas.

If Oliver had been thinking clearer, he would have grabbed for the lantern first. But he wasn't thinking. He was panicking. When he did scoot forward to grab at it, it was to throw it at the boy.

He threw the lantern as hard as he could but, with broken ribs, it hurt to raise a hand past his shoulder. Oliver had hoped the lantern's glass would shatter across Jackson's face. Instead the boy caught it neatly, as if Oliver had given it to him in a gentle toss.

Jackson let out a triumphant cackle. "Old man, you are a tough old fool, but you're a dead fool." Jackson raised the lantern high. The circle of light expanded and there, on the floor just out of Oliver's reach, the crowbar emerged from the gloom. He snatched it up and got up on one knee as the boy leapt forward.

Jackson came at him, ready with the lantern to smash it down on Oliver's head.

The old man didn't have time to draw back the weapon. He'd meant to swing it like a club and kneecap the boy. He was too slow for that. Instead he thrust it forward like a sword. The sharp, prying end jammed in deep, just below the boy's kneecap.

Jackson shrieked and fell back. Lantern light caught the sheer pain. The boy's face was a topographical map of agonized surprise and white shock.

Oliver heard voices upstairs. He couldn't make out what they were saying, but by their tone, he imagined a drunken, confused debate. If one of those guards overcame their laziness to check out the ruckus, Douglas Oliver would be made very sorry.

He stepped forward and grabbed the gas can he'd perforated with the little screwdriver. He made for the stairs in the dark.

The old man left Jackson crying and writhing in the lantern light, his eyes rolled up so only the whites showed. The crowbar stood up straight, bisecting the boy's knee. Oliver would have taken the bloody crowbar for a weapon, but he was afraid that, if he paused, the men upstairs might come rushing downstairs at any second.

A trail of gas from the leaking can followed Oliver up the stairs. He had to go by memory and feel, but in another moment he was at the back door and out into the cool air. He escaped into the dim angles and shapes described in the moonlight. Oliver limped away with a leaking gas can and his silver lighter gripped in a tight fist.

Say Farewell To Your Comfortable Home

As the goons from across the street jogged up behind Marjorie Bendham, Jack pushed Anna and Jaimie down the hall toward the door to the garage.

Theo swayed toward the front door, threw the deadlock and pulled Mrs. Bendham into the house. He thought he had more time, but the man in Bermuda shorts and the man in his wife's wedding dress were on her heels, shotguns at the ready. They breathed hard from their sprint, their white surgical masks puffing in and out with each drag of breath through the fabric. Theo could tell by their eyes they were smiling.

Theo tried to slam the door but one of them got the barrel of his gun in before he could close it.

"Get to the garage," he whispered to the old woman and leaned against the door, determined to buy his wife and children time. Mrs. Bendham kept going without looking back.

The men outside didn't push at the door but didn't let it close, either. "Hey, we'd just like to have a chat," one of them said in a reasonable tone.

"Go away," Theo said, gasping. It wasn't his strength but his weight that held the door. He was sure that if they really wanted in, he couldn't deter them. However, Douglas Oliver had already packed the van. He heard the van start up in the garage and a small smile came to the edge of his mouth.

The wolves at the door heard it, too. "Open the goddamn door or I'll blast right through," one said. His voice was so calm that Theo had no doubt the threat wasn't an empty one. He turned and slowly opened the door.

"Hi," the man in his wife's wedding dress said. He held his shotgun's muzzle level with Theo's chest. "We're a couple Jehovah's Witnesses. We wondered if we could come in and chat about your everlasting salvation for a minute? We don't miss a house, so you may as well open up." He let out a delighted cackle.

His companion snorted and gave a high, grating laugh. "You better yell to whoever's in the garage. Tell them they aren't traveling anywhere without you. Tell them quick!" He held up his shotgun for emphasis, as if he was giving a toast.

Theo stood before them, swaying and weak. "That's my wife's wedding dress you're wearing."

"So?"

Empty-handed and at their mercy, Theo struck at them with the only weapon he had. He coughed, long and hoarse and wet, into their faces.

They wore masks, of course, but still they turned away, cursing. Theo had hoped that anyone still left alive would have seen enough death. He hoped they'd run from him, that he'd be dangerous enough that both men would retreat. Instead, they nodded at each other, stepped back two steps each and raised their weapons.

"It's not murder if you're already dead, compadre," the one in Jack's dress said.

Theo closed his eyes, taking one last, ragged breath. How fitting, after carelessly killing Kenny with the blast of a shotgun so long ago, that he should die the same way.

That long ago meadow seemed close again. Theo had held his friend in his arms and watched the stars come out and listened to each halting, hitching breath get slower. The space between each breath stretched until it reached forever.

The men hesitated when they heard Jack rev the motor. Jack waited for Theo to race in — as if he could run at all. She prayed her husband would throw himself in the van's open side door and they'd make their Butch and Sundance escape.

Theo knew he wasn't up to a Hollywood escape. He knew Jack knew that, too. She should have already jammed her foot on the accelerator.

"Go! Just go!" Theo yelled. "Don't wait for me!"

He would be blown back by shotgun blasts. At the sound of the twin blasts, Jack would know what had happened. She would step on the gas and the van would shatter the garage door as she drove off, far away from these wolves who only looked like men.

Theo had expected to die on Douglas Oliver's couch of the wretched virus. He had waited for it for many hours. He'd had time to consider Death and taste it. He'd waited so long, he was impatient for it.

Then Theo heard the creak of a hinge behind him. He felt as if he was swallowing a stone. Even before he looked over his shoulder, he knew that his son had come back for him. Jaimie stood looking at his father, one hand held out, offering it to be held.

Theo's last words were, "Run! Go!"

Jack blasted the van's horn.

The man in Bermuda shorts cursed and started for the garage as the man in the wedding dress stepped forward, teeth gritted, aiming his weapon, his finger tightening on the trigger.

A deafening roar erupted as, across the street, the Spencer's house exploded in orange and red wrath.

Goodbye To Tea, Clotted Cream And Scones

Douglas Oliver's pants were on fire and he could barely breathe. Fire and debris rained down around him. He rolled and swatted at the lit cloth with his bare hands. Bending made his ribcage worse, as if all his nerve endings were on fire, as well. He rolled until he'd strangled the fire and snuffed it out.

He wanted to fill his lungs with the goodness of the cool air, but he couldn't. The bellows of his lungs were still working, but in shallow, painful gasps. He wanted to shout for help but the effort was too much. Pain shot up his left leg. It was more than a burn. His knee worked but the ankle protested with a sharp signal of agony when he tried to move it.

Still immortal, Oliver thought. *No one ever died of a twisted ankle. Not yet.*

His gas can was empty before he was halfway across the Spencer's back lawn so he flicked his Bic there, too close to the house for his liking. By then, the wounded boy by the furnace had regained his voice and was shrieking.

Oliver ignited the gasoline just in time. As he watched the trail of light race toward the house, he stood, too tired or more likely, too dumb with shock to run or even cower. The explosion blew him backward and off his feet.

Someone else screamed. If he could shut his ears, he would have. The wailing might belong to Bently, but it was impossible to say. For its pitch, it might have been a woman or even a small child's voice.

Still, in his mind's eye, Oliver saw Bently engulfed in flame, trapped under a burning beam. Though Bently had betrayed him, Oliver thought he was dying too horribly and far too slowly.

After what seemed like a century, the agonized wail stopped. "I'll remember that for the rest of my life," he said aloud.

He struggled to his feet. The Bendham's roof, Sotherby's house and nearby bushes were alight. Oliver would have moved left toward the Bendham's backyard if he could. Marjorie's pool would have soothed the raw burns on his arms and face. However, the heat of the flames pushed him back.

A high hedge behind him was already on fire from sparks, landing like huge fireflies. Bits of burning paper ignited the long grass in the yard. The only way out was over the fence, on to Sotherby's property, the absent pilot. Oliver limped toward what he hoped was Hell's exit.

He fell over the fence. If not for his enormous pain, he might have stayed where he'd fallen, enjoying the cool grass at his back and taking in the stars that emerged amid smoke and trails of fleeing clouds.

Instead, he forced himself to get up and move. The Spencers would be leaving and he had to leave with them if he was to survive.

The fire to his left spread, but not so fast that he couldn't get around the destruction. So much for my gasoline cache, he thought. He'd stored enough gas in the Spencer's basement to get them a long way toward the safety of Theo's father's farm. He'd planned to find another truck for carrying the fuel so he and the Spencers could merrily convoy all the way east.

Something to his right and behind him creaked, cracked and crashed. He guessed a burning floor joist gave way. He couldn't bring himself to look back. No matter the circumstances, he had just killed at least four people. Oliver didn't want to think about that.

The pain in his ankle and ribs helped crowd out most thought. It was as if his various pains competed for his attention.

There was another thought: he'd won. He'd lost his cache and God knew how many supplies, but Douglas Oliver, old and hobbled, had won the fight and escaped his captors. Victory, even a Pyrrhic one, was still victory.

Wait. At least four. *Four?* There had been four men in the house. Where was the officer who had condemned him to death?

When Oliver made it to the street, he dared a look left down Misericordia Drive, afraid of what he might see. Orange flames blossomed down the street.

The man in the wedding dress was a still form near Oliver's front door. The corpse was on fire. Jack Spencer's wedding dress was evidently quite flammable. The thug was beyond caring.

That's five I've killed tonight. The thought came at him unbidden, expressed before he could push it away. Killing people, even bad people who would have thought nothing of murdering him, was not the simple equation he'd convinced himself he should believe.

The man in Bermuda shorts was alive. He lay on his side on Oliver's driveway, trying to peel off his burning shirt with one hand. One arm was broken and useless, twisted up behind his head at a sickening angle.

Oliver rushed on as best he could to the corner of his front yard, picking his way through the field of debris. The rocker from the front room lay on its side. Beside it, he spotted a tennis shoe. He did not pause to find out if there was still a foot in it.

Oliver gasped for air and grabbed at his side. As he paused, he glimpsed someone in the street. It was the man who had sentenced him to death.

Lieutenant Francis Carron stood dumb in the street, his gaze locked on the flaming pile of brick and timber and possessions that had been the Spencer's home. Oliver's eyes weren't so sharp, but he was sure the man held a pistol in his hand. However, the man in camouflage stared, mute and numb, at the destruction. The heat and light bathed him in a red glow of shock. The old man hoped the officer's brains were scrambled by the concussion of the blast.

Every pane of glass at the front of Oliver's house had shattered. Though it was at the edge of the blast radius, falling embers were already glowing on his roof. Soon, his home would be consumed, as well. Oliver pushed off the wall of his house and limped to the backyard.

Each step was a jolt from his ankle and he gritted his teeth against the pain seething through his burnt arms. If he allowed a scream, though, he was afraid the pain from his ribs might make him pass out.

Oliver lifted the gate latch. The hinge creaked as the heavy, wooden door to his backyard swung open. Oliver closed it carefully behind him.

His yard seemed doubly large now after the field of fiery debris he had traversed. Oliver hobbled toward the porch, headed for the rear door. A flashlight popped on. The beam blinded him. Oliver dodged to his right as best he could but the pain through his chest almost drove him to his knees.

He held up a hand to shade his eyes and peered. Jaimie Spencer stood behind the screen door. The old man's tension loosened a fraction.

"It's okay, Jaimie. It's me. Superman." The old man wanted to scream as he stepped on the bottom step. He had twisted his ankle badly in the blast, but that was a concern for later. When things settled down, he would have a lot more pain ahead of him. That was the price of immortality.

Oliver's relief didn't last long. He made it up the three short steps. As he reached for the handle, Jaimie locked the screen door.

"Boy?"

The old man tried the door. "Kid! Unlock the door!"

The boy stared back at him. The boy gazed into the old man's eyes.

"Boy! Let me in! It's me! This is my house! It's Mr. Oliver. It's me! It's Superman! It's — !"

A growl rumbled behind Oliver. He turned, seeing nothing at first. Then Jaimie shone his flashlight out, playing it over the yard.

Five dogs, eyes bright.

Oliver spotted the form of another dog coming in under the fence. It was the same passage his pet had dug. Then another dog came. Then another and another.

The pack leader bared its teeth and bent to spring. A white froth dripped from its jaws. The alpha dog had been his German Shepherd. Douglas Oliver's dog had finally returned home, but he was sick.

"Steve?" Oliver said. "It's okay, boy. You're a *good* boy!"

The animal leapt, its mouth a deadly trap of teeth.

"Steve!"

The dog's jaws clamped tight around the old man's throat, bringing him down with a crunch.

Familiar, long fangs ripped and tore as the starving dog's big head shook back and forth. The rest of the pack closed like a noose, eager for meat.

Jaimie closed the heavy back door behind him and locked it, too.

Anna had gone so pale she looked like a white ghost coming at her brother in a rush. "Ears! C'mon! We have to go! We have to go! Move! *Move!*" She pushed her brother before her like a storm wave carrying driftwood to the shore.

Bewildered but with no time to think, Anna pushed Jaimie toward the garage and the safety of the van.

Over her shoulder, Jaimie could see his father, white and weak, still swaying, but following them to escape.

"Jaimie?" Theo Spencer looked at him with a reassuring smile and grasped the boy's hand. Jaimie no longer resisted his sister's insistent pushing. He walked to the van willingly.

"You okay, Jaimie?" his father asked.

The boy look up into his father's eyes, squeezed his hand and gave a tiny smile.

Jaimie allowed himself one word: "Kryptonite."

The Fruit Of War, The Wages Of Sin

The Spencer family did not talk. Jack slammed the accelerator to the mat. When the grill hit the garage door, it broke much easier than Jack anticipated. The van shot out of Oliver's garage in an explosion of splintered wood.

They drove over the man in the Bermuda shorts with a sickening *bump-thump*. Anna screamed, but they were already over him and down the driveway.

Maybe not so much over him as through him, Jack thought.

Jack spun the wheel and touched the brakes just enough that they avoided overshooting the road and driving into the inferno that had been their home.

The van tipped sideways, threatening to roll as Jack fought the wheel. As the van rocked, light on two right wheels, everyone in the van involuntarily leaned right, as well. Jack swore and overcorrected so they almost hit the opposing curb and fishtailed through burning debris. Jack bit her lip so hard she tasted blood.

The lieutenant's face flashed past the driver's side window. Jack shouted for everyone to get their heads down. However, the fat man in fatigues, suddenly ridiculous, stood in the street behind them with his arms limp at his sides. He was too dazed to shoot.

When they were safely around the next bend in the drive, Jack realized one of the headlights, the one on Anna's side, broke as they crashed through the garage door. Nothing compared to the loss of the Spencers' home.

Anna and Jack did not speak. Mother and daughter could not look at each other.

My mother and sister and the man in the street are like me now, Jaimie thought. The appropriate Latin phrase was: *Curae leves loquuntur ingentes stupent.* It meant: *minor losses can be talked away; profound ones strike us dumb.*

They drove in circles at first, through the seemingly deserted streets and meandering crescents and empty courts of darkened urban sprawl. The sound of their engine was a lonely comfort. Anna turned on the air conditioning. Cool air chilled their wet cheeks.

It was Mrs. Bendham who broke the crystal silence. "Was Oliver in your house when it exploded?"

"Yes," Jack said. "I'm sure he was. Those men took him."

"Should we go back to be sure?"

Jack shook her head. Jaimie looked to his father and Theo shook his head, too.

"Mr. Oliver was a good man," Anna said.

"No, he wasn't," Mrs. Bendham said.

"But he wasn't a bad man," Anna said.

Mrs. Bendham shrugged and her chin sank to her chest. She sighed. "No, I suppose not. He just did what most of us do. He thought of himself first."

Jack stood with both feet on the brake pedal. Tires screeched as they rocked forward. The van's nose dipping toward the pavement. In their single headlight beam, just a few feet ahead, stood a deer.

Time stopped. The doe eyed them cautiously, standing her ground. Behind the animal, the forms of more deer moved across the street: wet-black eyes, brown fur, ghostly white tails. When the others had moved out of sight, the deer turned and made for the other side of the road. They just glimpsed its white hindquarters as it leaped, effortlessly, over a low chain-link fence.

Jack drove forward again, slower now. "Where are we going?"

Anna pointed ahead and to the left. "I know a safe place."

"No place is safe," Jack said.

"I know a place for now," Anna said.

Jaimie looked at his father. Theo reached over and patted his shoulder. "Don't worry," Theo said in a thin-as-paper voice. "We'll get safe. We're going to get away."

Anna directed her mother to Trent's parents' house. Jack drove into their empty driveway and then, to everyone's surprise, wheeled around a narrow side yard, bumped through a rose bed and into the backyard.

Theo leaned close to his son. "Jaimie, I saw what you did to Mr. Oliver and I know why you did it. How do you feel about what you did, son?"

Jaimie bent his head and whispered so low only his father could hear. "*Vincam aut moriar.*"

Victory or death.

You Don't Yet Know What It Will Take To Win

Lieutenant Francis Carron awoke from his shocked trance when an ember from the explosion fell on his head. He brushed it away before it could light his hair on fire. The Spencers' van had disappeared around a curve and his men were gone. So much for getting hold of that pretty girl he'd heard so much about from Bently. He'd been saving her as a reward for his men's loyalty.

His men dead, Carron faced the plague apocalypse alone. The stolen police cruiser and the trailer full of food were still intact, but they wouldn't be for long unless he moved them. The explosion had lit secondary fires and the wind rose to feed them.

Through the smoke, he heard crying from across the street. Carron ran, drawing his pistol.

He found Bob Lockhart, also known as Wolfman, in front of the shattered garage door. He coughed up blood and his pelvis was turned to a startling angle, almost 90 degrees. He'd been wearing Bermuda shorts, but all Carron could see was blood and torn flesh.

"Bob?"

The weight of the Spencer's van had burst organs through his abdomen and destroyed his groin.

"I'm sorry, Bob. There are no medics and no hospitals. There's nothing I can do for you."

The man managed to shake his head and raised one finger.

"Yeah," the lieutenant said. "You're right. There is one thing. I'm sorry, Wolfman."

Carron raised his Parabellum and fired once. What was left of Bob the Wolfman Lockhart's body shuddered and he was released from torment. Carron began to cry.

Then the lieutenant heard the dogs. They snarled and snapped, fighting with each other. When he ran to Oliver's backyard hoping to find another of his men, he found the dogs feeding on Douglas Oliver. Carron shot three dogs dead and wasted five more bullets chasing the barking pack away.

There was no use checking Oliver's pulse. The man looked like he'd been torn apart by the steel jaws of deranged robots.

Carron felt no power. Douglas Oliver was beyond pain, so that left Carron only the sliver of satisfaction spite yields. The lieutenant put one bullet through the old man's forehead. It wasn't enough. The only joy left for him would be tracking down the Spencers and making them beg and scream before he killed them.

As Carron wandered back, he noticed Oliver's roof was on fire. The wind picked up even more, fanning the flames. The Bendham house was burning well, too. Carron hurried to close the trailer full of supplies and pull it out of harm's way.

He was about to leave when he heard splashing. He drew his weapon again and, wary for a return of the pack of wild dogs, slipped through the garage to Mrs. Bendham's backyard.

Amid the light and shadow of the flames, he found a crying man in the shallow end of the pool. Carron stepped closer for a better look and instantly regretted it. The man's face was burned horribly.

Lieutenant Carron raised his pistol. "Identify yourself!"

The crying man looked up. "Bently!"

"How?"

"I was blasted out a window. The gas...I threw myself in the old lady's pool!"

"Bently. I'm sorry this happened to you. You were a loyal soldier."

"S-s-sir?"

Carron did feel power now. He could give the man the gift he so desperately needed. He raised the Parabellum. It clicked empty.

"Sir!"

"That's a sign from God, right there." Carron shoved the gun home in its holster. "C'mon, Bently. We've got to get out of here before the whole neighborhood goes up. C'mere!"

Bently waded forward slowly, racked with pain. His clothes had been burned off. Carron squatted with a grunt and reached to grasp Bently by his upper arm.

As Carron pulled to help the man out of the pool, Bently shrieked. The skin of his arm sloughed off as one long glove, all the way to his fingertips. Carron fell back, one grisly evening glove in his hands.

The lieutenant turned on his belly and puked on the cement, the ragged model of an arm still stuck to his hands. Bently managed to stumble up the pool's steps and fell on top of him.

They screamed together.

Or Even Half Of The Trouble We're In

After driving over the Howler's lawn to hide the van behind the house, it seemed silly to knock on the back door. However, Anna did knock. "In case Trent's brother made it back from downtown and he's freaking out in there," she explained. "We don't want to freak him out."

"Would he have a rifle or something?" Jack asked, afraid but also hoping for a weapon.

"No, but he smokes a lot of weed. I can just imagine him in there all paranoid. With his parents and Trent disappeared and maybe leaving him behind..."

"You never told me Trent's brother did drugs."

"Not *drugs*, Mom. Marijuana."

Mrs. Bendham cleared her throat. "I wish I had some right now."

If it was a joke, no one laughed.

Jack and Anna told the others to stay still while they poked through the house. Anna knew the layout and Jack had the big Maglite, their heaviest and longest flashlight. No one was home.

"Trent's brother's dead, too, isn't he?" Anna said when they'd finished searching the house.

Jack didn't answer. Silence was answer enough.

Mrs. Bendham went straight for the kitchen and rifled cupboards for food. In a small pantry downstairs, she found three cans of peaches. She took the cans upstairs and, after failing to find a can opener, banged the tin against the inside of the sink.

Jaimie and his father watched her curiously. Mrs. Bendham handed Jaimie her flashlight and told him to keep the beam steady as she worked.

"I was on a camping trip when I was a young woman. Me and a gentleman. This was before me and my late husband were an item. This boy was in my choir and had a lovely bass voice. If he'd had lovely brains to go with it, who knows where I'd be now?"

Bang! Bang! Bang! Mrs. Bendham turned the can and hit it against the steel sink, chopping with a downward motion.

Bang! Bang!

"There we were, two kids in a tent miles from the road and he'd forgotten the can opener. I was angry that night and by the next night we were famished. We had water from a stream of course — you could drink from a stream back then. We had cans of beans and no way to get into them. I thought we'd starve," she said, "though, of course, I know what starvation is really like now."

She rotated the can and when she hit it this time, the top of the can lifted away. Mrs. Bendham smiled, peeled the circle of tin back and, without spilling any of the peach juice, she drank. She gobbled a peach half, then another. She pulled up the collar of her dress and wiped her mouth on the cloth. She handed the tin to Jaimie.

"You're a good listener," she said, watching Jaimie eat. "Anyway, I came back from this horrible weekend. I was so thin then it's a wonder I didn't die. I remember the hunger pangs curled me right up when I got home. My father said it served me right and then he showed me how to open a can without a can opener. He'd been in the army. People knew useful things in his generation."

She took the can from Jaimie and ate another peach half. "I never went out with that fool who forgot the can opener again."

Mrs. Bendham slipped the remaining two cans of peaches into her purse. "Try to get some sleep, dear. There's been too much tragedy to talk. Maybe we'll talk tomorrow. Maybe not. Up to you." The old woman reached out a hand and patted Jaimie's cheek. The old woman climbed the stairs, found the master bedroom and claimed it.

The boy turned to his father.

"It will be okay, Jaimie. We're going to do this together and I'll hold your hand all the way to Papa's farm. We'll be together, every step."

Anna closed Trent's bedroom door behind her, got into his bed and pulled the blankets tight to her chest. Then she pulled them over her head. Anna still wore her shoes, but left them on in case she had to run again. She wondered if she would ever get to go to sleep again without wearing shoes.

She put her face to her boyfriend's pillow, and inhaled deeply through her nose, taking in his scent. After a moment's silence, she began to gulp and sob. Anna pressed into the pillow until she thought she might smother. Anna Spencer screamed and screamed.

Jack wept for a long time until, just before dawn, she fell asleep on the couch in the family room. Jaimie found a blanket and slept on the floor by his mother with a throw pillow under his head. He hugged his big dictionary to his chest.

He woke several times through the night, unsure each time where he was. Jaimie shifted around on his side to accommodate the comforting bulk of his dictionary. Each time the boy opened his eyes, he found his father in a chair by the front window, peering out into the darkness.

The next day was an arid expanse of tears and silence. In the afternoon, Jack jumped in the van on her own and disappeared for several hours.

Anna eventually emerged from Trent's room. "I'm officially terrified. What if Mom doesn't come back?"

"She'll be back," Theo said, never moving from the window. "She's just going back to see what's left. Scouting to find what she can salvage. She'll find only ashes, but she'll have to look for herself."

Anna turned away, oblivious to her father's assurances.

Jaimie opened his dictionary and looked up the words *moribund* and *feral*. *Feral* slashed at his fingertips. *Moribund* tasted like the

335

smell in the air when the dog pack struck. The pool of blood spreading out from Oliver's throat had come in such great spurts, Jaimie thought of the word *exuberant*. The *x* in exuberant was sharp, too, but his hands searched out the word's soft serifs and that calmed him. It helped him ignore the smell of copper and acid under his tongue.

Acid and copper had risen from the old man's blood in a cloud. Their mark was indelible on the boy. He wondered how the Romans would say, *Remembering everything is a curse.*

When Jack Spencer returned, she held a large, red cookie tin with a faded yellow flower on its cover. The can was sealed with duct tape.

Anna was furious. "Where have you been?"

"Give me a moment to examine the irony, Anna. You forgot to say 'young lady.'"

"You left," Anna said.

"I'm back. With a plan."

"What's the plan?" Theo said.

"We've gotta get out of here."

"Good plan," Theo agreed, still scanning the street.

"Perhaps, before we discuss details," Mrs. Bendham said, "you folks would like to share my peaches? We should preserve our rations in the van, don't you agree?"

Jack nodded and, in the dim light of the late afternoon, they sat at the Howler's dining room table and planned for tomorrow. The peaches were sweet and good and not enough to fill them.

That night, Jack tucked her daughter into bed. "You haven't done this since I was nine or something," Anna said.

"You were thirteen."

"I wasn't."

"You were. It was your birthday. You thanked me and your dad very nicely for your presents. When I tucked you in, you said you were too old for getting tucked in anymore."

"Did you cry?"

"At first I was a little relieved it was deleted from the bedtime routine."

"Mom!"

"I got around to missing it later."

"I miss everything that was boring."

Jack clicked off her flashlight. "Trent kept a neat room. I can make my way to the door and around the house without tripping over anything. It's not like your room at all, is it?"

"You just complimented Trent."

"It's killing me," Jack said.

"This really must be the end of the world."

"Shut up," Jack said. "I was just pointing out how different you two are, actually. Is that wrong?"

"It would have been better if you'd left it at complimenting my boyfriend."

"Can I say hell froze over?"

"Sure," Anna said.

Jack got up to make for the door, but Anna held her at the wrist. "Mom?"

"Yes?"

"Have you noticed that Mrs. Bendham said *my* peaches tonight, like she was doing us a great, big favor?"

"Yeah. I noticed. I think she's doing what Oliver did, trying to suck us into owing her, underlining the debt."

"And did you notice that nobody pointed out to her that she gave away our hiding place?"

"Oliver's place is burned down. Her house is rubble, too. It's all gone. *Everything* is gone." Jack began to cry again. In the darkness, they couldn't see each other's faces. "You're right. Mrs. Bendham does seem to have a dangerous sense of entitlement. She could have at least had the brains to apologize or…something."

Anna sighed. "It's irrational to expect someone who does galactically stupid shit to have the brains to apologize for said stupid shit," Anna said.

"You sound so much like your father before we had children and he cleaned up his language."

"All I'm saying is, what can you expect from someone who doesn't expect you to use her first name?" said Anna.

"She did tell me her first name when we moved in and then I forgot about it and then we pretty much ignored all our neighbors. It's Marjorie, but to us, I think we'll always call her Mrs. Bendham."

"Or That Bitch."

"We have to depend on her."

"That didn't work out so well with Oliver," Anna said.

Jack's anger flared. "No, it didn't. And I don't know if Mrs. Bendham is any better, but I know I can't do this without help. Oliver was right about one thing no matter what else he did or didn't do. We need a tribe. Lovers get separated. Loners die. I know this is hard to swallow, but I'm thinking we need allies and I'll take what I can get."

"Even a stupid one?"

"Just think of her as your crazy grandmother. Everybody has one," Jack said.

"I'll try to think of Mrs. Bendham that way but at some point we owe her a few hard slaps across the face."

"Yes. For now, we need numbers. But...yes...I want to kill her, too."

"Mom?"

"Yes?"

"Don't run off again like you did this afternoon. I'll be okay. I can handle this. I can help. But for Jaimie, be here and do not freak out. Don't lose it. You say Jaimie is in his own world, but sometimes, the way Jaimie looks at me sideways when he doesn't think I notice? He's more sensitive to this world than we give him credit for. I think so. I'm not sure."

"What am I supposed to do?" Jack said. "With all we've lost, what would you have me do, Anna? Am I supposed to act like everything's normal?"

"Just keep calm. We'll grieve about everything later. When people die, even surgeons freak out after it's all over. They don't panic during the operation. We're in the middle of the operation now."

A moment of silence passed as Jack weighed her daughter's words. "You're right. I'm sorry I left. There were things I had to do. I won't leave you guys alone again."

Jack found her way in the dark, rushing faster than she should have, down the stairs. She didn't stop until she was outside in the cold, still air. Clouds blocked all light, as if even the stars had turned their back on Earth. She worked her lungs and expanded her chest to take in as much air as she could. The air felt so clean. It was like drinking ice water.

She stayed outside until her tears were too cold to bear.

Jaimie watched from the window, holding his father's hand. Briefly, he leaned into Theo's side. Theo squeezed his son's hand tight. "War makes monsters and ghosts, son. Don't become either of those things in the journey to come, please."

Jaimie turned to Theo. In a clear voice he spoke to his father, *"Coelum non animum mutant qui trans mare currunt." Those who cross the sea, change the sky, not their spirits.*

It was a promise.

He'd fail to keep it.

Save Your Strength For The Fight

Dr. Neil McInerney's wife Sheila was a youngish fifty with blonde hair and very nice teeth. She waved the refugees aboard the stolen sailboat."Thank you for calling us, Dr. Smith."

"Sinjin-Smythe," he said.

"Yes. Sorry. This psychosis...I guess the toll of the flu has become too much for some, hasn't it?"

"That what your husband told you, is it?" Sinjin-Smythe climbed aboard and was about to shake Sheila's hand when he spotted the bandage at her wrist. A spot of blood seeped through, stirring his fears of contagion. "How did that happen?"

"It's nothing," McInerney said from the quarter deck. "I'll stitch her up myself later. We got disinfectant on it right away."

Dayo stepped aboard, uncertain of her balance. "But what happened?" Dayo reached down and pulled up the little girls, Aastha and Aasa, one by one. Aadi, shivering in his light, Harrods security guard jacket, stepped aboard, eyes sharp for trouble chasing them.

"Where are we headed, Craig?" McInerney asked. "As your captain, it would be good to know."

"Is the Atlantic Ocean that way?" Sinjin-Smythe pointed west.

"Of course."

"Then that way. As soon as we're off the river, I think we should head north, but hug the coastline. Somewhere, I hope we can get more supplies, maybe find help or a refugee station or...I really don't know yet. First priority is not to get blown out of the water by a sodding submarine."

"What's the plan?"

"Go where the navy isn't looking."

"Brilliant," the dentist said, but his tone was sour.

"Tell me how you got hurt," Aadi asked Mrs. McInerney.

"A neighbor lady from down the way lunged at me as I got in the car."

Aadi looked at her bandage with his flashlight. "Was it the car door that caught your wrist or — ?"

"Oh, no, she bit me. Like some kind of animal, growling and all."

"It's nothing!" her husband repeated from the helm, which seemed to underline for everyone that the wound was not nothing. "Cast off," McInerney said in a stage whisper, "before more of them come! We'll raise the sails when we're in open water. For now, let's burn some petrol and get the hell out of here."

Dayo rushed to the side and untied one rope. Neil McInerney gunned the engine. Sheila McInerney stepped aft and untied the mooring line deftly.

Aadi stepped behind Sheila McInerney and pushed her into the cold water of the Thames as the boat surged forward.

"Daddy! Daddy! What did you do?" Aasa screamed. "The lady! That lady is in the water!"

Sheila screamed and choked on black water.

McInerney shut off the engine, turned and shouted for his wife.

Two zombies ran out of the darkness and leaped from the dock on Shiela McInerney's back.

Aadi covered his daughters eyes.

Sinjin-Smythe turned the spotlight on the water where the infected took her down. He saw churning and splashing, but he could only guess that the dentist's wife died screaming, either bleeding profusely, drowned or both.

With an anguished cry, McInerney abandoned the wheel and rushed aft. The dentist might have jumped in after his wife or attacked Aadi, but Dayo bashed McInerney across his shoulder blades with her length of lumber. The dentist fell heavily. Dayo stood in his way with the length of lumber.

"I'm sorry, Neil," Sinjin-Smythe said. "She's gone."

McInerney's gaze was fixed on the little man holding his hands over his crying daughters' eyes.

"How could you?"

"I'm Indian," Aadi said. "I'm good at math and I've seen every zombie movie ever made. Now get back to getting us away from here before those things come out of the water and drag us all down."

"Z-zombies?"

"I'm not saying they're the undead come back to life. I'm saying they're the closest thing to the real deal you can imagine, except they're faster than most zombies. And you already know what you're seeing is *not* simply mass psychosis."

The two monsters who had taken his wife had disappeared. However, three more of the infected appeared at the water's edge, panting and fierce.

"If not for your girls standing there —"

"You heard the boss, doctor," Dayo said. "Let's get going. It's done and, if we're lucky, we'll have plenty of time to talk about it later."

The dentist struggled to his feet and to the wheelhouse, cursing. Only when the zombies hit the water did he have the good sense to gun engines and pull away.

Lijon sauntered onto the bridge of the container ship, *Gaian Commander*, followed by two guards who escorted Edwin George Stanhope. An open cut bled into Stanhope's left eye. A tight ball gag with black leather straps cut into his face. Thick rope pinned his arms behind his back, hands and elbows knotted together.

Shiva turned and gave the prisoner an appraising look. She had changed into another seductive red dress meant for sultry nights out on the town, not for a woman five months pregnant at sea.

"Edwin! So good to finally put a terrified face to the name! Oh, please don't glower. It won't help your cause...though you might as well glower, I suppose, since nothing will help your cause."

She turned to Lijon. "You're sure this is the man who was brattish with you, Sister?"

"Yes, Dear Sister. This is the one."

"Very well. You look uncomfortable, Edwin, so I'll be brief." She circled Stanhope as she spoke. "First came Sutr X. You and your rich friends hid out and endured the first wave of the virus in comparative luxury. No foul there. We took precautions that played out well, too. Then Sutr Z arrived and it was time to escape to the haven your vast company had the foresight to invest in. However, for planet rapists such as yourself? There's been a change of plan. Please remove his gag, brothers. If he speaks, crush his left testicle. If he speaks again, we'll try a nail gun on the other one and see if that teaches Mr. Stanhope some manners."

Shiva stepped close to Lijon, cupped her oval face in gentle hands and gave her one deep kiss on the mouth. Lijon blushed. Her gaze fell to the floor. Shiva patted her cheek and smiled. "No worries of contamination there. Lijon has had her needles. No Sutr X or Z for our sisters and brothers."

Shiva stepped close to the prisoner. She began with a sweet kiss on his lips. Instinctively, he kissed her back. Then Shiva clamped down on his lower lip, bit down hard and ripped away his lower lip, shaking her head side to side savagely.

Edwin George Stanhope struggled and keened but the guards wrapped their legs around his, pinning him. When she was done, Shiva spit his lower lip on the bridge deck. "Lijon, darling, would you mind fetching me some vodka and orange juice, please? He tastes terrible. Too much aftershave, Edwin! And what have you been eating?"

Lijon nodded and hurried away, looking relieved to go.

"Funny thing. The sister you wished dead had her needles and she'll survive the entire voyage in fine style. You are *needless*. Amazing the difference a single *s* makes, isn't it? Soon, you will be without needs, which you'll find quite a relief after a lifetime of conspicuous consumption."

Stanhope let out a garbled cry and one of the guards delivered a vicious punch to the prisoner's groin, doubling him over.

"I think you got them both, Rory."

The guard gave a helpless shrug.

"Never mind. Small targets. What do you suppose he said?"

"I think he asked what we wanted with him?" the other guard suggested.

"It's good you caught that, brother. If I had to ask him for clarification, I suppose, on principle, I'd have to send you off to fetch me a nail gun, wouldn't I?"

Stanhope slumped in misery. It took both guards to hold him up.

"Very well. You're bleeding on my ship, so I won't keep you longer. I hereby find you guilty of treason to your race and, more importantly, Earth. You wanted a cabin instead of a container in the hold. You and your family shall have your cabin. It's quite fine. Your wife and two children will be locked in with you. Since you haven't had your shots, you'll soon turn into a rampaging animal with a desperate thirst for blood and meat. This will be an interesting experiment."

Stanhope looked at her, his eyes glassy.

Shiva wasn't sure he understood her, so she spoke slower and louder. "My hypothesis is you will be driven to bite your family as Sutr Z shuts down your neocortex and you are driven by the imperatives of your primitive, lizard brain. No need to be embarrassed on that score, Edwin. We all have a lizard brain. As the animal takes over, you will eat your family. Or maybe they'll fight you off. You can hope for that, though with a couple of little kids in the room, I'd be surprised if you don't bite at least one of them first. You're so used to being a *winner*, Edwin."

She leaned close to Stanhope's face. He flinched and turned his head away. "My guess is, by the time we get half way to New York, you'll have infected your wife and children. I suspect that, if you had a choice, you'd go after fresh meat. However, in the close confines of your cabin and with no other food source? Only one will be left for the end of the voyage. Maybe you'll succeed in putting your wife and children out of their misery quickly. Then you can feast at your leisure."

Stanhope cried harder.

"Don't worry. If you survive your family's ordeal in that nice cabin, you'll see me one more time when I throw you into the hold with all your fine, rich friends. When we get to New York, I shall unleash the surviving animals. It's time Wall Street got a taste of their own medicine, don't you agree, Edwin George Stanhope?"

He looked up at Shiva, confused. He'd already forgotten his own name.

Use Your Rage. Defy The Night.

Sinjin-Smythe stared at London as the boat rumbled toward the mouth of the Thames. He could see lights on here and there through the city. In other places, the streets were dark for blocks. Screams echoed over London's stone and concrete. Rage, carried on the howling wind, reached out to him across choppy waves. Only cries of utter anguish could compete with rage.

Aadi came forward and bent over Sinjin-Smythe in the bow.

"Are the girls okay?" the doctor asked.

"Good as can be expected. Dayo is with them. Dr. McInerney won't look at me."

"You understand why, don't you?"

"Of course, I do. I'm not an idiot."

"No. In fact, you did the smart thing."

"It was the right thing, too, doctor. If I didn't think it was the right thing, I wouldn't have done it."

"Yes. I just…we were…"

"You were alarmed at my perspicacity and sagacity."

"I — what?"

"I saw what needed doing and I did it right away. I have two little girls who are probably alive because I didn't wait for a debate about a woman who was already dead. She just didn't know it yet."

"Yes. Good."

"I don't need your blessing, doctor. I've got Aasa and Aastha. As long as I have them, you'll find I won't need your condescending forgiveness or understanding."

"Sorry. You're not what I expected, Aadi. I'm sorry if I was...we're all just having to adjust to a lot of change very quickly."

The security guard knelt by Sinjin-Smythe's side. "From now on, doctor, we learn to live with the Ghost and the Darkness or we die horribly. Do you know the story?"

Sinjin-Smythe shook his head.

"In Kenya in 1898, two rogue lions killed 140 people working on a railroad. There were only two lions, but they lived to kill. That's what the plague victims have become."

"I feel like we're more the plague victims now. More so than those...those *things*."

"I won't laugh at you if you call them zombies, doctor. That's what they look like to me."

Another shout reached them from the shore. Two of the infected chased a young woman, her long, blonde hair flew behind her like a flag. She screamed for help as she ran. "You! On the boat! I need a ride! Help me!"

Sinjin-Smythe began to stand but Aadi gripped his shoulder. "Don't even think about it. If we get close, those things will jump on the boat with her."

Before Sinjin-Smythe could reply, two more men, a woman and a child — zombies all — rushed to meet the fleeing woman. They crashed into her and brought her down.

The things were animals, yes, but as they pinned their victim, Sinjin-Smythe was sure he detected triumph and joy amid the guttural, snarled shouts. The joy of the violators competed with the terrified screams of their victim. Her screams followed the boat as they swept on and the doctor prayed the monsters would tear at her throat so her suffering would end.

The doctor and the security guard were quiet for some time before Sinjin-Smythe broke the thoughtful silence. "Maybe whatever they've become...maybe they are what we always were. What if Sutr just let the lion out of its cage?"

"I can't believe this is something at all natural, doctor. If I believed that, I wouldn't have had children."

"I don't have a kid. Not quite. If I did...."

Aadi patted him on the back. "If we're to survive, we must be clever and quick. We have to be smarter than the Ghost and the Darkness."

"But what kind of future are we fighting for? What are we fighting *so hard* for? To be eaten by monsters or...I mean, what if we survive those things but have to die slowly of something else? How many cardiologists and oncologists are going to make it?"

"You're a doctor for a start."

"Not that kind of doctor."

"And McInerney's a dentist, so there's that."

"You aren't hearing me, Aadi! If it's going to be like that," — Sinjin-Smythe pointed back to where the huddle of cannibals made a horrid meal of their victim — "why survive?"

"My answers are sleeping," Aadi said. He stood to go below with Dayo and his daughters.

Sinjin-Smythe thought of his flat in Cambridge and all his dead friends in the lab. If he'd thought to warn them to get out of the building before he called Merritt at the CDC, he'd have more allies now. All he had left were a few documents, the cruel note Ava left him and the memory stick with their lab notes on the Sutr virus.

He began to cry again. He thought about what he believed about the human race. He wished he possessed the young security guard's optimism. But, of course, Aadi had something to live for. Aadi had children so he didn't have the luxury of self-pity.

But Craig Sinjin-Smythe? He who had somehow let a worse variant than the world's worst plagues loose on the world? At that moment, it seemed not merely self-pity, but only right that he should drop over the side, swim to shore and receive proper justice by tooth and nail.

The doctor pulled out his phone, fished the cell's batteries out of his pocket and powered up the device.

Surely my beautiful Ava is dead by now, he thought.

On a whim, he texted Ava.

He wrote:

To my Juliet: I still will stay with thee, and never from this palace of dim night depart again.

I'm truly so sorry that, whatever you needed, I couldn't give it to you. I wanted so much more than this for you, for us and for our child. And so it comes to this.

The doctor pressed *Send*.

He climbed to his feet, dropped his bag to the deck and stepped to the rail, arms stretched to each side. The wind whipped his long hair, its cold fingers pulled at his shirt. He put one foot on top of the rail, ready to dive.

The phone rang.

To be continued in *Season 2* of
This Plague of Days
Robert Chazz Chute

To find more books of suspense and horror by
Robert Chazz Chute,
please visit AllThatChazz.com.

About the Author

After several years working in the publishing industry, Robert Chazz Chute took a long hiatus before founding Ex Parte Press. He has a degree in journalism and is a podcaster, award-winning writer, former magazine columnist and features writer. He is a graduate of the Banff Publishing Workshop.

This Plague of Days, Season 3 **will be released June 15, 2014.**

This Plague of Days, The Complete Series
**contains all three seasons. That collection
launches June 15, 2014.**

**Go to
www.ThisPlagueOfDays.com
for the latest apocalyptic news.**

Author's Note

Thanks very much for trying out my zombie apocalypse serial. There are many more twists, cliffhangers and surprises to come in this three-book series. Expect new villains as the pace speeds up and the virus continues to evolve.
If I'm your flavor, please leave a happy review wherever you bought this book.
Much love,

~ RCC

350